Letters
from the Past

Letters *from the* Past

KEITH J. WILSON

Clearly, many of the places, buildings and locations in this story are real.
Many others, although they may exist, do so here only in the author's imagination.
Most of the characters are entirely fictional and any similarity between them
and persons alive or dead, is entirely co-incidental

Matador
9 Priory Business Park
Kibworth Beauchamp
Leicestershire LE8 0RX, UK
Tel: (+44) 116 279 2299
Fax: (+44) 116 279 2277
Email: books@troubador.co.uk
Web: www.troubador.co.uk/matador

ISBN 978 1783061 754

British Library Cataloguing in Publication Data.
A catalogue record for this book is available from the British Library.

Typeset by Troubador Publishing Ltd
Printed and bound in the UK by TJ International, Padstow, Cornwall

Matador is an imprint of Troubador Publishing Ltd

Keith J. Wilson

CHAPTER 1

Summer 1802
Near Preston Capes, Northamptonshire

It was a fine warm day. The sun blazed down from a clear blue sky, bathing the lush green countryside in its shimmering heat. After a rather long period of cool, cloudy weather and occasional rain, this was the sort of day that summers should bring.

In a field, some distance from the village, an old gentleman was behaving in a manner that, to the casual observer, could only be described as odd. The clothes he wore were old fashioned but well-made and, being black and of a heavy material, seemed most unsuitable for the hot weather and for the activity in which he was engaged. He was, it appeared, frolicking about waving a stick to which was attached a large net. He approached a clump of nettles with all the stealth of a Red Indian Brave. Swinging his net down on to the nettles he let forth a shout of triumph, only to be followed by a cry of anger and frustration. Then, off he set again, dancing this way and that, waving his net in the air as he went. Once more he quietly stalked an unseen foe and then pounced. He repeated this ritual a number of times until, bending over the net, he laughed with satisfaction. Muttering to himself he produced a jar from one of the large pockets in his voluminous black coat. Carefully lifting the net, he placed it over the empty jar and watched with satisfaction as into it fluttered a brightly coloured butterfly.

James Somers of the manor house at Preston Capes was 75 years old, although he could have been taken for 60. He was somewhat taller than average, well-built and remarkably fit for his age. There was little left of the dark brown hair which in his younger days had made him a man of handsome, if not striking

1

appearance. That which remained was grey and somewhat unkempt. The grey green eyes, which now inspected his latest specimen, seeking vainly to escape its prison, told of a still alert and lively mind. His memory, he had to admit, was not as good as it used to be. But then, after 75 years, he did have rather a lot to remember.

'How fortunate!' James muttered to himself. 'It must be at least five years since I caught one of these little beauties.'

Still muttering to himself, he fitted a perforated lid on to the jar which he then replaced in his pocket. Head bent a little, clearly deep in thought, he set off briskly across the field towards the village some mile distant.

Twenty minutes later, he arrived perspiring under his heavy coat which he wore summer and winter. Hat in hand, he mopped his brow with a large, once white handkerchief, as he made his way to a side entrance of the manor. Pausing at the bottom of the stairs, he turned into the large, light and airy living room. Here his wife, some ten years younger than her husband but considerably less active, sat drinking chocolate with a friend who had called in for a gossip.

Poking his head through the doorway, James greeted his wife and her friend with a nod and a smile.

'I'm back, my dear. I have another little fellow in my pocket.'

His wife, Ellen, smiled indulgently and nodded encouragingly. She, of course, knew exactly what he meant, but her friend looked at the old chap in surprise. It was well known that James Somers was eccentric but there were times when his behaviour made her wonder about his sanity.

'I'll be in my den if you want me.' He patted his coat pocket. 'I must find a special place for this one amongst all my other little beauties.'

Smiling happily, he left the ladies to their chat and went up the broad oak staircase along the landing and to a passage leading to a room at the back of the large rambling house. The manor house dated back over four centuries, but had been rebuilt and extended over the years. The last addition had been made by his father when he built a wing on the side, making redundant some of the older rooms at the back which were now ideal storage space and provided a study for James' activities as a collector, naturalist and antiquarian.

The room that he now entered was in an indescribable state of confusion. There were books by the score, cases of butterflies, stuffed birds and stuffed mammals of all kinds. The stuffed birds were invariably set to perch on short lengths of branches with vegetation to resemble their natural habitat, mounted on a stand and covered with a glass dome. They surveyed the room with their beady eyes whilst a long dead and well preserved stoat eyed them hungrily. There were fishing rods, butterfly and fish nets, walking sticks, statuettes and a multitude of smaller items. One wall was dominated by a mounted deer's head. Underneath it in a frame, forever swimming in glassy stillness, was a stuffed pike of record size according to the plaque attached below. Prominent on the opposite wall was a large, ornately carved, escritoire or bureau. It was very old and had clearly been well used, but had stood the test of time and was still a handsome piece of furniture. Almost matching it for age and size was a large table which occupied the centre of the room and which was piled high with boxes, books and a representative sample of the clutter which filled the rest of the room. Next to the escritoire was a smaller table, equally laden with a miscellany of objects. The chairs in the room were not available for their intended purpose since these too were full of books and some items of clothing.

It was in the chair in front of the escritoire that James intended to sit to catalogue his most recent specimen. He removed the hat and coat which were draped over it and threw them over another chair. He picked up a pile of books which lay under the clothing and looked around helplessly for somewhere to put them. Finally, in desperation he turned to the smaller table and, resting the corner of the pile of books on a small area of available space, he shunted the table's contents along with the book pile to make enough room to accommodate them. They stood there, precariously balanced, like a miniature leaning tower of Pisa.

James pulled down the front of the escritoire to form a desk top and reveal an interior of small drawers and pigeon holes, mostly crammed with documents; small books, letters and other papers. Reaching for a large notebook, he thumbed through its pages which were full of sketches that he had made of various butterflies which he had caught over the years. James Somers was an artist as well as a collector, for some of the sketches were exquisite. Many were coloured and accurate in every detail. Unlike the room, the notepad was extremely neat and tidy. Each life size illustration was tabulated and numbered, whilst below the drawing there was, in each case, copious notes on each butterfly, stating where and when it had been caught and the habitat in which it could normally be found.

A noise outside in the passage made James look up. The door slowly opened and around it appeared the head of a chubby, fresh faced boy of somewhat less than ten years old.

'Can I come in Grandpa?' asked the small boy.

'Come on then, but be careful how you go. None of your jumping around mind. Where is your papa today? He was up early I believe.'

'He's gone in to Towcester, Grandpa.'

'I see. So he has left you to your own devices. Well then, you can help me if you behave yourself.'

Nothing loath, young Timothy Somers shut the door and came to watch his grandfather. Grandfather was always fun to be with. Anything could happen and often did. Half the time Timothy had no idea what the old chap was up to, but he never found him dull. To begin with, grandfather was always cheerful and busy with something or other. He never objected to Timothy helping him although, it must be said, that the 'help' was often more of an hindrance. The two of them would often spend an hour or more together. Timothy would ask questions and grandpa was never short of an answer. Most adults, with whom Timothy had dealings, normally ignored him or demanded silent obedience and, if they did talk to or listen to him, did so with a great deal of condescension. Not so grandpa who treated Timothy as a young adult, talking to him of things which he often didn't in the least understand, but in such an easy friendly manner that it didn't seem to matter to either of them.

'Now see what I have here, young Timothy. How about that? Isn't it a beauty?

James produced from his pocket the jar containing the large, multi-coloured butterfly that he had recently captured in the meadow.

'Oh, what lovely colours.' exclaimed Timothy. 'What sort is it?'

'Well now, I'll show you.'

Grandpa set the jar down on a shelf in the desk and reached for the book that he had been examining when Timothy had arrived.

'I was just looking it up in my catalogue. I'm almost sure that I caught one like this about five years ago. My word, you weren't so very old then, were you?

He leaned across to pick up the book and, in doing so, his elbow caught the pile of books which he had placed recently on the small table. These fell on to the floor starting an avalanche of boxes and books which had been stacked so precariously that they needed only a nudge to topple them. In spite of James' frantic efforts to stem the flow, much of the table's contents fell on to the floor and some on to the desk, shaking it and dislodging the jar containing the butterfly. This dropped from the shelf on to the desk top, rolled to the edge and fell with a crash on to the floor. The glass shattered and, miraculously, from the debris fluttered the butterfly.

With a cry of surprise and annoyance, James directed his attention from the cascade of boxes and books to the butterfly. Doubtless rejoicing in its unexpected deliverance, the butterfly fluttered around the room and settled on the arm of a chair. With a cupped hand James tried to capture it but, just as it seemed within his grasp, away it flew to settle on the escritoire. Picking up a hat from the chair, James cautiously approached it but, as the hat descended, up it rose and fluttered into the dark recesses of a pigeon hole inside the bureau. Now, surely, it must be trapped. There was a row of nine such holes, most of which were stuffed with papers but the one on the far left was almost empty and it was in this that the butterfly had sought sanctuary. There, on the

5

side of the recess towards the back, it clung to the rough dark wood, occasionally fluttering its wings and trembling, almost as if it expected recapture. Snatching up a thin book, James tried to cover most of the pigeon hole with it whilst he reached in with his other hand to try and gently grasp the butterfly. Trying to make sure that there was no escape for the creature, James pressed hard against the wooden side with his cupped hand.

Young Timothy had watched this pantomime with great delight. His face, a picture of merriment, changed to one of surprise; for, as James exclaimed triumphantly 'Got it', there was a click and a panel on the left hand side of the escritoire slid open.

'Oh look grandpa. There is a hole in the side of the bureau.'

James, still cupping the precious butterfly carefully in his hands, stooped to look at the side where Timothy was pointing.

'Why, bless my soul, so there is. Just wait a moment, while I put this little fellow safely away.'

Reaching up to a nearby shelf, James found another specimen jar and popped the butterfly inside. Putting on the lid, he placed the jar, this time more safely, at the back of one of the shelves inside the bureau. Then he bent down to examine the opening in the bureau more closely.

'Well, upon my word, I do believe that this is some kind of secret compartment. I must have opened it somehow whilst I was catching the butterfly.' On his knees now, he examined the interior of the compartment which the sliding panel had revealed. 'Wait a minute, there's something inside.'

Reaching inside, the old chap brought out a piece of folded paper sealed with red sealing wax and yellowed with age. He examined it closely. There was no writing on the outside of the paper, nothing in fact save the seal which was embossed with a small crest. The design of the crest appeared to be a large bird in flight with a small animal held in its talons. The motif was so small and rather indistinctly formed, that James could not make out with the naked eye exactly what it was meant to be. Placing the document on the desk, James sat down and regarded it thoughtfully.

'Well now, young Timothy, what have we here? This could

be quite valuable. Perhaps it contains clues to a hidden treasure or maybe it tells of secrets long forgotten.'

The boy's eyes widened with excitement.

'Aren't you going to open it, grandpa?'

'All in good time my boy. First of all, I need a candle and a sharp knife.'

Making his way across the room, taking care not to have any more accidents with the piles of books, from a small chest of drawers James produced a knife with a wafer thin blade. From the mantelpiece he took a candle in its holder. Setting this firmly on the desk, he lit the candle and heated the blade of the knife in its flame. With the hot blade, he proceeded to cut through the sealing wax close to the paper. This left the embossed seal intact, whilst releasing the folded sheet so that the document could be opened out. The old chap did this with great care, making sure not to damage the old and slightly brittle paper. He tried to read the document, but stopped and fumbled in his waistcoat pocket for a pair of spectacles which allowed him to examine the document more closely. Timothy looked on with increasing impatience as James became totally absorbed in the contents of what appeared to be a letter.

'Well, bless my soul. Well, I never did. Incredible! Goodness gracious me!'

'What is it, grandpa?' Timothy could scarcely contain his excitement. 'Is it about hidden treasure?

'No, Timothy, not about treasure, but something almost as exciting. It is very old. Look at the date, 3rd November, 1642. Why, that is 160 years ago, when England was fighting a civil war.'

'What's a civil war, grandpa?'

'Why, when Englishmen were fighting each other. Some were fighting for the King and some were fighting against him.'

'Is it about the war, grandpa?'

'Yes, I think it is; in a way.'

There was a noise outside the window which looked out on to the yard at the back of the house. Looking out James and Timothy watched a man, who had just arrived on horseback, dismount and hand the reins to a stable lad. Whilst the horse was led away, the man entered the house.

'Ah, there's your father back home. Let's see what he has to say about all this. Now, young man, run along and ask him if he will join us here.'

Timothy ran off shouting excitedly to his father. A minute or two later he was back, urging his father to hurry and tugging at his sleeve. William Somers was in his middle forties. He was a well-built man of good appearance and medium height. He wore a wide skirted coat of navy blue and tight riding breeches. His manner, especially with strangers, was usually a little reserved. However, with his family he was relaxed and his easy going, good nature, became immediately apparent. Seeing the three generations of Somers together, a family likeness was clearly visible. William greeted his father with a bewildered smile.

'What's all this Timothy has been telling me about hidden treasure?'

'It's true enough.' replied James, as he directed his son's attention to the document lying on the desk. William studied it for a while and then began rather haltingly to read it out aloud.

3rd November 1642

"Sir,

I understand from one who has this day been with the Earl of Essex that it is the Earl's intention to march with his army to London and join with the forces that have been raised there in support of Parliament. He will break his journey at Dunstable where he will wait and rest until his baggage train and ordnance have caught up.

The army, lying at Warwick with the Earl, is comprised of….."

Here the writer gave details of the number of men at arms, both foot soldiers and cavalry. He listed the artillery and other items of ordnance. He gave his opinion of the strengths and weaknesses of the army and of its morale after the recent battle with the Royalist army at Edgehill which, although prolonged and bloody, had ended without clear victory to either side. The letter ended with a hint that the writer was in some danger.

"My presence here is not without suspicion and I must therefore be circumspect in the manner in which I gain this information and in transmitting it to yourself. Nevertheless, I will endeavour to discharge my duty by the best means that God allows. Your most obedient and nameless servant."

'Well, I never did.' exclaimed William. For a minute he stood lost in thought. Then he enquired of his father, 'Do you think that it is genuine? Where did you find it?'

James indicated the still open panel in the side of the escritoire, which they both proceeded to inspect minutely.

'I never dreamt of any such hidden compartment.' exclaimed James. 'I've been using this bureau over the years and never known of its existence.'

'What were you doing, father, to make it open?' asked William.

'Well, I don't really know.'

'He was catching a butterfly in there, papa.' said Timothy, pointing at the end pigeon hole.

'In here?' asked William, examining the place which Timothy had indicated. 'There is nothing here. What, exactly, were you doing?'

William continued to inspect the pigeon hole and felt inside. There was no catch or lever; nothing that might be used to operate the door of the compartment. There was nothing but the plain, rough side of the recess.

'The butterfly had settled on the left hand side there towards the back. I cupped my hand over it to catch it.' volunteered James, trying to think exactly what he had been doing.

William felt the side of the recess, poking and prodding at the wood. As his hand moved towards the front of the pigeon hole side wall, while he was pressing on the side, there was a faint click and the panel, which had swung open, swung back into place. They bent down to examine the panel more closely, but not even the closest inspection gave any indication that this was a door or, indeed, that the panel was anything else other than a fixed part of the body of the bureau. The panel and its carving had been so cleverly arranged that when it closed, it did so with the edge of the panel forming the door covered by beading, so that no gap could be seen and there was nothing to indicate that it was any different from the other panels.

'How did you do that?' asked James.

'I'm not sure. I was feeling the inside and pressing the wall of the recess. The whole side seemed to move very slightly.'

He pushed the side again with no effect. He continued to explore the side of the pigeon hole with his fingers. Methodically he covered the whole of the wall on the left hand side. It was some ten inches high by twelve inches deep. As his probing fingers reached towards the back of the side of the pigeon hole, there was a click and the hidden panel swung outwards. He pushed again; nothing happened. Again he pushed, but still with no results. Once more he began to move his hand methodically over the wall. As his hand moved towards the front, with a click, the door swung to.

William examined the side of the pigeon hole very closely. It was sometime before he was able to open and shut the panel at will. Finally, he felt that he had mastered the secret.

'The whole side of this pigeon hole seems to be hinged to pivot slightly about the middle. Pressure towards the back of the side wall moves it slightly causing the door to open. Presumably it works by some system of levers and counterbalance weights. Pressure towards the front of the side pivots the side back and the door closes.

'Well, how amazing! All these years and I never knew.' Old James was looking at the bureau as if he had never seen it before.

While they were talking Timothy could restrain himself no longer. 'May I have a go papa, please?' His father motioned him forward and Timothy laughed with glee as he quickly found the trick of opening and shutting the panel.

'That's enough.' warned his father. 'We don't want it broken. Where did the bureau come from father? You had it before I was born, didn't you?'

'Yes indeed, my boy. It was here in my grandfather's time.

It's always been here. I've no idea how old it is, but it must be over a hundred years. My grandfather, old Julian Somers, had it downstairs in the big living room.'

'This document, then; It must be genuine, so it seems. It certainly looks old enough to me. How long ago was the Civil War, father? Does this date, 1642, make sense?'

James looked at his son very much in the manner of a displeased school master. 'I thought you learned some history at Dr Frazer's academy. It seems that I wasted my money on your education. The English Civil War took place in the 1640's and, to some extent into the 50's. That's 150 to 160 years ago.'

'Well now, I wonder how it came to be left inside a secret compartment in this escritoire. It could have been put there after the war, but that seems unlikely, especially since it was unopened. In view of its contents it seems more likely that it was put there for secrecy and safe keeping. I wonder by whom. Was it put there by one of our ancestors? The bureau may well have been in their possession at that time. I wonder why it was never reclaimed.' James spoke hesitantly, as he pondered upon the mystery that the discovery of the letter had presented.

'Possibly the person who put it there was, for some reason or another, unable to or didn't want to remove it.' suggested William. 'Perhaps it was put there by the person for whom it was intended. The owner of the bureau would be the most likely person to know about the secret compartment and clearly he would not be likely to tell many other people, if anybody. So, it has remained hidden there for all these years until you stumbled across it purely by chance.'

William spoke thoughtfully, almost to himself, as he searched his mind for any probable reason for such a document to have been put into the bureau in the first place and to have remained hidden there for so long. Plainly, it was not a secret that could easily be discovered. Neither the panel nor the side of the pigeon hole showed any trace of their purpose and it was not a secret that could be easily found by accident. The chance, that had led James to press the side of the pigeon hole in just the right place, was a very remote one indeed.

Since the bureau was known by James to have been in the possession of his grandfather, that took them back to the 1720's. A further 80 years brought them to the 1640's. There was no good reason why the bureau could not be that old. As for the secret compartment, people did need a safe place to hide their valuables, money and documents of importance. 'What about the Civil War connection?' wondered William.

Still thinking aloud, he demanded of no one in particular. 'Why shouldn't our ancestors have been involved in the Civil War? Doubtless it affected the lives of many families in this area. There were few areas where the soldiers of either side did not march, whilst Northamptonshire and the Midlands were heavily involved in the fighting. Why, Naseby field is less than 20 miles away. The Somers have been landowners in these parts for centuries. It would have been difficult for people of their standing to remain aloof from the conflict. All the same, it would be fascinating to know more about this letter and the secrets that it holds. Who was the writer? Why, was it not signed? Was he some kind of spy? That seemed to be the most obvious explanation. Was he a long forgotten Somers? Was it one of our ancestors who had received the letter? Why was it never opened and why was it never retrieved? So many questions and so few answers! I doubt that we or anyone else will ever find out the truth behind this mystery.'

'The Reverend Mr Tilson is something of an antiquarian. He might know how to find out more about it.' suggested James, 'At any rate, it's worth a try.'

* * *

It was about a fortnight later, when the Reverend Henry Tilson, the local vicar, was making one of his pastoral visits, that William showed him the letter and told him how they had found it.

Mr Tilson was greatly interested but, as he modestly asserted, pretended no great knowledge in such matters.

'Remarkable! Most remarkable!' he observed, adjusting his glasses to better examine the letter. 'It would certainly appear genuine, especially having regard to the place and the manner in which you found it. From the contents of the letter, giving details of the Parliamentary army under the Earl of Essex, together with the fact that the letter is neither signed nor addressed, suggests that the writer was engaged in some form of espionage. The only clue lies in the seal.'

Producing a magnifying glass from his pocket, Mr Tilson carefully examined the seal.

'It is, I see, the impression of an eagle in flight holding a small animal, a lamb perhaps, in its talons. On reflection, I doubt if this will help us much. In such circumstances, the very purpose of the seal was to allow the writer of the letter to remain anonymous to all except the recipient who, seeing the seal, would know from whom the letter came. The design might be part of a coat of arms, but that is unlikely since that, in itself, might give a clue to those finding this correspondence if theirs were not the hands for whom the letter was intended. Clearly, the utmost secrecy was called for. More likely the design was chosen at random. The letter would almost certainly have been carried by some trusted servant who, apart from the sender, would alone know for whom the letter was intended.'

'What of the bureau or escritoire, as I believe it is more properly called, Do you know anything of its history?' asked Mr Tilson.

'Only that it is as much part of the Somers family as the house itself. My father tells me that it was here when his grandfather was a boy. That must be over a hundred years ago. People alive then would have their own memories of the Civil War.'

'Do you know anything of the Somers' family history?' The more he thought about the letter, the more frustrated became the Reverend Henry Tilson. That it was genuine, he had no doubt. That it told of bygone intrigues, he was quite certain. Further than that, he could deduce little; but, to Mr Tilson, it was a small thing like a letter, such as this, that gave the breath of life to history. It was a shaft of light which gave dimension to what, otherwise, might be regarded as a rather flat and featureless episode in history books, such as the Civil War. Here, in this letter, lay the key to stories of people whose lives were caught up in the turmoil of a war from which there had been little escape. For, it is true to say, there was little room for neutrality in that conflict. The saying that 'he who is not for me, is against me' was probably more true then, than during many other wars. If more could be found out about those who were connected with this letter, that may well tell a story of those participants in the conflict; how they lived and how they loved, how they fought and how they died in those tumultuous times.

William was no less intrigued to find out more about the letter. His sense of history did not prompt him, as did Mr Tilson's; but this was a mystery on his own doorstep, probably about his own ancestors and, for William, mysteries were there to be solved. However, he could offer Mr Tilson very little help.

'Beyond my grandfather I know very little. Doubtless, my father can tell you more; but even he will know nothing of our ancestry one hundred and sixty years ago. We have always lived here. The Hall has been in the Somers' family since it was built sometime in the 16th century. I believe that parts of the hall predate that period and, as far as I know, it was occupied by Somers even then.' William puckered his brow into a frown as he tried to think of anything more that he could tell Mr Tilson. Surely there was a way of finding out about one's family. Then the thought struck him. 'Why, Mr Tilson. What about the parish records? Will they tell us nothing?' William's face lit up with excitement at the idea, but it was short lived.

'I have thought of that, but what could they tell us? Even if it were recorded that one of your ancestors had been killed in the Civil War, what then? It would still not prove any connection with this letter. Nevertheless, it is worth looking to see what we can find. Meanwhile, you ought to take great care of that letter. I would advise you to frame it so that it can be seen clearly without having to be handled and unfolded. Also protect it from light to prevent it fading.'

So saying, Mr Tilson rose to leave. William ushered him into the hall where he fetched his hat and cane. Wishing him good day and thanking him for calling, William watched Mr Tilson make his way thoughtfully along the drive.

* * *

It was a day or two later that Mr Tilson was, once again, a visitor at the Hall. William was at work in his study when he observed him approaching the front door. Eager for news, he met Mr Tilson as he was being received by the maid. Having wished him 'good morning' and seen him seated in a chair in the drawing room, he called his father, who was as interested as William to know if any more light could be shed on the mystery of the letter. The old man soon joined them.

'May I ask you, sir, if you have any further news with regard to our mysterious document?' asked James.

Mr Tilson cleared his throat and looked first at James and then at William for a few seconds before he replied.

'I have looked through the parish records and have found that, as you have said, the Somers' have lived here since well before the days of the Civil War. At the time in question, you will recall that the letter was dated 3rd November 1642, the owner of the manor here at Preston Capes was a Henry Somers. His death is recorded as having taken place on the very day after the letter was written.'

Both James and his son gasped in surprise.

'What an extraordinary coincidence.' observed James.

'Coincidence?' replied Mr Tilson. 'Well, perhaps, but I doubt it.'

'Who inherited the property?' asked William.

'As far as I can make out,' replied Mr Tilson, 'Henry Somers had a sole heir, his son, Ralph.'

'When did he die?' asked William.

'The records are sketchy, give very little information and, not least, are often very difficult to read after all these years. The records are damaged over that period and, although they begin again in the early eighteenth century, I can find no records that contain mention of the death of a Ralph Somers. His birth was

15

however recorded in 1624. They were troubled times for the church during the years of the Commonwealth. Churches were sometimes looted and vandalised in the name of religion. However, this Ralph's descendants obviously continued to live in the Hall, for later Somers are recorded and, of course, your presence here today confirms that the family still holds the lands.'

'And that is all that we can find out from this source?' asked James.

'Yes sir, I'm rather afraid that it is.' replied Mr Tilson sadly. He felt aggrieved and frustrated; for behind the letter there was, he felt sure, a tale worth telling; but he could see no further avenues for exploration. 'No,' he spoke as much to himself as to his listeners, 'In all this there lies a mystery, with intrigue, adventure and perhaps romance. Your ancestors were, I am sure, much involved, but what it was all about and what exactly happened, we shall never know.'

CHAPTER 2

Spring, 1959
Just North of Salcey Forest, Northamptonshire

Frank Reynolds liked his job. The pay was good and the work, well, not so bad. In the cab of his Caterpillar tractor he was warm and dry, whatever the weather. He even had his small transistor radio, although for much of the time it could scarcely be heard above the roar of the diesel engines which powered the huge machine. The hours were long, but that was because of the overtime where he made his real money.

About thirty years old now, Frank had always worked on road and bridge construction. He had started during the war when he had been in the Royal Engineers. It was a steady job, if you were prepared to move around. Really, it was the only sort of work he knew. The pay had always been pretty fair, although he had had to put in the time to make the sort of money that he wanted to earn. Up until now the money had gone on beer with his mates, a few quid on the horses and flashy clothes. Easy come, easy go; but Madge had changed all that. Now that he had met Madge, he had something to save for.

With these thoughts in mind Frank waited his turn to fill his trailer with earth. At this point, the motorway which was the first to be built out of London, was to pass through a shallow cutting. Although the need to level the route was not so imperative as it had been while building the railways, it was still desirable to level the route to some extent to avoid steep inclines. A procession of earth movers, like the one Frank was driving, were being used to dig out to the required level. By dropping the huge cavernous trailer which was part of the vehicle, and using the tremendous traction that the large wheels provided, driven by a powerful diesel engine, Frank was able to grub up several tons of earth and rock as the mouth of the trailer bit into the earth when it was pulled along. Then, when the trailer was full, it could be lifted hydraulically, so that Frank could drive the load of spoil along the track of the 'motorway to be', to a point some half a mile away where a small embankment was being built to carry the motorway up to and over a bridge spanning a small stream.

Frank emerged from his day dream as he became aware that there was something happening ahead. 'What's the matter with Charlie?' he wondered as he saw, rather than heard, the shouts of Albert, the foreman. He watched as Charlie, the driver in front of him, stopped, then started and stopped again in response to Albert's shouts and hand signals. It was Albert's job to show where each driver was to scoop out the next load of earth. He seemed, for some reason, to be having difficulty in making his mind up with Charlie.

After a while Frank could restrain his curiosity no longer. Jumping down from his cab, he joined Albert to find out what was going on.

'What's the matter, Albert?'

'Charlie has hit a pile of stones just here. He pointed to a patch of ground, half covered by Charlie's trailer. Frank could see that there were indeed some quite large lumps of dressed sandstone which might have been from a wall or building. 'I've told him to back off a bit and take a shallower bite. It looks like the remains of an old building. It's funny, because there was nothing to see here before we started.'

With the din in his ears of the diesel engine and the rumble of the sandstone and earth tumbling into the vast, resonant steel trailer, Frank watched the machine scythe a path through the ground below. When Charlie had passed over the stony patch and moved on a dozen yards, Frank could see clearly that these stones did form the remains of a building. With the loose stones cleared from the top, the rough outline of the two walls forming the front and back or perhaps the two sides could be seen. The stones that had fallen inside the building appeared to go deeper still.

Albert inspected the remains. 'We need to go down several

feet yet,' he observed turning to Frank. 'Take another slice off this part, Frank.' Albert indicated with his hands precisely where he wanted Frank to cut into the ground. 'We'll see if we can bottom it.'

Frank walked back to his tractor and climbed into his cab. He eased the vehicle forward to position himself in front of the area of ground indicated by Albert. He felt the sudden tug as he lowered the shovel to bite into the earth and then he heard the engine strain as it hit the pile of stones from the old building. In his mirror he saw Albert watching intently as the tractor moved slowly through the wall and into what had been the building's interior. Suddenly Albert signalled urgently for him to stop. Coming quickly to a halt, Frank leaned out of the cab to hear what Albert was shouting.

'What's up then, Albert?'

'Hold it a minute Frank. There's something in amongst this rubble. It's bones of some kind. Maybe it's nothing but you'd better hitch up your trailer and back off so that we can have a better look.'

Frank reached for a lever in the cab and watched the rubber hoses flex as the hydraulic pressure lifted the huge bucket. Revving the engine he rolled slowly over the pile of stones until he was quite clear. Leaving the diesel idling in neutral he jumped down from his cab and walked over to join Albert. He watched as Albert gently lifted a large sandstone boulder to one side. Scraping the earth away from a smooth, round object underneath, Frank watched in amazement as Albert uncovered what appeared to be a human skull.

'Blimey mate!' exclaimed the startled Frank. 'It's a body, or part of one. Do you reckon it's human? Hey, look at this!' Frank moved a stone and scraped away until he could release a bowl shaped object, very rusted and distorted, but clearly recognisable as a helmet. Plainly it was a very ancient helmet and appeared to have been quite elaborate. It bore no resemblance to the type of helmet Frank had worn during his army service. Meanwhile, Albert continued with great care to clear the earth away to uncover more of the remains. He revealed bones that appeared to form the shoulder and the chest and which were covered in part by the remnants of clothing fabric and, in some areas, by the remains of rusty armour.

Albert stood up, scratched his head and looked at Frank.

'I reckon we had better tell the boss about this. We can't just forget about it. Look, you hang on here a bit while I go and find out what's to be done.'

So saying, Albert jumped into his Landrover and set off down the brown ribbon of half built motorway, stirring up a trailing cloud of dust. Watching him go, Frank stretched himself out on the cool green grass beneath the shade of a nearby tree. Well, this was fine by him. They could take as long as they liked. He was on the firm's time and this was as good a way of spending it as he could think of.

'Funny business though.' thought Frank. 'What the hell would a body be doing buried in that pile of rubble? Perhaps he had been murdered, or maybe there had been some kind of duel if, as it seemed, he had been some kind of soldier. One thing was certain, the poor devil had been dead for a very long time. Frank had never interested himself much in history. He had always been concerned more with today; problems enough now, he reckoned. Now, he had visions of soldiers swaggering around in armour, some on horses, jousting, or whatever they called it. He watched, in his mind's eye, as an insult was offered, swords drawn and the two men fought as he had seen Errol Flynn fight duels in films. Well, maybe. Frank looked across at the grinning skull as it lay there laughing at the sky. With a gesture of dismissal, he tossed a pebble at the remains. Then he got up, stretched himself and walked to the brow of the hill some thirty yards distant.

Frank looked across the fresh green Northamptonshire countryside. The trees were not yet fully in leaf, whilst the fields were, as yet, mostly brown with, here and there, a hint of green corn emerging from the soil. Because spring had not yet given way to summer, Frank could see through the trees over the rolling landscape of meadows and trees to a large old house built from the local sandstone. The mellow, golden brown stone blended harmoniously into the landscape. Some old manor house, supposed Frank. It had that look of permanence. Frank had no doubt that it had been there for donkeys years and, although he would not have been able to decide for himself that it was an Elizabethan building, he knew instinctively that it was a few hundred years old. Beyond the house; the hedges, fields, spinneys and copses formed a patchwork quilt in which lay a farm or two, other isolated buildings and, as a background to all this, Frank could see some mile or two distant a wall of trees that seemed to form the edge of a forest.

As he contemplated the view, Frank heard the sound of the Landrover returning. He sauntered back to the ruin in time to meet Albert, who had brought with him a youngish chap, perhaps in his late twenties. He nodded with a smile to Frank; then he looked at the skeleton.

'What've you been up to Frank?' he enquired cheerfully.

'Better ask him Mr Johnston.' replied Frank, nodding at the skeleton.

Bill Johnston knelt down to study the uncovered bones. He examined the remains of the metal and the fabric which covered the rib cage. Carefully he turned the rusty helmet over in his hands. Then he turned his attention to the skeleton and moved a few more stones to uncover more bones. 'Look here,' he exclaimed with a whistle. 'If I'm not mistaken that's the hilt of a sword, or what's left of it.'

Bill was keen on his job and as anxious as any of his men that they should keep up with the work schedule. The men's bonus depended on this. At the best of times, it was a battle either with the weather or some other obstacle that unexpectedly prevented their progress. Bill was well aware that this could prove a bigger obstacle than all the rest put together, if it attracted the attention of serious archaeologists and proved to be a find of some importance. He knew that it could mean weeks of delay, while the site was excavated and its secrets laid bare. However, Bill was no Philistine. In fact, he had always been interested in history. He had no idea what the find could be, but he realised that the helmet was quite old. He had not heard of there having been a battle of any sort in this area. Nevertheless, the fact that there were human remains made it imperative that he inform the authorities. It was possible that they had stumbled upon something of importance and it ought to be properly investigated. He quickly decided that his men could, for a while, work elsewhere and, provided that investigating the find took no longer than a fortnight, any serious delay could be avoided.

Having cleared it with his superiors, Bill's first contact was with the police. When the age of the deceased had become apparent, they lost interest and put Bill in contact with a local historian by the name of David Gibson. My Gibson was a youngish man in his early thirties, a teacher at the local grammar school. He had contacts whom, he declared, would quickly organise a "dig". He assured Mr Johnston that he quite understood the need to complete his investigation of the site as quickly as possible and anticipated that it would take perhaps as little as a week. He seemed quite excited at what was so far apparent, but reserved comment until more could be discovered about the find. The skull and the pile of stones were covered temporarily with a tarpaulin, which was held down with some of the larger chunks of masonry. Having done this, Gibson declared that he would make sure that work began early next morning.

Mr Gibson was as good as his word. The following morning, at nine o'clock, he arrived with some half dozen of his older students and two or three adult volunteers. They commenced in earnest to excavate the site. Within two days, he had revealed the foundations of an old building, with a cellar, into which had collapsed most of the walls together with part of the timbers from the roof and the floors above. The stones were blackened and where pieces of rotting timber were to be found, they were charred. Everywhere, the blackened debris pointed to the building having been destroyed by fire. One or two old tools were found, all badly rusted and, in some cases, unrecognisable.

The skeleton was the important find. The rib cage was crushed and a leg had been broken by the falling masonry, but it was complete. In addition to the helmet they found, as Bill had suspected, the very rusty remains of a sword and an old flintlock pistol. The soldier, for that is what he had undoubtedly been, was in light armour, of which only traces were left covering the upper part of his body. Here and there were fragments of clothing and around the skeletal remains of his feet were what was left of his leather boots. Around his neck, or rather lying inside his mangled ribs, they found a golden crucifix, whilst on his finger was a ring. It was the presence of these two items which led Mr Gibson to suppose that the soldier had been a cavalier fighting for King Charles 1st in the English Civil War. The period was easy to fix from the helmet and pistol, but these were common to both Roundhead and Cavalier. It was, however, unlikely that a soldier of Parliament would have carried a crucifix.

'Well, what do you reckon he was doing here then?' asked Bill.

'Oh, your guess is as good as mine.' replied Gibson. 'However, since he was under the masonry, it seems likely that he was in the cellar, or trying to get out of it, when the house collapsed. From the blackened stone and burnt timber, it also seems likely that the fire was the cause of the collapse. The pistol was loaded. It was strange that the fire hadn't set it off, but perhaps that was because it was underneath the blaze. Anyway, the ball is still in the muzzle. He could have been hiding, I suppose. The fire may have been connected with his presence. We haven't a hope of learning the whole story. As you saw, the body was partly crushed by the fallen masonry. This may have been the cause of death but, again, we cannot be sure. He may have been killed and put into the cellar. Who can tell? All we know is what the remains tell us and that is virtually nothing about why he was here.'

'What about the various things that you found with the skeleton?' enquired Bill. 'Were they of any great interest?'

'These things are always of interest, but they were only what we might have expected. Probably, the most interesting of these is the ring. At first glance it is an ordinary, ornamental ring, commonly worn by gentlemen of that period. On closer examination, you can see that the rather large engraved cap is a hinged cover.'

Gibson showed Bill the ring which he had cleaned. Looking closely, Bill could see that there was a joint at the base of the engraved cap.

'How does it open then?'

Mr Gibson pressed the side lightly with his thumb. The cap lifted a little at one side.

'I'm afraid that the spring isn't as strong as it was. Perhaps, with more cleaning, and a touch of oil, we might get it to work again. Originally, the cap would have sprung right back.'

He had to push the cap to get it to open fully, revealing an embossed design.

'There we are.' exclaimed Gibson. 'You see, it's a signet ring, used to put a pattern into sealing wax. It is a personal seal; a device to ensure that a letter could not be opened by a third party without the recipient being aware of it.'

Bill listened with great interest and, in his imagination, he saw the tall, imposing figure of a 17th century soldier, with armour protecting his chest, a helmet with some sort of visor, whilst in his right hand he carried an unsheathed sword, with his left hand resting on a pistol in his belt. Bill's imagination was limited by his lack of any real knowledge of the period and not a little coloured by the swashbuckling heroes of the films he had seen. He tried to imagine how the countryside would have looked in those days. Certainly, there would not have been the patchwork of fields that he could see now stretching into the distance. It was likely that there would have been more trees and, probably, that the forest would have been a little bigger and closer. Other than that Bill doubted if things would have looked much different.

'Would you call this an important discovery?' asked Bill.

'Well yes, quite important. This sort of thing is far from being an everyday occurrence. It hasn't added much to our knowledge of the period but, nevertheless, it's all most interesting.'

They both turned as they heard a car draw up at a gate some

fifty yards away across the field through which the motorway was being built. They watched a figure get out of the car, clamber over the gate and make his way towards them. It turned out to be a young man, perhaps in his early twenties with sandy hair and a freckled face. His glasses gave him a somewhat studious appearance, although this was tempered a little by the cheerful smile with which he greeted them.

'Good morning. Mr Gibson, isn't it?'

'Yes, that's right.'

'My name is Smithers, Frank Smithers. I'm a reporter from the Evening News. We heard that there had been some sort of find here by the chaps working on the motorway. Can you tell me anything about it?'

With Gibson at his side to point out the more interesting features, Smithers viewed the hole in the ground which had once been a cellar. He looked with interest at the skeleton which had been laid carefully to one side. He listened intently and took notes, as Gibson and Bill Johnston explained how the ruin had been discovered and subsequently excavated. He asked a number of questions regarding the significance of the find and showed particular interest in what they had found on the skeleton. The ring seemed to interest him most of all. He studied it carefully and, using his handkerchief, tried to clean up the embossed crest, or motif, which had been used as a seal.'

'Can you make out the crest?' he asked David Gibson.

'Well, it seems to be some kind of bird, perhaps an eagle in flight. It's holding something, a small animal, maybe a lamb, in its talons.'

Frank handed back the ring. 'You'll no doubt have taken photographs for your records, but I would like to get our staff photographer along to take a few for the paper.'

'You go ahead.' replied Gibson. 'We have taken several, but it might be better if you get what views you think best.'

'Have you connected this in any way with Hartington Hall?' Smithers nodded in the direction of the Hall which, although less than a quarter of a mile distant, was hidden by the brow of the hill.

'Well, nothing that we have found suggests any connection, but Hartington Hall is Elizabethan and so would have been there when the fire occurred and the soldier was killed.'

As Frank had done, Gibson and Smithers walked the twenty or thirty yards to the crest of the rise and looked through the trees across the meadow towards Hartington Hall.

'Ah yes, there it is. Yes, I suppose that there might be some connection.' Gibson spoke thoughtfully. 'I seem to remember that there was some sort of skirmish there towards the end of the Civil War.'

'That's right.' replied Smithers. 'The Cressley family still live there. They were Royalists, I believe. They were besieged for a short time and the house was sacked by Cromwell's men. We did a series of articles about a year ago on local historic homes. That's why I'm so knowledgeable about it.' Smithers ended with an apologetic smile.

'That ring you showed me,' he continued, 'Can you identify the design on the seal? Have you seen it before?'

'No, I'm afraid I can't; but I'd certainly like to follow it up.' David Gibson warmed to Smither's friendly manner and shared interest in local history. 'Have you any ideas?'

'Well, I may be wrong, but I think that a visit to Hartington Hall could perhaps be worthwhile. The eagle and the lamb, which are included in the design of the seal, seem somewhat familiar.'

'You mean that they are in the arms of the Cressley family?'

'No, that design is not part of the family crest, but I seem to remember that in one of the old panelled rooms there are some wood carvings with similar designs to the one on the ring; that's unless I'm confusing it with something I have seen elsewhere,' answered Smithers thoughtfully.

'Well, I shall certainly check on that and thank you for the tip. Isn't the present Cressley a military man?'

'Yes, that's right. General Sir John Cressley is the present owner. He is retired now and, I believe, that he is a widower living in the Hall with his daughter. He has a son who has followed in his father's footsteps and is also in the army. He may be a retired general, but he is still very active, as I have found on the one or two occasions that I have come into contact with him. Nice old chap though; I think you'll like him.' replied Smithers.

'How much longer will you need to finish excavating the site Mr Gibson?' asked Bill Johnston.

'Oh, by tomorrow we shall have found out all that we can hope to find from this sort of dig. There weren't too many items left to find after the fire and three hundred years have taken their toll. We were lucky to find as much as we have. A few more measurements and some further notes and it's all yours again.'

'Well, I must say that is good news. I'm pleased and surprised that you have finished so quickly. The one thing that worried me was the delay that a lengthy investigation might have caused. I have put the men to work on another section of the motorway. So, as it turns out, you haven't held me back at all.' observed Bill with a cheerful smile. 'Well, I must be on my way.'

'Thanks again,' replied Gibson. 'We must co-operate with you people as much as we can; otherwise we can't expect your help in the future, can we? Well now, I must get going too.'

'Yes, I must get back to work,' added Frank Smithers. 'Thank you for all the information. If you do find anything more about the ring or, indeed anything at all, I'd appreciate hearing about it. Oh, by the way, what will you do with the skeleton?'

'That has bothered me. It doesn't seem right to just throw it back into the foundations of the old house. I suppose the right thing to do would be to get him a proper burial. Have you any suggestions?'

'Would you like me to have a word with the local vicar? I'm sure that he will arrange for the remains to receive a Christian burial.'

'Yes, indeed, that's an excellent idea. Thank you very much.' replied Gibson appreciatively. 'Oh and I intend to try to see General Cressley as soon as possible.'

CHAPTER 3

Spring 1959
Northampton

Frank Smithers sat at his desk in the reporters room of the local newspaper. He was gazing out of the window on to the bustling scene below. It was market day in Northampton and the Market Square was full of life and noise. The stalls were all up and business was brisk. In one corner of the square, near to the newspaper's offices, under a green awning to protect his wares from the hot sun, a man stood holding a large cauliflower which he was displaying to its best advantage for the benefit of a somewhat reluctant customer. Nearer to the window, from which Frank stared with unseeing eyes, was a large man juggling an incredible number of plates, shouting to attract the attention of those who passed within earshot. One or two passers-by paused and gazed at him with some interest, as he vowed that he was not asking the usual price of £5 for the complete set, nor would he insult his customers by asking £4, nor yet £3, but the first one to step forward could have the lot for £2. 10s. He pointed to someone at the back of the crowd, which had now grown in numbers and declared that the set had been sold to the lady at the back. The lady came forward, paid for and received her crockery. No one noticed her when she later replaced them in the trader's van with the rest of his stock. She had started people buying and, within those few minutes, another five or six sets of crockery had been sold to genuine customers before the trader finished with that particular type of crockery and turned his attention to another line.

All of this went on below his window as Frank watched, but he saw none of it. His mind was far away. His imagination had been fired by the recent discovery from a bygone age. In his mind he conjured up all kinds of explanations for the presence of a cavalier soldier in the burnt out remains of an old stone cottage. Why, too, had the soldier's presence remained unknown all these years? The ruins must have been visible for years after the Civil War and, surely, someone would have known that there was a body in the ruins but, plainly, this was not the case. Why had he been there? What were the events that led up to his death? Why had he died, not on the field of battle, but apparently crushed by the falling masonry of a burning building? It might have been his home. If so, why was he in armour and why in the cellar? No, he must have been in hiding. Perhaps he was trapped down there, even perhaps a prisoner locked in that dark, dank hole until the building fell in on top of him. The possibilities were endless.

With a sigh, Frank turned his attention yet again to the paper on his desk. He had a story to write. A local football team had won a cup and the Sports Editor had asked him to write up two or three paragraphs. What a chore! He found sport a little tedious at the best of times but now, with so much more interesting thoughts and possibilities to occupy his mind, it required an immense effort to bring his mind to concentrate on such an inconsequential matter. The dreariness of it overwhelmed him and yet it was his job to make it an interesting and newsworthy item for the benefit of the readers, but the sporting activities of a local football team held his interest like a sieve holds water. With a yawn he tried, once again, to piece together a coherent story on this sporting triumph.

It was three days since he had been sent out to cover the motorway find. He had made quite a story of it and, to be fair, although the editor had cut it far more than Frank thought justified, it had still made quite a good centre page story. That was fine as far as it went, but Frank was convinced that there would be a follow up story when Gibson went to Hartington Hall. So far, he had heard nothing. Frank wondered if he should phone Gibson. No, Gibson would certainly contact him if there was anything more to tell. On the other hand, perhaps he would think it not worth bothering the newspaper again. Frank's hand reached out to the phone and hovered above it as, undecided, he considered what to do. Before he could come to a decision the phone rang beneath his poised hand.

'Reporters' room, Smithers speaking.'

A voice crackled at the other end of the line.

'Oh, good morning, Mr Smithers, Gibson here. I thought that you might be interested to know that I went to see General Cressley yesterday. It seems that there is more to be made of this motorway find than we first thought.'

Frank could scarcely contain his excitement. He knew it, in his bones; the find was just the beginning.

'What did the General have to tell you then?'

'Oh, it's too involved to go into over the phone. Look, the general has agreed to see us both either tomorrow or, if you can make it, at about 4 o'clock this afternoon. Can you spare the time?'

'You bet I can.' replied Frank enthusiastically. 'Will I see you at Hartington Hall?'

'If you wish; but let me give you a lift. No point in taking two cars. I'll call for you at your office.'

'Fine.' agreed Frank.

'Would half past three be alright?'

'I'll be waiting.'

Frank replaced the phone, rose from his desk and resumed his vigil over the market square. Once again he took no account of the scene below but this time, although the far-away look remained on his face, there was also a smile of triumph.

At about a quarter to four that afternoon, Frank Smithers and David Gibson were motoring along the quiet country lanes beyond Wootton. It was not long before they saw Hartington Hall, golden and dreaming, in the spring sunshine. Behind the old house, to the west, the tree covered parkland rose in a gentle slope to a low ridge behind which, unseen from the house, lay the line of the new motorway. To the south, some mile or so distant, was the edge of Salcey Forest. Turning off the road, David Gibson drove up the gravel covered drive and parked by the large and impressive front porch, covering a pair of ancient oak doors. Frank wondered if they had been there since the house was built.

In response to hammer blows with the large brass knocker, the door was opened by a distinguished looking middle aged man whom, Frank was sure, must be the original Jeeves. Gibson was immediately recognised.

'Good afternoon, sir. The General is expecting you. May I enquire the name of this other gentleman?'

After Gibson had explained that the General had invited Frank Smithers to accompany him, the butler led them into the drawing room, the walls of which were entirely covered with rich, dark, wooden panels, mostly decorated with intricate carvings. Despite the dark walls, the room was well lit by the sunlight pouring in through the large leaded bay windows; making the interior bright and airy. The General was seated in a chair by one of the south facing windows looking out over the garden to the fields beyond. As the butler announced the two visitors the General rose to greet them.

'Ah, Gibson, good of you to come!'

He shook Gibson's hand and looked enquiringly at Frank.

'It is good of you to see me again. As I mentioned to you over the phone, Mr Smithers of the local newspaper has a great interest in this matter. It was he who wrote the recent report of the find. He tells me that you have met once before.'

The General looked at Frank rather doubtfully.

'Yes, yes, I believe we have, now you mention it.' he replied without conviction.

'You may recall sir, that I did an article about your home. It would be some two years ago,' Frank interrupted tactfully. 'It was part of a series about local historic houses.'

'Yes, by Jove, yes, now I do remember you. Yes, indeed. Did us proud; damned fine article. Yes, I remember you.'

When they were all seated it was David Gibson who began by saying 'Mr Smithers can scarcely wait to hear what we have to tell him General. He has been quizzing me all the way here but I have refused to answer any of his questions until I had all of the evidence in front of me. Perhaps you will allow him to see the letters.'

31

'Certainly, I have them ready on the table.'

He motioned them towards a table near the window on which lay a number of faded documents held between a piece of board beneath and glass on top.

'We normally keep these well covered against the light. I am afraid that they are already very faded and, I suppose, the day will come when we can't read them at all. I have had them photographed, so we shall continue to have a record of their contents. This one,' said the General, pointing to the one on the left, 'was found by my ancestor, a Sir William Cressley, in a dusty old book somewhere in the library. I think that you will be able to make most of it out, although some of the words are a little bit difficult to decipher, whilst fading in parts has already become a problem.'

Frank studied the letter with great interest. It was, as the General had remarked, not easy to read but, with perseverance, Frank soon got the gist of its contents. It was in a spidery hand, written as Frank guessed with a scratchy quill pen. The spelling would not have been acceptable to Frank's editor but, in spite of all this, the letter still served to convey its message.

'Fascinating!' he remarked; half to himself. 'This Francis, the one who has written the letter; I assume that he is one of your ancestors. Who then, I wonder, are the others to whom he refers? Jack and Mary are clearly his son and daughter and Ralph must be the boyfriend. Do you know anything more about them?'

The General smiled at Frank's obvious excitement.

'Well now, we have looked at the family tree. That is one of the advantages of having an upper crust background; your family history is fairly well recorded. In 1642 this Hall and its lands were in the possession of a Sir Francis Cressley. After the defeat of the Royalists many sympathisers were dispossessed of their land and property, whilst many were exiled abroad. This seems to have been the case with Hartington Hall. The Cressleys fought on the losing side and paid the penalty. However, after the restoration of the monarchy, the Hall and lands were returned to a Jack Cressley. Unfortunately, like so many churches, ours suffered at the hands of Cromwell's puritan zealots, records were destroyed so that information about our family during that period in history is somewhat scanty. There are, of course, other sources of information but family details are best covered by church records for births, marriages and deaths during that time and, indeed, up to the middle of the last century when the state took over the task and registration of these events became compulsory.'

'There is a suggestion that some valuables may be hidden in the house.' observed Frank.

'Yes, indeed,' replied the General. 'In fact, probably due to this letter, there has always been a legend of hidden treasure, but the tale is unlikely to have any foundation. I'd wager that any valuables hidden during the Civil War were retrieved long ago.'

'Have you noticed the date and the address on the letter, Frank?' asked David Gibson.

'York, 1st July 1644. My word that's a long way from here! Is it of any significance?'

'The battle of Marston Moor was fought just outside York on the 2nd July 1644.'

'My goodness, so that's the battle to which the writer refers.'

Frank gazed at the letter deep in thought until the General directed his attention to the second letter.

'This one was found comparatively recently; at the end of the last century in fact. My grandfather was having some structural repairs carried out to the wall and ceiling of one of the bedrooms on the east side of the house. Underneath one of the wooden window seats, a workman found this letter.'

Frank studied the second letter with great care. For a while, he sat deep in thought. Then he turned to the General.

'Do you think that this letter is connected in any way with the first one which is plainly a letter from your ancestor, Sir Francis, to his wife prior to this battle of which David has told us? This is a love letter but it has a warning of some danger in which the writer finds himself. It seems likely that the Mary referred to in both letters is one and the same person and it may well be that the R.S., who signs the second letter, is the Ralph spoken of in the first.'

'Yes,' replied David Gibson, 'these are the same conclusions that we have drawn; but look at the seals.'

He pointed to the red wax seal at the bottom of both letters. In each case, the letter had been folded over at the bottom so that the relatively undamaged seal could be seen. Both seals were embossed with a design, which upon close inspection, although different, were very similar. The motif on each was that of an eagle in flight with a lamb in its talons, but the surrounding design and the embellishment were quite different. The seal on the first letter was somewhat larger and grander than the one on the second letter.

Now David Gibson handed Frank the ring which had been taken from the finger of the recently uncovered skeleton. It had been cleaned and polished since he had last seen it. When David touched the side of the gold dome with his thumb, it flew back quite freely, having now the advantage of a drop of oil. Frank looked at the sealing wax die revealed underneath the dome.

Frank took the ring and inspected it closely. Then he looked again at the second letter. The look of disbelief on his face was such that both the General and David Gibson laughed out loud. The dawn of realisation crept slowly over Frank's face, replacing the look of puzzlement. 'Why, it's the very same pattern. It must have been this ring that was used to seal the letter from R.S.'

It was his journalistic training that prompted his next remark. 'Why, this will be one hell of a good story for the paper.'

He looked again at the first letter.

'Both have very similar designs; a big bird, probably an eagle, with some small creature in its claws. But this ring definitely has the same pattern as on the second letter. Of course, there could have been more than one ring with an identical seal.'

'I doubt it. You see, these were made to be unique; so that those in the know could identify the owner and therefore the sender of the letter.' explained David Gibson.

Frank nodded. 'I see. Well, with such similar patterns there must be some very close connection between the two rings and their owners.'

'Undoubtedly.' agreed David Gibson. 'We don't have far to

look for that connection either. Obviously the General has always known about this.'

David Gibson walked across the room to the large fireplace and peered closely at the intricate carvings on the wooden surround. Frank, who had followed him, looked at the area David had indicated. There, in the pattern which repeated itself around the edge of the surround, was the self-same device; an eagle in flight with a small creature clutched in its huge talons.

Frank's mind was racing. What did this all mean? There must be answers to the many questions which entered his head and yet no obvious solutions came to mind.

'Well, plainly, both letters are closely connected with the occupants of this house at that time and one, at least, was written by the owner.'

It was the General who spoke next. He had been watching Frank's reaction with some amusement. These letters from the past had intrigued him for years and this recent discovery, far from shedding any light on the mystery surrounding the letters, had served only to raise far more questions to which he had no answers. He could well understand the fascination and frustration that Frank now felt.

'Members of my family, and not least myself, have puzzled over those two letters for years. There is so much suggested but so little told. Ralph was obviously in love with Mary, but the affair was under some veil of secrecy.'

'And yet,' interrupted David Gibson, 'the father knew and speaks highly of Ralph. Certainly it is a puzzle.'

'It is a puzzle that will intrigue our readers. Have I your permission General to run a story on this?'

'Yes, certainly. Why not? As you say, it is a good story which I'm sure your readers will find most interesting.'

'If I may, sir, I'll have our photographer call to get a picture of the two letters with a close up of the seal and the ring.'

'Why, yes, of course.' agreed General Cressley.

At this point in the conversation the door opened and a very attractive young lady entered carrying a tray with a teapot and cups.

'I thought that you and your visitors might be ready for a cup of tea by now.' she said with a smile.

'Well timed, my dear.' General Cressley returned his daughter's affectionate smile. Then, to Frank and David, 'This is my daughter Mary'; adding with a laugh, 'Oh no, not the one in the letters.'

CHAPTER 4

Spring 1959
Northampton

Two days later, seated at his desk in the reporters' room, Frank was finishing off a short story to catch the late edition. He was so utterly absorbed in his work that he scarcely noticed the office boy throw down, on his desk, the first edition of the day's paper. Scribbling furiously, he concluded the final paragraph and then put down his pen. He made to grab the paper lying on his desk but, remembering his priorities, he checked his article and took it into the sub editor's office. Seconds later he was back at his desk scanning urgently through the pages of the paper. There, in the centre, was his big story.

This time the editor had done him proud. Two columns had been devoted to his write up of the story about the sequel to the discovery of the skeleton. Adjacent to his two columns was the photograph of the skeleton on the site. This was simply a reprint of the earlier photograph. Below this were photographs of the two letters and a close up of the ring, showing it with its cap closed and also with the cap open revealing the sealing die.

Frank had started with a short history of the Civil War and how it had affected this part of the country and, in particular, what known facts there were about events during that period at Hartington Hall. Other than that an ancestor of General Cressley had fought for the Royalist cause, there was little enough to tell on this score. Frank had briefly related again the details of the find on the motorway construction site. From there he had gone on to tell how he and David Gibson had visited Hartington Hall and how they had discovered a connection between the ring found on the skeleton and at least one of the letters which had been shown him by General Cressley. He posed many of the obvious questions that arose from this discovery and ended with some possible explanations. He concluded with an invitation for readers to contact him with any further information that might throw more light on the events of those long forgotten days.

Later that day Gibson phoned.

'I'm just ringing to congratulate you on a well written article.'

Frank felt a glow of satisfaction.

'Thanks. It's a lot easier when you're really interested. It seems a pity that it will probably end here. I wish that there was a way to find the background to this whole business.'

'Yes,' agreed David Gibson. 'There are so many unanswered questions. It's like catching a fleeting glimpse of something in the half-light. There is so much more to know, but I expect most of it will always remain a mystery.'

The two men chatted for a few minutes longer after which, with mutual expressions of thanks, they rang off. Putting down the phone, Frank sadly reflected that that was probably the end of the matter and no more would be heard of the dead cavalier, or of those mysterious letters.

* * *

The unexpected happened the next day. Frank had not yet dismissed the matter altogether from his mind but he was, nevertheless, surprised when he answered a call in the office only to hear the unmistakable voice of General Cressley at the other end of the line.

'Is that you, Smithers? Ah, Cressley here.'

'Oh, hello General. This is a pleasant surprise.'

'I say old chap, I expect you're frightfully busy but I wonder if you can spare time to come over here. Something most interesting has turned up, entirely I may say, as a result of your story in yesterday's paper. I know that it is very short notice. I've already contacted Gibson and he is on his way. If you can make it, I am sure that you'll find it worth your while.'

'Have you received some further information about the

skeleton or your letters?' asked Frank with ill-concealed excitement.

'Yes, indeed. It really is most remarkable.'

'Right, I'll be over in twenty minutes.' Frank replied without hesitation, although he had just arrived back in the office from an interview with a local councillor and had a story to write before three o'clock. There were times, thought Frank, for decisions and this was one. Plans for new methods of sewage disposal could wait. Obviously, the General couldn't.

Motoring over to Hartington Hall in his new little Austin A30 car, Frank pondered about the sort of further information that the General could have received. He was more than a little uneasy about what the editor would say when the article he was expecting about sewage disposal failed to turn up on his desk and enquiries about Frank revealed that he was not even in the office. Well, 'sufficient unto the day is the evil thereof,' thought Frank and turned his mind back to the more attractive consideration of this new turn of events.

Soon Frank found himself once again in the drive at Hartington Hall. He noticed that David Gibson's car was already there. Another car was parked alongside it. Two minutes later Frank was being ushered into the same drawing room in which he had sat two days ago. This time there was no sun to lighten the room and the panelling, even with the benefit of electric lighting, looked somewhat darker. However, the atmosphere in the room was far from gloomy. On the contrary, there was a warmth and friendliness which was reflected in the welcome that Frank received from the General.

'Ah, Smithers, so glad you could make it. I'd like you to meet Mr Robert Somers. He farms over at Preston Capes. Mr Somers, this is Mr Frank Smithers, a gentleman of the local press.'

Robert Somers was a man of medium height and of sturdy build, more rugged than handsome. Frank guessed that he would be in his middle to late twenties. He was well dressed without being smart. He greeted Frank with a friendly smile and a firm handshake. There was about him an air of casual confidence; of one who has the ordering, rather than serving of others.

The General saw Frank seated and offered him a drink before

beginning with an excitement that he was scarcely able to contain.

'I asked you and Mr Gibson to come over since, as I said over the phone, something of considerable interest has come to light in connection with my letters and our friend the skeleton. Mr Somers read your article in yesterday's paper and, as a result, has brought something for me to see that has been in his family for donkey's years and which, I can imagine, has been as puzzling to him and his family as my letters have been to me. Now, Mr Somers, perhaps you had better explain.'

There was, in spite of Frank's first impression, a hint of shyness about Robert Somers as he began to speak, but it was well under control and soon he revealed a pleasing, outgoing personality.

'My family have lived at Preston Capes in the old manor for many years; centuries in fact. The records are by no means complete but they are sufficient to show that there were Somers in Preston Capes during Elizabethan times. Just over one hundred and fifty years ago the owner of the manor was a James Somers. His grandson, Timothy Somers, was my great, great grandfather. It seems that one day, completely by accident, he came across a secret compartment in a bureau which had been in the house for as long as could be remembered. Within the compartment was a letter. The letter, because of its obvious interest, has been preserved. I've brought it with me for you to see. It is dated the 3rd November 1642'

Opening a case, Robert Somers took out a letter which had been placed for safe keeping, rather like General Cressley's letters, between two pieces of glass. He laid it on the coffee table in front of him.

'The letter,' he continued, 'was neither signed nor addressed. It contained information of a military nature, relating to the forces of Parliament during the Civil War. Those of you who study history will perhaps have realised that the date of the letter, 3rd November, 1642, is about a fortnight after the battle of Edgehill. The writer describes the state and strength of the army under the Earl of Essex, lying in Warwick, where it was licking its wounds after the first major encounter of the war between the King and Parliament. The writer was obviously a spy and states that at the time of writing he is under some suspicion. For whom the letter was intended, and by whom it was written, has remained a mystery and may always be so. The tale about how the secret compartment was discovered and the finding of the letter has probably lost nothing in its telling over the generations. It seems that, of all things, they were trying to catch a butterfly that had flown into the bureau. Well, the truth is often stranger than fiction, so perhaps that is what happened. I had the tale from my grandfather who, in turn, had it from his own grandfather, Timothy, who was a young lad of eight or nine at the time and was actually with his grandfather James when the discovery was made. Whatever the truth of all that, the fact remains that the letter has been in our family since those days. It contains a mystery that has intrigued several generations of Somers. The only clue we have as to the writer lies in the seal.

Here Robert Somers looked up. He smiled when he saw the look on Frank's face.

'Yes, Mr Smithers, you've guessed it, the eagle and the lamb; the very same as the seal on one of General Cressley's letters and originating, almost certainly, from the ring found on the skeletal fingers of that unfortunate soldier. Having a general interest in local history I read your article, Mr Smithers, with great fascination. You can imagine my excitement when I saw in the enlarged picture of the seal an exact replica of the seal on my letter. I can assure you that I lost no time in contacting General Cressley and arranging to see him.'

Neither David Gibson nor Frank Smithers could contain themselves any longer. They were soon beside Robert Somers, gazing spellbound at the letter on the table in front of them.

'It's incredible.' murmured David Gibson.

'To think,' added Frank, 'that after all these years, a chance find of a skeleton would bring all this evidence together.'

'Not without your assistance, Mr Smithers,' observed Robert Somers, who seemed to find some amusement in the obvious astonishment evinced by both Frank Smithers and David Gibson. That is not to say that he, himself, was indifferent to the recent discoveries, but his was a more quiet satisfaction at having found out at last something more about that enigmatic letter, which had for so long puzzled the Somers of Preston Capes. David Gibson's initial surprise now gave way to a studious appraisal of the facts. On the other hand, Frank Smithers, who was always on the lookout for a story and who had an interest in the human angle, was now beginning to consider what sort of people were these ghosts of the past, who had walked these lanes and pastures and who had occupied this very room. They had been real people with loves and hates and ambitions, like so many others; but, much as these letters told, there was much more to know about them. How had they fared in the horrors of a civil war? Had Ralph and Mary married? Did Sir Francis Cressley and his son Jack survive the battle of Marston Moor? What was the peril in which Ralph stood?

The General brought out his two letters and laid them by the side of the letter belonging to Robert Somers. Both Frank and David joined the General in a detailed inspection of the three documents. They spoke almost in whispers as they discussed each detail or drew attention to something of significance. Robert and Mary seemed content to discuss the matter in more general terms and appeared as much interested in each other as in the letters.

For a while, time stood still in that ancient room, as the events of those long forgotten times were reviewed in the building which had been their mute witness. It was David Gibson who broke the spell when he spoke to Robert Somers.

'Have you anything else to tell us about this letter, Mr Somers? For instance, have you or anyone else investigated your family records during the period when the letters were written? Have you ever shown the letters to an expert or sought advice about its contents?'

'Indeed yes. It has been shown to a number of authorities, but none has been able to shed further light on the mystery. No one, who has looked at the letter, has ever cast any doubt on its authenticity; that is to say, no one has suggested that it is not a genuine letter from the Civil War period. The details that are contained in the letter, relating to the make-up and strength of the Earl of Essex's army, are fully borne out by historical records. We have been told that, during the Civil War, there were many men spying for both causes, as you would imagine. As to the identity of the writer, that was obviously meant to be a secret and it seems is likely to remain so.'

'The circumstances in which it was found vouch for its authenticity.' observed David Gibson. 'In any case, it would be a very elaborate hoax, to very little purpose. No, I'm sure that it is genuine, but it doesn't help us to any greater knowledge of the writer. Were any of your ancestors involved in the Civil War, do you know, Mr Somers?'

'I haven't the slightest idea. There is, however, one other point of interest which I haven't yet mentioned. It doesn't add anything to our scanty knowledge of the writer, but it is intriguing all the same. When the letter was discovered, my ancestors were as anxious as we are to find out what they could about the letter and who wrote it. Naturally, one of the first sources of information they turned to was the parish records. These are a bit sketchy around the period in question. It is a long time since I looked at them. However, it was soon discovered that the manor at Preston Capes was at that time in the hands of one, Henry Somers, and his death is recorded as having taken place on the 4th November 1642; the very day after the letter was written.'

'What an extraordinary coincidence.' declared Frank.

'Well, it might have been. I doubt that we shall ever know.' observed Roberts Somers shaking his head.

'Had he a son?' asked David Gibson.

'Yes.' replied Robert. 'His name was .....' He paused as the sudden dawn of realisation spread across his face. 'Yes, he had a son. His name was Ralph, Ralph Somers, R.S.'

'Of course!' echoed David Gibson. 'It must have been Ralph Somers then who wrote your letter and that is at least one good reason why it was found in an antique piece of furniture in your home.'

'Yes.' agreed Mary excitedly, 'And it was your ancestor who was in love with Mary, old Sir Francis Cressley's daughter.'

The General was just as excited as the others in that mysterious old room, as it now seemed to Frank.

'It can't be coincidence.' declared the General. 'The seals are identical. The writer in my letter signs himself 'R.S'. My other letter refers to a Ralph and now your letter arrives on the scene with, by the way, exactly similar handwriting and you tell us that the man who inherited your home in 1642 was called Ralph. Why, it all fits together like a jigsaw puzzle.'

'Surely there must be more that we can deduce from these letters.' murmured David Gibson thoughtfully.

'Mr Somers' letter doesn't give any further clues to the possibility that there is hidden treasure here at Hartington Hall.' remarked Mary sadly. 'I've always hoped that one day something will be found.'

'No.' agreed David Gibson. 'It adds nothing to that story.'

'No, I'm afraid that it doesn't.' she agreed, 'but it certainly makes the possibility more credible. It's as if the events and the people in those letters are coming to life.'

'There's one who is not.' observed Frank Smithers.

It was the manner in which he made the remark that made the others turn round and look at him.

'What do you mean?' they asked almost simultaneously.

'Our skeleton, of course. He's very dead and yet he must be our central character.'

'I'm sorry, I'm not with you.' replied Mary, wearing a somewhat bewildered expression.

'Well,' explained Frank, 'we now have three letters; two with the same seal and the other with a rather different, but similar one. The third letter, with the different seal, we know to have been written by Sir Francis Cressley. The other two, having the same seal, are presumably written by the same person. As the General points out, the handwriting compares exactly. This person we know to be R.S. or Ralph Somers. On the skeleton we find the ring that sealed both letters. It therefore follows that the skeleton must be the remains of.....'

'Ralph Somers.' declared Mary, excitedly, interrupting Frank before he could finish. 'Why, don't you see Mr Somers. That skeleton found out there must be the remains of your ancestor, Ralph Somers.'

CHAPTER 5

Spring 1642
Northamptonshire

It was a happy day for Ralph Somers as he rode on his favourite mare, Jezebel, through the rich green countryside in the month of April. The rain which had dogged the first few miles of his journey was clearing up. The clouds were becoming lighter and in the distance was a definite patch of clear blue sky. Soon, he felt sure, the sun would be shining. A short distance behind him Jethro, his man servant, rode horseback, leading a pack horse which carried a small leather bound chest containing Ralph's clothes, a few presents and one or two other necessities which Ralph had insisted on bringing.

In spite of the weather Ralph wore a sense of elation like a jaunty hat. He smiled as he thought of the holiday and pleasures ahead of him and, as he smiled, the sun broke through. He rose exultantly in his saddle and shouted to Jethro to stop dawdling. But, truth to tell, there was no need for hurry, especially when the sun was shining and spring had cast its green mantle across the rolling Northamptonshire countryside. He relaxed in his saddle and let his mare plod at her own pace; for he was on holiday. He was on his way to stay with his uncle who lived within the confines of Salcey Forest which, with Whittlebury Forest, covered the greater part of the south of the county and much of North Buckinghamshire. For a whole fortnight, Ralph would be shrugging off the burden of care which he had carried for these past six months and relaxing in the company of his favourite aunt and uncle. He looked forward to his uncle's companionship and to riding with his cousin in the forest. He remembered with pleasure the excellent food which, thanks to his aunt's well-ordered kitchen, was always on the table at mealtimes. He looked forward to at least one visit to Northampton and to any of the social activities that his aunt and uncle might arrange.

Since Christmas, Ralph's father, Henry Somers, had been in poor health. Indeed, for several weeks during the long winter months, Ralph had feared that his father would not live to gain the benefit of the summer sunshine. During all of this time Ralph had had not only the worry of nursing his father, but also the ordering of his father's estates. At eighteen years old Ralph had had little experience either of nursing people or of managing the land, but necessity is a harsh teacher and had found Ralph an able pupil.

Ralph had not minded the work. He was no idler and cared for nothing better than the prospect of managing the farms and the land which one day he would inherit. Ralph loved his father dearly; the more so for not having known his mother who had died when Ralph was born. The elderly nurse who had cared for him as a child had died when Ralph was fifteen. This had been a grievous loss to him, for he had bestowed on her all the love which he would have given to his mother. The anxiety about his father and the disturbed nights, when Ralph had sat with him, ministering to his needs, trusting no other; together with the long hours of work during the day, had all taken their toll and his own health had begun to suffer.

Now, thank God, his father was mending and was well enough for Ralph to leave him behind in the care of his housekeeper. It was thus that Ralph was able now to leave the estate to run itself for a while and leave his father to convalesce in their home at Preston Capes in the west of the county. He felt that, at last, he could indulge himself in a holiday at his father's brother's home, scarce fifteen miles from his own. This was far enough for a change, but near enough for a quick return in an emergency.

So, today Ralph's spirits were high. He was bursting with youthful zest. Why must they dawdle at this snail's pace when he itched to gallop his horse over the damp green turf.

'Come along, Jethro. Can you not get that beast to trot a little faster? We shall not be at my uncle's house before nightfall if we do not make haste.'

'Nay master, he will travel at his own speed or not all.' Jethro was forty years of age and, truth to tell, he had long since lost the desire to gallop around the countryside, when he could arrive at his destination only a little later while travelling at a more restful pace.

Ralph knew this too and resigned himself to making haste slowly. He also knew that there was plenty of daylight left and, indeed, it would be less than half an hour before he would catch sight of his uncle's house half hidden in the trees and sheltering behind its high trimmed hedge.

The forest began to close in on them shortly after passing through the little village of Hartwell, where the forest was a source of livelihood to many of its inhabitants. Indeed much of Ralph's route had been through forested country and his own home lay on the edge of Whittlebury Forest. Between his own home at Preston Capes and Salcey Forest, much of the forest had been cleared over the centuries, especially adjacent to the Watling Street which had brought settlers since Roman times. To the east of Hartwell the trees grew more thickly and they spread with little hindrance for some miles towards Olney. A mile or so from Hartwell, Ralph came to a crossroads where his path crossed the road that traversed the forest from north to south. It was another mile or so further on that Ralph caught a glimpse of chimneys and then the leaded windows and the ornately carved masonry at the gable ends. This was Bullshead Farm, his uncle's home.

It was a small but attractive building, situated on the western edge of a small clearing in the forest, close to the track from Hartwell along which Ralph was riding. Some distance away, on the eastern side of the clearing, was the busier highway used by travellers going south from Northampton to Newport Pagnell and on to London. The house had clear views over the farm and parkland which sloped gently away to the south and east to where, some half a mile distant, the forest closed in once again.

Their coming had been looked for. As they were half way up the drive, the front door burst open and a curly haired boy of some eight or nine years old ran shouting to greet them. It was Hugh, Ralph's cousin.

'Ralph, you've come at last. Father said that you would be here soon. I've been keeping watch for you from a bedroom window. I've got lots to show you. Come and see my rabbits. There are five now. I keep them in one of the stables. Thomas built a hutch for them. He calls them conies. I sometimes let them out for a run around.'

Hugh was already tugging at Ralph's sleeve.

'All in good time you young rascal.' boomed a voice from the doorway. Charles Somers, Ralph's uncle, stood there beaming a welcome to his nephew. He was a large jovial man; a man of stature in every sense of the word. He was the sort of man who would call every other man his neighbour. He was quick to anger, but bore no malice. He despised idleness, but his servants loved him. He hated waste, but was generous to a fault. He was a man of principle, but never dogmatic. He was a man whom Ralph had grown to love and admire. Between them there had always been a bond, almost as close as between father and son.

'Ralph, my boy, you're looking more the man each time I see you. Come along inside.' He ushered Ralph into the light and airy hall. 'Nathan, where is that man?' A door opened at the back of the hall and in came Nathan, the long suffering servant to Charles Somers. 'I'm coming, I'm coming as fast as these two legs will carry me. I heard you the first time. How be you, Master Ralph?' Nathan had the measure of his master and would not be bullied. He knew his worth, as indeed did Charles.

'You come too slow, you idle fellow. Now fetch Master Ralph's trunk whilst Jethro attends to the horses.' The words held no anger, neither was Nathan cowed. Nevertheless he went quickly out to do his master's bidding.

Charles led Ralph from the hall into a pleasantly furnished living room. Ralph found a seat in the window looking out into the garden and the pastures beyond. Hugh sat beside him, waiting to ply him with the many questions that he was desperate to ask and drag him off to see the many wonders that he was itching to show him.

'Well now, how is your poor father? I believe that he is

somewhat improved since I saw him last month.' Charles enquired with obvious concern for his brother.

'Much improved, I'm glad to say, and getting stronger by the day. He has been very ill indeed and there was a time when the physician feared for his life. But now, thank God, he is on the mend and will soon be about his business once again. The physician warns that he will have a weakness in his heart now and must avoid heavy work and stress but, with that proviso, he can look forward to a life as good as new.'

'Well, that is good news indeed. Now you must make sure that he takes care of himself. He is not a young man anymore. It will be hard to hold him back. I'm sure that he will wish to be back at work soon. When there is work to be done, your father was never one to shirk. It was, I think, his business and worries of the estate that brought him so low. He works too hard and plays too little. Work and worry take a great toll of a man's health and strength; but I suppose that there is always work and worry in these troublous times. Parliament is against the King and the King is against Parliament. There is open talk of rebellion. I wonder sometimes what use it is to work and plan when all may come to ruin.'

Ralph was surprised to see the genuine concern on his uncle's face about the rift between the King and his Parliament which is threatening the peace of the realm. Ralph had always thought of his uncle as a born optimist. He was usually the first to see the bright side of the most gloomy situation. He had thought that the news of his father's improved health would have raised a smile on his uncle's face. Yet here he was, lost in thought, his brow furrowed as he worried about the future and what it might bring.

'This is but talk, surely uncle. Englishmen would never rise in rebellion against their King.'

'Let us pray that you are right, but we live in fearful times and I have grave doubts about the future.' Uncle Charles sat for a moment thoughtfully shaking his head and then dismissed his reverie with a shrug of his shoulders and, with the smile back on his face, declared. 'These are heavy matters to discuss, you have only just arrived! Where is my wife, your aunt. Surely she heard you come.' Charles strode to the door. 'Maria.' One felt the walls shake as his voice thundered in the hall.

'Hugh, go and find your mother.'

Hugh had scarce left the room when a door opened on the other side of the hall and Aunt Maria appeared.

'Come Maria, your nephew is here. Come and bid him welcome.'

Aunt Maria was not a small woman but beside her husband she seemed so. She was in her early thirties and younger than her husband by six years. She was no great beauty but rather a pleasant motherly soul, kindly and content with a good husband and her young son. With a smile she welcomed Ralph with arms extended.

'Ralph dear, how happy I am to see you.'

She embraced him and then held him at arms-length as she viewed him with a gentle smile, which spoke of a genuine warmth and affection. She enquired after his father and his own health. Then, with a reminder that dinner would be served within the hour, she released him to the patient Hugh.

What was left of the day was spent in looking, eating and talking. Before darkness fell, Hugh took Ralph to see his rabbits, his cat and his dog, as well as the small garden which he cultivated. Ralph had watched his cousin grow through the years and marvelled at how little time it seemed since he had first seen him as a babe in arms. In spite of their difference in ages, the two got along well together. Ralph dutifully admired the rabbits and gave Hugh some advice on how to rear the young. Then he helped Hugh make a bow and arrow. They spent the last half hour of daylight practising their archery.

As the light faded from the sky they heard the call that dinner was about to be served and went indoors. Dinner over, Hugh was dispatched to bed leaving Ralph to a quiet chat with his aunt and uncle. The larger candles used at the dinner table were blown out and, by the light of two or three rush candles, they talked of family and friends, of the problems on both Uncle Charles' farm and Ralph's father's at Preston Capes, of the troubles that beset the country and, most interesting of all, they talked of how they could entertain Ralph during his stay. It was quite late for the Somers of Bullshead when Aunt Maria decided that it was time for her to seek her bed. Ralph and his uncle chatted for half an hour longer before they too felt it time to get some sleep.

The next day Ralph took his time in rising. As a rule, he was reluctant to lie abed in the morning. Indeed, it was seldom that he had the chance. However, he was on holiday and, since his aunt had made a point of telling him to sleep for as long as he wished, he found some pleasure in this indulgence.

After breakfast, with Hugh for company, he went for a stroll in the forest. The two of them wandered along the ridings finding something of interest at every turn. Ralph was careful to note the way they went for he was all too well aware how easy it was to lose one's way in so large a forest, where one riding looked very like another. He had, however, little need to worry for, in spite of his tender years, Hugh was as much at home in these leafy glades as Ralph was on his father's lands.

The sun hid behind a layer of clouds and the day was dull but mild. The rain, which had come in the night, had cleared up leaving the grass wet and the paths a little muddy in places, where the grass was worn. Now and then the clouds thinned as the sun tried, without much success, to break through. In spite of the dullness of the day, the forest was a picture with the trees now clad in the fresh green of spring time. The only sounds to disturb the peace of the forest were the sounds of nature; the song of the birds, the hum of the bees, the wind in the trees and the occasional noise in a thicket of some small creature startled by the sound of their footsteps or of their voices.

During their wanderings the only person they met was old Tom Kiteley, the local game keeper. He was a quiet spoken fellow who was happier with the creatures of the forest than with people. Ralph soon saw that he had a soft spot for young Hugh. They both shared an instinctive love of the countryside and had a feeling of kinship for the wildlife which roamed the forest. The two often spent hours together walking the ridings;

the one doing his job and the other listening and learning. Already Hugh was wise beyond his age in the ways of the forest and its inhabitants. For these two there were sights and wonders of nature reserved for only those who had learned the art of stealth and knew where to look.

Home for lunch, Ralph heard with pleasure that the next day they were to ride horseback to visit some friends of the family who lived at Olney, some six miles away. The friends were a family of six. The father was a prosperous trader in this small country town. He ran a business in which his older sons helped, supplying the needs of the local farmers. His wife was a fat, jolly woman who had been a friend of Aunt Maria in her younger days when, as a child, Maria had lived with her parents at Olney.

Aunt Maria's mother and father had died some six years ago and the family home had been sold. At her request, they had detoured from the path to look at the small house, which had been her home some sixteen years ago. She was pleased to find that it was still trim and well cared for. Some few minutes later they were being welcomed into the home of her friend.

The day passed very pleasantly, talking and strolling along the banks of the sluggish river Ouse. They looked around and sat for some time in the large garden in which the house was set. On more than one occasion Ralph found that he had been left alone with Alice, the oldest daughter in the family. She was slim and attractive. It was soon plain to Ralph that his aunt was match making and had hopes that the two might strike up a friendship and perhaps something more. She was a pleasant enough lass and Ralph enjoyed her company, but she stirred no deep feelings within him. She was just another girl. Ralph had had little time during the past six months to interest himself in the fair sex. Like most lads of his age, Ralph had been out with a number of girls whom he had partnered to dances and parties. He had had his fun with the village girls but it had never been serious. Indeed, Ralph sometimes wondered why youths of his acquaintance lost their hearts and their senses to some black haired beauty, whose sole aim seemed to be to get their suitor into church and into bed; preferably in that order. Perhaps there was something amiss with him, but Ralph had never been thus smitten. So, sadly, Aunt Maria's schemes came to nought.

However, the day passed pleasantly enough and, after an evening meal, they saddled their horses and set off to ride the short distance back to Bullshead farm. The days were lengthening and so it was that they were able to delay their departure until just before seven o'clock, giving themselves over an hour of daylight to make the journey home. Hugh was anxious to show off his pony and challenged Ralph to a race. Side by side, the two of them galloped through the mostly open countryside, skirting the occasional cluster of cultivated strips, usually close to some small hamlet. After about a mile they reined in their mounts to rest them and to wait for Uncle Charles and Aunt Maria to catch up. They preferred to let their horses amble along side by side while they chatted and enjoyed the evening ride. They had timed their journey nicely, for a red and yellow sky in the west hid the setting sun and betokened, if proverbs be true, a fine day tomorrow. Bats were on the wing and, in the trees, owls hooted as they rode into the yard at Bullshead farm. There was just enough light to stable their horses before they went indoors to lighted candles. For an hour or so they reviewed the day's events and then they found their beds.

A day or two later Ralph was up early. He had by now had his fill of lazing in bed. A couple or so mornings were quite enough for a while and, after an early night, he was glad to be up, breakfasted and out before Hugh was awake. Ralph was fond of his cousin, but he was glad to be on his own for a change and savour the silence or sounds of the forest without the constant chatter of Hugh's tongue. He had walked for some miles in a circular route and found himself, once again, within sight of Bullshead farm. He could just see the gable end through the trees at the end of the riding and smoke curling lazily upwards from one of the tall chimneys. Then, of a sudden, he became aware of the drumming of horse's hooves and looked round to see a horseman galloping hell for leather in his direction. A deer grazing in the undergrowth some fifty yards away also heard the horse thundering towards him. In a panic, the frightened beast leapt from the undergrowth, across the path of the horse and disappeared into the trees on the other side of the riding. Startled by the deer's panic stricken flight, barely a dozen yards in front of it, the horse reared, threw its rider and bolted.

This all happened within seconds and, being some distance away, Ralph could do nothing to stop the horse. However, seeing the rider lying motionless on the ground, he ran to see what help he could afford. As he approached the rider, who lay still on the ground, Ralph feared that perhaps he was dead. It was with considerable relief that he saw signs of life. By the time he reached her (for in spite of her attire, the rider was a young lady), she was sitting up and attempting to get to her feet. Ralph took her arm.

'Are you able to stand?'

The girl rubbed her arm and shoulder which had taken the brunt of the fall.

'I thank you, yes.' she replied with a smile which, in spite of the mud on her cheek, was the loveliest smile Ralph had ever seen. The smile changed to a wince as she moved her arm.

'You are hurt.' said Ralph. It was more an observation than a question.

'A bruise or two, that is all; I think.' she said, smiling again, as she took a few tentative steps to make sure that her legs were in working order. That ravishing smile so enthralled Ralph that he could scarce take his eyes from her. She was a girl of about his own age. She wore breeches and a lace trimmed shirt much as he might himself have worn, but her long golden curls were not all which showed that she was no lad, whilst her speech betrayed her breeding. Her eyes sparkled as she smiled and spoke with a low enchanting voice. Ralph's manners had gone with his wits.

'My dress surprises you, I see. I'm not what you thought.' She tossed her lovely head and smiled at Ralph with some amusement.

'Your pardon mistress....' Ralph paused, tongue tied and foolishly lost for words, but the young lady came to the rescue.

'Mistress Cressley, sir, at your service!' She introduced herself with a curtsey delivered in fun and which, from another in breeches, would have appeared foolish. But it was done with such grace and again, that enchanting smile, which left Ralph spellbound. When he gathered his wits to reply his voice seemed not to belong to him, but came unbidden from within.

'Ralph Somers, at **your** service, Mistress Cressley. I am glad to see that you have come to no harm from your fall. Have you got far to go? What of your horse?'

'The mare will find her own way back to her stable, but I have now a mile or two to walk.'

Mistress Cressley seemed little concerned at the prospect which, after all, was none too fearful. Ralph, however, had other ideas.

'If you will walk with me a short distance to my uncle's house, I am certain that we shall be able to find a horse for you to ride. I will accompany you home and lead the horse back again.'

'There is no need to put you to so much trouble Master Somers. It is not the first time that I have been thrown and needs must find my way back home on foot.'

'It would be a great pleasure for me to be of assistance, mistress.'

Ralph looked eagerly for a chance to prolong this new acquaintance. Mistress Cressley, for her part, saw before her a handsome young man with a very pleasing countenance and quite a gallant manner. She felt that it would be churlish to refuse his help and besides, although she herself was scarcely aware of it, there was about Ralph Somers a charm which was already captivating her. Moreover, she was flattered by the obvious sincerity of his desire for her company.

'Then sir, I shall be happy to accept your help.'

Ralph flushed with pleasure and pointed in the direction of Bullshead farm. Mistress Cressley strode along beside him in her boots and breeches, but her walk was disconcertingly feminine. None of the young ladies of Ralph's acquaintance would ever have dressed so. When they rode horse-back, they did so decorously, using a side saddle, without abandoning their feminine attire. Not so Mistress Cressley; she always rode her horse like a man, spurning the use of a side saddle.

'I have not seen you in these parts before Master Somers. Are you paying your uncle a visit or have you come to live here?'

Ralph told her of his home at Preston Capes. He talked of his father and of the house where they lived in a way that told of his love for both. She, in her turn, told him of her family and more of herself. Her name was Mary and she lived with her father, mother and brother, some two years older than she, at Hartington Hall near the tiny village of Quinton, just north of the forest on the way to Northampton. Her father, Colonel Sir Francis Cressley, had spent much of his life soldiering in the Low Countries, just across the English Channel. He had given up active service a year or so ago and now devoted his time to the management and care of the large family estate.

They were soon at Bullshead farm where Ralph took Mary to meet his uncle. He was not surprised to find that they already knew each other. Living within a few miles, the two families had met from time to time at various social functions. Ralph observed, too, that his uncle found nothing odd in Mistress Cressley's attire. It seemed that she had quite a reputation as a tomboy and was often seen galloping along the forest ridings. Uncle Charles was happy to be of assistance and smiled knowingly when Ralph explained that he had offered to accompany Mistress Cressley on the short journey back to Hartington Hall.

They mounted and rode off together. As if by mutual consent neither attempted to trot their horse nor in any way speed the journey, but happily they allowed their mounts to dawdle side by side.

They talked, as young couples do, of their likes and dislikes, of their fears and their fancies, of their hopes and their ambitions. They had no trouble in making conversation, but talked as if they were old acquaintances. Mary showed a great interest in Ralph's home which was in a part of the county that she did not know well. She asked many questions and seemed curious to know all about Ralph and about his interests. Ralph readily supplied the answers and showed an equal interest in her and her life at Hartington Hall which, like so many big houses in the country, was the centre of life in the nearby village.

They talked and they talked. Although their horses merely ambled along the time flew by until, after what seemed only minutes after leaving Bullshead, they suddenly emerged from the forest. Pointing, Mary said. 'There lies Hartington Hall.'

Looking in the direction indicated Ralph saw, through the trees which were scattered across the meadow land, a large sandstone building of grand appearance and built in the style of fifty years earlier. It had lawns, gardens and pleasances well laid out and well maintained. The whole was surrounded by a sandstone wall. From a gated opening in the wall, a short drive led to the imposing front door of the mansion.

As he looked, Ralph saw a horseman ride out of the courtyard at the rear of the building and turn up the drive to the muddy road which wound past the mansion grounds. Tethered to his own mount, the rider led another horse which carried its own saddle and stirrups. Gaining the road to the forest, he urged his horse to a gallop and started in their direction.

'Why, 'tis brother Jack with Midnight. I knew that she would find her way home. Jack,' cried Mary, rising in her stirrups, waving and shouting at her brother who, having seen her, waved in return.

They waited while he galloped up to meet them. He was about Ralph's age, maybe a little older. There was in his manner a slight haughtiness which, Ralph discovered later, was his defence against strangers to cover his shyness. He was finely dressed in the gay manner so much in the fashion of the time. He wore a large, wide brimmed hat with a bright feather. His tunic was the colour of claret, which he wore over a lace trimmed shirt. His breeches were made to match and were tied with a ribbon below the knee over white stockings. He wore calf length riding boots with ornate spurs. He looked every inch the gentleman.

He had no need to ask what had happened. 'Surely, sister, you will come to grief one day if you continue to ride about the countryside so madly.' He looked enquiringly at Ralph.

'Don't be cross with me Jack. You ride at least as recklessly as I. Meet Master Ralph Somers who helped me when I fell, almost at his feet. He is nephew to Charles Somers of Bullshead. They were kind enough to lend me a mount and Master Somers has brought me safe back home.'

'Then we are in your debt Master Somers and I am very glad to meet you. Will you refresh yourself with a glass of wine in my father's house?'

'That I will, gladly, sir.'

So, the three rode to Hartington Hall. It was a very grand house, the home of Sir Francis Cressley but, thought Ralph, it hadn't the charm of his own home, even though his could not rival Hartington Hall for its size and grandeur. In the great hall, Ralph met Sir Francis, a man in his early forties; vigorous, strong and obviously still in his prime. He looked every inch a soldier. He had a military bearing and a manner of addressing others which commanded instant obedience and also respect. He seemed to Ralph to be the sort of man to inspire confidence in others and to be a born leader. His welcome was friendly and he expressed his gratitude for the help which Ralph had afforded his daughter. Like Jack, he reproved his daughter for her wildness and forecast that she would break her neck if she didn't ride a little more sedately. But, in his tone, Ralph detected a hint of pride in having such a daughter. He showed a genuine interest in Ralph and his family. He seemed to think that he had, upon some occasion, met Ralph's father but could not pretend to recollect him.

Having finished his wine Ralph rose to leave. He bid good day to Jack and his father, who were content to let Mary show him to the door and to his horse and the one that Mary had ridden, which were tethered outside. As he was about to mount he paused and then turned to speak to Mary.

'Mistress Cressley, forgive me if I seem somewhat bold, but I have little time left before I must return home. I would be very sad to think that I would not see you again. I go this Thursday to the Spring Fair in Northampton. I would be honoured if you would come with me.'

'Why sir, you are bold, to be sure; but I, too, would be sad for us not to meet again and I would love to go to the fair. I fancy that my father will not hinder me, so I shall be glad to go with you.'

'Then I will call for you on Thursday. Will you be ready for an early start? Shall we say two hours after sunrise?'

'I will be ready.'

She smiled at Ralph and his heart leapt. With thanks and promises to meet early on Thursday, Ralph mounted his horse and rode off with the other on a tether at a canter. As he headed back through the forest to Bullshead he could scarcely contain the joy that rose up within him. He shouted aloud with sheer elation and, although he scarce recognised the fact, he experienced the first sweet pleasure of being in love.

* * *

Thursday dawned clear and dry, if a little overcast. The dull weather did nothing to dampen Ralph's spirits. He rose at dawn and dressed in his finest clothes. He, too, could be just as much a peacock as Jack Cressley. He surveyed himself in the mirror. The suit he wore was a shade or two darker than that worn by Jack. However, it made up for what it lacked in brightness by the rich lace trimmings at the neck, cuffs and knees. His leather boots were ornately buckled. At his side hung the sword which his father had given him some years ago and which, if the need arose, Ralph was able to use with good effect.

He was greeted cordially when he arrived at Hartington Hall. This time it was Mary's mother, Lady Elizabeth Cressley, who met him as he was ushered by their man servant through the hall into the living room. She was friendly enough towards him but, thought Ralph, somewhat reserved. Doubtless, she would regard him with some suspicion and wonder, perhaps, if he was a suitable escort for her daughter.

Mary was bubbling with excitement at the prospect of the day's outing. She burst into the sitting room where Ralph sat talking to her mother and waiting while she finished her preparations. Like most of her sex the final embellishment of her appearance inevitably meant that she was not ready until sometime after her escort had arrived. In this case Ralph did not begrudge a second of the time he had been kept waiting. For now, he saw her dressed as a young lady should be and she looked more lovely than any girl he had ever seen.

She wore a pink satin dress with a low cut neckline emphasising the curve of her breasts. It had long sleeves puffed to the elbow. The bodice was embroidered with gold thread and decorated with lace. Her golden hair was in ringlets and held in place with ribbons. As she entered she threw over her shoulder a dark green cloak, tied at the neck and with a hood hanging down at the back.

Ralph thrilled with pleasure as he escorted her to the horses, which were held by a groom outside the front door in readiness for their departure. Seeing her safely mounted, this time on a side saddle, he was soon astride his own horse and by her side.

'Take good care of her Master Somers.' called Lady Cressley as they set off. 'Enjoy yourselves and make sure to be home before dusk.'

At the end of the drive they stopped to wave and turned their horses' heads in the direction of Northampton. They rode gaily together with the joy of youth, with the joy of spring and the happiness of a young couple testing for the first time the pleasure that a man and woman can find in each other's company.

It was not long before they came to the small village of Wootton and then, skirting Hardingstone, away off to the east, they paused by the old stone cross to look down on Northampton nestling in the valley on the far side of the river Nene.

Ralph dismounted and helped Mary down, as they stopped to examine the ancient monument.

'It's said that a king once camped here while taking the body of his dead wife back to London for burial. He had this cross built to mark where her body rested for the night.' said Ralph as he examined the cross with some interest.

'Yes, so I have heard. He must have loved her very dearly.'

They stood side by side in silence for a while looking now at the cross and then at the town some mile distant and then at each other. They were not alone on that grassy and sometimes muddy track. Others were also up early and on their way to town to make the most of a day at the fair. Taking her hand, Ralph led her back to the horses tethered nearby and grazing so contentedly that they were reluctant to continue the journey. They descended the gentle slope, by now a wider but ill kept road that led through the trees to the river's edge. They passed over the ancient stone bridge by old St John's and entered the town. Their horses bore them slowly up the steep hill of Bridge Street, passed the old church of All Saints and into the Market Square.

It was by now well past nine o'clock and the fair was in full swing. Town's folk and country folk jostled together in high good humour, determined to enjoy the day. The Market Square was packed. There was wrestling, bear baiting and cock fighting. There were jugglers and acrobats, gypsies and fortune tellers. Everywhere there were gaily coloured stalls where men and women with noisy animation cried their wares, vying with their neighbour to attract the attention of the passing crowd. There was all manner of food and drink to be bought; fresh fruit and vegetables as well as pies and cooked meats. At one end of the square a side of beef was being roasted on a spit over a blazing fire.

Ralph and Mary gave themselves over to the pleasures of the day; each enjoying themselves very much more because of the other's company. At midday they found an inn nearby where they waited patiently with other folk to be served with a mug of ale, a slice of meat and some bread.

There was little to choose between the commotion and bustle in the inn and the noise of the milling throng outside. Taking Mary's hand, because he wanted to as well as for fear of losing her in the crowd, Ralph led her to a stall which attracted his attention. They watched with fascination as a tall, dark, foreign looking man appeared at first to be either breathing or consuming fire with no ill effects and then, in a further demonstration of his obvious imperviousness to the normal laws of nature, contrived to swallow the whole blade of a sword with apparently no ill effect, although he had demonstrated by shaving wood how sharp the sword was. They paused to watch a bloody duel between a bear with several wounds bleeding freely and a snarling, biting dog. The great, frightened, lumbering beast had been goaded to a fury by the pain, the noise of the crowd and the vicious attacks from the dog which, in spite of stunning blows from the huge paws of the bear, kept leaping and tearing at the creature's throat. Both Ralph and Mary watched the spectacle with fascination and some pity for the distress of the bear. They laughed, however, as they watched the local youths clinging desperately to a greasy pole, trying to shin up to the top and pluck the prize which had been placed there for them to reach. They marvelled at the wrestlers, particularly one giant of a man, who challenged all comers and quickly dismissed anyone who dared to take him on.

So the day wore on. They could have stayed until after nightfall, for the revelries would continue far into the night by the light of torches. Mindful, however, of the need to impress Lady Cressley and her husband, Ralph declared that they ought shortly to begin their journey home. There was, however, time for Ralph to look over the horses for sale and for Mary to see some of the latest fashions on display in the Drapery. They made time too for more refreshments at one of the many stalls selling food and drink. Then it really was time to go.

Collecting their horses from the ostler at the inn where they had left them, they retraced the path which they had ridden earlier that day. As they rode, they chatted happily about all that they had seen and done. Then they fell silent for a while, each one with thoughts of the pleasures they had enjoyed. What a glorious day it had been, thought Ralph and how much more he had enjoyed it being with Mary. Had she enjoyed it too, he wondered. She seemed to have done. What of the future? Soon he must return home to Preston Capes. Was this to be the last he would see of Mary? Not if he had his way.

As they rode, Mary's thoughts were also on the future as well as the fun she had had that day. Why had she enjoyed it so much? She had been to fairs before. They had always been fun, but today had been special. What was it about this man that affected her so? He was handsome, charming and fun to be with, but she had met handsome young men before. So what was it about this one? Would he ride out of her life as abruptly and as quickly as she had ridden into his? He wouldn't care for her. She was but a convenient companion to pass a day of his holiday. Soon he would return to his father's home and she would probably never see him again. This turn of thought sped the last vestige of happiness from her mind and sadness seemed to enshroud her.

'Why so sad?' asked Ralph, seeing the doleful look on her face.

'Oh, I am just sad that the day is nearly over. I've enjoyed it so much.' Her words were faltering and there was a hint of tears in her eyes.

At the top of the hill, a little beyond Queen Eleanor's Cross, they stopped to let their horses drink from a wayside horse trough. Ralph dismounted and helped Mary down. They looked back at the town they had just left. It lay there in the valley so quiet and still, as if hiding the secret of all the bustle and gaiety going on within those now crumbling town walls. The spire of the church of the Holy Sepulchre could be seen surmounting the old round church which, it was said, had been built as a copy of a church in Jerusalem. Away to the left stood old St Peter's on the slope to the river Nene. Ralph had learned at school that those fierce Saxon invaders had penetrated inland following the Nene as far as they could until the river divided into two. Here they had built their settlement which was to be the start of Northampton. Romans had built their villas nearby and earlier man had camped on Hunsbury Hill to the south, but the Saxons were the first to build where Northampton now stood. Beside St Peter's, a little to the west, stood what was left of that once proud castle where kings of England had stayed and held court and from whence, Thomas a'Becket had fled for his life. Away to the right, Ralph could see the road leading from Derngate to the Midsummer Meadows bordering the river. Here, two hundred years before, men had fought and died in one of the many bloody conflicts of the Wars of the Roses and where, as so often was the case, treachery had won the day.

Ralph and Mary sat side by side on an old tree trunk as they surveyed the scene before them, but their thoughts were more for each other than what they saw. Ralph's arm slid around Mary's shoulder. Words passed between them. Their heads moved closer. Before long their lips met in a kiss and their bodies joined in a sweet embrace.

Slowly, reluctantly, they remounted and rode on. As dusk fell they approached the gates of Hartington Hall. Neither was willing to end that precious day one moment before the curfew of approaching night.

It was Ralph who broached the subject that was uppermost on both their minds.

'May I call on you again Mary? I've so enjoyed today and I shall enjoy the rest of my holiday so much more if we can spend some more time together.'

'Yes, I'd like that. I'll show you some parts of Salcey Forest that I'll wager you have never seen before.'

She smiled again; that lovely smile. Her eyes were inviting. Ralph leaned across, as the horses walked side by side, and caught her in a last embrace which nearly toppled them both from their saddles. He snatched a last lingering kiss.

'We'll meet tomorrow?' he asked. 'You can show me the secrets of Salcey.'

Mary nodded her agreement with a happy smile. She turned her horse into the drive.

'Don't lie abed. I shall be calling early.' were Ralph's parting words as he watched her ride to the front door where a groom took her horse. The door opened and, as she went inside, they exchanged a final wave. With a glow of pleasure and anticipation Ralph turned his horse's head towards the forest and, in the fading light, set off at a canter for Bullshead farm.

CHAPTER 6

22 August 1642
Northamptonshire

Augustand the trees were in the full leaf of summer. Everywhere the countryside wore a rich mantle of green. Greens of every hue abounded. Although it was early in the day, it was already quite warm and there was a stillness as nature rested to enjoy the warmth and peace that such a day can bring. Only the insects seemed to be busy.

Ralph rode the quiet of this summer's morning in the certain knowledge that, for him, the day would be even more delightful because he was on his way to see Mary. It was now four months since their first meeting. During that time he had been six or seven times to stay for two or three days at Bullshead farm, from whence he had been able to meet Mary.

Where before, Ralph had been a carefree young man, able to turn his mind and body to the pursuit of any pastime that took his fancy, now, on his own admission, he was a love sick youth. He had become the sort of person who four months ago he would have despised. But now he revelled in the joy, the misery, the frustration and the longing of being in love and he thought only of those happy hours that he could share with Mary.

He had left home early in the morning to make the most of the day. Two hours ride brought him within the confines of Salcey Forest. Another twenty minutes and he would be through its shady depths and at his uncle's house. Both his uncle and aunt were delighted to watch the growing attachment between their nephew and young Mary Cressley. Charles had often remarked that she might have been born astride a horse. At first she had ridden the countryside with her brother Jack and later had ventured out alone, riding further and faster as the years rolled by. She had been a proper tomboy, but not now. Since meeting Ralph she had blossomed into as lovely a young lady as Charles had seen for many a day. Little wonder, thought Charles, that young Ralph should take so much time off for the sake of her company. Aunt Maria had watched the relationship develop with especial interest. She was a born romantic and already had them walking up the aisle. Truth to tell she had encouraged Ralph to come and stay as often as he liked. To some degree, at least, she could then hear first-hand how things were between them. As for young Hugh, he regarded the whole affair with ill-concealed disgust. Where before, Ralph had always been ready to join him in some joyous adventure or new scheme now, when he was not with Mary, he was mooning around the house counting the hours to their next meeting. Hugh had found that his idol had feet of clay.

After an early lunch Ralph was on his way to Hartington Hall and was soon knocking on that now familiar studded oak door at the front of the building. Minutes later he was with Mary.

They rode out together in the warm summer sun. In a secluded part of the forest they tethered their horses and walked hand in hand.

'Darling Mary!' Ralph paused to look into the face of that one person who could cause such tumult within him. 'You don't know how much I have longed for our next meeting whilst I have been miles away at home.'

'I could scarce wait your coming.' Mary's voice was soft, a little breathless. She blushed a little, as their eyes met.

'My father has been asking about you.' declared Ralph. 'He wishes to meet you. Will you come to stay for a while at Preston Capes. Our home is not so grand as your father's, but it is big enough and has a charming garden where you may sit in the sun. Please say you will come, if only for a short while.'

'There is nothing that I would rather do in the whole world.'

Happiness shone from her eyes as she spoke. Indeed, she longed to see the place where this young man lived, to meet the people that he knew and to walk where he walked. She wanted more than anything to see his home where, if only he would ask her, were it a hovel, she would be mistress.

Ralph held her at arms-length and revelled in her loveliness. His arms enfolded her as he hugged her to his breast. Their lips met in a sweet, lingering kiss which said all those things lovers have to say and for which there are no words to wield the matter.

'You are invited to dinner tonight.' said Mary breathlessly when he released her from his loving embrace.

'I shall be happy to go anywhere, if it is with you.'

'My father has invited some friends. He is concerned at the possibility of rebellion against the King and wishes to discuss what should be done if the worst happens. I understand little of these matters but father says that the country is heading for civil war.'

'Yes, your father is quite right in his foreboding, I fear. I heard only yesterday that the King is gathering around him all those who will fight for him against Parliament, should the need arise. He has left London and is travelling through the Midlands to the North and West where his support is strongest.'

'It is hard to believe that Englishmen would take up arms against each other. I know of men who condemn the King for his stand against Parliament and believe that there should be religious freedom outside the established church, but I cannot believe that they would fight other men like my father because of it.'

Ralph was not a little surprised to hear Mary express these profound thoughts. Such matters were not thought to be the concern of women. Indeed, he was surprised to find that she knew so much about the dispute between King Charles and his Parliament. Nevertheless, he was pleased to find that she took an interest in these matters and saw no reason why she should not.

That evening Ralph rode over to Hartington Hall quite early. He was made very welcome by Lady Cressley who, by now, had overcome her reserve towards him and, indeed, had taken quite a liking to him. She ushered him into the large drawing room where Sir Francis Cressley and three other gentlemen sat in conversation.

'Welcome Master Somers. Allow me to present my good friends.'

67

Ralph was introduced with all ceremony to Sir Francis Cressley's guests; a Squire Bennett from Piddington, a local vicar, the Reverend Smallwood and a certain Doctor Murchison, a serious looking man who took himself even more seriously. He was large of girth and small of stature. They greeted Ralph cordially and accepted him into the conversation. The talk was all of rumours of war and who might be relied upon to support the King. It was hard to know, when it came to the point, which side to take. Many had been critical of the King over the past year or so. Many believed that he had gone too far in assuming powers which rightly belonged to Parliament. They were unhappy, too, at the powers which the Roman Catholics wielded under his protection. There were many grievances to air, but to rise in arms against the King was quite another matter and this was a step too far for many. Others looked to the example set by some of the local gentry, who had already declared themselves for Parliament and held themselves prepared to fight for that cause. If they would fight for their beliefs, why should not others? It was a conflict in which the enemy was not so much other men as ideas and, this being so, who could say how men would choose?

'I hear, Sir Francis, that His Majesty has already had many flock to his side and receive his commission. Many are coming to his aid with bands of soldiers, armed and accoutred at their own expense. It is confidently expected that he will soon publicly proclaim his defiance of this Parliamentary rabble.' Doctor Murchison expressed himself in a manner which proclaimed the high opinion he had of all of his own views.

'Aye and not before time!' observed the Reverend Smallwood. 'It is an abomination that these canting, hypocritical puritans, who defy our bishops and revile our King, are allowed to go unpunished. They should be taught a lesson with hard steel. The Lord's vengeance shall surely fall upon those who defy his anointed one.'

'That vengeance may not fall upon the King's enemies as surely as you expect Master Smallwood.' It was Sir Francis who spoke. 'He has my support and that of many others, but he does not have the support of the majority of the common folk in his realm, especially in the towns; nor does he have the support of so large an army as his opponents. It's said that they have made fast the city of London and its arsenal of weapons and are holding it against His Majesty. His supporters will need much zeal to make up for their lack of numbers. What say you, Master Somers, will you fight for the King?'

'If I have to choose, I would sooner fight for the King than against him. I would, though, prefer not to have that choice thrust upon me. It is hard to conceive of a greater evil than one Englishman taking up arms against another. Such a war will cause strange and unexpected divisions, for it will be a war between people of different beliefs. It will not be war of north against south or rich men against poor, or even one class of people against another. It will be a war which will set neighbour against neighbour and will even split families. It will be a war where a man's friend will become his foe. It will be a war that we can do without, but it will come all the same, I fear. Some may be able to remain neutral but many will be forced to choose sides.'

Sir Francis seemed impressed by this short speech.

'You are wise beyond your years, Master Somers. I have seen much war and have been in the thick of the fighting. It has always brought misery and suffering. There is little glory in war. However, what is a man to do when all that he holds dear is threatened? I fear that the time for discussion is over. This is not a matter that can be settled without bloodshed. I also believe that you are right when you say that to be neutral may prove impossible. When all around you men are choosing sides, it will be a case of those who are not with me are against me. Then a man must quickly decide where to place his allegiance.'

At this point a servant entered to announce that dinner was ready. They joined the ladies at the large table in the dining room. The Squire's lady and Mistress Smallwood were deep in conversation with Lady Cressley. Mary also listened with less enthusiasm to the gossip, around which so much of their lives revolved. As they were taking their seats at the table, Jack Cressley entered and apologised for having come so late from some business with one of his father's tenants.

During the three or four months that Ralph had been visiting Mary and her family, he had got to know Jack a little better. The more he knew him, the more he liked him. Beneath that haughty, rather reserved exterior lay a warm and friendly nature. Indeed, Ralph liked, without exception, all of the Cressley family who had readily accepted him and seemed to approve of, or at least did not resent, his friendship with Mary. This encouraged him to believe that there would be no opposition when he asked Sir Francis for Mary's hand in marriage. He had determined that, if he could find the right moment, he would ask Mary this very evening if she would become his wife. He had no doubt of his love for her and feared only that she might reject him. She may think little of what he had to offer; a house at Preston Capes, which was no match for the grand mansion which was now her home. If her family did not approve of the match, he had wild schemes for elopement, but what if she were to refuse him? His heart sank at the thought, for then all would be lost and his world shattered.

Seated now at the table he had no time for such gloomy thoughts as the business of eating had begun and good manners dictated that he should be attentive to the needs of those ladies nearest to him. The table was laden with a great variety of dishes of meat, poultry, fish, pies and pasties, sweet meats and fruit. Wine was served with each dish. Servants were on hand to replenish those dishes which were emptied and serve the wine as required.

Ralph sat with Mary on his left and Mistress Smallwood on his right. Next to Mary sat Doctor Murchison, whilst across the table was the Squire Bennett and his lady. The good doctor, between mouthfuls of goose which he gnawed from the leg of the bird, lectured those who cared to listen upon the evils of those who meddled with the teachings of the Church, for it was the Church alone that was entrusted with the task of interpreting the bible and the meaning of the Christian message. Those who, usually with little knowledge, (which everyone knows is a dangerous thing), set themselves up to criticise the teachings of the bishops, the clergy and others who are their betters, inside and outside the Church, were servants of the Devil. He went on to condemn those amongst the labouring classes who incited their fellows to think themselves better than their station in life dictated. They were getting above themselves and a few examples should be made of their ringleaders.

Squire Bennett was interested to know if Doctor Murchison thought that farm workers had no right to education if they could get it. Did he not believe that every man had a duty to exercise his brain, if he was able to?

Dr Murchison thought that he had no such right or duty and that any encouragement to education was tantamount to an incitement to revolution. Squire Bennett thought that there were some revolutions that were long overdue; at which Doctor Murchison's annoyance became visible. His complexion, already ruddy from high living and over indulgence in alcohol, became almost purple.

'The common people should know their place, sir. Give them these notions of equality and the day will come when every man is as good as his master and that will be an end of all law and order in the country.'

'It might be the beginning of a better order.' The Squire was determined to press his point.

'Damn it, sir. It will be the beginning of anarchy and it will be the likes of you and others with your nonsensical liberal notions who will be the cause of our downfall.'

Doctor Murchison was now livid.

Mary perceived that this quarrel could get out of hand. She knew the Squire of old. He was loyal to his class and to the crown. He would never betray them. However, he did have very liberal notions and a genuine concern about the right of the working classes to better treatment. He believed that those in authority must allow a fairer society for, if it was not given freely, it might be taken by force. His views on the subject were a mixture of altruism and pragmatism. He encouraged any of his tenants who showed an interest in becoming literate. These were few in number, since work filled most of their waking hours and there was little time for relaxation. The Squire also liked a good argument and if it finished up in violence, well, what of it? Mary thought that it was time that she intervened.

'I hear, sir, that you have had more than your usual success in the hunt of late.' she said, addressing the Squire. 'It is said that you have killed six foxes this past month.'

'That is so, Mistress Cressley. Luck has been on my side but the hounds have been.....' His voice trailed away at the sound of a commotion in the hall. Both Sir Francis and his son rose to see what was afoot. Before they got to the door however, it burst open and a man in mud spattered riding attire entered the dining room.

'Your pardon, Sir Francis, but you will, I know, wish to hear the news that has just reached Northampton. His Majesty, the King, has this day raised his standard at Nottingham and declared war on the rebel Parliament and its supporters. I fear that the conflict is now in the open.'

'When did this news arrive in Northampton and how did you hear these tidings?'

'I do not know how it came, sir, but it was given out this very evening by the town crier. Northampton, as you expected it would, has declared its support for the rebels. It's said that the Earl of Essex, at the head of the rebel army, plans to rally support in the town.'

'So gentlemen, as we expected, it has come to open war. Let us talk and make our plans.'

Sir Francis dismissed the messenger to the kitchen for refreshments and gave him thanks for the speed with which the news was brought. He then ushered his guests into another room. The ladies returned to the withdrawing room, doubtless to speculate on how these events would affect them.

Although he had been expecting the news, Ralph was stunned to know that his worst fears had been realised. The rosy future that he had envisaged now faded like a dream. Tonight he had intended to ask Mary to be his wife and seek her father's permission. After their marriage he had intended to take her back to Preston Capes, there to live in peace and contentment, raising a family just like any other young couple.

He realised that all this was now impossible. Certainly he could ask Mary to marry him. Both she and her father might agree, but he could not sit at home safely with Mary, playing the coward's part, whilst her father and brother were away from home fighting for the King. Besides, what time would Sir Francis and Jack have for a wedding now? The King stood in need of their help and they were not the sort of people to stand idly by when such duty called. Ralph had no liking for war and no great allegiance for one side or the other. He had always supported the King's cause, mainly because he supported law and order which the King represented. Nevertheless, he could see the justice in many of the arguments put forward by those who supported Parliament. The more he thought on the matter, the more he saw clearly the truth of his earlier observation; that it would be very difficult for any man to remain neutral. If he wished for any respect from the Cressley family he had no alternative but to fight for the King. As he sought to absorb the initial shock that the news had brought, these thoughts passed quickly through his mind.

Having closed the door behind him, Sir Francis Cressley turned to face the five men.

'Gentlemen, I shall ride to Nottingham to seek the King and offer my services. I already hold his commission and flatter myself that, having seen some action in battle, I might be of some especial service to His Majesty. Who amongst you will accompany me?'

Jack immediately volunteered. Ralph, having come to terms at least in part with the situation, also indicated his willingness to join Sir Francis. Doctor Murchison shuffled awkwardly and with many sideways glances at Sir Francis said, 'Sir, I would gladly accompany you to offer my services too, but I have much unfinished business at home which requires my urgent attention. When this is completed, I will gladly put myself at His Majesty's disposal.

'I trust, Doctor Murchison,' replied Sir Francis, somewhat coldly, 'that your business will not detain you overlong lest His Majesty be delivered from his enemies before you can assist him.'

The good doctor looked even more uncomfortable as he replied that he hoped, of course, that the King would speedily quell this villainous rebellion. He then rose and announced his need to depart, which he did with unseemly haste.

'And you Squire, will you ride with us?' asked Sir Francis of Squire Bennett who had been pacing the floor, his head bowed as though deep in thought.

'No sir, not if I can persuade you otherwise. I will ride to Nottingham alone, or perhaps with one other, taking a message to the King offering him your support and giving His Majesty the intelligence that you are raising men and arms for his cause in South Northamptonshire. It would be pointless for us all to ride to Nottingham only to come back in a few days to find that the countryside had been recruited to fight on the side of the rebels.

'That is sound advice.' agreed Sir Francis. Jack will you ride with the Squire to Nottingham and carry my message to His Majesty. Ralph, tomorrow you and I will ride forth to rally support for the Royalist cause and find arms wherever we may.'

'And in what way may I be of assistance to His Majesty's cause, Sir Francis, pray?' enquired the Reverend Smallwood in a quiet, serious voice.

Sir Francis Cressley looked surprised for, to be honest, he had not expected the vicar to be of any help.

'His Majesty would not ask a man of God to take up arms in his cause.'

'Nor would I expect to do so.' replied the reverend gentleman in the same mild and serious manner. 'However, his cause is God's cause and it is therefore my duty to serve where I can. May I suggest that I might help you in your task of persuading the local country folk to answer His Majesty's 'call to arms'. It may be that there are some who are blind to their path of duty and I may, by the grace of God, perform some minor miracle by opening their eyes to see which road they must take.'

All this was said with such a serious countenance and in such pious tones, that others might have thought of the vicar's offer as nothing more than a gesture of help that would be of little practical value. Sir Francis and his son, who knew the Reverend Smallwood of old and had witnessed his methods of persuasion on his own flock, saw the twinkle in his eye and could scarce refrain from smiling.

'God moves in mysterious ways, His wonders to perform.' replied Sir Francis in equally pious tones. 'It is not for us to question His servant or the means that He employs. We shall welcome your company, Master Smallwood, on our ride tomorrow.'

So it was decided and, in this manner, the Civil War began for those at Hartington Hall on that warm August night.

CHAPTER 7

22nd October 1642
Wormleighton Manor, Warwickshire

A shot rang out in the dark. 'There,' shouted one of the horsemen riding alongside Ralph. 'There is another of the rogues. God's death, there must be more than a score of the villains.' The rider shouted as more shots were heard coming from the direction of the building where the cavalry troop, in which Ralph was riding, hoped to find quarters for the night.

The captain in charge of the troop halted his men.

'Godber, go with your men round behind that copse and ride towards the house from that direction. When we hear your attack we will come at them from the flank.'

The young lieutenant quickly withdrew, accompanied by some fifteen horsemen. Ralph and the others waited anxiously. Three minutes passed; they seemed like thirty. Another eternity crept by. Then came the sound of charging horsemen and the cry of men thirsting for battle, mingled with the clash of steel and the crackle of pistol fire. At a signal from the captain, Ralph spurred his horse forward.

With what was left of the troop, some twenty horses, they charged towards the side of the house where there was a cluster of outbuildings. It appeared to Ralph that they were riding through what were well laid out gardens which, in better times, were doubtless the pride and joy of the owner of this small mansion. It crossed Ralph's mind that a troop of horsemen riding across flowerbeds and lawns must be wreaking a terrible havoc. Access to the gardens appeared to be through an ornamental gateway in a wall that joined the outbuildings to the house, forming a courtyard between. The gateway was narrow, slowing the charge almost to a halt as the troop was forced to pass through in single file.

Forewarned by the preliminary skirmish, with what Ralph supposed must have been guards, the element of surprise was not complete. As Ralph, in his turn, rode into the courtyard, he found it a scene of complete confusion, lit by the few rush torches which had been placed in brackets around the yard. That the enemy had not expected such an attack, and had had little time to take advantage of the warning the guards fire had given them, was quite evident. Those on horses were mainly of Ralph's troop. Men on foot ran out of the house, many half-dressed, but with sword in hand ready to deal with the attackers. A few had been quicker off the mark and wore breast plate and helmet. Some wielded the vicious fourteen feet long pikes. Very few had had time to find their horses and mount. A pistol exploded nearby and one of Ralph's comrades riding by his side screamed in pain as a bullet entered his body. He clutched at the wound, slumped forward in his saddle and lay for a second or two across the neck of his mount before sliding to the ground where he was dragged for some yards before his foot slid from his stirrup. Ralph watched in horror as the now rider-less horse, with others, rushed headlong into the melee.

Reaching the far side of the courtyard, Ralph discharged his pistol at one of the two men who appeared from behind the corner of a stable and advanced their pikes to impale the approaching horsemen. He had a fleeting glimpse of pale faces and expressions which conveyed an impression of terrified resolution to make a stand against their enemies. One fell to the ground with an agonised cry as Ralph's shot found its mark. His comrade held his ground and thrust his pike at Ralph's horse. The pike is the infantryman's best defence against charging horsemen and proved effective in this case. The horse reared away from the point. Ralph fought to retain his seat and control his mount. Drawing his sword he sought to deflect the pike and get below the point of this lethal weapon. Ralph then aimed a savage blow at the pike-man, who had drawn back his weapon and was renewing his attempts to dislodge Ralph from his saddle with another vicious thrust. Swinging in his saddle, Ralph managed to avoid the thrust and struck again at his adversary.

The blow missed and his horse carried him on passed the pike-man back into the milling crowd in the centre of the courtyard. Other lanterns appeared as the defenders tried to throw more light on the confusion that reigned.

Immediately in front of him, two men sought to topple Lieutenant Godber from his saddle. Ralph spurred his horse towards them. So engaged were they in dealing with Godber that Ralph was upon them before they saw him coming. His first blow found its mark between the head and shoulders of one of those attacking his lieutenant. The other rebel, seeing himself outnumbered, took to his heels. He had taken only a dozen steps across the yard to seek the sanctuary of the stables, when Godber discharged his pistol at the fleeing man. The ball struck him full in the back. With a scream he flung out his arms. The pike fell from his grasp and he sprawled face down in the mud of the yard.

From the corner of his eye Ralph saw a figure running towards the entrance to the house. The remaining enemy in the yard were now all engaged by the superior Royalist force. Some had fled into the night. Others looked to find refuge in the stables or in the house. The rest of the battle would now have to be fought on foot. Jumping from his horse Ralph, sword in hand, raced after the figure retreating into the lighted porch which covered the entrance to the hall. The man whom Ralph had seen escaping into the hall saw that he was pursued and turned to make a stand on the steps into the porch. For a moment the two men paused to survey each other. Ralph glimpsed beneath the helmet a man not more than a year or two older than himself. His expression was of neither fear nor hate. He was, thought Ralph, the sort of man whom, under other circumstances, one might be happy to greet with a friendly word and a smile. But this was war and the man who confronted him was an officer in the service of Parliament.

The man struck. Ralph parried the blow. He struck again and again. Under his murderous attack, Ralph retreated a step or two drawing the man down the steps towards him. Then he lunged to penetrate the man's guard but the thrust was skilfully parried. They fought furiously for an age, as it seemed to Ralph. The man's guard seemed impenetrable and Ralph was hard put to keep his flickering sword at bay. Fit as he was, Ralph began to weary from the exertion. He wondered how much longer he could continue this duel before, worn out, he received a fatal thrust. Then, more by luck than skill, a cut from Ralph's sword caught his adversary's arm just below the shoulder causing him to loosen his grasp on his sword. In a second Ralph was on him, pressing the sword to the man's throat.

Their eyes met. There was still no trace of fear in those cool grey eyes, but now Ralph could detect a gleam of hatred. The man had dropped his sword and was nursing the wound in his arm with his left hand. The hatred was now masked by a look of haughty disdain as the man stood there passively awaiting Ralph's next move. Ralph knew that he could not kill him; not like that, in cold blood. However, he could not let him go. Fortunately he was delivered from his predicament when he heard steps behind him. He wheeled around to face new adversaries but saw to his relief that two of his companions were coming to his aid.

'The Captain has ordered that all prisoners are to be held in that stable across the yard until they can be questioned. Here, we'll take him, you look spent. Are you alright?'

Ralph nodded, but it was with considerable relief that he watched the two troopers escort the Roundhead prisoner at sword point to the temporary gaol where two armed guards stood by the door.

Looking around the courtyard, it was apparent that the skirmish was over and the Royalist troops were now in command. Ralph sheathed his sword. This was his first taste of war. His heart was still pounding and he seemed very alert in spite of his weariness. Although he knew only too well that the outcome could have been very different, there had been an excitement and intensity during the last ten minutes, which he had found exhilarating, in spite of the horror with which it had filled him. Now he looked around the yard and it was the confusion of that scene which now imposed itself upon his mind. In the flickering light of the torches he could see the lifeless bodies of fallen friend and foe. He could see and hear the wounded, some lying groaning where they had fallen; others trying to move with broken limbs. There were those who reached out as men passed by, piteously imploring assistance. He bent to help one man whom he recognised. He was bleeding copiously from a stab wound in the chest from a pike. Ralph cradled his head in his arms and tried to listen to what he was trying to say. The words were faint and, before Ralph could begin to understand, they were lost in a flow of blood from his mouth. With a sudden convulsion the man's body arched in pain, his face distorted in a final agony before he relaxed in death.

Ralph released the body of his dead comrade on to the ground. What a squalid end to life in the filth and mud of this yard. He was glad to have been able to offer him some comfort in his final moments. Ralph stood up and looked about him to see if there were others to whom he could offer help. He saw more prisoners being escorted to the stable. He was about to go to another man, lying crying in pain, when Captain Parker, Ralph's senior officer, strode up. In his hand he carried his sword still stained with blood and on to it fell his own blood from a gash across the side of his face. In his hand he carried the dented helmet which had almost certainly saved his life. He seemed unconcerned by his wound and still very much in command.

'Godber, take ten men and bring the wounded into the house. Bring both friend and foe. Find quarter for them in a room where their wounds can be tended.'

He turned and addressed another officer who had joined their group. 'Connel, see to it that guards are posted and relieved regularly throughout the night and guard well the prisoners in the stable. The enemy were surprised. Let us make sure that the same does not happen to us.'

'Somers, leave as many men as Connel needs and then find quarter for the rest in these stables and outbuildings. There should be hay enough to bed them down for the night.'

It was two hours later that Ralph found himself relaxing in a chair by a blazing fire having dined on a rough and ready meal of passable pork, bread and ale. With him were Captain Parker and Lieutenant Godber by whose side he had recently fought.

They were in the manor of Wormleighton in Warwickshire, not far from its border with Northamptonshire and not so very far from Ralph's own home at Preston Capes. They had been the advance guard of Prince Rupert's cavalry which was now fully in possession of and quartered in and around the manor. It had been a surprise to both parties to find a troop of Roundhead soldiers in occupation when they first arrived. However, the prisoners had provided the intelligence that the Earl of Essex was quartered with the Roundhead army at Kineton, not ten miles distant. This explained the presence of the Roundheads at the manor. It appeared that they were a patrol out scouting for the main force of the Royalist army. Having been overtaken by darkness they decided to spend the night at Wormleighton.

'What about that fellow I fought with, did he talk?' asked Ralph of the Captain.

'Not he. We could have torn him to pieces ere he would have given us the time of day. He did, however, tell us that he was Lieutenant Burns and asked me to present his compliments to the gentleman with whom he had had the honour to cross swords. He says that he will remember your face and pray that you and he will meet again one day. He showed no sign of fear, but the whole time maintained a lofty contempt for us. The troopers were another matter. With their lieutenant out of the way, and setting one against another, we learned a great deal about my Lord of Essex, his army and its whereabouts. I fancy that tomorrow, or the day after, his army and ours will meet on the field of battle. His Highness, Prince Rupert, would have fallen on him tonight if wiser counsels had not prevailed.'

'What plans has His Majesty?' enquired Godber.

'Nay,' laughed Parker, 'I am not privy to the thoughts of our King. He lies this night, as well you know, at Edgecote, with his armies camped about him. Essex is at Kineton, as we now know, with his army only a few miles hence. Without doubt the Roundhead army will advance by Banbury to try to secure London, which has already declared itself for Parliament. The King will almost certainly try to bar his way. Where, how and when, I do not know.'

Other officers from the Prince's cavalry entered the room. Among them Ralph espied Sir Francis, now once again Colonel Cressley, with his son, Jack. He had left them earlier that day, when he had been ordered to ride forward with the advance guard.

'I hear Ralph that you have just drawn blood in our cause,' declared Jack as they greeted one another. Both Jack and his father were obviously pleased at Ralph's success, the more so since he remained unscathed.

'Thank God you came to no harm. I am told that it was you who disarmed their lieutenant.' Colonel Cressley clapped him heartily on the back.

'I must confess, sir, that luck was on my side.' Ralph replied, with more truth than modesty.

They talked together for some time. It seemed to be generally held that a battle would soon take place between the two armies and most thought that tomorrow would be the day.

The talk and laughter flowed around Ralph as he sat gazing into the dancing flames of the log fire. He was lost in thought, not about the forthcoming battle, but about Mary who was never far from his mind. What an age it seemed since last they met. It was an eternity since that fateful night scarce two months ago when his world had collapsed beneath his feet. In his thoughts, he went over for the hundredth time the events of that evening. After the somewhat abrupt end to their meal and the urgent plan of action had been hastily put together, Sir Francis Cressley's visitors had left to attend to their affairs and make ready for an early start the next day. However, in all that worry and excitement, the Cressley family had not been insensitive to the especial sorrow that the news of the outbreak of war had brought to Ralph and Mary. They had gone to some trouble to ensure that those two young people had had some time to themselves before Ralph had to leave for Bullshead Farm.

Ralph had taken Mary into the garden, where the evening was cool and they could be alone. In spite of the moonlight, the sadness of the parting, which both knew was to come, hung between them like a dark veil. Ralph's knowledge and interest in poetry was minimal but he remembered the line from Shakespeare saying that "parting is such sweet sorrow" and knew that it was no such thing. It was a bitter sorrow, from which neither he nor Mary could find any solace. It was all the more bitter because he was off to fight a war and in war there are no guarantees of a safe return. Seated beneath the stars and not far from the flickering light of the candles in the house, Ralph had told Mary of his love for her, of his plans for their future together and how, if she agreed, he had intended to ask her father that very night for permission to take Mary as his wife. There had been little need for Ralph to seek an answer to his proposal from Mary. It had shone in her eyes as brightly as the stars that twinkled overhead. Then tears had filled her eyes, as they were forced to consider the reality of the situation. Ralph would be off to war the very next day. Mary's father and brother, too, would be away to serve the King. What chance was there for a wedding? There was little they could do but promise that each would wait for the other and pray desperately that the war would be over soon. For some time they had clung to each other and, for a while, time had stood still. Mary had determined not to make the parting harder by yielding to tears. She would put a brave face on it and smile when the time came to part. As the servants began to close the doors and put out the candles, the time came when part they must. With a final squeeze of his hand, the ghost of a smile, Mary went indoors and rushed to her room where she wept in joy for his love and misery at his leaving.

* * *

The next day Ralph had ridden forth with Sir Francis and the Reverend Smallwood to enlist all those who could be persuaded or cajoled into the service of the King. Their task had not been an easy one, for they had found much support for Parliament and, truth to tell, Ralph had feared a premature start to the conflict. He saw only too clearly how bitterly this war would set neighbour against neighbour and even sunder family loyalties. For the most part they found ignorance and bigotry but amongst a few, even of those who opposed them, sound reasons which he had been bound to respect for supporting their chosen side. In such cases Ralph felt an even greater sorrow that men, with honestly held convictions, must resort to violence to settle their dispute. There were too many, with whom Ralph shared a secret sympathy, who wanted nothing to do with this quarrel. They saw that no good would come from such a war and were horrified to think that the differences between King and Parliament could not be settled by peaceful means.

Finally, with a small band of men, they had set out to join the King whom, they were told, had left Nottingham for Shrewsbury. They had avoided Northampton where the Earl of Essex was marshalling the rebel forces which were to fight for Parliament. They had made their way unmolested to join the swelling ranks of the King's army. The King had been pleased to receive the news that Sir Francis Cressley had recruited men to join his cause and had renewed the commission and rank of colonel which Sir Francis had previously held. He had assigned their party to the army under the command of Prince Rupert of the Rhine.

* * *

Several weeks had passed and, up to now, life in the army had been very dull. There had been a little training and reports of one or two minor skirmishes. Ralph had missed the one at Powick Bridge near Worcester. For the most part they had done little, but to march across country in pursuit of what appeared to be only the changing objectives of their leaders. In reality, Ralph knew that the main difficulty was in finding the elusive rebel army in order to bring it to battle. Now the two armies were almost within sight and a battle was soon to take place. Upon the result of this engagement might rest the outcome of this tragic war.

Later that night, the intelligence arrived from the King's headquarters that the army was to rendezvous the next day at a place called Edgehill, on the road south from Warwick to London, just south of Kineton. It was doubtless here that the

King intended to block the path of the Earl of Essex in his advance with his army towards London. This news caused an uproar of excitement and enthusiasm amongst the men of Prince Rupert's cavalry. They were a wild, devil may care bunch, who would ride to hell and back with their leader if they were promised a good fight and plenty of plunder. They were, for the most part, recruited from the gentry and were fierce in their support for the King. Each one was brave to the point of recklessness, proud of his skill at arms, his horsemanship and eager to prove his valour. In these qualities lay the strength of Prince Rupert's cavalry but, in them too, lay its weakness. For of all the qualities a fighting force needs, above all, it is discipline and this is a quality which they lacked.

Ralph discussed these tidings eagerly with Jack and Sir Francis.

'It will be a great battle tomorrow. It's said that Essex outnumbers us and has more cannon than we can bring to bear.' said Ralph.

'And yet, his is an army of peasants. When our cavalry charges they will run like rabbits for their burrows. The sooner we meet them the better, say I, for then we can give them the thrashing which they so richly deserve.' Jack spoke full of enthusiasm for the victory which he fully expected would go to the King.

'To think thus of the rebel army is to court disaster.' observed Colonel Cressley.' 'They will for the most part stand and fight, just as we will for the most part stand and fight. With God's help, we shall win the day; but it will not be easy and before it is finished many will die.'

This somewhat gloomy prediction from Sir Francis, whose knowledge and experience of military matters was generally accepted by those who knew him, dampened the enthusiasm of the young hotheads spoiling for a fight. However their spirits rose again with new boasts of valour and promises of martial deeds. Fighting is a primitive instinct in young men who see nothing of the pain, the suffering and the misery which must result, but think only of the thrill and the glory that they are sure will be theirs. Ere long the promises of victory and the routing of the enemy filled the room.

'Father, if we can bring the rebels to battle tomorrow, or the day after, do you think that it could end this war?' asked Jack.

'It could be so if our army can bring about a great rout of the rebel forces and capture their arms and equipment and bring their leaders to book. If this were followed by a swift march on London, which is their main stronghold, the rebels may surrender; but I doubt it. The feeling against the King in the country is very strong; there is much division that will not easily be healed. I think it is more likely that this will be a long war. Pray God that I am wrong, for already I miss the comforts of my own hearth and it grieves me to think of the danger in which you and Ralph, and thousands like you, will stand when we meet our enemies tomorrow. I say it with a heavy heart but I think that there will be many tomorrows before this war is at an end. Come, though, let us not end the night on such a dreary note. Let us drink to the King and confusion to all his enemies.'

Having thus drunk a glass or two of wine they fell to talking, once again, with those about them; for none were disposed to sleep. Jack was soon deep in conversation with two other men; one about his own age, the other several years older. Doubtless, they were also father and son, thought Ralph, who was once again deep in thought. He didn't notice Colonel Cressley take his leave of the group, with whom he had been sitting, and make his way to the door. Ralph did not notice him that is, until he paused at Ralph's side and spoke casually to him.

'I would speak with you Ralph on some serious matter. It is too secret for this place. Come with me where we can talk quietly and privately.'

Wonderingly, Ralph followed the Colonel out of the noisy room into the great hall of the manor house and up the grand staircase. Some way along the corridor, off to the left, a door opened into a small, well-furnished bedroom which was presently serving as Colonel Cressley's quarters. The Colonel invited Ralph to enter and motioned him to a chair whilst seating himself on another chair which he had drawn up opposite.

'Ralph, today His Majesty spoke to his Highness, Prince Rupert of the need to have intelligence of the enemy; to know his whereabouts, his plans as far as it is possible, his strength, the morale and disposition of his troops. This information we badly lack. For nigh on ten days the two armies have marched, scarce twenty miles apart across the country, and yet it was a chance encounter which told us that the rebel army was so close. Had it not been for that, and our encounter with the enemy patrol here earlier this evening, we should not, even now, know that Essex and his army lie tonight at Kineton.'

'Prince Rupert recommended to His Majesty that I should make what arrangements I think fit to keep him supplied with the information, that he so sorely needs, of the rebel army and its movements. He wishes, if possible, to know before Essex himself what is happening in the Roundhead camp.'

'I have a plan whereby, with your help, we can provide His Majesty with that information. As you have heard, it is likely that tomorrow there will be a battle. If by God's grace we win a great victory, we shall need to know where the King's enemies have flown to lick their wounds and plot to renew their struggle against the King. If we lose, we shall have an even greater need to know his plans to further his cause against the King. Will you go tomorrow to offer your services to Parliament?'

Ralph was stunned. It was several seconds before he realised what the Colonel was asking of him. He resisted the temptation to refuse point blank and sat for a minute or two considering the implications. Objections came flooding into his mind.

'But surely it will appear to my friends that I am playing the traitor. What will Mary and Jack think of me? What of my father? Do you know what you ask of me?'

'I have thought of all this. Jack will hear from me that you have gone away in the King's service. He will suspect much, and may ask more, but will learn nothing more than that from me and that is the information which he will pass on to your friends. Mary is safe at home and need not know. As for your father, he is the one person in whom you may confide. He is, I know, an elderly man who does not venture far from home. He shows no strong attachment for either cause and keeps his opinions very much to himself. He is not a man of politics and takes very little interest in affairs outside his estate. He is also, I fancy, one who could pretend to a disinterest in his son's affiliation with the Roundhead cause.'

'You seem, sir, to pretend yourself to know a great deal about my father.' replied Ralph curtly. He was angry that Colonel Cressley should ask him to perform such an impossible task. Death or glory on the field of battle was something that he was prepared for but deceit, probably shame and disgrace for himself and the name of Somers, not to mention the possibility of an inglorious death at the end of a rope, should he be discovered; all this was something for which he had not bargained.

'Ralph, you must hate me for this and justly so.' answered the Colonel softly, 'but do you not see the importance of this work? Any agent who works for me must be a man of integrity, one in whom I can repose complete trust and one with the skill to match the task. You are such a man. As for knowing about your father: I, the father of the girl you hope to marry, if I mistake not, would have been failing in my duty to my daughter had I not acquainted myself to some degree with your family.'

Ralph was somewhat mollified by the reasonableness of this reply but argued. 'Surely sir, you have men of more cunning and wit than I for this subterfuge?'

'I know of few. At least, I know of few who would serve me and whom I could trust. The man to serve me in this matter must have the brains and the brawn, aye and the valour to match the task. His loyalties to our cause must not be published far and wide. Jack, my son, is one other who could perform this task, but he is known and it is known where his loyalties lie. There are, as yet, few who know of your associations with the Cressleys. As I have said, your family has no widely known opinions and might be expected to serve one side as likely as the other. Listen lad, I know what I ask. There will be peril for you, not on the field of battle as for every common soldier, but during every minute of the day and night. You will have to act with stealth and guard your tongue. It may prove difficult, if not impossible, to get the information which I need but you, I know, will do as much as anyone can. I will not hold it against you if you refuse me. You can serve in other ways. If you do decide that this is a job you cannot do, we will simply forget that this conversation ever took place. But please, think on it for a time. Give me your answer ere we march tomorrow.'

Ralph took a deep breath and, disbelieving his sanity, heard himself saying to the Colonel, 'No sir, you may have my answer now. If this is the best way that I can serve the King, then I am yours to command.'

A warm smile lit Colonel Cressley's rugged features. Quietly he said 'Thank you, Ralph. God send that you may safely discharge this service.'

He then gave Ralph some ideas and instructions on how he might proceed.

'I suggest that you go this night to your father's home since it is but a short ride from here. None should see your arrival there at this late hour, but take no chances and wear nothing to show your attachment to the Royalist cause. Tomorrow leave, with whatever ceremony you wish, to go to join the armies of Parliament at Kineton, if they are still there. Get the best position with them that you can for our purposes and send back whatever intelligence you can find out. We need, above all else, to know the strength of their army, its spirit, its determination and, whenever you hear it, the intentions of its leaders. This is the news that we must have. Numbers of infantry, of cavalry and ordnance, stocks of powder and balls, number of horses, supply of victuals and the health of the soldiers; all such news will aid us in finding the weakness of our foe and show His Majesty when and where to attack.'

'How will I get such reports to you sir?'

'I am short of men of quality and intelligence but I am not short of faithful servants. One such is Jim Peabody, a lad whom I have known all his life. He and his father and his father before him have served my family. He will meet you at any time and at any place that you appoint and carry any message which you give him back to me.'

'What if he is captured or the message falls into the wrong hands?'

'Any message that you send to me must be without address and without signature. The address is unnecessary if delivered into Jim's hands. I shall know that it is you by your writing but, as an added precaution, lest you be forced to write under duress, take this ring.'

Colonel Cressley handed Ralph a gold ring. At first glance it appeared to be a plain band of gold surmounted with a rather large engraved cap. Colonel Cressley pressed the side with his thumb and the cap flew back to reveal an engraved crest which was obviously intended for use in embossing hot sealing wax with a distinctive seal. In this way, because of the unique design of the crest, Ralph could assure the Colonel that any letter he received had indeed come from Ralph and had been freely sent without coercion. Such a ring was not extraordinary and seals were often used to give authority to, and identify, the originator of a document. Ralph had seen many such sealing dies before, although the one he had been given was somewhat different to the others he had seen. He studied the design closely by the light of a small candelabrum. It was, of course, in reverse but, as far as he could make out by that none too bright light, the motif was an eagle in flight clutching between its talons a small lamb.

The Colonel watched Ralph studying the ring. 'It is a motif used in some wood carvings at home. It would need to be someone very familiar with Hartington Hall for them to recognise it and associate it with me.'

Ralph and the Colonel sat for short while discussing the problems and difficulties which Ralph might encounter in the task ahead of him. As he spoke, Ralph realised what a daunting task it was. There was really little advice that the Colonel could offer. This was something in which Ralph would have to use his imagination and ingenuity to the full, if he were to accomplish anything worthwhile. After a while there seemed little more to be said other than for the Colonel, yet again, to express his gratitude to Ralph and wish him all the luck that he would surely need. As he rose to see Ralph to the door he said.

'Oh, one more thing before you leave; Jim Peabody waits below. You will need to make his acquaintance.'

Sir Francis escorted Ralph to a room near the kitchen on the ground floor at the rear of the house.

'Jim knows you and he is not a man to forget a face, but you must see and remember his and arrange your first rendezvous. He is not a man who seeks company and we shall find him in a quiet corner on his own where I told him to wait until we came.'

'You seem to have been very certain, Colonel, that I would do as you asked, or was Mr Peabody told to wait on the off chance?'

'No, Ralph,' replied the Colonel softly, 'I told him you would come.'

CHAPTER 8

23rd October 1642
Burton Dasset Hills, Warwickshire

Seated astride his horse on that rather chill autumn day, Ralph surveyed the scene before him from the top of the Burton Dasset hills. From this vantage point he had a clear view of the countryside to the west. Below him and a little to the right lay the village of Kineton. This was where the rebel army had spent the previous night and where, he guessed, they would have left some sort of picket to guard their weapons and supplies. Away to the south of Kineton, some two miles distant, Ralph could see the smoke of battle and the flash of armour, although the conflict was too far away to see clearly what was happening. Across the plain rolled the thunder of cannon and with it came the continuous roar of a multitude locked in mortal combat. From where he sat, Ralph had a grandstand view of this, the first major conflict of the Civil War, which was now taking place around the village of Radway at the foot of Edgehill.

After his interview with Colonel Cressley and a brief meeting with Jim Peabody, Ralph had left Wormleighton Manor to ride to his home at Preston Capes. It was well after midnight when he arrived and crept into the house quietly, disturbing only the stable boy and the housekeeper. Then he found his way to bed. So, it was not until the next day when he saw his father who, as always, was delighted to see his son whom he missed more than he was prepared to admit; not only for his help on the estate, but also for his company. After having been away for some two months, Ralph found that his father had aged considerably. He had lost all the vigour of former days and was now a tired old man. It grieved Ralph to see him like this, the more so since he was unable to stay and help. However, it seemed that he was able to make his way about the house and even go for short walks, provided that he did not exert himself too much. Any strenuous exercise would bring on pains in his arms and chest. His physician had warned him to take life steady but, complained his father, how could he when there was work to be done.

Ralph did not wish to worry his father with the news of his new assignment, but he had to offer some explanation for his presence and for the fact that, within an hour or so, he must be leaving in rather more sober dress than the one in which he had arrived. He merely told his father that he was on special duties for the Royalist cause. He asked his father to be vague with all who enquired about his activities in the present conflict. He would prefer as little as possible to be known about which side he had chosen to support.

Henry Somers was not as wholly disinterested in affairs outside his estate as Colonel Cressley had imagined; nor was he so senile that he failed to grasp the implication of what his son had just told him.

'You are playing a dangerous game, my son, but you say it is in the King's cause. Well, it is the better cause; but it is my belief that no cause can be served by fighting and killing. However, it is difficult to stay neutral, especially when your heart is given to one of the Cressleys. You are a grown man and you must do what you think is best. Your secrets are safe with me. God go with you and keep you safely.

Ralph left late in the morning. He saw no need to hurry. If, as seemed almost certain, there was to be a battle today, he would have to await its outcome before he could join the rebel forces. He left without ceremony. Fortunately there were few servants in the house. Only two lived in the manor, apart from the stable boy who bedded down above the stables. There was Mistress Gurney who served his father as housekeeper and, of course, Jethro Knight who was a jack of all trades and served the Somers in many different ways. Mistress Gurney doted on Ralph, but her mind was too full of her household duties to wonder about his comings and goings.

It was therefore with a mixture of apprehension, sadness and excitement that Ralph set forth that day. He was sad, not only to have to leave his father in ill health, but sad to leave in the knowledge that his father did not wholly approve of Ralph taking up arms for either side. Nevertheless, it was plain his father understood that, given his love for Mary, Ralph had little choice. In any case, Ralph was reasonably certain that he would not have been able to stand aloof from the war, regardless of his involvement with the Cressleys. Although Ralph would not have seen it so, it was inevitable that the ardour of youth and the craving for adventure would disregard the wisdom of old age. For these reasons, not fully resolved in his mind, Ralph was glad to shake off the dust of Preston Capes and make a start on his new task which, truth to tell, he had little hope of fulfilling. He felt that the Colonel expected more of him than he could give and he had only the vaguest ideas about how he might obtain the information that he was expected to provide. It was such doubts which filled him with apprehension. However, he was by nature an optimist and had the confidence of youth. It was the challenge of the task, and the element of danger which it held, that filled him with excitement.

So it was that on that Autumn morning, in the year 1642, Ralph left the home that one day he hoped to call his own and set forth to lose his identity and work as an agent for the King within the forces of Parliament.

Although he had seen no need to hurry, now that he was on his way Ralph made haste to seek out the rebel army to see if indeed a battle was taking place as had been predicted. Ralph knew that the city of London had been seized by its citizens, the majority of whom supported Parliament. It was important that the Earl of Essex should join up with those forces now in control there and consolidate his hold on this, the capital city and major port through which supplies for his army could be brought. The King, of course, knew of the importance of this move to the Earl of Essex and the urgent need therefore for him to stop the rebels. This done he could, himself, march upon London. There must surely be a battle this day.

When Ralph arrived the battle had just begun with an

exchange of cannon fire. The noise rolled across the plain like thunder. Ralph marvelled at the sound and wondered that any men could stand against the venom of these instruments of death. Distant though he was, he saw something of the splendid charge of the Royalist cavalry led by Prince Rupert. He watched with some excitement as the horsemen, with whom he had recently served, chased the enemy into Kineton itself and harassed the picket guarding the baggage train. Then, he watched the two armies engage one another in a conflict which was confused and in which it was impossible to decide what was happening and which side was winning.

The conflict was far too distant for Ralph to discern much, other than battle had been joined by the two armies. The outcome of the conflict would, he supposed, become apparent if he saw either side making significant advance against the enemy or one side being routed. While the noise of battle echoed across the countryside, Ralph could do little but wait. He was not able to witness the capture of the Royal Standard and its heroic recapture. He could not see the reverses suffered by one side and then by the other and which neither was able to turn to their advantage. He was too far away to hear the screams of the wounded and the dying, neither could he see the blood and the horrible wounds inflicted on living flesh.

Ralph could neither see nor hear the horrors of war. All these details were lost in the wider panorama of the battle set out before him. He was not, however, so lacking in imagination that he gave no thought to the real meaning of war for those who fought in it. He wondered how Colonel Cressley, Jack and his many other comrades were fairing in the combat and he feared for their lives.

So the battle continued until evening when darkness brought it to an inconclusive end. The same darkness forced Ralph to descend into Kineton and make his first contact with the rebel forces, of whom he enquired how he might join their number.

* * *

Two days later Ralph was still in Kineton. The battle was over.

Neither side could claim a victory although both did and, of course, it was true that neither need admit defeat. The King had stopped the rebel force from advancing south to London; although he did not hasten there himself. On the other hand, the rebel army was far from being defeated and lived to fight another day. Instead of taking the initiative and marching straight on London, the King retired south only as far as Banbury, which surrendered to him after only a token resistance. Meanwhile, the bulk of the Parliamentary forces travelled the few miles north to Warwick.

On the day that he presented himself to join the rebel forces, Ralph had been brought before a Captain James who questioned him about his background and his reasons for wishing to join their cause. Ralph answered most of the questions honestly where he could, but was more guarded when questioned about his home and family and revealed no more about himself than he felt obliged to. He thought it best not to give his real name. He was a little uncertain in this respect and said that he came from near Daventry. Perhaps he ought to have given a wholly fictitious address. However, it was unlikely that they would take the trouble to check. He felt that a false name was an appropriate precaution, since his name would be known to all and it was just possible that someone might have heard of Ralph Somers. He therefore introduced himself as Robert Snaith. Fortunately, the interview was short and it seemed to Ralph that his story was fully accepted. Recruits were always welcome and Ralph was a recruit; a volunteer at that, unlike many who came because of the master whom they served. Those in authority had little leisure to enquire deeply into the background of all who wished to serve their cause. Ralph pleaded his enthusiasm for the cause, rather than any fighting skills. Indeed his health was not as robust as he would have wished and hoped that a way could be found for him to serve in non-combative duties. He stressed that he could read and write and was good with figures. He was used to keeping accounts and accustomed to the ordering of his father's estate. He suggested that he might serve Parliament better in some modest administrative position, where his pen might be of better value than his inept handling of a sword.

As luck would have it, the Wagon Master was in need of help with the business of obtaining and transporting supplies. He was even more hard pressed with the task of requisitioning provisions for the growing army of men. He badly needed someone who could, not only read and write, but who could keep accounts and attend to the business of requisitioning and paying for the huge amount of supplies needed to feed an army. Like most armies, the forces of Parliament were obliged, to some extent, to live off the land. Unlike many armies, Parliament was prepared to pay for the food it demanded; at least in theory. The job of obtaining such supplies was not always easy and needed the efforts of a man with a persuasive, or on some occasions, a coercive manner. Ralph looked as though he might fit the bill and he soon made himself very useful in this role.

Such a job suited Ralph better than any that he could have been given. His main concern, from the time that he had been asked by Colonel Cressley to join the rebels, was that it seemed inevitable that he would find himself in an armed encounter with the forces of the King. In such an event there would be no alternative; it would be kill or be killed. He viewed the prospect of killing men serving the cause to which he had offered his allegiance with great dismay. However, he had made up his mind that he had no choice. The game he was playing was an unpleasant one, with unpleasant consequences for himself, if he were discovered. He hoped desperately to be able to avoid such a confrontation but, if it came, he must play his part as best he may. It seemed now, however, that his duties may, thankfully, never bring him to the forefront of the field of battle. Nevertheless, Ralph was well aware that the chance still existed that he might see action in defence of the wagon train, but this prospect concerned him far less than being in the front ranks against the Royalist army.

There were also other advantages that this particular job offered him. It gave him access to pen and paper. As a common soldier, he would have no apparent use for these materials and it would be thought odd if he were seen to be using them. As an assistant to the Wagon Master, what more natural than to be seen daily scribbling some note of demand or credit to one of the army's suppliers. The need to contact local merchants and visit farmers would also be part and parcel of his daily round. Thus he might travel unchallenged about the countryside, affording himself ample opportunity to hand his dispatches to Jim Peabody in some quiet place, where the two could arrange to meet without fear of observation.

Ralph slipped out of the farm house, which had been the billet for the Wagon Master and his staff during the past four days. Tomorrow they were due to move north to join the main force at Warwick. Since the battle their task had been to salvage what was still serviceable of the ordnance, collect what small arms that had not been looted from the dead and, in general, retrieve whatever might be usefully had from the aftermath of the battle. Ralph sauntered along the road out of the village and up to the Burton Dasset hills. His path led him along the same road by which he had descended only four days ago. It seemed more like four weeks since he had joined the rebel army.

The weather, as it had been on the day of the battle, was fine but very cold for October. Today had been fine again. The sun had risen out of the morning mist and offered light and a little warmth to the countryside. Amongst the dying bracken and long grass the sight and smell was unmistakably of a summer gone and winter not too far away. The trees were now resplendent in their autumn colours, enriching the greens and browns of nature's canvas with their reds and gold to form a breathtakingly beautiful landscape. Now these same trees were trembling in the chill wind that began to blow. Here and there a withered leaf fluttered to the ground, adding to the rich brown carpet which rustled beneath Ralph's feet. Summer had gone and, all around, nature prepared for the coming of winter.

With evening, what little warmth there had been in the sun had now gone and the mist was rising again over the lower land behind him. Now, Ralph began to walk briskly. Somewhere ahead Jim would be waiting. Up the hill, a little further on, the path led somewhat to the left around a bend behind some low bushes. The slope of the hillside began to ease and the village fell out of sight behind him. Ralph was alone. He shivered apprehensively and looked around. Ahead lay more bushes. As he approached, he detected a movement behind them. Without hesitating he continued forward, allowing his right hand to feel for the dagger hidden within his leather jerkin. Before he reached the bushes however, Jim Peabody emerged from behind them with a welcoming smile.

'Give you good day, Master Ralph.' The smile on his face was warm and friendly. There was little servility about him and yet he was prepared to serve loyally. Ralph liked what little he knew of him. It was a first impression, but one that was to last and grow stronger during their short acquaintance.

'Good day, Jim. What news of the Colonel and Jack? How did they fare in the battle? Were they injured? Ralph looked anxiously to Jim for a reassuring reply.

'Both hale and hearty; never a scratch from the battle, though Jack was in the thick of the charge and saw some of his comrades fall. The Colonel stayed as an aide to the King.'

Ralph heard the news with a great deal of relief, which was revealed in his smile and words of thankfulness. 'Where lies the Colonel now and the rest of the King's army?'

'They are all safe at Banbury town where I am to meet the Colonel tonight, if this fog doesn't thicken and cause me to lose my way.'

'Well, God give you a safe journey and here is a message to take to Sir Francis. It does not tell him anything of great import but it will show him at least that I have been able to join the Roundhead army.'

'What did they say when you presented yourself to the Roundheads, Master Ralph?'

'They asked but little. Volunteers are hard to refuse.'

'How long do you stay at Kineton?'

'We leave tomorrow for Warwick where the Earl of Essex and his army are now camped. Watch for me in the market square in Warwick in three days' time. I will try to meet you there at this hour. If I fail, wait again the next day or the day following.'

With that Ralph handed Jim the letter which was folded,

sealed with wax and embossed with the ring given him by Colonel Cressley. He watched Jim walk back up the hill and untether his horse which he had left behind a dilapidated old barn. He watched him mount and ride away at a canter.

When Jim had disappeared from view, Ralph turned and continued his walk, descending into Kineton by another route. In spite of the thickening fog, Ralph took great pleasure in the solitude and beauty which the countryside afforded him.

* * *

Two days later, Ralph found himself in Warwick. It had always been a busy little market town, where country folk came to sell their produce and buy the necessities of life that were to be had from the merchants and tradesmen of a town such as Warwick. Now it was even busier. Everywhere there were soldiers. For what, it was hoped by the majority would be a short time, the town was playing unwilling host to the army of Parliament. Nevertheless, the work of the town must go on and so markets were held and shops were opened for business; war or no war.

Ralph was returning from a visit to a local grain merchant, with whom he had reached an agreement on the supply of grain for the army. One hundred bushels were to be sent to a local miller, ground into flour, and collected by the army in two days' time. At this stage in the war, such matters were being conducted in a very civilised way. The army was being mostly paid and supplies were being obtained through the normal commercial channels. There was every chance that both the grain merchant and the miller would be paid.

These, however, were not the thoughts that were occupying Ralph's mind as he strode through the town to the house on the outskirts where he was billeted. He was more concerned at present with what he should be doing in pursuit of his true purpose within the Roundhead camp. His job was to get information, in short to spy; but for the life of him he had no idea how to go about it. He was not privy to the plans of the Earl of Essex, nor had he any way of reading his mind. Few people confided anything to him that would be of great use to his masters. It seemed to Ralph, that all he could do was to keep his eyes and ears open and use his native wit to make whatever deductions he could from the evidence that they provided. Estimates of numbers, both of ordnance and troops, the morale of the army, troop movements, marching orders and the availability of provisions; all of these should be of use to the King in assessing the strength of his enemies. If Ralph could provide this information on a regular basis, then he felt that he would be of some use.

That night he made a start. On the pretext of compiling lists of supplies to be obtained, he began to write his report. It was a task not without danger. He worked by candle light in the back room of the large house, which served as both office and billet. Outside were camped the men who, under the orders of the Wagon Master, tended the horses that pulled the huge carts or trundled the heavy canons.

As he wrote, Ralph was acutely aware of what the future would hold for him were he to be caught with his half written report. Just beyond the sheet of paper on which he wrote, were a number of other sheets dealing with the supplies which he had yet to order. Should he hear steps in the passage he could quickly cover his report with these and appear to be diligently pursuing his proper task. It would be a great relief when the report was completed, although he still had little worth telling. Much as he disliked having a half written report on his person, Ralph felt that it was pointless sending Jim back to the Colonel with very little information.

* * *

The next day Ralph stood in the market place watching the bustling scene and listening to the cries of the traders. In spite of the town's invasion by the army, the town's folk tolerated the soldiers with fairly good grace. After all, they did bring a bit more business into the town. The war was still young. In spite of Edgehill, comparatively few had been killed and its full impact had yet to be felt. Many had still not taken sides and hoped to remain neutral. So, apart from the influx of soldiers, life in the town was still fairly normal.

Ralph watched a large, red faced man unloading crates of chickens from his cart. Nearby, another man led a cow passed a barrow loaded with apples, behind which the owner was crying his wares. A sudden noise and movement in the crowd startled the cow which jerked backwards against its tether. The owner responded by pulling the rope sharply. The cow skittered against the pull and moved sideways into the barrow load of apples, knocking it over and throwing the contents to roll in the filth of the street. Within seconds pandemonium broke out. Ralph watched with interest and amusement as the owner of the cow squared up to the apple seller. With a push the larger man sent the cowman sprawling into the crates of chickens, some of which broke open. Seeing his livestock making the most of their unexpected liberty, the chicken seller set upon the cowman who, perforce, let go his hold on the tether giving the cow a chance to join the chickens in their bid for freedom. It was while Ralph was enjoying this comedy of errors that he saw, beyond the crowd, beneath the overhanging timbers of one of the houses that surrounded the market, the figure of Jim Peabody who was clearly waiting to catch Ralph's eye.

Ralph turned and walked out of the market place with a casual backward glance at the scene of chaos, noting at the same time that Jim was following. Without turning his head again, Ralph walked on down the hill towards the river. He stopped on the bridge in the shadow of the huge old castle. Nearby one its towers loomed over him. He leaned over the parapet and gazed into the sluggish dark waters below, where he caught sight of a few small fish which darted back and forth in search of food whilst two larger fish, with their heads into the current, lazily held their station as the water flowed slowly by. There were few people about. Some yards away, along the bank, three boys played at the water's edge as young lads are wont to do. Further away a boy and two girls threw a stick for their dog. A few soldiers were making the best of their stay in Warwick by escaping the noise and turmoil of the town to seek the relative tranquillity of a stroll by the river. Although he couldn't be sure, Ralph thought that he recognised one of them who had just arrived on the river bank, and had seated himself on a fallen tree, where he gazed into the river contemplating the quiet waters.

Soon Ralph was joined by Jim who paused on the other side of the bridge. He spoke to Ralph as a stranger might speak to another man of whom he enquired the time of day. For the benefit of passers-by, they spoke of the weather and other general matters. Ralph appeared to find something of interest in the river when Jim joined him in searching the waters that passed beneath the bridge.

'I have nothing for you yet, Jim. We march south quite soon. I suspect that it will be to London. The whole army is to go, but I do not know when. This is no safe place to talk. Meet me tomorrow evening after dark at the sign of the Ram's Head. You'll find it in one of the alleys leading off the market square.' Ralph nodded towards the town and the market they had just left.

Jim nodded and pointed to something in the water. Then with a laugh and a shake of his head he bid Ralph 'Good day' and strode off across the bridge, continuing on his way. Ralph spent another half hour watching the flow of traffic across the bridge and strolling along by the placid waters. Then he turned back towards the town and made his way across to his quarters on the far side.

* * *

The next day at dusk Ralph left the warmth of the room that he was sharing with four other soldiers. Not without some difficulty he found his way through the narrow streets to the tavern where he had arranged to meet Jim. It was a cold and damp night after a little rain, which had done nothing to dispel the evil smells arising to assail his nostrils from the filth in the streets. The refuse, which was discarded there, combined with the wet surface to make a muddy and slippery path. Once on the main streets walking was a little easier, not because they were free from refuse, but because they were cobbled and so were mostly free from mud. Most of the streets were narrow. The overhanging upper stories of the houses on either side almost met in places to exclude what little light the sky afforded. Here and there at a corner, or a cross roads, the way was lighted by rush torches which were placed in wall brackets. These were few and far between and, except for the light that occasionally shone from a window, Ralph had to grope his way in complete darkness.

Fortunately it was no great distance but, as Ralph felt his way between the occasional dim beacons of light, he wondered if he would be able to find his way back. All of his journeys in the town, since his arrival, had been in daylight. Now, he would have to test his memory to find his way in often complete darkness. Soon he heard the babble of voices with some raised in laughter and song. Further along the street he saw light from the door of the tavern he sought and, above it, dimly lit by the light spilling from the open door, just visible in the gloom, hung the sign of the Ram's Head. He stooped to enter through the low doorway and found himself in a noisy smoke filled, ill lit room, already quite crowded. He ordered a tankard of ale and took it to a corner, not far from a cheerful fire which did much to dispel the gloom and make the room a little more welcoming.

Some of the clientele were soldiers. The pleasures of the ale house were not encouraged by the puritan leaders of Parliament's army, but soldiers must find some way of amusement during their leisure hours and gambling, whoring and drinking were their traditional pursuits. There were also a goodly number of locals whose resentment at the take-over of their hostelry by the army was beginning to show itself.

'Plague, take these rebel soldiers.' Ralph heard one man say to his companion. 'A man can't find a quiet corner for a drink and a chat since they came to town.'

'Hold your peace, man.' whispered his friend. 'They be quick to quarrel. We don't want no trouble. Anyway, they'll all be gone ere long. 'Tis said that they march for London soon.'

It was so noisy in the large room that it was only because

one of the two men had spoken loudly, perhaps to let the soldiers hear of his displeasure, that Ralph heard what was said. The man's companion glanced apprehensively at Ralph as they found a seat on a bench at the side of the fire, where they had been standing for a minute or two warming themselves. Ralph, knowing none of the townsfolk and, for that matter, none of the soldiers, made no endeavour to join in the conversation. Instead, he sat quietly drinking his ale and gazing into the fire. Here it was warm and, almost mesmerised by the dancing flames and relaxed by the ale, Ralph sat comfortably dreaming idly of the events of the last few days.

'A cold night, young master! Mind if I join you.' said a voice by his side.

He looked up with a start and saw the smiling face of Jim Peabody, who sat down beside him and joined in his quiet contemplation of the glowing logs in the hearth. They sat thus for a time in companionable silence. Ralph looked casually around to ensure that they were not likely to be overheard before speaking.

'I still have little worth the telling. For what good it may do our master, I am writing it down in my report. I am writing something of the numbers of soldiers here, together with the best information that I can get of the rebel leaders' plans.'

Ralph tried to speak as though their conversation was casual and inconsequential gossip.

'We march on Saturday, but I still have no firm knowledge of where our destination is to be. I do know that our way lies by Daventry, where I am to call upon a horse dealer whom I fear may know me. This may prove difficult. However, it does mean that I shall pass near my home at Preston Capes. I have written a letter to my father who will give you shelter while you await our arrival. Our progress will be slow and I doubt that we shall be in Daventry until late on Monday. Our wagons are laden and the roads will be difficult after this rain.'

Such was the noise in the room that it was easy for Ralph and Jim to talk freely without the risk of being overheard, except by someone very close to them. The two locals had been joined by friends and were now so busy with their own gossip, that they had no ears for what others might have to say. However, Ralph noticed a movement to the right as a soldier slid into a seat just behind Jim and himself. A quick glance revealed that it was the same soldier whom Ralph had noticed by the river.

Ralph allowed nothing in his countenance or his demeanour to betray the anxiety that this 'coincidence' caused him. He continued his conversation with Jim, but now he began to discuss the price of food, the day's happening in the market, the weather and other general topics. Jim looked somewhat surprised at this abrupt change of subject but quickly realised, from Ralph's cryptic glances and furtive nods in the direction of the soldier, that the man was eaves dropping. After a few more minutes of idle chat Ralph rose from his seat.

'Come sir. I will walk with you for as far as our paths lie together. We will help each other on this dark night to find our way home.'

Jim nodded and rose with Ralph to leave. They stepped into the darkness of the street. Quickly, Ralph hustled Jim into the blackness of a nearby doorway.

'Watch the tavern doorway.' he whispered urgently, 'I am being followed.'

Sure enough, within seconds, they saw the figure of the soldier, who had seated himself behind Jim, suddenly framed in the doorway. He paused for a few seconds to let his eyes become accustomed to the darkness, listening as he did so. In the shelter of their doorway, less than six yards distant, Ralph and Jim froze, scarce daring to breath. After some hesitation, which seemed a lifetime to Ralph, the soldier set off along the street leading out of town. When they were sure that he had gone, the two men emerged from their hiding place and breathed a sigh of relief.

'We shall need to be very careful from now on.' observed Ralph grimly. 'Plainly I'm under suspicion. I wonder why. I can't think of anything that might have given them cause to suspect me. I wonder who that man is and who is his master? Perhaps all who have freedom of movement, such as I, are watched closely for some time. Well, I must keep my eyes and ears open and my mouth shut. Here, take this letter which will introduce you to my father at Preston Capes. He will give you lodging. When next we meet, it were better if it were after dark. Let that be in three days' time, one hour after sunset. I fancy that we shall not be far from the village of Badby, only three miles from my father's house. I will wait for you there by the church.'

'Take care, master. This be a dangerous game we play. There's little gain for us if we win and a rope's end if we lose. God send us both a safe deliverance.' whispered Jim.

With that the two men parted. Ralph found his way, in all but total darkness, back to his quarters and Jim to an inn on the other side of the town. Ralph took comfort in the fact that for anyone to follow him on such a night would have been nearly impossible and yet, he recalled, that he must have been followed to the tavern.

CHAPTER 9

31st October 1642
Warwick

Jim rose early the next day and set off on his journey to Banbury to see Colonel Cressley to keep him informed of the arrangements he had made with Ralph. After a brief rest and refreshments, at a hostelry in Banbury, he rode to Preston Capes. Jim had a good sense of direction and had also some knowledge of the Midlands from earlier trips with Sir Francis, or Jack. However, he was glad of the directions that Ralph had given him, since he had never been to Preston Capes before. Doubtless, he could have found his way without Ralph's instructions but, having been told the best route, he found the journey that much easier.

Had it not been for the weather he would have enjoyed the ride. After leaving Banbury the drizzle, which had been with him since he left Warwick, became a heavy persistent rain. Within an hour Jim was soaked to the skin and feeling very cold.

When he finally reached his destination and stood at the door of the Somers' home in Preston Capes, rain water was running from him in streams. An elderly lady answered the door in response to his knocking. It was Mistress Gurney, the same old soul who delighted in fussing over Ralph. She wore an amiable smile as she answered the door and enquired of Jim his business.

'I bring a letter from Master Ralph Somers.'

'Mercy on us.' cried the old lady in some alarm. 'He's not ill or hurt, is he? Come you inside. Where did you see him?'

Jim reassured her that Ralph was quite well when he had last seen him only the day before. She guided him into the kitchen and motioned him towards the hearth where there was a blazing fire.

'Why, you be soaked to the skin, so you be. You'll catch

your death of cold. Stand you there by that fire and get dry while I tell the master.'

Leaving Jim to the friendly warmth of the fire, she hurried away. Two minutes later she was back.

'The master will see you now.' She beckoned Jim to follow her through the hall into a large and pleasant room where, as in the kitchen, a cheerful log fire held the damp and cold at bay. Seated in the chair before the fire was an elderly man. He rose unsteadily to meet Jim. His face had a pallor and his eyes reflected the pain he endured. His welcome was, nevertheless, warm and sincere as he bade Jim take a place near the fire. With a shaking hand he took the letter, broke the seal and began to read its contents. When he had finished, he spoke.

'So, you serve my son. He asks me to offer you hospitality for three or four days. You are then very welcome in my house. I will not enquire your business, for I may guess that it is intrigue and the less I know the better; but my son, did you leave him safe and well?'

The old man's face lit up as he spoke of Ralph and it was with obvious concern that he listened for Jim's reply.

'I did, sir; never better. You've no need to fear on that score. He's a man who can look after himself, that's certain.'

'Yes, yes, I hope so; I do indeed.' said the old chap shaking his head. 'He is still young and lacks the wisdom of years. This may prove his undoing. Well, well, we shall see. He must make his own way. But you, sir, your clothes are wet. You look perished. You must have dry clothes, ere you take a fever. Come, I will call Mistress Gurney. She will see to your needs.'

Henry Somers rose and called for his housekeeper who showed Jim to a bedroom, where she gave him a change of clothes borrowed from Ralph's wardrobe and took away his wet ones to dry.

Jim spent the next two days exploring the countryside around the village. He found the church at Badby, which was in thickly wooded countryside. Whilst offering excellent cover, Jim saw that it would be easy to get lost and he especially wanted to be sure of his bearings, so that he might find his way back to

Preston Capes after his meeting with Ralph.

During his stay, Jim got to know the servants in the household of Henry Somers. These were Mistress Gurney, the housekeeper, Jethro Knight, the gardener and handyman, also the stable lad, Jack, who spent most of his time in the stables. He was a good-natured simpleton, who seemed to have a way with horses and was useful for little else. He divided his time between the stables at the manor and his mother's home in the village. He was something of a law unto himself, but he was accepted in the village for what he was. A young girl came to the manor each day, from her home in the village, to help Mistress Gurney. Jim soon found that Henry Somers was not only thought well of by his servants but was a loved and respected figure in the village. Ralph was also held in high esteem. Jim found it necessary to be circumspect in his conversations with the villagers. He was not by nature a gregarious person and kept to himself as much as possible but, nonetheless, did not wish to appear surly and unfriendly. This might have increased any interest which his presence in the village aroused. He would have preferred to have his stay in the manor kept secret but, in such a small place, this would be difficult and might again attract more interest. He decided to take the middle course by appearing openly in the village, giving it out that he was a distant relative of the family. He told those who showed interest that he was travelling north and had turned aside to spend a few days at the manor. In so doing he hoped to attract little attention to himself.

The day came when Jim was to meet Ralph. He explained to Mistress Gurney, with whom he was now on the best of terms, that he might be late back and would certainly not return before dark. Being the most incurious soul, she was not in the least concerned to know what it was that would delay his return.

He arrived at Badby church at dusk. He tethered his horse to a small tree at the edge of the forest and well away from the spot in which he had chosen to wait. As the last of the daylight faded from a clearing sky, Jim settled himself on a log beneath a tree some fifty paces from the church yard gate. The church at one end of the small village occupied a clearing in an area that was otherwise thickly wooded. Fortune favoured Jim that night. For, as the daylight ended, the full moon rose and sailed like a pale yellow orb in a clear sky on a black velvet cloak; pierced with a myriad of twinkling stars. From the vantage point that Jim had chosen, he could see anyone who approached the church where the open ground was bathed in pale silvery light, whilst he was lost in the Stygian darkness of the shadow beneath the tree.

The song of the birds had long since ceased and now, save for the hoot of an owl that patrolled the sky on silent wing, it was only the noises of the nearby forest that broke the still of the night. Wrapped in a thick coat against the cold, Jim waited in silence.

Suddenly he heard the sound of approaching voices. There was laughter and a woman spoke. Jim shrank further back into the cover that the tree and the bushes behind afforded.

'Why, Walter Taylor, you be a saucy devil. No you don't. No, you keep your hands to yourself.'

There followed the sound of a scuffle and shrieks of laughter. Peeping from his cover Jim saw a lad, still short of twenty, with a lass no older, pass by arm in arm. So wrapped up were these two young people in each other, that an army could have lain hidden by the roadside and they would have been none the wiser. They wandered slowly on their way, laughing and talking, until they disappeared from view among the small cluster of cottages, some two hundred yards distant, that was the village of Badby.

Once again all was silence except for the bark of a fox. As Jim shivered and drew his cloak more closely around him, he began to hear all those small noises of the nocturnal woodland creatures for which the night was the time for hunting and feeding. A rustle in the carpet of leaves, the snapping of a twig, the squeal of some unfortunate prey; all this and the sighing of the wind in the trees kept Jim company during his lonely vigil.

It was therefore a relief when, after an hour or more of waiting, he heard the approach of a horse ridden slowly over the turf. Looking cautiously from his vantage point Jim saw, by the ample light of the moon, a horseman ride into view and halt near the church some thirty paces away. From that distance Jim had no difficulty in recognising Ralph Somers. Noiselessly, he detached himself from his shelter beneath the tree and called softly to Ralph. The horseman turned swiftly in his saddle. Jim saw that Ralph held a pistol which pointed straight at him.

'Tis I, Master Ralph, Jim Peabody.' called Jim, a tone of urgency in his voice. To his relief, he saw Ralph relax and lower the pistol.

'We must be brief.' said Ralph, without ceremony, as he replaced the pistol in its holster on his saddle. 'I am certain that I am being watched. I have noticed that same fellow who followed us in Warwick. He suspects something, that's certain. Here take this letter for Colonel Cressley. It contains the best information I can find about the rebel army. I was lucky to come across some information about its strength and the number of men under arms. It was in an order to the Wagon Master to aid his provisioning of the army. It gave details of the number of men there were and how many horses were to be used to pull the canons. We march south to London. Look for me in Dunstable, by the church, in four days' time and, if I am not yet there, wait for my coming.'

Ralph thrust a letter into Jim's outstretched hand.

'Take care. They may even now be watching our meeting. If so, you too are in danger.'

'Let them come, an' they will. I am armed.' replied Jim, with a hint of menace in his voice. 'I'll take one of them to hell with me.'

'A reckoning must come soon, I fear.' Ralph's voice betrayed the anxiety he felt. 'I must be off. Farewell.'

Turning his horse, Ralph rode swiftly away.

'Take care of yourself.' Jim called as he watched rider and mount vanish into the dark shadows of the track through the woods. Turning, he walked quickly to his horse which was grazing contentedly where he had left it.

Swiftly, Jim mounted and set off back along the road to Preston Capes. In the bright light of the full moon, he had no difficulty in following the road, along which he had feared that he might lose his way by night. Even on the soft turf, or mud, the tread of his horse's hooves sounded like thunder in the still of the night. The wind had dropped and the moon, more brilliant than ever, lit the landscape almost as bright as day. Tonight, there would surely be a frost. Jim felt an eerie thrill in riding alone through that black silhouetted landscape. He was not a man given to wild imagination. A countryman, born and bred, the countryside held no fear for Jim, either by day or by night. For all that, in spite of telling himself that there was nothing to fear and that it was a grand night for such an errand, his imagination ran riot, as he plunged from bright moonlit meadow into inky darkness where his road ran through woodland. Perhaps it was Ralph's obvious anxiety that had unnerved him. Was it his imagination or did he really hear the drumming of horse's hooves behind him? He glanced backwards over his shoulder. There was nothing. He excused his fears by comparing the work that he now did in the Colonel's service to his nightly escapades on the Colonel's estate. He had little fear of the game keeper there who turned a blind eye to his occasional poaching.

Jim reined in his horse for a moment and listened. No, his hearing wasn't playing tricks. There were horsemen behind him. Riding on again he waited until, once more, he was swallowed up in shadow and the road behind was bathed in moonlight. Turning he saw, some hundred paces behind him, two riders following the path that he rode. He spurred on his mount and sought to outpace them. Willing, however, as was his horse, Jim was unable to increase the gap between himself and his pursuers.

Feeling inside his cloak, Jim closed his hand over the butt of the pistol which he had loaded before leaving Preston Capes. It gave him some reassurance to know that he could defend himself. For yet another mile he rode, first seeking to outpace his pursuers and then allowing his horse a somewhat steadier gallop. Behind him still rode the two men, keeping pace, some two hundred yards distant. It became apparent to Jim that these two riders did not wish to apprehend him, but rather to find out where he went. His mind was racing as he rode and he guessed that these must be the men who had been watching Ralph. They were now following him to find out to whom he would deliver the letter which he carried. They had probably watched his meeting with Ralph and the passing of Ralph's report. They could easily have taken them both but, by following Jim, they would discover who it was that Ralph was working for and so secure the evidence to condemn him. Having dealt with Jim and his contact, they could take Ralph at their leisure.

Coming to a thicker area of woodland, Jim looked for an opportunity of eluding his pursuers. The track took a sharp turn to the left and, for a moment, Jim was out of sight of those who followed him. Quickly he turned his mount in among the trees and waited. Soon the two horsemen came into view. Alas, Jim had failed to notice that the road ahead was brightly lit for several hundred yards. It was obvious therefore that, since he was nowhere to be seen on the road ahead, he must have turned off. It was too late to make amends. The two riders reined in their horses and halted only a few paces from where Jim sat astride his horse hidden from view. Jim's fears were realised as he recognised one of the riders as the soldier who had followed Ralph to the tavern in Warwick. There was a brief exchange of words as the soldier directed his companion to search the other side of the road.

'So, the fellow tries to escape us. Well, he won't get far. I'll have him and that letter and then I'll have Master Snaith, if that be his name, for the spy that he is. He must be hiding nearby. I heard no sound of his horse and I doubt that he could get far through this woodland.'

Dismounting, and leading their horses by the reins, the two men began to examine the trees close to the road. Quietly Jim withdrew the pistol from his belt. He bent low over his horse's neck, patted it and whispered softly in its ear. 'Steady now, stay quiet.'

Jim noticed that both men had pistols in their hands as they commenced their search among the foliage. On came one of the soldiers peering into the dark shadows beneath the trees. In grim silence Jim sat motionless on his horse which must also have sensed the danger, as it too remained completely still. Slowly the soldier worked his way passed the spot where Jim was hidden in the darkness. Indeed, he was some short distance beyond when he trod on a piece of dead branch which snapped with a loud crack. Jim's horse shied a little, then snorted and tossed its head. Immediately, the man turned and, with a cry, ran towards the place from which the noise had come.

Not waiting to be discovered, Jim urged his steed forward. Startled by the crashing of Jim's horse through the undergrowth the man staggered backwards. He recovered himself and fired at Jim from less than a dozen paces. Crouching low on his horse Jim heard the ball sing passed his head, missing him by inches. In his turn Jim levelled his pistol at the other man, who had turned and was now raising his pistol to fire. Without the leisure to take careful aim but, at less than four yards when he could scarcely miss, Jim beat the other man in the race to fire first. With a scream the man stopped in his tracks as the ball struck him in his chest. He stumbled and then fell lifeless to the ground.

The second soldier, who had run to join his companion, paused by the body lying in the damp grass. Finding his companion beyond help, he turned and dashed back along the track for his horse. Jim now had a good start on his pursuer and spurred on his mount with an urgency born of rage which, for the moment, was a rather stronger emotion than the fear he also felt. The village was scarce half a mile from where the encounter had taken place. As Jim pressed on with all speed he could hear no sound of pursuit nor see any sign of the remaining horseman following. It was with a great deal of relief that he came upon the village and the Somers' house, where a friendly light glowed in a downstairs window.

Quickly, he stabled his horse at the rear of the house where the stable lad was nowhere to be seen. Then, knocking at the backdoor, he was soon admitted by the smiling Mistress Gurney.

'Why, Master Peabody, you'm back then. Come inside and I'll find you a bite to eat.'

'No, mistress, I thank you. First I must speak with the master.'

He strode quickly ahead of her to the room, where he knew that he would find Henry Somers. Opening the door of the living room he saw the master of the house in his usual seat by the fire place. Henry Somers looked up in some surprise at Jim's abrupt entry into the room and was about to remonstrate, when he realised from Jim's manner that something was amiss. Quickly and without ceremony, Jim told Henry Somers what had passed that evening and of the letter that he carried for Colonel Cressley.

'It is possible that the rogue may track me to this house.' Jim reached inside his leather jerkin and pulled out the letter which Ralph had given him less than an hour before. 'Should this fall into his hands and he work for Parliament, as I'll wager he does, then Master Ralph's life will be forfeit. Take it, I beg you, sir, and, if they come, burn it. As for myself, Master Somers, you have shown me great kindness during the past three days. I have no wish to bring peril to you or to others in this house. I will leave immediately.'

'No, you serve my son and it would ill become me to abandon you to your fate at such a time. I have a better plan which may throw them off the scent. Give me the letter.'

Henry Somers seemed to become once again a young man. He spoke with a firmness of tone and walked with a sense of purpose as, taking the letter from Jim, he strode across the room to a large writing desk. It was a magnificent piece of furniture, exquisitely carved and finely made. The front of the desk lowered to form a writing table, revealing dark recesses and drawers which were filled with documents and papers relating to the Somers' land and property. Jim did not see exactly what Henry did but, suddenly, a small panel in the carved pattern on the side of the desk swung open, revealing a compartment inside. In this Henry placed Ralph's letter. Then again, as if by sleight of hand, the panel closed, leaving no visible evidence that such an opening existed.

'There, now! I fancy that your letter will be as safe there, as anywhere in this house.'

'Nevertheless, sir, I think it were better if I left your house immediately. Now that Master Ralph's letter is safely hid, should my pursuers call here and I am gone, there will be nought to cause suspicion against your household. The fellow, whom I left alive, may well go for help. Were he and his companions to find me here, it would go hard for you; for remember, I have killed one of their number. If I leave now, I can find my way back to Colonel Cressley and return for the letter at some later time.'

While he was talking Jim took out the pistol that he had recently discharged so effectively against one of his assailants. 'With your permission, sir, I would like to make sure I am armed before I leave.' Taking a small powder horn and pouch of shot from his jerkin he busied himself with the task of reloading his weapon.

'What you say makes sense.' replied Henry thoughtfully. 'You should be safe now, unless you have the bad luck to run into this fellow again and, after this time, it is unlikely. The letter is safely hidden. Should the Roundheads call and search this house they will find nothing. You have your pistol. Here, take this sword. It is the one that Ralph used for practise but it should serve you well enough, if pushed.'

Lifting the lid of a large chest, Henry Somers took out a sword which he handed to Jim.

'I thank you sir. It may afford me some defence but, truth to tell, I have little skill in the art of swordsmanship. I trust that I shall have no cause to use it.'

Jim set the loaded pistol on the table by Henry Somers' chair and proceeded to buckle on the belt to which the scabbard was attached. As he was doing this they heard a loud banging on the front door of the house. They heard a raised voice demanding that the door should be opened in the name of Parliament. Too late now for Jim to leave. Henry Somers motioned him to take a seat opposite his chair by the fireplace. It was into this apparently tranquil scene that the soldier, who had been following Jim, now unceremoniously entered followed by an agitated Mistress Gurney. Seeing her master and Jim in the room she closed the door and left them to it.

'So the fox has found its den.' sneered the soldier with a hint of triumph in his voice. 'That vagabond did not play me false. He swore that it was to this house, the home of one Henry Somers, that he had seen a horseman ride in great haste, less than ten minutes ago. Lucky indeed that he should have seen you and I seen him. Come sir, the letter which Snaith gave you. I demand to see it in the name of Parliament.'

The truculent manner and insolent tone adopted by the soldier, roused Jim to a fury. His hand went to the sword which he had recently acquired.

'God's death, sir. Dare you, a common footpad, show your face in the home of decent people?'

So enraged was he that, throwing caution to the wind, Jim began to draw his sword from its scabbard. He felt a restraining hand rest on his arm. It was Henry Somers.

'Softly, good sirs.' He said gently. 'There is no need of violence.' He turned to address the soldier. 'What is your business with this young man?'

'My business is to apprehend him as a murderer and an enemy of Parliament. And you sir if, as I take it, you are Henry Somers, the owner of this house, would do well to be mindful of the fact that you are harbouring a murderer and a traitor under your roof. This man has just received a letter from one, Robert Snaith, whom I suspect is in the pay of those who follow the King against Parliament. I doubt not that the contents of this letter conveys intelligence of our army to those whom Snaith serves.'

'I am Henry Somers and Robert Snaith is my son. He adopted that name in deference to my wishes that our family should remain neutral in this dispute between the King and Parliament. You say that your interest is in a letter which Master Peabody brought from my son?' Old Henry Somers eyed the soldier with a hint of disdain. 'Certainly he brought a letter from my son, whom he met by arrangement this evening; but I see nought in this that should concern you. However, since you suspect some mischief; here, read it yourself.'

So saying, the old man held out a letter to the soldier that he took from his writing desk. It was eagerly snatched from his hand. With a surprise, that he could ill conceal, Jim recognised the letter that he had brought three days ago from Ralph and by which he had been introduced to Ralph's father.

The soldier's face registered first disbelief, then disgust and finally suspicion. He threw the letter contemptuously aside.

'I like this not. It is strange indeed that a man with seemingly so little to hide should act in so furtive a manner. Not withstanding; there is the death of my comrade and for that you will be charged with murder.'

'You may recall, sir,' answered Jim, who had by now regained his composure, 'that it was your friend who shot first at me. This gives me the right to defend myself.'

'These matters can be debated with my captain. I have much to report on your comrade Snaith or Somers, if that be his true name. When Captain Davis hears what I have seen in these past few days, I doubt not that you will both be closely questioned. Come sir, I take you to my captain.'

'That you will not.' answered Jim, defiantly drawing his sword.

With a smile and licking his lips in anticipation of an easy victory, the soldier unsheathed his own sword. With a vicious swing of the blade, he sought to knock Jim's weapon from his grasp. Jim parried the blow which was followed by another and another as the soldier pressed home his attack. It soon became clear that Jim had not been modest when he declared his lack of skill with the sword. Although the soldier relied more on strength than art, he was more than a match for Jim. For a moment though luck was on Jim's side. Defending himself as best he could, Jim retreated behind the table. Intent upon penetrating Jim's wavering defence, the soldier failed to notice a footstool in his path. He stumbled and fell. In a second Jim was on him to exploit to the full this extraordinary stroke of providence. Placing his foot firmly on the man's outstretched wrist and with his sword at his throat, he called upon him to yield.

The soldier's eyes flashed murder at Jim, but yield he must.

He let the sword fall from his grasp, whereupon Jim allowed him to rise. In doing so the soldier half turned away from Jim, apparently to support himself on the table as he gained his feet.

The events which followed were perfectly timed, like a well-rehearsed scene from a play, and lasted less than ten seconds.

Unseen by Jim, the soldier's hand went for a pistol which he had tucked in his belt. As he straightened himself with his other hand on the table, he swung round revealing the pistol which he now levelled at Jim. Realising his danger Jim lunged at his adversary with his sword. Too late; with a crash the pistol fired, filling the room with noise and smoke. Jim fell, a ball lodge in his brain. As if in echo to the first, another explosion followed. The soldier staggered and clutched at his breast, from which oozed an increasing circle of blood, staining his light brown tunic with a blotch of vivid red. He coughed and a trickle of blood ran from the corner of his mouth. Horror, surprise, as well as pain were all mirrored in his eyes as, looking up, he saw Henry Somers holding the smoking firearm that had once been Jim's and, which now, all but fell from Henry's trembling hand. Realisation had scarcely dawned on the soldier's face before the dark curtains of death banished all light from his eyes. He sank to the floor and lay still.

Allowing the pistol at last to fall from his hand, Henry Somers staggered across to his chair, into which he collapsed, as a spasm of pain convulsed his body. He sat there, his face contorted with the rending pain which filled his chest. The door slowly swung open. Mistress Gurney, hearing the noise, had plucked up courage to investigate. Puzzled by the silence, she cautiously peered around the door and surveyed the scene in horror and disbelief. Her eyes fell on her master, to whom she looked questioningly for an explanation, not realising immediately that the two men prone on the floor were dead.

'He would have condemned my ....' but the words would not come. Shoulders hunched, his hands clutching at his breast, Henry reeled back in the chair. Deathly white, he fought for breath. His chest heaved. Then suddenly he lay still.

Mistress Gurney looked away from where her master lay

slumped, dead in his chair, rid at last of all pain. Her eyes fell on Jim's shattered face where the ball had entered his head. She saw the staring eyes of the soldier, whose head lay in a pool of blood. The only sound in the room was the ticking of the old grandfather clock as Mistress Gurney, her face flushed and her eyes bulging in horror and revulsion, surveyed that arena of death. Then, as if released from some spell of silence, she let forth a piercing cry. She fled from the room, filling the house with her shrieks of terror, as she sought to escape from that ghastly scene of murder and death.

CHAPTER 10

Late Summer, 1643
North Buckinghamshire

R alph sat on a stone at the side of the road and enjoyed the warmth of the sun on a golden day in September. It was very peaceful alone in the north Buckinghamshire countryside. The war seemed almost an illusion; like a nightmare from which one can awaken to more pleasant realities. Ralph was awaiting the arrival of the troop of horse soldiers to which he had been attached for two or three days. The patrol was searching the area north of Newport Pagnell for news of the Royalist army. Ralph's purpose in joining them was to investigate what supplies were available to help feed the armies of Parliament during their stay in this part of the country. He had separated from the patrol an hour ago to call on two farms in the area. In the meantime, Captain Hurst had detoured to follow up a rumour that Royalist troops had been in a village two miles to the east. So pleasant was the day that Ralph was happy to wait, at the arranged meeting place on the road north, for as long as necessary

The cross-roads, at which he sat, was deserted. Lazing in the sunshine, Ralph contemplated the events that had brought him to this peaceful place. Three days ago he had arrived at Newport Pagnell, from London, with a detachment of Lord Essex's army under the command of Sir Samuel Luke, who was intent upon besieging the small town which had been held by Royalists. However, when Sir Samuel arrived, he had found to his surprise that, rather than fight, the Royalists had abandoned their defences and marched north. This had puzzled Ralph considerably. The year had been a good one for the King whilst Parliament and its forces were in a state of disarray, with scarcely a battle won. Why, then, would Sir Lewis Dyves choose to resign the town so recently captured by Prince Rupert and offer no resistance to the Roundheads. Well, Sir Lewis no doubt had his reasons but they were a mystery to Ralph and, he suspected, to Sir Samuel Luke as well.

From puzzling over this mystery, Ralph fell to thinking of the past year. He thought, as he so frequently did, of Mary. When he had set out that morning, he had experienced some pleasure in the knowledge that the day's march was likely to take him over the border into South Northamptonshire and, maybe, within a few miles of Hartington Hall. Whilst in this area, he had determined that he would try to visit Mary. Perhaps it would be a rash adventure; certainly one that he would have to undertake in complete secrecy. He so longed to see her, to hold her and to tell her of that love which had never failed during the long, long year since they had been forced to part. Perhaps, too, he could tell her something of the part that he was playing in this war; just enough to make her realise, in case she heard any rumours, that he was no traitor to the cause for which her father and brother fought. He missed her so much and he wondered if she ever thought of him.

Being young, the privations of war caused Ralph little concern. He had soon learned to sleep rough and to eat when and where he could. The double game he played troubled him more than he cared to admit to himself. He did not like to think that he was playing the traitor to the friends whom he had inevitably made. He felt it impossible to regard these men as his enemies. These were his comrades, who shared the hardships and pleasures that came their way. It was not the men who were his enemies, but the cause that they followed. With a sigh he longed for the day when the war would end and he could go back to Mary and take her for his wife. It seemed impossible that it was over a year since last he had seen her, so fresh and alive in his mind was the memory. Would she, he wondered, still feel as much for him as he did for her?

Time made nonsense of memories, thought Ralph, as he let his mind wander back over the past year. On the one hand his memories of Mary were as fresh as ever and yet, those early days of the war seemed a hundred years ago. He recalled the days that he had spent riding with the King's army. Then he had not ridden under false colours, but proudly in the ranks of Prince Rupert's cavalry. In spite of the gloomy forecast of Colonel Cressley and others with more experience, Ralph had been among the many who thought that, when the rebels were brought to battle, the matter would be quickly settled in favour of the King. Those were heady days when, it seemed, that there might be honours to be won in a short, glorious conflict after which he could ride home in triumph. Alas, this was not to be. Colonel Cressley had been right in forecasting that a long and bloody war was the more likely outcome. It was the Colonel, too, who had had other more inglorious ideas for Ralph. Ralph remembered how those plans had nearly come to grief, almost before they had been properly started.

Ralph shuddered as he remembered his last meeting with Jim Peabody, by the church at Badby. For the best part of a month, he had expected to be charged with spying and be confronted with the letter giving irrefutable evidence of his guilt. He had, of course, no knowledge of the events that had taken place near Preston Capes and at his home. It was well over four weeks later that he had been accosted in Dunstable by one of Colonel Cressley's agents. When Jim Peabody had failed to return, the Colonel had sent one of his men to make discreet enquiries in Preston Capes and at the manor house, where he had known that Jim had intended to stay. It was this man whom the Colonel had sent to find Ralph and relate to him those terrible events.

It seemed that after Mistress Gurney had fled hysterically from the room in which she had seen her master breathe his last and join his two companions in death, Jethro had arrived on the scene. It was to Jethro whom Ralph owed a debt of gratitude that he could never hope to repay; for it was he who had taken the steps that had undoubtedly saved Ralph from being arrested as a Royalist spy. Jethro knew nothing of the business upon which Jim Peabody had been engaged but, in his limited conversations with Jim, he realised that he was in some way serving Ralph. When Mistress Gurney's screams had brought him to the scene in the living room and he had seen the three bodies, he had managed to calm her down. He had taken her back to her kitchen, given her a brandy and helped her to tell him what had happened. After a while she had regained her composure. Both quickly realised that the events which had obviously taken place in that room must never be generally known and that, if they were ever revealed to a rebel supporter, Ralph's life would be forfeit and they themselves would be in grave peril. Jethro had found the letter that Henry Somers had received from Ralph introducing Jim Peabody and which Henry had shown to the soldier. Neither Jethro nor Mistress Gurney could read and they dared not show the letter to anyone else in case it contained something incriminating. They decided therefore not to destroy it, but to hide it until it could be given back to Ralph.

Jethro Knight was not normally known as a man of action, but he proved to be one that day. While the village slept, later that night, Jethro had taken the body of the soldier in a horse drawn cart and dumped it unceremoniously at the side of the road well to the north of the village. As for Jim Peabody, reluctant as Jethro was to bury him in unhallowed ground, there was nothing for it but to bury his remains in a quiet corner of the large garden belonging to the manor house and over which Jethro was the master for the time being. He and Mistress Gurney made a careful note of the position of the grave so that, at a later date, if possible, the body could be exhumed for a proper Christian burial. By now Mistress Gurney had regained her self-control. She was not a stupid woman and was, like Jethro, very loyal to the Somers whom they had both served for the greater part of their lives. She realised the importance of secrecy and would keep her own counsel if any questions were asked.

Neither Jethro nor Mistress Gurney had any knowledge of the other soldier whose body was found the next morning on the lane to Badby. The discovery of two bodies the next day had caused rumours to spread like wildfire through the village. Fortunately, none of them connected the Somers' household with their deaths. The news that Henry Somers had died caused little surprise in the village for it had been generally known that he had been in poor health. The response in the village had been simply one of sadness at the loss of a well-respected member of the community and the whole village turned out for his funeral. A few days later a Roundhead officer had arrived to enquire into the deaths of the two soldiers. He asked questions cursorily in the village and called at the manor house, more out of duty than in the expectation of any information. There were no witnesses to question and no further information to be had. So the officer, who had much more pressing matters to attend to, left none the wiser.

By the time these events had been related to Ralph there was nothing that he could do, even if he had been able to return home. His father had been buried and life at the manor house had, to all appearances, returned to normal. All Ralph could do was to mourn, in private, at the loss of his father and thank God for two quick-witted and loyal servants. From the fact that he had not been apprehended, Ralph concluded that the two soldiers had acted alone, perhaps waiting for proof before reporting the matter to their captain. He therefore concluded that he was free from suspicion but, nevertheless, he was infinitely more cautious after that event. It had been agreed with the Colonel, through his new contact, that the courier would not always be the same person and, in some cases, he would leave his report in an agreed hiding place. He soon got to know the three or four couriers whom the Colonel employed and any new man would introduce himself to Ralph by a prearranged exchange of statements and responses.

It was the delivery of his report that Ralph feared most. If he were to be caught in the act of handing it over to the courier or if it were to be found on his person.......... Ralph was no less brave than most other men, but when he thought of the consequences of such a misfortune, fear gripped him. Once the report was out of his hands, he experienced a great sense of relief for, provided that the courier was not caught, interrogated and forced to speak, then there was nothing to connect him with the document.

Meantime, Ralph could only keep his eyes and ears open for any information that might prove useful. Rarely was he able to supply more useful information than details of the army's strength, an approximate estimate of its armaments, the morale of the troops, their state of training and, when he knew it, the route along which they were to march and, perhaps, their destination. Nevertheless, Ralph fancied that this information would be of help to the Royalist cause. He knew that the Colonel had others like him elsewhere in the armies of Parliament. The sum of information he received could build a very useful picture of the enemy and allow an informed guess as to its intentions.

Ralph surveyed the countryside about him. Autumn was almost here and winter not far behind. The days were becoming shorter and the evenings cooler and mistier. In spite of this, Ralph reviewed his surroundings with pleasure. Pleasure because he had for too long endured the crowds, the filth and the stench of London, so that it was pleasure enough simply to be in the peace and solitude of the countryside. Pleasure, also, because this particular piece of countryside was the border with his own county. Here he was near, not only to his own home, but nearer still to Mary's. That thought, alone, made his face light up with a smile.

Ralph was awoken from his reverie by the distant sound of horsemen approaching from the south. He rose and looked in the direction from whence came the noise. He took care not to reveal himself. In these days it paid to be careful. His caution proved unnecessary for he recognised the patrol in whose company he had that morning left Newport Pagnell. Ralph stood in the road, where he could be seen, and waited for Captain Hurst and his men to arrive.

'Well, Master Snaith, have you found anything for our bellies?' asked the Captain cheerfully as he greeted Ralph.

'A farm or two have agreed to provide the necessities.' replied Ralph with a sardonic smile.

The farms in question had had little option but to supply whatever they were unable to hide. However, they were still likely to be paid, although this was not entirely certain. Victualing both armies was not always a profitable business.

When it came to billeting troops, especially where a house was known to be owned by someone whose sympathies lay with the enemy, the owners could feel grateful if all they lost were consumables and their possessions were left intact. In some cases payments were made, or dockets given, which could be redeemed through the army paymaster. Wherever possible, the Roundhead army paid for its keep but soldiers, especially those who were ill disciplined, were apt to take what they wanted as spoils of war.

'Have you heard any news of Royalist forces?'

'They have been seen by none to whom I have spoken.' replied Ralph. ''Tis plain that they did not pass this way.'

'Then mount and let us continue with the search.'

Ralph mounted his horse and fell in with the ranks at the rear of the column.

'How now, Bob?' A cheerful looking fellow, little more than a boy, greeted Ralph as he joined the column and rode alongside him.

'What news then, Bill. None of the Prince, I gather.'

'None in the world, but it's a lovely day for a ride.'

They jogged along chatting merrily of past events, of the latest news and of what they saw as they rode. They exchanged cheerful banter with those who rode near them and looked forward to what pleasures a small town like Newport Pagnell could offer them when they returned that night. Indeed, as Bill had observed, it was a nice day for a ride.

Soon they re-joined the Newport Pagnell to Northampton road. The captain led the column to the right, heading north.

'If our captain takes us much further north, we shall not see Newport Pagnell tonight.' remarked Ralph.

'He does seem determined to find out which road those plaguy Royalists took. For my part, I care not if they have gone to Hell so long as we don't have to follow,' replied Bill with feeling.

It was the middle of the afternoon before they reached the small village of Stoke Goldington. There the Captain gave orders to dismount and the men were allowed to rest and eat any refreshments that they had brought with them. Ralph joined the others drawing water at the village well. Meanwhile, the Captain was busy questioning the villagers who were looking cautiously from their cottages to see what new arrivals the war had brought to their doorsteps.

They came out shyly and timorously at first, not daring to do more than peep at the crowd of noisy troopers gathered around their well. One or two of the braver souls strolled up to chat with the soldiers whom, it became clear, intended them no harm. When the Captain began to question them in courteous and friendly tones, they quickly lost their reserve and it was not long before the whole village was talking, laughing and shouting exchanges with the Roundhead patrol, almost as if an impromptu party was taking place. So engrossed was everyone in their conversation and banter that Ralph was certain the King could have ridden passed and no one would have noticed.

Standing next to the Captain, Ralph was able to hear how easily he gained the information that he required. There was for him no formal inquisition, no stern questioning of each villager in turn, but a relaxed and friendly chat about life in the village during the war, about the state of the harvest and the increased traffic which passed by their small cottages; for their village lay on an important highway leading south to London. 'Yes, indeed. It was only yesterday that a very large body of armed men had passed through, marching north.' volunteered one man.

'That must have caused a stir.' observed the Captain. 'Did they ride in good order? Some of the soldiery in this war behave little better than cut throats. Was their captain in full command? Did they behave properly towards you?'

'They seemed in some haste. They scarce found time to exchange a word or pause for refreshment.'

'Yes, many were on foot, but mostly they were mounted.'

'Yes, there were several large wagons which were heavily laden, whilst teams of horses hauled some large cannons.'

'Did their leader have aught to say? I suppose that no one heard his name.'

'Twas said that they were some of Prince Rupert's men, but

he was not amongst them. Of that I'm quite sure.' A quiet, rather elderly man joined the conversation and seemed only too ready to help the Captain with his enquiries. 'I heard one of their number address their commander as Sir Lewis.'

After about an hour the Captain gave the order to mount, well pleased with what he had learned. With the curious stares of the village folk on their backs and some shouts and waves of farewell, the patrol rode north away from the small cluster of cottages.

'Surely it is now time the Captain turned south. It's not long before dusk. If he continues much further north, we shall be riding back in the dark.' observed Bill to Ralph as they jogged along side by side.

'We'll not see Newport Pagnell tonight.' another soldier declared, joining in their conversation. 'Our brave Captain has got news of the Royalists and he'll not give up until he has found where they lie. He's hot on the scent and he'll run them to earth ere he seeks the comfort of his own bed.'

There was a murmur of agreement amongst those who knew and had served under Captain Hurst for any length of time.

As they rode further towards that part of the country with which Ralph had become so familiar, just over a year ago, he did not know whether to be scared or glad. Certainly, he was pleased to pass by the scenes of his past happiness but another three miles and they would be within sight of his uncle's house at Bullshead. What if he were to be seen and recognised? What would his uncle make of it, were he to see Ralph riding in the ranks of a Roundhead patrol, when he had been led to believe that his nephew served the King? How would Ralph react himself? He could hardly pass his uncle by without some acknowledgement. As the column got nearer to Bullshead farm, Ralph became more anxious. He thought of dashing away from the column, but quickly dismissed that idea. Perhaps he could excuse himself on business but, having not mentioned it previously, it would not sound very convincing. The house was a short distance from the Northampton road so, with luck, Ralph should not be recognised.

At a turn to the left, where the road through the forest parted from the Northampton road which continued north, the column halted. Ralph could see the Captain talking to a labourer from the forest, who was trudging homewards, axe in hand. The man was nodding and pointing along the road through the forest. Ralph could hardly believe that the Royalist force would have taken that road. Indeed, it seemed much more likely that they would have continued on along the main road. However, upon reflection, he realised that the Royalist's welcome in Northampton might well be a hostile one, which they could avoid by skirting around the west of the town.

Looking in the direction indicated by the woodsman, Ralph saw the roof of his uncle's house peeping between the trees at the edge of the forest. At a command, the column moved forward and, led by the Captain, turned left towards the dark wall of trees that led deeper into Salcey Forest. Slowly the patrol drew nearer to Bullshead farm. To Ralph's immense relief they passed by it without seeing a soul and, apparently, without being seen by anyone in the house. Ralph could only assume that his uncle and family had decided that it was more prudent to remain out of sight. Like his brother, Charles Somers would doubtless prefer to remain neutral in this conflict. It seemed most unlikely that none had seen the patrol approaching.

They rode through seemingly endless woodland along a well-used, somewhat muddy, track which could have been caused by a large party of men and wagons, but Ralph rather doubted it. He wondered what exactly the old forester had told the Captain.

Either side of the track the trees were still in full leaf, but here and there was a tinge of light brown as the leaves began to lose their green with the end of summer. Soon the trees on either side would be bare, revealing the darkness of the forest beyond. To many, the dark recesses of the forest were gloomy and foreboding whilst, to others, the forest was a wonderland in which to escape the world and be alone. Ralph loved the forest for many reasons, but most of all because it was here that he had met Mary.

What if she were out riding today? What if she, as on that fateful day last spring, were to come bounding from the depths of the forest, right into the arms of the patrol? The very thought caused Ralph's heart to miss a beat. But no, she would be at home now, for the day was nearly spent and within an hour it would be dark.

With this thought Ralph wondered again what the Captain intended; for it now seemed hardly likely that the patrol would ride all the way back to Newport Pagnell in the dark.

'Do you think the Captain intends to search all night for the King's army. We shall find little in the dark.'

Ralph spoke to Bill who had been riding by his side in silence for the last mile or two. It seemed that the same thoughts had been passing through his head.

'I think that Richard here has the right of the matter. The Captain is on the track of the Royalists and we shall not go back to Newport Pagnell until he has found them. Doubtless he will persuade some poor souls to offer us food and shelter for the night.'

After a while, they came to the cross roads near the middle of the forest. Surrounded as they were by trees, the Captain was not to know that only a mile further straight on lay the small village of Hartwell. The column halted and Ralph could see the Captain arguing with his two lieutenants. From the way they pointed and heatedly debated, it was plain that they could not agree on which way they should go. Finally, the Captain made up his mind and, jerking his horse's head to the right, led the column along the road that Ralph knew would pass right by Hartington Hall.

Ralph's mind was in a turmoil as he rode with the column along the muddy track. The light was now fading and the captain must surely decide soon where the patrol should camp for the night. When they emerged from the forest, he would not fail to see Hartington Hall and where better to shelter some forty men for the night and expect to find food. Another quarter of an hour and the patrol came to the edge of the forest and into more open meadow land with only the occasional cluster of trees. By now

132

the sun had an orange and red cloak, as it started to dip below the western horizon. Soon it would be twilight. In the distance Ralph could see Hartington Hall shining golden brown in the reflected rays of the setting sun. From his place towards the rear of the column, Ralph could also see the Captain pointing in the direction of the Hall. Once again he halted the column to confer with his lieutenants.

At a shouted command the patrol moved forward again. Although it had been clear to Ralph that the Hall would be an obvious choice for the patrol to shelter for the night, it was no less to his horror when the leading horsemen turned into the drive, through the ornamental gateway in the wall surrounding the Hall.

Ralph's mind was in a whirl. He scarce knew whether to shout for joy or cringe with apprehension. Soon he would see Mary and that would have been a pleasure beyond words in other circumstances. But she would soon see him and then what? To find Ralph, a soldier in the armies of Parliament, when he had ridden away with her father and brother to fight for the King. How could this be? Was he a turncoat, a traitor to the cause her family espoused? Ralph could see the contempt in her eyes and hear the scorn in her voice. He could imagine how that love, which he had hoped she would cherish for him, would fade and die. At the obvious evidence of treachery, that love would be replaced by hatred and loathing. What could he say? How could he tell her the truth? Perhaps her father had told her of his mission. Hope rose within him at this thought, but quickly died as he remembered her father's words. 'Mary need not know what work you do.' In any case, the Colonel would not have seen her since the war began. So busy was he in the King's service, that he would certainly not have had time, nor the willingness to explain the matter in a letter. If he had had time to visit his home, he might have told her.

Captain Hurst led the patrol along the drive to the front of the house. This was the very path along which Ralph and Mary had passed together so many times. Ralph's thoughts flew back to the day when they had ridden to the Midsummer Fair in

Northampton and when they had both first felt that strange and wonderful attraction to each other.

Already there were signs of stir within the house, as faces appeared at the windows and two serving girls scuttled indoors. At the large oak front door, the Captain dismounted. He hammered on its timbers with his gloved fist. The door swung open revealing the figure of one of Colonel Cressley's elderly servants.

The Captain spoke in firm and uncompromising tones, backed by the power that he so obviously wielded.

'In the name of Parliament, I require food and shelter for my men and their horses this night.'

The old man who had opened the door was obviously startled, but was about to make a spirited reply when Ralph heard the voice of a woman. Before she appeared at the door, Ralph knew it was Mary.

Gently but firmly, she ushered the elderly servant inside.

'Where is the master of this house?' demanded Captain Hurst.

'My father is not here. He is away fighting for his King as befits any loyal subject of His Majesty.' replied Mary, without fear and in a haughty manner which yielded nothing to the arrogant demands of the Captain.

'If indeed your father is fighting for the enemies of Parliament, then he can make some amends by providing for our needs. Mistress, I must trouble you to find food and shelter for my men and fodder for the horses. If you will not help then, perforce, we must help ourselves.'

'It would seem sir, that Parliament takes what it wants whether given or not. I have no power to stop you, so you must make what shift you can for yourselves.'

With that, Mary withdrew, leaving the Captain standing somewhat helplessly at the door.

Ralph's heart swelled with admiration for the magnificent way in which Mary had dealt with the Captain and, from the Captain's demeanour, it seemed possible that there might be also a certain grudging respect from him. However, he quickly recovered himself and turned to his two lieutenants.

'Have the men dismount and find quarters where they may around the back. Then, raising his voice somewhat, the Captain shouted in Ralph's direction. 'Master Snaith, come with me, I have work for you.'

For a moment Ralph hesitated. He watched the lieutenants give orders to their sergeants and then re-join the Captain who stood waiting on top of the few steps leading into the house. He had hoped to remain hidden amongst the forty or so troopers; but it was of no use. He heard the Captain bellow.

'What ails you man, come forward.'

Ralph came forward. He joined the Captain and his lieutenants. The four men entered the large entrance hall.

Mary was standing at the foot of the great staircase. As they crossed the hall, she spoke.

'Alfred, will you show these gentlemen which rooms are not in use.'

She motioned to the Captain to follow Alfred and was about to continue up the stairs when she saw Ralph. He was standing at the rear of the group. Recognition was instantaneous. He saw her lips frame his name, but the sound did not come. With a look, he silenced her. How he looked, Ralph knew not. How he conveyed those thoughts and fears racing through his mind, he could not say but, in that instant, the silent message that passed between them was as clear as the spoken word.

For a second Mary paled and almost staggered, as if struck by some unseen hand. She grasped for support at the ornate pillar on the end of the banister rail. Then, with a tremendous effort, she calmed her trembling body, gathered together her tumbling thoughts and spoke above the pounding of her heart.

'Alfred will find you what you need.'

With that she turned and almost ran upstairs.

Ralph watched her go and then turned his attention to the others there. If they had noticed anything amiss, they did not show it. Ralph wondered about Alfred, the man servant. He must have recognised Ralph. Doubtless, he would now follow the lead given by his mistress and say nothing. The four men followed Alfred through to the dining room, where Ralph had been with Sir Francis and his guests when they had received the news of the outbreak of war.

The Captain spoke.

'It seems that we are in a Royalist household but, for all that, I insist upon proper standards of behaviour from all of my men. We will show these people how the soldiers of Parliament behave towards all unarmed people, especially women and old men. There will be no plunder and no brawling. Simonds, go to the kitchen and see what food can be found. Arrange for the men to be fed in turns and make sure that they are properly quartered for the night. Evans, go with this servant to see which rooms can be found for us to pass the night, then find Simonds and arrange meals for the three of us. We shall have it in my quarters where we can discuss our plans for the morrow.'

The Captain turned to Alfred, who stood silently by the door awaiting instructions.

'Show Lieutenant Evans what rooms are available to us, but first bring paper, pen and ink.'

Before long, Ralph was seated at the large dining table with paper before him and a quill pen, ready inked, in his hand.

The Captain dictated a letter to Sir Samuel Luke, in which he told him of the news that he had received during the day, indicating that the Royalist forces had withdrawn north west from Newport Pagnell, probably towards Towcester and that he, Captain Hurst, was on their trail and hoped soon to be able to report to Sir Samuel their exact position and strength. Having finished the letter, the Captain bade Ralph seal it for dispatch at first light tomorrow by special messenger.

'Find food in the kitchen and enquire of Lieutenant Simonds where you may find quarters for the night. Be ready for an early start.'

'Gladly sir but, by your leave, I will first set down details of the supplies I have ordered to be sent to the army at Newport Pagnell. The same messenger that carries your dispatch to Sir Samuel Luke can take my report to my captain.'

'As you wish then, I'll bid you good night.' With that, the Captain left the room to see if his orders were being carried out.

Ralph sighed with relief. Alone now, he could give way to the emotions pent up inside him. It had been a great effort to appear indifferent to all that had happened since the patrol turned into the drive and the Captain had hammered on the door of Hartington Hall. He had set out this morning without the slightest idea of coming nearer than a few miles to Salcey Forest with all its memories and now, here he was in the house of the girl he loved most dearly in all of the world, but as a stranger and an unwelcome guest at that.

While he had been writing the Captain's letter his mind had been in a whirl, but now he had time to think clearly. He dearly wanted to see Mary. He was desperate to assure her of his loyalty to the King and of the constancy of his love for her, but he knew that it might bring disaster on them both, were they to be seen talking urgently or in a familiar manner together. He could hardly go looking for her and dare not ask a servant to take him to her room. He might well, however, pass a letter to a trusted servant to take to her. A maidservant might surely be approached and a note passed furtively to her. It would be a poor substitute for the soft touch of Mary's hand, for a sweet embrace and the warmth of her smile. It would, however, serve to assure Mary of his love and loyalty. Ralph could not contemplate the idea of leaving Hartington Hall the next day without having told Mary some of those things which he so urgently desired her to know. A note might fall into the wrong hands and, if so, he was sure that it would not be long before Captain Hurst would guess who had been the author. It was a risk, but one he must take.

Seated at the table Ralph commenced first to write an account of his day's work in obtaining army provisions. Then, before he sealed the letter to his captain, he took a fresh piece of paper and began to write.

'*My Dearest Mary,*

I have little time to say all that is in my heart. If you love me as I love you, what you have seen this day must have caused you grievous hurt. I beg you to believe that things are not entirely what they seem. There is a need for secrecy and so I can say no more at present except that I wait only for the time when, once again, I may hold you in my arms. With this letter goes all my longing and all my love R. S.

Ralph re-read the letter. He had couched it in such language that its meaning would be clear to Mary and yet, if it were discovered, he could plead simply an affair with the daughter of a Royalist household, where his attentions would not have been tolerated were they known to the family. Ralph now had three letters for dispatch and he took the utmost care not to get them muddled. The first one, which he had written for his Captain, he sealed with the official army seal and addressed it to Sir Samuel Luke. The second letter to his own Captain, he again sealed with the official seal and addressed it to the Wagon Master at Newport Pagnell. The third one, to Mary, he sealed with the ring her father had given him. She would know nothing of the reason for his having such a seal, but she would recognise the motif and, perhaps, understand that he was still working for her father. He addressed it simply 'To Mary'. Taking great care not to mix them up he put the letter to Mary carefully into an inside pocket. Taking the other two in his hand he went in search of Lieutenant Simonds, not only to find his quarters for the night, but also to give him the letters for the courier who was to ride to Newport Pagnell at first light the next day.

Having thus discharged himself of his duties, he found his way to the kitchen by the light of the candle which had been left for his use in writing the letters.

In contrast to the gloom of the ill lit dining room from whence he had come, the kitchen was a scene of warmth and merriment. On one side in the great open hearth was a glowing fire over which, on a long spit, a pig was being roasted. Not far from the fire, at a huge wooden table, sat a dozen or more soldiers noisily dining on the fare provided in his absence by Colonel Cressley. Bustling backwards and forwards across the flagstone floor, two kitchen maids served the soldiers with cuts of pork from another ready roasted carcass and put out platters with small portions of bread, which were all that was left of the day's baking, when the thought of providing for forty hungry men had been last thing on the mind of the Cressley's cook. In the oven by the fire, chickens were also being roasted so that there was no shortage of meat. Ale too was in plentiful supply, at least for now. Doubtless, there would be little left for the Cressley household by tomorrow. So it was a rough and ready, but satisfying meal to which Ralph sat as he squeezed himself a place on the bench at the table. The ale had not only quenched the soldiers' thirst, but also loosened their tongues. It seemed to Ralph that soldiering offered few pleasures, so soldiers took them avidly when the opportunity arose and this was one of those occasions.

Ralph wondered if the food had been willingly supplied or whether it had been simply found and taken. He guessed that Mary would be shrewd enough to supply the soldiers' needs with what she felt she could spare since, if she did not, they would probably take everything and leave her with nothing. Certainly, the two maids were doing their best to keep the soldiers supplied with food and drink. Perhaps they were acting under Mary's instructions. He guessed that Mary and her mother, whom he assumed to be in the house, would be keeping to their bedrooms and counting the time until the soldiers left. The kitchen maids plainly enjoyed their task of serving food to a group of lusty young men. Life at Hartington Hall during the past year must have been dull enough with all the young men from the estate, and from the surrounding villages, away fighting in the war. Now, here were men in plenty, but only for tonight. There were shrieks of laughter as the two maids disentangled themselves from the clutches of one burly trooper who wanted to pull them both down on to his lap. Ralph guessed that neither one of those two maids would spend the night alone. The kitchen, lit by the fire as well as a large round candelabra hanging from the ceiling, was aglow with good humour and companionship. As he ate his meal Ralph felt that he, rather more than those around him, had a greater right to partake of the provender provided willingly or not by the Cressleys.

Ralph recognised neither of the two scullery maids who

brought his food and drink. With all the noise around him it was impossible to talk without shouting but, feeling unwilling to do so, Ralph ate in silence wondering how he might get his letter to Mary. The meal progressed and, as Ralph was draining his second mug of ale, he noticed a woman in her late twenties about to leave the kitchen, having just delivered some instructions to the two maids. He recognised her as one of the two women who attended to the needs of Lady Cressley and Mary. Here, surely, was one he could trust.

Quietly he rose from the table and walked quickly towards the door. Seeing his approach the woman withdrew, pulling the door to as she left the kitchen. Ralph seized it ere it shut. He passed quickly through, closing it behind him. He found himself in a dimly lit corridor, confronting a startled woman who plainly feared the worst from him. As he saw the fear in her face, he also saw the dawn of recognition as she realised who he was. She stared at him in disbelief.

'Why, 'tis Master Ralph ....'

Ralph silenced her with a finger to his lips.

'Be silent, I beg you. I must not be known here.' he said quietly and, seeing her obvious alarm, continued reassuringly. 'Do not be alarmed. I have a message for Mistress Mary. Will you see it safely into her hands?'

Less frightened now, the woman looked at him wonderingly.

'But sir, what do you here with .....'

Again Ralph motioned her to silence.

'Here, the letter.' He thrust it into her hands. 'It must be seen by no other than your mistress. Bid her destroy it when she has read it. Now, remember, you do not know me.'

No longer frightened, but somewhat curious about his presence and the obvious secrecy that went with it she replied, nevertheless, with a confident smile.

'You may trust me. I may not know you, but I'll see your letter safe into Mistress Mary's hands and right welcome it will be too, I'll warrant.'

So saying, she plunged the letter into the folds of her dress, turned and ran swiftly down the passage.

Inside him Ralph's heart turned a somersault and near burst for joy at the woman's parting remark. 'She cared; Mary still cared for him. Why else would the servant have said such a thing? Mary would be glad to hear from him.'

In a daze of happiness, he turned back into the kitchen. Without realising it, he was grinning from ear to ear. His return, therefore, after apparently leaving in hot pursuit of a woman gave rise to some ribald comments as he resumed his place at the table. The good humour of his comrades, with whom he sat, was now matched by his own high spirits at the news he had had of Mary. He joined in the conversation and the laughter, as he enjoyed an evening as merry as any he had spent in the last twelve months.

Ralph was far from sober when he finally rose from the table and, led by others offering mutual support, they stumbled, staggered and wove their way across the yard to the stables which were to provide their shelter for the night. An abundance of fresh hay required little preparation as they collapsed into their ready-made beds. The warmth and comfort of the hay, together with the effects of the ale, ensured that, within seconds of stretching himself out, he was sound asleep.

The next morning Ralph awoke with a thick head, a furred tongue and a foul taste in his mouth. He felt less jovial than the night before and less inclined to eat what little breakfast had been provided, mainly from last night's left overs. This did not stop him thinking of Mary and wondering if he would see her. It would be better, he concluded, if he did not. It was difficult enough knowing that she was in the house, but to see her and not be able to talk to her and hold her in his arms would be unbearable. If she felt the same way, Ralph guessed that she too would stay out of sight.

Ralph saw Lieutenant Simonds talking to a trooper and hand him the two letters, after which the man mounted his horse and left the yard on his own. The Captain and his two lieutenants had appeared from the house where, doubtless, they had spent the night in soft beds. The order came to mount and the patrol began to move out of the courtyard. As they rode along the drive, Ralph looked wistfully back towards the splendid building they were leaving behind. Here lay his heart and his real self. One day, God willing, he would return and collect both.

CHAPTER 11

Late Summer 1643
Hartington Hall

I t had been a long hard winter, a long hard spring and a long hard summer for Mary. Indeed, she could scarcely believe that it was only a year since she had been left, with her mother, to manage the affairs of Hartington Hall as best they could. With her father and brother had gone every able bodied man on the estate, leaving only the women and old men for the same amount of work. But of all those who had left, she missed Ralph most of all. She had known him for only three or four months, but in that time she had learned to love him. She wanted no other man than Ralph and no other thing than to be his wife and live in his house at Preston Capes. So often had he described it to her, that already she seemed to know it well and felt sure that she would be at home there. She could picture herself in the spacious garden on a summer's day, or before a roaring fire in the living room on a winter's evening. She saw the two of them walking arm in arm through the neatly kept flower garden. She saw and she dreamed so much; but she feared too. On that fateful day in August last year, when the beginning of the war had shattered their lives, Ralph had taken her into the garden on that cool summer evening and told her of his great love for her. The love in his voice, the rapture of his embrace, had been like a glimpse of heaven for Mary who loved Ralph just as dearly as he loved her. Now he was away fighting. What if he were to be killed? The panic welled up inside her. It was a thought that she could not bear and, yet, it was one that she must face.

Slowly the year progressed and the war passed them by. The news came slowly too, but it was old when it arrived; although news is always fresh to those who have not heard it and news always has an eager audience, even when it is not always good. They had heard of the battle of Edgehill and of other small encounters. News had come of battles in various parts of the country, mostly in the south of England, as far afield as Cornwall. Of her own folk, how they had fared, whether they had been in some of the fighting, she had heard nothing for the past five months since a brief visit from her father, when he had been passing near enough to call. He had brought some news, of course. He was able to tell Mary how, with her brother Jack, Ralph and all the others whom he had taken with him, they had joined the King's army. He had spent much of his time at Oxford where the King had made his headquarters and where he held court. Jack was fighting with Prince Rupert. Other than that, he had little to say and even less about Ralph, except that he served the King bravely, being engaged in very important work for the Royalist cause. Having thus added only very little to their stock of knowledge about the war, the Colonel departed, leaving his wife and daughter once again in charge of the Cressley estate.

Soon after her husband's leaving Lady Cressley had begun to ail. She complained of griping pains in her bowels and, after a while, she had had to retire to her bed. The physician was called and, for a time, it seemed that she was improving; but the sickness never really left her. Mary had, therefore, virtually the whole responsibility of the house and the estate on her shoulders. Fortunately, Mary was the sort who rose to a challenge although, truth to tell, the burden of these responsibilities weighed heavily on her at times.

So, for the past year, Mary had tackled the job which had been thrust upon her. She organised the women, and such men as there were left, to do the jobs that were most urgent, leaving other jobs to be done when time allowed, which usually meant never.

So to those remaining at Hartington Hall the war was something remote. They waited avidly for news and every rumour was eagerly passed from mouth to mouth, where it generally lost nothing in its telling. To them, the only reality of war was that they had lost their men folk and must make do without them. Of soldiers and of battles they had no first-hand experience. From time to time one of their number, perhaps on a visit to Northampton or some nearby small town, would see soldiers ride by but the soldiers had no business with them nor they with the soldiers. At the outbreak of war, when the Earl of Essex had assembled his forces in Northampton, there had been more news, but now the soldiers were gone and even Northampton was relatively quiet.

One strange tale which had come to Mary's ears was from one of the older men left to work on the estate. He had, one day, been riding along the Watling Street near Towcester when he had encountered a group of Roundhead soldiers. Riding amongst their number was one, whom he had positively identified as Ralph Somers. The man said that Ralph had not recognised him, but that was not surprising since Ralph had had little time to get to know all of those who served on the Cressley estate. Mary had closely questioned the man, who was certain that Ralph had been one of their number and not a prisoner or there under duress. Mary had been disturbed and puzzled by this report and had finally come to the conclusion that it must be a case of mistaken identity and thereupon dismissed it from her mind.

Summer had given way to the early days of autumn. Harvest time had come and gone with great difficulties. Old men and women had been co-opted to undertake the tasks with which they had previously merely helped, but now they had to organise and accomplish them without the strong arms and experience of the men whose work it had normally been. The days were shortening. Soon there would be frosts and the land would succumb to winter's icy grip. Mary was sitting upstairs with her mother when one of the servant girls knocked at the door and, upon entering, exclaimed breathlessly that a troop of horsemen could be seen approaching the house. Mary rose and crossed to the window. Sure enough there, almost at the Hall gates, was a column of horsemen riding in their direction from the forest. For whom did they fight, wondered Mary. It was very hard to tell from their uniform, except for those knowledgeable in military matters, whether they were soldiers of King Charles or of the armies of Parliament. Mary had no idea to whom they owed their allegiance until they were close enough for her to see the orange scarves which she understood were worn by Roundheads.

She watched the patrol ride towards the Hall. When it reached the gate at the entrance to the drive Mary saw, to her horror, that instead of riding by as she had imagined they would, the soldiers turned into the drive and made for her front door. Whatever could they want at Hartington Hall, she wondered, but the lengthening shadows and the failing light suggested to her that they probably sought shelter for the night. She quietly left her mother, who was fortunately asleep, and went to the head of the wide staircase leading down into the hall. She heard the imperious knock on the front door and watched Alfred go to answer the summons. She heard the Captain demand food and shelter in the name of Parliament. Alfred, although now ageing, still had a forthright tongue in his head. A servant all his life to the Cressley family, he shared his master's loyalty to his sovereign. Mary knew that his heart often ruled his head. She also realised from the Captain's tone, that his demands would brook no opposition. This was a time, she quickly decided, when discretion was the better part of valour. Acquiescence would doubtless leave them with considerably less food, but resistance could leave them without a roof over their heads. She quickly decided to intervene.

Resist, she could not, but cower she would not. At least she would meet her family's enemies under her true colours and own her allegiance to the King.

Having gently removed Alfred, she turned to face the Captain. She saw before her a man in his early forties and, in his looks and to some extent in his manner, he reminded her of her father. She could not help but consider that such a scene might well be enacted elsewhere in the country, with her father playing a similar role to this Captain. Mary, having declared herself, thought the Captain's manner and his reply not altogether unreasonable under the circumstances. She felt that if he and his officers could control their men, apart from the loss of food, the house was unlikely to suffer.

Although loyal to her family, Mary had no very strong views as to the rights and wrongs of this awful war. Being her father's daughter, she shared his loyalty to the crown, but this did not blind her to the fact that sections of the community had good reason for complaint. She thought that Parliament had a right to rule, pass laws and make its voice heard. While she could never support the idea of taking up arms against the King, she realised that men must have been very hard pressed to do such a thing.

So, as she confronted the Captain, it was with no great feeling of animosity that she bade him make shift for himself. It was more with a feeling of intense annoyance that men of either faction should be able to invade and plunder private property. She spoke quietly to Alfred, persuading him that resistance was useless and that the sooner the soldiers were fed and on their way, the better.

She passed to the foot of the stairs, intent upon leaving them to it and returning to her mother's room to ensure that she had not been disturbed by the commotion. As she heard the Captain and some of his men enter, she turned to tell them that Alfred would show them what rooms they might use. It was then that she saw Ralph.

At first she could not believe her eyes. Then, from the expression on Ralph's face, she knew that her eyes did not deceive her. Her heart leapt within her and it seemed that it might stop. A thousand thoughts sprang into her mind, confounding wonder with surprise and joy with disbelief. But he was there amongst the other soldiers. His name formed upon her lips. Then, again their eyes met; if indeed they had ever parted. There was a warning there, no joyous welcoming smile, but a look, an unwritten message. It was as if his whole being spoke with a deafening silence. 'Be quiet. I must not know you.' With it and in it, was the unmistakable menace of hidden danger.

She turned and, without knowing what she said, or if she

spoke at all, she fled upstairs. She did not go to her mother's room, but went instead to her own. Throwing herself on a couch she lay trembling and afraid. Gazing out into the sky, she half expected to find the answer written in the clouds. Ralph here, but with the armies of Parliament. Was he then a traitor to the King and to her father? No, that she would not, she could not believe. Had he declared himself for Parliament, she would have been sad, but she would not have ceased to love him. To marry him might have been impossible, but he would still have had her love and respect.

She thought of the tale told nigh on a year ago by the servant who had seen Ralph with Roundhead soldiers, near Towcester. Perhaps it had been true. Perhaps Ralph had decided to fight against, rather than for the King. Yet her father, who had called six months ago, had firmly declared Ralph to be serving the King well. Notably now, she remembered, he had not told her how. What, then, did he here?

Plainly he did not wish to be recognised by her. What did this mean? If he were fighting for Parliament, what need then for secrecy? Perhaps he thought it better that his connections with a Royalist household were not known. If he was a turncoat, he would not wish to speak to her. But there had been such urgency in his mute appeal. He must not be known to her. If he were a spy, then surely there would be an urgent need for his identity to be kept secret.

All of these thoughts crowded into her mind, demanding answers which she could not give. However, there was one question above all others to which she craved an answer. Did Ralph still love her, as she loved him? She cared not what he was, nor what he had done. She wanted only to be, once again, alone with him and in his arms.

How long she sat lost in thought she had no idea; but it was quite dark when a knock at the door jolted her out of her reverie and back to the realities of the moment. It was Amy, her maid, bringing a candle.

'Why mistress, all alone in the dark?' asked Amy in some surprise. 'I thought that you had been carried away by one of those soldiers.'

'No, Amy, I have been sitting here quietly thinking. I scarcely noticed that it had grown dark.'

'Most of the soldiers have made beds in the stables and other outbuildings.' Amy seemed quite excited at the turn of events, which had shattered the dull routine of life at Hartington Hall. 'Olive and Mabel are serving food to some of them in the kitchen. They be a merry lot for all that we've heard of them. I've yet to hear any of them sing a psalm, or try to preach to us.'

'What of the Captain?' asked Mary.

'He is in one of the spare rooms and his two lieutenants are sharing another.'

'They seem to be well behaved. We might have expected rougher treatment from them since they know that my father supports the King.'

To this Amy had no comment. Life during the past year at Hartington Hall had been so dull that she had, at times, thought herself to be in a nunnery. Now, all around her downstairs was life, stir and merriment.

'Will you come downstairs for a meal, mistress?' Amy asked persuasively.

'No.' replied Mary sharply; then more gently, 'No, Amy, I must go to my mother. You shall bring a platter to her room with food sufficient for us both.'

Mary went along to the room where her mother lay in bed. Her illness had left her weak and listless with very little appetite. There was very little sign now of the improvement which Mary had hoped for. Amy returned downstairs to prepare the food that Mary had asked her to bring. Soon she carried it upstairs to Lady Cressley's bedroom. Mary helped her mother to a sitting position in her bed and tried to tempt her to take a goodly share of the food. Anxious to return downstairs to see what was going on, Amy excused herself, leaving Mary alone with her mother.

Truth to tell, they were poor company for each other. Neither showed much interest in the food. Mary, whose appetite was usually considerable, ate but a morsel; her appetite supplanted by her fears and worries about Ralph. Her mother ate even less. Nor did they make up for their lack of food by their conversation. Mary tried to interest her mother in recent events, although she did not mention the presence of the soldiers and hoped that any noise would be too distant to reach her mother's bedroom. Mary's mind was too much in a whirl to concentrate on anything her mother had to say, whilst her mother had little inclination to conversation and showed almost no interest in what Mary had to tell her. It was a sombre meal and Mary was glad when her mother fell asleep. Taking the candles, she left quietly and returned to her own room.

Mary had little idea what the hour was, but felt unready yet for bed. However, she was unwilling to leave her room, lest she risked an encounter with Ralph. Plainly he had not wished to be known by her and she felt instinctively that, to oppose his wishes, might bring danger.

As she sat wondering what she should do, there came a knock at the door and Amy entered. She was plainly in a state of great excitement.

'Mistress, you'll never believe who I've just seen with those soldiers. Why, 'twas Master Ralph. He gave me a letter for you. He said, most particular, that it was for you only and that you were to destroy it when you'd read it. He said that he couldn't see you himself and that it must not be known that you and he had met before. What 'tis all about, heaven knows, but it be plain to me that he doesn't want it known that he's a friend of the family.'

Mary almost snatched the letter.

'Then Amy, if Master Ralph does not wish us to know him, we must make sure that we don't.'

Desperate to open the letter, but determined not to read its contents until she was alone, Mary gave Amy leave to go.

'You may go Amy and, remember, not a word of this to anyone.'

'Trust me, mistress.' replied Amy eagerly. To her it was just another part of the excitement of the evening which she was enjoying to the full. She scurried out of the room anxious not to miss any other adventure that might come her way.

Mary was relieved to see her go. She clasped Ralph's letter

to her breast for a moment as if she held Ralph himself. Carefully she lifted the seal, which reminded her of a similar one used by her father. She unfolded the paper and began to read. Tears of joy glistened in her eyes as she read that he still loved her. He begged her to believe that things were not what they seemed. Together with his wish not to be known at Hartington Hall, this surely could mean only one thing, He must be spying for the King in the Roundhead army. What else could be the reason? What did all that matter to her anyway? He loved her and longed to hold her once again. Her heart sang with joy. If he were a spy though, what of the risks he ran? What if he were caught? Mary's blood ran cold as she thought of the peril in which he stood were he ever suspected. Well, they would never learn the truth from her.

She re-read the letter several times over. To write this had been a risk. Ralph had taken this risk, just to put her mind at rest. If only she could see him; just for a few minutes to be in his arms. But it could not be.

She turned her thoughts again to the letter. What should she do with it? It was addressed to her and had Ralph's initials. There was also the small distinctive pattern on the wax with which the letter was sealed. She held the letter closer to the candle, the better to examine the embossed design. Yes, she thought that she recognised the motif imprinted in the wax. It was one she had seen in a similar form many times before, used by her father. The wood carvings in the fireplace in the living room downstairs had very similar designs to this. Such a seal must surely have been given to Ralph by her father. Was Ralph then acting for him in this business?

The letter, she decided, must not, at all costs, fall into the wrong hands. She ought to burn it immediately, as Ralph had instructed, but that she could not bear to do. It was the first contact she had had with him for over a year. It was her reassurance that the bond between them had grown, not weakened. To destroy something from one so precious was almost a sacrilege. She could put it in a drawer or a chest, but in these places it could be found. She looked around the room for a better hiding place. The room was wood panelled as were most of the rooms in the house. Where the panelling from the floor met the window seat there was a small gap. She tried sliding the letter in there. It went in easily. In fact, it went in so far that she could not get at it to pull it out again. No matter, she thought. There, at least, it would be safe from prying eyes. Later, with the aid of a needle, she would fish it out.

With that, she prepared for bed. Sleep was a long time coming. Her mind was so full of the day's events; of soldiers, of letters, of the Captain and, above all, of Ralph. But with the young, sleep is never too elusive and soon it carried her through pleasant dreams to the light of a new day.

She awoke to the sound of voices and of horses' hooves. Running to the window she caught sight obliquely, for her window faced the wrong way, of soldiers preparing to leave. Rapidly she dressed. Amy came to her assistance and to tell her that the Captain wished to see her.

She descended the staircase to meet the Captain who awaited her in the hall.

'We are about to leave, Madam. Thank you for the hospitality that we obliged you to offer. I have inspected the stables and outbuildings and I can assure you that my men have caused no damage. If we meet again, I trust that it will be in happier times.'

'Sir, you were not welcome guests, but I thank you for the courtesy that you have shown us.' replied Mary, gravely.

The Captain bowed, placed his hat upon his head, turned and strode out of the hall. Mary heard the command to mount and then the clatter of hooves, as the patrol moved off along the drive. She looked eagerly from the window as the patrol rode away. She drew back a little, without knowing why, as she caught sight of Ralph turning in his saddle to steal a glance at the house he was leaving.

With a sigh Mary sat in a chair and, for a while, let her mind dwell on the events of the past twelve hours and the bitter sweet, but remote, contact that she had had with Ralph. By nature, however, Mary was not much given to idle dreaming, so she quickly pulled herself together and turned her thoughts to the mundane tasks of a normal working day.

Half an hour later she was in the kitchen, discussing the depleted food stocks, when she heard outside a tremendous commotion. She went quickly in the direction of the noise and found the courtyard filled once again with armed men on horseback. For a moment she thought that her guests of the previous night had returned. This time, however, the soldiers wore scarlet sashes. The officer in charge was questioning the servants, who were excitedly gesticulating and pointing in the direction taken by the departed Roundhead patrol.

Before Mary had a chance to intervene, the officer shouted an order to his men. The group of riders thundered out of the courtyard, following their officer who spurred his horse to a gallop.

The meaning of all this came instantly to Mary. Plainly the Royalist forces had received news of the Roundhead patrol lodging under her roof and were now in pursuit. Her first thoughts were for Ralph. Now he stood in danger from both sides and there was nothing Mary could do to warn him. She watched helplessly as the Royalist horsemen rode away. Tears of fear and misery filled her eyes.

CHAPTER 12

Late Summer, 1643
South Northamptonshire

An hour had passed since the patrol had left Hartington Hall. As he had yesterday, Ralph rode towards the rear of the column alongside Bill Sheppard. For the most part they rode in silence, enjoying yet another fine day. Now and then a word passed between them and, although they talked but little, the companionship which had grown between them gave them both some pleasure. The night had brought a slight early frost which, having quickly cleared, left a crispness in the morning air. Now the sun was bringing some warmth to what had been a chilly start to the day.

It seemed clear from questioning the few folk whom the patrol had met on their way, that it was on the trail of a considerable Royalist force. From the information thus gathered it was apparent that, as anticipated, the Royalists had skirted to the south west of Northampton. Captain Hurst led his patrol from Wootton across to Milton Malsor and along the road to Towcester. It was not long before they reached the small village of Blisworth, where they stopped while the Captain made further enquiries of the villagers.

The patrol dismounted and, as usual, the men and women came, timidly at first then more readily, to talk to the soldiers and to hear at first hand news of the war and to tell what they knew of passing troops. They stood in groups, laughing and chatting, while others chose some sunny corner to sit and rest where they gossiped in comfort. Ralph, as usual, stationed himself near to the Captain, the better to hear what information the villagers had to offer him. Ralph was avid for news from any source. Much was to be learned from the information that flowed from the Captain's amiable interrogation. Upon his return to Newport Pagnell, Ralph expected to be approached by one of Colonel Cressley's agents, when he would dearly love to have something of real value to report.

As the patrol thus relaxed in the morning sunshine, Ralph became aware of the thunder of horses' hooves. A shot was fired, then another and another. A yard or two from him, a man fell with a scream and lay moaning on the ground. Wheeling around, Ralph saw a large force of mounted soldiers charging towards them at full gallop through the narrow village street. The Captain shouted an order for his men to run for cover while he drew his sword and prepared to defend himself.

Surprise was complete. Had it not been the outcome could have been very different, for the houses and alley ways between them offered ideal cover for protection against charging horsemen. However, there was no time for the Captain to organise any sort of defensive posture for, within seconds, the Royalists were upon them. A yelling horseman bore down upon the Captain, his sword thrust forward ready to impale him. Quickly drawing a pistol from his belt, Captain Hurst calmly took aim and fired at point blank range. The ball entered the man's body in the region of the heart. Instantly dead, the horse carried his body passed them until the lifeless corpse slid from the saddle, into the mud, and in the path of the pounding hooves of horses which followed in their wild charge. Replacing his spent pistol, the Captain once again prepared to use his sword.

Ralph had no weapon and, uncertain what to do for his own safety, stood somewhat behind the Captain. Before he could decide how best to defend himself the Captain staggered back, wounded in the shoulder by a pistol shot. He collapsed at Ralph's feet, blood pouring from his wound.

Ralph looked at the Captain lying in the mud, half rising on his elbows, trying desperately to escape from the virtual certainty of death in his exposed position. Already, another horseman was bearing down on him. Throwing caution to the wind Ralph dashed forward, bent down and, catching the Captain under his unwounded shoulder and by the collar of his tunic, dragged him to safety at the side of a nearby cottage. The

Royalist horseman, unable to finish the Captain, swung a vicious cutting blow at Ralph's head. Sensing his danger, Ralph dodged but was unable to entirely avoid the savage blow. The tip of the sword bit through the cloth of his sleeve and sliced through the flesh of his upper arm. The blood spurted.

Cursing, Ralph managed to drag the Captain to the comparative safety of an alley way between two cottages. Taking the wounded officer's sword he prepared to defend himself. Fortunately, it was his left arm that was injured, leaving his sword arm intact. His wounded arm throbbed painfully and bled profusely. No time to consider his dilemma; like it or not he was now a rebel soldier and must fight or die. Ralph was not yet prepared for death and determined to fight hard for the life he still had.

Peering cautiously around the corner of the cottage which offered him some shelter, Ralph saw that the battle had passed on some fifty yards or more along the village street where, what men were left of the patrol, were fighting for their lives whilst others were seeking to escape in any direction that opportunity afforded them. Obviously the day was lost to the Roundheads and escape could be the only successful outcome.

About to make good his own escape, Ralph heard a groan behind him and saw that the Captain had managed to rise to his feet. He swayed drunkenly as he staggered towards Ralph. Abandoning thoughts of flight, at least for the moment, Ralph considered what he could do to ensure the Captain's safety. At that moment a rider-less horse came careering towards them along the narrow village street. Wild eyed and crazed with fear at the noise of battle and scent of blood, the animal sought to escape the commotion. In the narrow confines between the cottages that hemmed in the street, Ralph was able to grab the bridle as the frightened creature passed. Speaking softly into the horse's ear, Ralph tried to calm it and lead it to the passage between the cottages where the Captain lent for support against a stone wall.

'Can you mount, sir?' demanded Ralph, looking fearfully at the battle still raging but, fortunately, moving away from them.

'With your help.' replied the Captain striving to place his foot in the stirrup.

Blood ran freely down Ralph's arm. His sleeve and hand were now red. It was with great difficulty that Ralph managed to heave the Captain into the saddle. Neither was it easy for Ralph to mount behind him, for the pain in his arm was now considerable.

Ralph turned the horse's head in the direction from which they had come, away from the end of the village where some men were still fighting. The Captain swayed in the saddle and, without Ralph's help, would have fallen.

'How fare you, sir? Can you ride?'

'I must.' came the agonised reply. One arm hung uselessly by his side while, with the other, the Captain strove to retain his seat.

Ralph's first thought was to ride in any direction that would allow them to escape from the Royalist troops, who were now revelling in the savage joy of hounding a beaten foe. Having put a quarter of a mile between themselves and the horrid scene of slaughter back in the village, Ralph began to wonder where he should go. The Captain was all but fainting in the saddle, whilst Ralph was himself in poor shape. He felt faint from loss of blood and his arm throbbed unbearably. Fortunately, he knew the countryside. He had ridden this way many times in the past year on his way to visit Mary. Across to the north of Courteenhall it was barely three miles to Hartington Hall. During the morning the patrol had ridden by a somewhat circuitous route before arriving at Blisworth. Hartington Hall not only offered sanctuary, but there he would find Mary. The choice was obvious. Ralph turned the horse towards his goal and prayed that they would not encounter any marauding Royalists.

'Hold tight, Captain. I think that I can find rest and help for you, if you can but stay the course.'

The Captain muttered incoherently. He reeled so violently in the saddle that Ralph feared they would both be toppled. The miles crept slowly by. Ralph dared not urge the horse to a trot, lest they should fall. The journey was a nightmare, eased only a little when the Captain lost consciousness and slumped forward on the neck of the horse, where Ralph found it easier to hold him. After what seemed an age, Hartington Hall came into sight. Ralph entered the courtyard without delay and was about to shout for help, when Mary burst from one of the doors that led into the yard from the house.

'Ralph, oh Ralph, thank God you're safe.'

One of the men and two women came forward to hold the horse's head and support the Captain. Gently, Ralph allowed the unconscious body to fall into their outstretched arms when it was carried into the house. He then slid from the saddle into Mary's arms. Weak as he was, he felt an overwhelming joy and relief at being reunited with the girl he loved. But, as they clasped each other in rapturous embrace, the red mist rose before his eyes and Ralph sank unconscious to the ground.

* * *

When he came to, it was to find himself between clean sheets tucked warmly in a soft bed. By his side sat Mary. Her anxious face lit up with a smile when she saw his eyes flicker open. He tried to speak.

'Quietly, now. You must have lost a lot of blood. You have quite a deep cut on your arm. I have bandaged it and now you must rest.' She spoke softly, but still with anxiety apparent in her expression. 'What a fright you gave me!'

Ralph smiled at her. His arm hurt like the devil, but let it hurt if he could be with Mary.

'What of the Captain?'

'Poor man; he's badly hurt. There is a ball lodged in his shoulder. I've sent a boy to fetch the physician. If he can remove the ball, and his wound heals cleanly, he should live but I doubt that his right arm will be of much use to him again.'

Ralph took her hand as she stood by his bed and looked up into her eyes.

'I've missed you sadly and longed to see you again, but I never thought it would happen this way. I've so much to tell you.'

'And I have so much to ask you, but it were better if you slept now. Our talking will wait until later.' replied Mary firmly as she rose to leave the room.

'Mary,' called Ralph as she reached the door. She turned; the door half open.

'Yes,' she looked towards him. Their eyes met.

'I love you and want you.' He uttered the words with a simple sincerity.

'Just as I love and want you. Now sleep.'

With that, she left the room.

The days that followed were like an interlude in Paradise for both Ralph and Mary, following the rigours and hardship of the past year. They spent hours in each other's company and the more time they spent together, the more their love for one another grew.

Three days after his arrival Ralph was sitting with Mary at his side in the comfortably furnished living room. They were completely alone, sitting silently together in pleasurable companionship. Ralph's mind turned over the events that had brought them to this extraordinary, but happy, state of affairs. His wound was healing, although still quite sore and painful to touch. Nevertheless, it seemed to be free of infection and he was sure that quite soon it would be better. Happy as he was to be at Hartington Hall, he knew that this idyllic situation could not continue indefinitely and he wondered what his next move should be. News of the way in which the patrol had been ambushed would by now, quite possibly, have reached Sir Samuel Luke in Newport Pagnell. Possibly, some stragglers would have managed to get back to the town, or perhaps a second patrol had been sent out to seek news of the first. A message had been sent to Sir Samuel Luke by Captain Hurst before the patrol had left the Hall, so it was possible that, at any time, an officer might arrive at the front door seeking information.

Ralph saw no great peril in being found at the Hall. He himself had been injured whilst Captain Hurst lay upstairs being cared for in the best possible manner. The physician had removed the ball. At the time, the Captain had been mercifully unconscious. Poultices of herbs had been applied to draw out any poisons from the wound. However, he had been weak from loss of blood and a fever had developed. In between bouts of delirium he slept fitfully, knowing nothing of what went on around him. Should an officer of Parliament call, Ralph felt that he had nothing to fear. The presence of his wounded officer in the Hall justified his remaining here. Although his own wound was healing, Ralph reasoned that his duty would surely be to stay, at least until it was clear that his Captain was going to recover. Then he would have to return to Newport Pagnell.

Ralph reflected upon the absurdity that war, the ultimate stupidity, made of life. To think, that he had gone to so much trouble and taken such risks to save Captain Hurst when his duty, if his true allegiance were known, was to kill him. Yet Ralph did not hate him. Indeed, although Ralph did not know him well, what he did know of him he liked. Now the Captain was upstairs, fighting for his life and a greater authority than them both would decide whether he should live or die. The Captain had no need to concern himself on the best course of action. His worries were at a different level. In that grey world of limbo between the living and the dead, he had his own personal battle to fight; not with his sword, but with his will to live. The enemy was the fever that racked his body and which sought to rid it of the life that it owned.

Ralph wondered if he should desert. Now would be as good an opportunity as any. There were none within the Roundhead army to say whether he was alive or dead. But what purpose would that serve? He had sought to find a place in the rebel army, where he might gain intelligence for Sir Francis and had done so with some success. So far, he had been able to provide the Royalists with some useful intelligence and, if he returned to the rebel army, he may continue to help in this way. If he deserted now, he would be failing in his task. No, soon he would have to go back to Newport Pagnell. However, he could extend his stay until it became clear what the Captain's fate was to be.

What if the Captain recovered? It would surely do Mary no

harm if it were known that she had nursed a Roundhead officer back to health. Even the Royalists would surely not hold that against her. Ralph was concerned for Mary's safety and was most unwilling to leave, but soon he must go; not yet however. With that thought he must, for the time being, content himself.

Rousing himself from this contemplation, Ralph looked up at Mary who was busy with the household accounts. The Roundhead patrol had made considerable inroads into the provisions held in the house. It had been an expensive visit. She had to decide what must be replaced. Ralph gently touched her hand.

'Much as I would like to, my sweet, I fear that I cannot stay here for ever.'

Mary nodded sadly. She, too, had thought of Ralph's situation and had come to the same inevitable conclusion. Oh, that this insane war would end and the two of them could be left to live their lives together in peace. Ralph had told her the reason for his presence in the Roundhead army. It gave her little comfort to know that he was spared the perils of battle when he, daily, ran the worse peril of discovery and death. She trembled with fear at the thought. Knowing nothing of this when Ralph had arrived, she had said nothing to the servants and let them assume that Ralph fought for Parliament. It was not uncommon for even families to be divided in this war, let alone friends. Only she knew the whole truth. Amy knew that things were not quite what they seemed. Mary had warned her again to keep the matter to herself and not gossip about it to the other servants, including Alfred. They must think what they liked. She had no choice but to rely on Amy's discretion. For the rest, Ralph was a soldier of Parliament, who had been and still was her friend.

* * *

Two days later, Ralph's wound was sufficiently healed to allow him once again to ride a horse, so he and Mary rode out together. Usually, neither were short of words but, today, they were both saddened by the knowledge that the time for parting was close at hand. Their horses ambled side by side along the forest track. It was a dull, damp morning which heightened their mood of depression. The ground was wet and the track muddy, as their horses plodded through large puddles.

'How was Captain Hurst this morning?' asked Ralph.

'The fever has left him but he is very weak, although Amy tells me that he is now sleeping more peacefully. I think that he is on the mend.'

'Then I must think of going. If his wound is healing and his fever gone, then surely he will live. There is little that I can do for him and, once he is conscious and rational again he will, I am sure, not expect me to stay. It will be a week or two before he is fit to leave you, but he will wish to go as soon as he can. I expect that he will want me to take a message back to Sir Samuel Luke, when he sees that I have recovered; although I doubt he knows that I am here. I expect he will remember little of what took place.'

Ralph paused and glanced at Mary.

'Although he may be our enemy, I wish the Captain well and hope he makes a full recovery but, if he does, there are dangers. Clearly, it is essential that he knows nothing of my purpose in his army. What if, while he is convalescing, he talks to the servants? What will they tell him about me? The subject is bound to come up and servants will talk. Even though they are all loyal to you, some chance remark may give rise to suspicion.'

'Yes, I have thought of this and it worries me.' Mary's face clouded with concern. Some of the servants will remember you. Only Amy knows that you might have something to hide, even if she has no idea of your real work. Without making an issue of it, I have asked her not to discuss you with the servants. If the Captain does learn that your name is Somers and not Snaith and, if he does discover that you and I were friends and that you have visited Hartington Hall before, well, what of it? This war has come between many friends and split many families. So Captain Hurst will not find the situation so very odd.'

Mary paused and glanced anxiously at Ralph.

'Anything that puts you in danger is the cause of countless

fears to me my dearest but, in this case, I cannot see what else we can do but brazen it out. If Captain Hurst asks if I knew you before you came with his patrol to the Hall, I shall not deny it but I shall not volunteer the information. The worst case would, I think, be to deny it. If he pursues the matter I shall freely admit that we were friends before the outbreak of war, but your conscience led you to fight for Parliament, whilst my family chose to support the King.'

Ralph, no less worried than Mary, tried to cheer her by professing a confidence that was rather less than real.

'Yes, you are right. As for my name, we can say that I changed it to save embarrassment to my family and friends who mostly support the King. Surely, he will be satisfied with that. Anyway, if I leave tomorrow as it now seems I might have to, assuming the captain is out of danger, then he will have little thought of me when I am gone. He will be content to regain his strength and leave Hartington Hall as soon as he may.'

'He is bound to wonder why you brought him to Hartington Hall.' It was a point that obviously worried Mary.

'You may answer that it was pure chance. Truth to tell, when I caught that rider-less horse and fled from the carnage at Blisworth village, I rode in the direction that took me most quickly away from danger. I had covered some distance before I stopped to wonder where I should go and found that I was already on my way to Hartington Hall. True, the thought of you quickly decided me that the Hall was the best place to look for refuge, but you need not tell him that. If he presses the point, then tell him that we were acquainted before the war. If he hears this from your lips and accepts your version of the story, he may not seek to find out more from others.

Mary smiled. The story was not unreasonable. Doubtless, if Ralph had sought shelter in some labourer's cottage it is likely that the Captain would have died for the want of proper nursing. Still, for all that, a Royalist household was a strange choice of shelter for a wounded Roundhead. It was to be hoped that the Captain would be too grateful for his restored health to pry too much into the reason for his good fortune.

'Will you be able to visit me again? Newport Pagnell is not too far away.' Mary enquired hopefully.

'If I can come, I will; but with Captain Hurst your guest it might be unwise to call without a good reason. I fear, though, that I shall not be long in Newport Pagnell. A garrison will be left to guard and hold the town for Parliament and the army will move on. If I am to learn anything of the armies of my Lord of Essex, I must make sure that I move with Sir Samuel Luke. I shall learn little for your father by watching the war go by in Newport Pagnell.'

Mary knew that Ralph must go, but that knowledge did little to repair the misery she felt because of it. There was no use in wishing. Go he must and she must smile bravely when the time came for him to leave.

'You have had no contact with your father.' It was more of a statement than a question.

'No, I haven't heard from him since he was here in the spring.'

'I was wondering if he should be told of what has happened, indeed is happening in his house.' Ralph spoke pensively.

'Well, there is little he can do about the patrol's visit and it might be better if he doesn't know about Captain Hurst's presence, at least until he has gone. He will hear about it all in good time. Meanwhile, doubtless he has enough to worry about.'

They rode on through the forest towards Bullshead farm. Ralph would have gladly called upon his uncle, but there would have been too many questions which he would not care to have to answer. The less his uncle knew, the better. So, sadly, they avoided passing close by.

Ralph glanced at the sun which had passed its zenith. Time, he thought, to turn back to Hartington Hall.

After a meal Ralph and Mary went up to the room where Captain Hurst lay. Amy had just looked in to see how he fared.

'How is he?' Mary whispered the question to her maid.

'He's been sleeping sound as a babe, mistress.'

The Captain stirred at the sound of voices. Ralph looked at

his pale face and drawn features. He seemed to have aged ten years. Ralph knew little of sickness except for that suffered by his own father but, as the Captain spoke, although his voice lacked its former strength, Ralph sensed that there was now hope that he would recover.

The Captain looked at Ralph and Mary and then around the room in which he was lying. The struggle to make sense of his surroundings was plainly mirrored in his face.

'Why, Master Snaith, what do you here?'

'Do you not remember sir? You were wounded in the fight with the Royalist troopers. I brought you here. You have been very ill, sir. We feared for your life. It was the wound in your shoulder which brought on a fever. But, you may rest easy now, sir. You are, I'm sure, over the worst and are set fare to recover. You are in good hands.'

'My shoulder?' The Captain turned his head to look at his shoulder, but the movement caused a sharp pain to surge through his chest and shoulder like a knife. With a groan, he let his head fall back on to the pillow. 'I can't remember much. The Royalists, they fell on us in that village. There was a shot. How did you bring me here? Where are we?'

'Try not to move sir. Your shoulder needs a chance to heal. The ball has been removed and poultices have drawn out the poisons, but I'm afraid that the bones are shattered. The physician says that the wound should mend, but you are weak and need to rest. You are at Hartington Hall, where I brought you to seek help. This is Mistress Cressley. Do you not remember her?'

'Hartington Hall; Mistress Cressley. This is a Royalist household. Why came we here? Why did they take me in?'

Mary drew up the covers on the Captain's bed.

'Master Snaith was wounded too and was weak from loss of blood. He managed to catch a rider-less horse that chanced by and which carried you both away from the fight. Your patrol was routed and I'm afraid that many were killed. By chance, his flight led him in this direction. He was near fainting from pain and weakness from loss of blood and could scarce sustain himself in the saddle. This house was the first he came to where he thought that he might get help.' explained Mary to the Captain with a reassuring smile.

'Why so, mistress? Your house is for the King; we fight for Parliament.'

'Captain, in this house we support King Charles, but that does not rob us of concern for our fellow men. Your conscience has led you to take up arms against the King. Would to God that it were possible for men to settle their differences in peace. If they must fight, we would not refuse succour to anyone when the need was as great as yours.'

Mary spoke sincerely. The fact that it was Ralph who had brought the Captain to her doorstep altered the case somewhat but, had Ralph not been there, help would have been offered all the same. Mary was not short of compassion. She did not hate those who fought against the Crown so much that she would refuse them help in such a plight.

'You are a welcome guest in this house until you are well enough to leave.'

'Mistress, you are very kind. I trust that I shall not be a burden upon you for too long; and what of you, Master Snaith?'

'I received a flesh wound in my arm from a sword cut. I was faint from loss of blood but now the wound has nearly healed. I did but wait to see you on the path to recovery ere I return to Newport Pagnell. Now, I see that you are improving so I shall ride there tomorrow. But come sir, you have talked enough. You must rest. I will see you before I leave.'

The following morning Ralph was up and breakfasted soon after the sun had risen. He went up to see the Captain before he set out on his journey. Captain Hurst lay on his bed supported in a slightly raised position by several pillows.

'Good morning, Captain. I trust that you are feeling better than yesterday.'

'A great deal better, thank you.'

Indeed, thought Ralph, the colour was already returning to his cheeks and his voice sounded stronger than yesterday.

'I think that it will not be long before you are once again on your feet.'

'I trust that it will be so quite soon. Do you leave now to return to the army at Newport Pagnell?'

'Indeed, sir, I do. Now that you are clearly improving, there is no longer any need for me to remain here. Is there any message that you wish me to convey?'

Captain Hurst gave Ralph a few instructions and a message for his commanding officer. They spent a few minutes chatting, during which time the Captain questioned Ralph further about the skirmish with the Royalists at Blisworth and the manner in which he had been brought to Hartington Hall. The loss of his patrol saddened him greatly. Ralph tried to put the best possible view on the events and suggested that, as might well have been the case, whilst some men had been killed, many might have managed to escape as had both of them.

'It seems, Master Snaith, that I owe you my life and no man can ever repay such a debt. For now I can only give you my thanks, but if ever I can offer you some more substantial proof of my gratitude, I shall be most happy to do so.'

'You owe me nothing, Captain. What I did for you, I would have done for any man. If we must fight, then I trust that no man would ever want for my help when he is sorely wounded. Would that this war were over and this horrid slaughter at an end!'

Ralph felt that he had probably said too much and promptly changed the subject.

'I must leave now, sir. I shall attend to your instructions and I shall pray for your speedy recovery.'

With that, Ralph bade the Captain goodbye and left the room. Mary was waiting for him in the hall. Her face was sad and tears glistened in her eyes. At the foot of the stairs they embraced.

'God keep you safely.' she whispered.

'And you, my love. I pray that this parting will not be for as long as the last and that soon I may return to you for good.'

Quietly and without further ado, Ralph mounted the horse captured at Blisworth and rode off to Newport Pagnell.

CHAPTER 13

June, 1644
Stow-on-the-Wold, Gloucestershire

"Sir,

This day, the 6th of June, at Stow-on-the-Wold, the Earl of Essex has held a council of war with his generals. In spite of great protest, he has divided his army in two. At the head of one half, it is his intention to ride to the relief of Parliament's forces in Lyme. The other half he has given to Sir William Waller and charged him with the pursuit and harassment of His Majesty's forces at Oxford.

The Earl marches south tomorrow, leaving Sir William to make the best shift he can in the discharge of that duty entrusted to him. I have been ordered to remain with that part of the army which will keep me nearest to yourself."

Ralph added what further information he had, then quickly re-read the letter that he had just written. He was alone in the room of a small cottage on the edge of the bustling town of Stow-on-the-Wold. He was, so it was supposed, bringing his accounts up to date and listing some of the produce held by local farmers which, Ralph intended, would shortly be requisitioned for Sir William Waller's new army.

Satisfied that all was in order, Ralph folded the letter. Removing the signet ring from his finger, he pressed the catch at the side when the cover flew back, revealing the engraved seal. Lighting a candle, he held a stick of red sealing wax in its flame, heating it until drops of the molten wax fell on to the letter and spread across the bottom edge of it at the back of the folded sheet. Quickly setting down the candle and the stick of wax, he took up the ring and pressed it into the molten wax, covering the edge of the folded sheet before it set. The wax quickly hardened and Ralph saw, with satisfaction, a clear imprint of the pattern in the seal. He checked that the wax firmly held down the top of the folded sheet on to the back, so that the letter could not be read without breaking the seal. He then placed it carefully in a pocket inside his shirt. He would not feel easy now until he had met the agent and delivered to him the letter to be carried to Colonel Cressley. The hour was late and Ralph must keep the letter hidden on his person until tomorrow, when he was to meet the courier by the church in the town.

The timber cottage, with its low ceilings, had two rooms upstairs and two down. As usual, Ralph was somewhat privileged beyond his rank when it came to allocating quarters. Normally, he would be expected to rough it, sharing with the other soldiers whatever accommodation was available. However, when his work for the Wagon Master involved clerical duties, as was usually the case, necessity demanded that he be found a make shift office, which he invariably made his own quarters as well. This downstairs room at the rear of the cottage, which served as his office, was sparsely furnished. It had a bench, a table, a chair and a low bed; but to Ralph it was a haven, where he could find solitude and peace, not only for his secret work, but also for the privacy which he found so essential. Ralph liked companionship, especially with chosen friends of whom he made but few. Nevertheless, he was not fond of the communal living, which army life imposed on all but the higher ranks. There were times, especially at night, when he yearned for the quietness of his own company. The satisfaction that he now felt came not only from having completed his report, but also from the peace of his surroundings, far away from the noise and hubbub of a crowded room shared with his comrades. He sighed with relief as he stood up, stretched himself, pushed the chair back under the table to make more room and threw himself on his bed.

The failing light of the long summer's day faded into dusk. The room, which an hour ago had been bright with the rays of the evening sun, was now filled with the gloom of approaching night. Outside, Ralph could hear the murmur of voices from the troopers who sat around the fire, on which they had cooked their evening meal. As he lay on his bed, deep in thought, he could see the reflected light from the flames dancing on the ceiling. When would it all end? Ralph wondered. The war was now nearly two years old and in its second summer. It was about eight weary months since he had last seen Mary. He had managed to see her just once since that happy week at the beginning of last autumn. The thought of their time together had sustained him during the long winter nights but, with the coming of spring and summer, the memory of that week grew more distant until now it seemed but a dream.

For most of the winter, Ralph had again been with the Earl of Essex's army in London. Since the beginning of spring the army had been campaigning from London to Reading and Abingdon, manoeuvring to contain the King's army in Oxford. Essex had been joined by Waller, after his successful encounter with the Royalist forces at Cheriton. The Scots had now entered the war to support Parliament. After a year of some success, the King was now on the defensive and it was Parliament which was taking the initiative. The outlook, Ralph decided, did not bode well for the King. The one bright spot was this recent decision of Essex to march off to the relief of Lyme. Had both he and Waller stayed with their combined armies to continue their action against the King's forces in Oxford, Ralph feared that the outcome would have been grave for the Royalists. However, Essex had decided to march south west and this was good news indeed for the King. Ralph felt that it should be immediately made known to him. Fortunately, he had arranged to meet his courier tomorrow, so this new intelligence should reach the King with little delay.

Ralph was not up at dawn, which was a little too early at this time of the year, but it was not long after that he was out and on the way to see his new captain. When Ralph had heard that part of Parliament's army was to march off to the south west, he was somewhat dismayed lest he should be ordered to go with them. He believed that, important as the relief of Lyme was to

Parliament, the more important part of their campaign would be fought in the Midlands and this is where he would glean the most useful information. He had, therefore, pointed out that he had a better knowledge of the Midland counties and would be more useful in that area. When he discovered that he had been selected to stay with Sir William Waller's army, he was fairly certain that this had more to do with army organisation than the rather feeble reason that he had put forward. Well, for whatever reason, he had been selected to stay in the area that best suited his purpose and he was glad to accept the decision. He had been told today to report to the new captain, from whom he and the Wagon Master would now receive their orders. The meeting was a formality to allow the new captain to get to know his men. He complimented Ralph on the good reports which he had had of him from his previous captain and hoped that he would prove to be as useful under his command. It pleased Ralph to know that he was accepted in the rebel army but thought, with a wry smile, that it was indeed an odd situation that he was giving satisfactory support to the army which it was his duty to help defeat.

Having visited his new captain, Ralph excused himself on the grounds of duty, telling the officer that he had to visit one of the merchants in the town. This was perfectly true, but he omitted to say that his appointment with the merchant was at the somewhat imprecise time of mid-morning, whereas another appointment at the church was more pressing. As he left for the church, Ralph once again reflected that his job in the Roundhead army could not serve his purpose better and he rejoiced in the freedom it gave him.

The small town of Stow-on-the-Wold consisted of a cluster of houses, a market place and a church, all located at the intersection of a number of roads. It was always a busy place, which became busier on market days. Now it was full of soldiers who appeared to occupy every building and every corner of the town. Whilst many appeared to have little to do and seemed happy to pass their time pleasantly gossiping with the townsfolk, there was, nevertheless, much going and coming of officers expediting the orders of the Earl of Essex and his war council. Soon there would be the stir and commotion of an army about to march out of town. Ralph noted with interest that preparations were already well under way for many of the soldiers to leave. He made his way from the market place towards the church where, for the want of a better place, he had agreed to meet Colonel Cressley's courier. Ralph had never been to Stow before, but every town had a church. So, without knowing the town, he was able to arrange a meeting place.

Away from the bustle of the market place there were fewer people about. As he entered the churchyard, it was almost as if he had shut the door on the hubbub of a busy town. Underneath his arm Ralph carried a roll of paper. It was only an account for payment for horse shoes supplied to the army by a local blacksmith. On this occasion it served no other purpose than as an additional source of identification since, in this case, neither the courier nor Ralph knew each other. Walking along the path between the wooden crosses with which all but the graves of the richest folk were marked, Ralph came to the church door. Inside the porch were, on either side, stone seats on one of which sat a man who regarded Ralph with some interest before he spoke.

'Good day, young sir. 'Tis seasonable weather.'

'For the month of June.' responded Ralph.

'Or for July.' re-joined the other.

'But not for winter.' replied Ralph.

With this unlikely, prearranged exchange of conversation, Ralph identified himself to Joseph Grimshaw, one of Colonel Cressley's most experienced and trusted couriers. Joseph Grimshaw was a man of medium height, brown hair and coarse features; probably older than Ralph by some fifteen or twenty years. In disposition, he was cast in the same mould as his predecessor, Jim Peabody. The Colonel seemed to choose men of a solitary nature, who had few words to offer and preferred their own company. The less they got involved with others, the better. Joseph was indeed a man of few words and of a somewhat gloomy nature. His face rarely allowed itself a smile. As well as liking his own company best, he also liked to be his own master.

He had no skill at arms, but he had a wide knowledge of the roads and byways of England, along which he was well travelled. His loyalty to the King and to Colonel Cressley was complete and unquestioning. He would do any service they might ask, but he did it better alone. Thus it was that the work upon which he was now engaged gave satisfaction, both to his master and to himself.

'Where lies our master now?' asked Ralph. He was always curious to know the Colonel's whereabouts. It gave him some idea of the proximity of the royalist command.

'He's gone with a message from His Majesty to the Lieutenant General, Prince Rupert, to urge him to join with the Scots loyal to Montrose and hasten to the relief of York. The Prince's army is presently camped in Stockport and, it is there, that I am to find Colonel Cressley to deliver your report.'

'And His Majesty, where is he to be found?'

'He is gathering his army about him at Woodstock.'

'The intelligence contained in this report will be of the greater value to His Majesty, rather than Colonel Cressley. Will you carry this message first to the King?'

Joseph Grimshaw answered gruffly. There was a stubbornness in the look he gave Ralph and in his tone of voice. 'My orders were to carry your message to Colonel Cressley. He said nothing about going first to the King.'

'Then I must confide in you.' said Ralph softly. He realised that he was in no position to bluster and command. Subtler tactics must suffice, if he was to get his way. 'The armies of Parliament are now to be divided into two parts. Only one part will remain near Oxford, and in the midland counties, to oppose His Majesty. The King waits now at Woodstock, scarce fifteen miles distant. With this knowledge that the Roundhead army is now weakened, he can strike a crushing blow at Sir William Waller; but only if he moves swiftly. You will see then, that there is little point in your riding all the way to Stockport, only to receive instructions to take the news from there, in all haste, to the King who is only an hour's ride from here. By the time you get back from Stockport, the news will be a week old. Any opportunity for a surprise attack on a disorganised and weakened army will be gone.'

As he spoke, Ralph saw the light of understanding dawn on Joseph's rather dull countenance. Joseph was not a clever man, but he had a large measure of native cunning which made up for otherwise slow wits. Loyalty and determination were the better part of Joseph Grimshaw's character.

'Aye master, there be good sense in what you say. I'll to the King first and then ride to my master at Stockport; 'tis a year or two since I rode so far north.'

Ralph looked around. There was no one to see them, partly hidden as they were by the church porch. Quickly, Ralph removed the letter from his pocket and handed it to Joseph who, equally quickly, concealed it on his person.

* * *

It was a sultry summer's evening, as Colonel Cressley sat lost in thought in one of the rooms of Lathom House near Stockport. The rich tapestries and paintings which covered the walls gave the room an atmosphere of rather sombre splendour, but did little to brighten it, lacking the sun's rays which normally lit it at this hour. The sky was overcast and in the distance could be heard the rumble of thunder.

For once, the Colonel was not busy. Today, he had decided, he would rest and review the situation. He had arrived only yesterday at Lathom, entrusted by the King himself to deliver, verbally to Prince Rupert, information about the present military situation and to express to the Prince some of the wishes of his royal master. The King had felt that Colonel Cressley could convey his desires to the Prince better by word of mouth than he could express them in writing. Furthermore, His Majesty had expressed the view that the valuable organisation, which Colonel Cressley had set up, would be of more use to the Prince in his campaign in the north than to the King who was to remain in the Midlands. The Colonel was sure that this was not the case and even went so far as to suggest to the King, in the most tactful manner, that his agents were better placed to give news of the rebels in the Midlands and the south, but not the north. The King had said that, if this were the case, the Colonel ought to seize this opportunity of travelling north to rectify the situation. Thus defeated, the Colonel had little choice but to surrender gracefully to his sovereign's will and commence his journey north.

Yesterday, the Colonel had had an hour long interview with Prince Rupert, who had been keen to learn as much as he could of his uncle's mind. He had last seen him in April, since when their only contact had been in writing. He was particularly interested in the King's remarks about the relief of York, upon which he placed much store. The Prince fully intended to relieve the city from siege by Roundheads, but first he must recruit more men. Hence his march through Cheshire and Lancashire to gain that support which he must have for a successful campaign. He was heartened by the news that the Earl of Montrose was leading an army south from Scotland to support King Charles.

The Prince had received Colonel Cressley with considerable cordiality. The Colonel had earned himself quite a reputation with the leaders of the Royalist cause. Since the early days of the war, indeed soon after Edgehill, the Colonel had built up an organisation of agents which had brought him information from Parliament's forces in most places where they were active. Time and again he had been able to give positive, accurate information of the position and strength of the enemy. The Colonel expressed to Prince Rupert the hope that he would be able to continue to keep him, as well as the King, informed about the rebel forces.

So far, apart from Edgehill, the Colonel had seen very little fighting. His work had been clandestine, where the exercise of his agile mind had been of far more use than his prowess with the sword. For Colonel Cressley, the time had flown. Whilst other officers had moments of excitement, fear and action during battle, followed by weeks of tedious inaction, the Colonel's life was one of continuous work. He sat for hours during the day, and often long into the night, studying the reports which he had received; sifting information, setting one report against another and analysing the purpose behind the enemy's movements. Then, often purely by a process of deduction from this gathered information, he had been able to forecast the rebel's next move.

He had had little time for day dreaming but now, in the peace and solitude of his present surroundings, he allowed his thoughts to wander to memories of home; of Hartington Hall and of the rich Northamptonshire countryside with its forests and pastures. He thought of his wife, Elizabeth, whose health had given him some concern when he had called in the spring of last year. Goodness, was it that long ago? Thank goodness that she had Mary to look after her. He had received a letter from Mary, carried to him by one of his agents who had been passing that way and had called to deliver a letter from the Colonel during the earlier part of this year. He had felt that Mary was not telling him as much as there was to tell about her mother and he was anxious to know if his wife's health was now improved. That Mary could manage the affairs on the estate, he had no doubt. She was a capable girl and, although she would not enjoy such a task being thrust upon her, she would make a good job of it. Doubtless, she was eating her heart out for young Somers. Damn the war, thought Colonel Cressley. How it was devastating people's lives! Ralph and Mary had been so much in love. That had been plain, even to him, and he was not very observant in such matters. Now they were apart and for how long; God alone knew. To make matters worse it was he, Mary's own father, who had asked Ralph to undertake such an inglorious and perilous role as a spy. Each moment of the day and night he would be in peril; death a certain reward for failure and no expectation of glory if he should succeed. But, men like Ralph were rare. The Colonel had all manner of men to serve him, but few with those exceptional qualities of courage, loyalty and discretion coupled, above all, with the intelligence and initiative to perform the task of supplying the information, which the Royalists needed, if they were to wage a successful war against the rebels.

These were gloomy thoughts and the Colonel had little time for negative thinking. It was not that he was an unkindly or unfeeling man, far from it; but there was a war to be fought and won. Each man's first duty was to his King and, as a soldier, Colonel Cressley was not one to shirk his duty.

There was a knock at the door. Already Colonel Cressley's train of thoughts was turning to matters of work.

'Come in.'

The door opened and in walked a soldier whom he instantly recognised.

'Why, Jack, my boy, my dear son. How are you? You look fine. I'd hoped soon to see you again and now here you are.'

'Yes, father, here I am and very pleased to see you too.'

After a warm embrace, Colonel Cressley took his son by the arm and led him to a chair.

'Sit yourself down. You've time to stay and talk, haven't you?'

'Yes, I'm off duty now. I have just returned from a recruiting sortie. We rounded up another two score men who will bear arms for the King.'

'Well done. Now, how long is it since we last saw each other? It was early spring or late winter, I'll be bound; in March, I think, at Oxford. Well, God be praised that he has kept you safely.'

The two men talked until it was quite dark and then continued by candlelight. It was past midnight before they parted to go to their beds.

* * *

Two days later, the Colonel sat during the afternoon in the same room, but this time he was busy pouring over maps and other papers. Gloomy thoughts had given way to the serious work of collating the various reports that he had received and relating them in place and time, until a clear picture emerged of the Roundhead's disposition, their strengths and their weaknesses. Once again he was immersed in work.

A knock at the door caused him to pause and bid the visitor enter. It was one of Prince Rupert's staff officers.

'His Highness sends his compliments and requests that you attend him in the study.'

Lathom House was the spacious home of the Countess of Derby and had lately been under siege by the Roundheads, until relieved by the arrival of Prince Rupert. Colonel Cressley walked along its stately corridors until he reached the study, where the Prince held a daily council with his officers and directed the affairs of war.

The officer preceding the Colonel knocked at the door and straightway entered.

'Colonel Cressley, Your Highness.' Colonel Cressley entered the room and bowed to the Prince. As he did so, he observed that there were two aides whom he recognised and, also, Joseph Grimshaw.

'Good day, Colonel.' Prince Rupert's greeting was cheerful and friendly. 'This fellow claims to be one of your couriers and has, furthermore, brought me a letter from my uncle, the King. He reiterates the message that you carried from His Majesty upon your arrival. He writes,' and here the Prince referred to the letter from the King.

"If York be lost, I shall esteem my crown little less."

'Strong words, would you not say Colonel? You did not express these sentiments so strongly.'

'I pray your forgiveness sir, if my message lacked the forcefulness with which it should have been delivered, but I did try to convey His Majesty's concern about the siege of York.' replied the Colonel somewhat defensively.

''Tis of no matter, I was not then ready to offer proper assistance to those within the walls of York. I still lack the strength I need for such an encounter with the rebels but, God willing, Lancashire will supply my needs.'

'Master Grimshaw here also bears a letter from one of your agents in the army of Sir William Waller. It tells how Essex has divided his army so that one half may go to the relief of Lyme and the other to attack our army in the Midlands. Realising the urgency of this news, your man and Master Grimshaw decided that the letter should first be taken to the King at Woodstock and then be brought north to us. I compliment you on the manner of men you employ. Would that we had more like them! Here is the letter. You will see that it now bears the royal seal. If my uncle acts swiftly, he has a distinct advantage which, I trust, he will exploit. While he is dealing with Sir William Waller, I shall be free to route the northern rebel forces. Tomorrow, we march north. We shall travel the length of Lancashire, raising men and arms. Then, we shall turn east for York. Meanwhile, Colonel, I look to you to keep me informed of the enemy and his movements.'

'I shall strive to ensure that you are as knowledgeable of the rebel forces, as are their leaders.'

'I'm sure that you will, sir.' The Prince received the Colonel's reassurance with a smile. 'Thank you for your attention and thanks to you, Master Grimshaw, for your services. Doubtless you will wish to accompany the Colonel. Good day, gentlemen.'

Both the Colonel and Joseph Grimshaw bowed and withdrew from the Prince's presence.

'How fares Master Somers?' enquired the Colonel of Joseph, as they walked back along the corridors to the Colonel's room.

'Sufficiently well to tell me my duty, Colonel. 'Twas Master Somers who bade me take the letter to the King.'

'It was a wise decision by you both.' replied the Colonel diplomatically. 'Where was Master Somers when you collected his report?'

'At Stow-on-the-Wold, sir, with the hordes of the rebel army.'

They entered the Colonel's room, where he offered Joseph a glass of wine. 'When did you last eat?'

'Not since I broke my fast, soon after first light.' came the somewhat aggrieved reply.

'Away to the kitchen then and tell that cook, from me, to fill your belly with some of his excellent food.'

Grimshaw needed no second bidding and, within a moment, the Colonel was left alone to read his letter.

CHAPTER 14

Late June, 1644
Skipton, Yorkshire

For the next week the Colonel was in the saddle most of the hours of daylight. Such unaccustomed exercise taxed his strength. In his younger days, he would have thought nothing of such riding. Indeed, often had he ridden for two weeks or more, for hours on end, but he was too old for such tricks now. It was, therefore, some relief for him when the Prince decided to rest his army at Skipton castle and look to their weaponry and, for a few days, to the training of the new recruits.

On the third day at Skipton one of Colonel Cressley's agents, who had been attempting to find the Royalist army, arrived at the town bringing news that reinforcements were riding to the assistance of the rebels, who were besieging York. These forces, it was reported, were led by the Earl of Denbigh and Sir John Meldrum. On hearing this news the Prince decided to press forward without delay. From then on, for the next few days, there was little rest for any man in the Prince's army. Indeed, on the 1st July, the infantry marched twenty two miles during one day, in a swift dash to side step the rebel forces, who had abandoned the siege of York to meet the Royalist army as it approached the city. In a rapid encircling march, Prince Rupert led his army around the enemy to gain the safety of York and join there with the Duke of Newcastle and his besieged army. It was, therefore, to their considerable surprise and dismay that the Roundhead commanders found the Prince's army behind them in York and the crossing over the river Ouse snatched from their grasp.

Like the days in the saddle before Skipton, the past few hectic days during the march to York had taxed Colonel

Cressley's stamina. He was thus relieved to find himself able to rest for a short while inside the city. The town was crowded with the newly arrived army of Prince Rupert, as well as the Duke of Newcastle's army which, until now, had withstood the siege alone.

The Colonel found quarters in a small house in the city and was delighted to share his accommodation with Jack. Jack was fresh from yesterday's attack on the Roundhead's bridge of boats over the Ouse at Poppleton. It had been a short sharp action, in which the Royalist cavalry and some infantry had been dispatched across the bridge to keep an eye on the movements of the Roundhead army near the village of Long Marston.

The quarters, which father and son shared with Joseph Grimshaw, were cramped and uncomfortable, totally unlike the luxury which Colonel Cressley had enjoyed at Lathom House but, at least, it was a roof over their heads once again, rather than a tent.

'I thank God to see you still safe after yesterday's fighting.' Colonel Cressley greeted his son, who arrived at the lodgings in the late afternoon. 'Were there many killed in the action?'

'Not so many, father, at least not on our side. We have fought bloodier battles. Do you know the Prince's plans? Will he seek to bring the rebel forces to battle?'

'I do not know, nor do I think that the Prince himself knows yet. At this moment he is holding a council of war with the Duke of Newcastle. But if I know His Highness, he will fight. 'Tis the others of whom I am uncertain.'

'York is relieved.' observed Jack. 'We are in occupation. Surely it would make better sense to rest our men, await the Scottish army and attack the rebels when we are strong enough.'

'Such tactics may be wiser and, moreover, would afford rest for my old bones but I fear that, since we do not now lack strength in numbers, we shall be called upon to fight quite soon.'

The men sat for a while discussing the possibilities facing them and exchanging gossip. Joseph Grimshaw had not been asked to act as a courier since their march from Skipton. He was now assisting the Colonel in the more mundane position of servant and was presently preparing a meal from the meagre rations that they had been able to obtain. The food which Joseph had supplied was basic, but edible, which was all that Jack and his father expected under the circumstances. They ate in comparative silence whilst, outside in the streets, there was noise and commotion. Many of the soldiers belonged to the garrison which had recently been relieved. The disappearance of the rebel forces outside the city walls represented to these men a victory, which they now celebrated by drinking and feasting on what food they could loot from the hastily abandoned enemy lines. They were, for the most part, ignorant of the possibility of a battle in the near future.

There came a knock at the door. At the Colonel's bidding a young officer entered. He was, as the Colonel quickly recognised, one of the Prince's aides.

'His Highness, Prince Rupert, has ordered me to inform you that he intends to pursue the enemy at first light and requests that you attend him at that hour prepared for battle.'

The message was delivered courteously, if somewhat officiously.

'I thank you sir. I shall do as His Highness commands.'

Jack wondered if he should leave to join his regiment at the same time as his father. 'Do you know sir, if Colonel Anstruther also rides with the Prince at dawn?'

'I understand, sir, that all the Prince's men will ride with him from the city at daybreak.' The officer withdrew, doubtless to acquaint the remainder of the Prince's staff with this decision to engage the enemy.

'So, tomorrow, we fight.' observed the Colonel. 'Well, I had hoped for a little rest behind the stout walls of this city, ere we took to horse again, but it seems that is not to be. There was a time when I would have welcomed the opportunity to see some action; heaven knows that I have seen little enough during the past year. A few more days rest and then I fancy that the chance to strike a blow for His Majesty would have been more welcome.' The Colonel looked gloomily into the flames of the fire which Joseph had lit in the hearth for the purpose of cooking, rather than heating the room which was already warm on a sultry summer's evening.

'What is the rebel's strength, father?'

'I do not know the exact figure but I do know that, if our two armies meet in full strength, it will be as big as any battle fought in this war.'

'Do you think that they will stand and fight?'

'I think that they will. They now have the Scottish army under Lord Leven, which gives them some advantage in numbers and they already have shown that they seek to bring us to battle.'

The Colonel shook his head. The doubts and reservations that he had at the prospect of such an engagement showed clearly in the worried look upon his face. 'The Prince would have been wiser to await the arrival of the Earl of Montrose with his army from Scotland.'

'It will be a hard and bloody battle then?'

'Yes, my son, I fear that many will die.'

'Not us, father.'

Like most young soldiers the thought that death or injury would fall upon them was not to be contemplated.

'If God wills it, Jack.'

The Colonel looked at his handsome young son and wondered if he would see the sun set upon another day. It was a grim thought, but the Colonel was more than twice his son's age. His experience, on battle fields and skirmishes in Europe, had taught him the truth about war and the grim harvest it reaped. However, Jack had also seen action in a number of minor engagements and more than one large battle. It was strange, therefore, that he should believe himself beyond hurt. Well, perhaps it was a good thing that he should think so. This was the confidence of youth. For Colonel Cressley there was no illusion about the glory of war. He knew that war was as inglorious as it was horrible; but wars must sometimes be fought if the cause was just and sometimes if it was not. He also knew that young men would see only the glory of battle and realise its horror when it was too late, or with advancing years if they lived that long.

'I would that your mother and Mary were here to see and speak to us now. It is more than a year since I saw them both. That was when I chanced to be passing by and able to call. You haven't seen them since the day you left to join the King, nigh on two years ago.'

'Aye, that's true, father. I sometimes weary for our home and the countryside I know so well. I wonder how fares mother and what of young Mary? She'll sadly miss Ralph Somers. She's head over heels in love with him. Is he safe and still working for the King?'

'He serves the King and does so bravely. I can say no more, save that when I last heard from him he was fit and well.'

Jack knew something of the work that his father did to aid the Royalist cause and, since he seemed to know of Ralph and what he was doing, Jack had a pretty shrewd idea of the way in which Ralph might be serving the King. He, therefore, wisely refrained from pursuing the matter further knowing that, in any case, he would learn no more from his father.

'Let us hope that tomorrow's battle, if a battle there is to be, will crush the rebel forces and bring their leaders on their knees to plead for peace.' Jack spoke fiercely. He was keyed up with the thought of what the next day may bring.

The Colonel stirred himself from the train of thoughts that his conversation with Jack had set running through his mind.

'Get some rest, my son. I will write a letter to your mother, which Joseph shall take when next he journeys south.'

Amongst the few possessions that it was possible to carry with him, the Colonel found paper, ink and quill. Until now, these had been more essential to him than his sword. Seating himself at the table, by the light of a candle, he commenced to write,

"*York, 1st July, 1644.*
My Dearest Wife,
Tomorrow we march at daybreak to meet the enemy. It is likely that the battle will be long and hard fought. Jack, who is here with me, will also ride with Prince

Rupert. We shall endeavour to serve him and our royal master, in every way, as best we can. I know it is possible that one of us, or both, may not survive the conflict. Know you then, that we are both in good heart and go forth gladly to do our duty for God and the King. My dear Elizabeth, you may be very proud of our son; he is a most gallant gentleman.

To you, I send my love and pray daily that we may soon be reunited. To Mary, I also send my love and affection for a daughter of whom any father may be proud. I can tell her that her Ralph, whom I know she loves dearly, is serving the King in a different way to us and is doing his duty most bravely.

Remember wife, should I not survive tomorrow's battle, all our money, valuables, papers and any documents of importance are hid in that secret place in our house to which only you and I have the means of access.

May God be with us all in his goodness and mercy. Your loving husband, Francis."

The Colonel read the letter over again and nodded with satisfaction. Searching in the bag in which he carried his writing materials, he found a stick of sealing wax. He folded the letter and then, with the aid of a candle, he secured the folds of the paper with droplets of the molten red wax. Using a small jewelled seal, he imprinted into the wax a motif which depicted an eagle in flight carrying in its talons a small lamb.

The Colonel then called for Joseph Grimshaw and handed him the letter.

'Joseph, you have attended me for the past fortnight, acting during that time more as a servant than a messenger and I know which task suits you best. Take this letter and keep it safe. Wait upon the outcome of the battle, which it is expected will be fought tomorrow. If all goes well, I shall see you when the fighting is done. There will be other messages then to carry, as well as the one you have. If the day goes ill for me, you must decide for yourself the best course of action. You should first seek to serve the Prince in any way he commands. If you can find no one to direct your actions, go then to the King to give him news of the battle. Next, find Ralph Somers and my other agents and tell them that they can no longer serve me. Ralph must decide for himself whether, perhaps, the time has come for him to return to the Royalist army. Then take this letter to my wife at Hartington Hall.

That is enough of gloom. God send that we all stand here tomorrow after the battle, safe and well. However, it is wise to be ready for the worst, if ill fortune strikes.'

'You may rely on me sir. May God keep you and Master Jack safe tomorrow.'

Joseph's loyalty to the Colonel made him reluctant to stand by and do nothing, but he was not a fighting man and there was nothing else he could do, except wait upon the outcome of the battle and then act accordingly.

'Amen to that Joseph. I thank you for the service you have given me. I trust that there will be many more years to come.' The Colonel promised Joseph that he would seek him out as soon as possible after the battle, if all went well. He then furnished him with a goodly supply of money and bade him seek some rest. The Colonel then found his own bed and sleep, before the dawning of the next day.

* * *

It was still dark, when the commotion in the street awoke them. The noise of men on the move and the passage of wagons allowed no further rest.

Joseph brought them food and drink, as they prepared to set out and handed them both a parcel of wrapped meat and bread to sustain them during the day ahead. Dressing as they ate, Joseph helped them pull on their knee length boots. Over their tunics of stout buff leather both father and son wore a steel breast plate. The one that Joseph fastened on to Jack had several dents in it in addition to the proof mark, bearing witness to the action that he had already seen. On their heads, they wore a 'Lobster Pot' steel helmet, with both neck and face guards. As means of identification, they wore the red sash of the Royalist army. Their weapons consisted of a sword, which hung in its sheath, attached to the thick leather belt around their waists. Tucked into the belt each had two pistols, yet to be loaded from the pouches of powder and shot which they also carried. Jack had two of the more reliable flintlock pistols, while his father had only one pistol with the flintlock mechanism and one of the older wheel lock type.

Breakfasted and dressed, the two men bade Joseph farewell and left to separately find their way to their appointed places. As usual the progress of the army was a slow business. It soon became clear that the rebel army was prepared to stand and fight so that, by noon, the two armies were drawn up facing each other, prepared for battle, on a stretch of open ground known locally as Marston Moor. This was some six or seven miles to the west of the city of York, which Jack and his father had left at dawn. On the opposite side of a shallow vale, the rebels could be seen making the final preparations to their battle order, separated from the Royalist army by a deep ditch, in which meandered a sluggish stream.

It seemed to Jack that there was a reluctance for either side to commence hostilities. This was, perhaps, because other contingents were still arriving to strengthen each side. Unknown to the Royalist leaders, the commanders of the Parliamentary army were holding a council of war on a small hill overlooking the battlefield. Both armies had set out their ordnance and placed men in the forward position approaching the ditch. In some cases, these 'Forlorn Hopes' were within a hundred or two hundred yards of the enemy. Their purpose was to harass the enemy and try to break up any charge before it could gain its full momentum.

For hours, the soldiers of both sides had the harrowing ordeal of waiting and watching. Came the evening and still no move had been made. Prince Rupert, with whom the Colonel had been commanded to ride, finally made up his mind that the day was too far spent for the battle to commence in earnest. So far, there had been some minor skirmishing for positions. After consultation with the Duke of Newcastle, the Prince withdrew to the rear of the army for refreshments and the Duke of Newcastle retired to his coach. The tension in the ranks of the cavalry had grown as the day wore on. Seeing their leaders retire the troopers began to relax believing, too, that there would be no battle that day. Not far away Jack, in Prince Rupert's reserve cavalry, slid from his saddle to stretch his legs.

* * *

The sky darkened with the approach of a summer storm. After a flash of lightning came a rumble of thunder in the distance. Then, as if in answer to the thunder, the ordnance of the Parliamentary army spewed forth its own bolts of iron which fell amongst the Royalist forces. Their cavalry, under the command of Lieutenant General Oliver Cromwell, began to move forward. Gradually gathering momentum, it rode to engage Prince Rupert's front line cavalry opposing it. Taken by surprise the Royalist cavalry, under the command of Lord Byron, reformed and commenced a counter charge to meet the Roundhead onslaught.

The opposing forces met in boggy ground just by the ditch. The Royalist cavalry was broken by the impetus of the Roundhead charge. For a while they stood sword to sword with the enemy, but only briefly. Like a wave crashing on the beach, the Roundhead forces paused and then smashed through the Royalist front line. Some horses floundered in the mire, reared and threw their riders, but the Roundhead charge continued.

Hearing the commotion Colonel Cressley, with the Prince and other officers, raced to their horses and spurred their steeds to the scene of battle. As they rode, they met the fleeing horsemen from the routed Royalist cavalry. Livid with the turn of events, Rupert drew his sword and rallied his men.

'Swounds, do you run. You cowards; follow with me.'

In the melee, Colonel Cressley saw Jack sitting composed at

the head of a squadron of reserve cavalry. At the Prince's command they charged, hurling themselves through the remnants of the initial conflict, at the victorious Roundhead regiment. As the lightning flashed and the thunder rolled, they threw themselves on Cromwell's men.

Jack, in the van of the charge, led his men forward over the dead and the dying. Once his horse stumbled, as a wounded Roundhead rose up in its path. The soldier made a vain attempt to thrust his sword at Jack as he passed. Like a mirror to the lightning, Jack's sword flashed as he cut the man down and gathered up his horse all in the same second. On they rushed. With a great leap Jack's mount cleared the ditch and charged up the gentle slope on the other side. Then, within seconds, they were into the main force of Roundhead cavalry.

Before him Jack saw the face of an enemy horseman, resolute but fearful. The man aimed a vicious blow at Jack who swayed in the saddle to avoid the deadly blade and, at the same time, found his own mark with his sword in the man's throat. The impact of the blow almost dragged Jack from his saddle but, desperately regaining his balance, he charged on. A frightened horse in front reared and turned, leaving its rider defenceless to the blow from Jack's sword which fell between the head and the shoulders, almost severing the neck.

Now, in front of him, Jack saw a Roundhead officer of high rank, riding with two Colonels. Drawing one of his pistols Jack took deliberate aim and fired, watching with satisfaction as the man fell back and started to fall from his saddle. Jack had no time to look back and see the man recover his seat, aided by the two officers riding with him. Nor did he realise that it was Cromwell, himself, whom his ball had struck, causing a flesh wound in his neck from which much blood was now pouring.

Jack seemed now to be through the thick of the Roundhead cavalry. Ahead of him lay the baggage train of the Parliamentary forces. A foot soldier ran forward seeking to dislodge Jack from his mount by thrust of pike. Swaying in his saddle to dodge the vicious point which he knocked aside with his sword, he then brought the blade down ferociously upon the head of his adversary. So forceful was the blow that it bent the nose guard and bit into the flesh. With a frightful scream, the man reeled back clutching a horrid gash across his face. A ball from a musket sang passed Jack's head. He pulled up his horse to rally his men. To his dismay, he saw immediately behind him a scene of confusion and slaughter. The Royalist cavalry had, for the most part, been brought to a standstill and were fighting sword to sword with their opponents. Surveying the scene and deciding what best to do, he watched as some of his troop turned to flee; the impetus of their charge having been overcome, leaving them outnumbered by the rebel cavalry. Realising that he was virtually alone behind the unbroken ranks of the Roundheads, he turned his horse and charged back into the fray.

On either side, dismounted and mounted horsemen sought to drag him from his horse. Above the clash of swords, the frightened whinnying of horses, the shot of pistol and musket, came the cries and screams of wounded and dying men. Desperately using his sword to fend of those who beset him, Jack sought to find his comrades. He espied a small group of horsemen duelling with swords and, in the middle, he saw his father who had evidently been cut off from the Prince. Setting his horse at the group, Jack arrived just as a Roundhead horseman was about to strike his father from the side. Attacked as he was by two other rebel troopers, the Colonel had not seen the third attacker. Before the blow could fall, Jack thrust his sword under the armour that covered the upper part of the man's body, entering just under the ribs. He felt' the blade grate on bone and then, with devilish satisfaction, twisted the sword and watched the body of the soldier arch and his face contort with agony. Then, withdrawing the sword, he brutally pushed him from his saddle.

Now he turned on the other two horsemen, whom his father was seeking to hold at bay. This time he no longer had the advantage of surprise. One of the two spurred his horse to meet him and aimed a cutting blow at his head. Unable to parry the blow in time, Jack tried to dodge, but the blade fell with tremendous force on the side of his helmet. He swayed in his saddle as his senses reeled. Frantically, he clung to his steed as it reared in fright. Turning his horse, before his opponent could attack his rear, Jack aimed a blow which the horseman deftly parried. His horse was somewhat steadier now. Using his left hand, Jack drew the second pistol that he had in his belt. His adversary, intent upon pressing home his attack, failed to notice this move. He raised his sword for another crashing blow and skilfully changed it to a thrust below Jack's guard. Ere the murderous steel could find its mark, Jack's pistol fired and the man fell violently backwards from his horse.

Jack turned to his father who, relieved of two of his opponents, had little difficulty disposing of the third.

'Come father. If we stay here, we are lost.'

Reluctant as they were to leave the field, they were now isolated with only the enemy for company. A ball whistled between them. Needing no further bidding the Colonel followed Jack.

Another obstacle lay ahead. The discipline of the Roundhead troops had allowed their commanders to halt the cavalry rather than pursue a beaten foe before regrouping. Now Jack and his father found themselves galloping straight for the midst of the Roundhead troops. Such a course was madness. Wheeling their horses, they veered to the left. In the confusion of the battle, they were able to ride around the flank of the enemy cavalry. Keeping at least two hundred paces distance from the Roundhead horsemen, they were able to return to the depleted ranks of their own squadron which Prince Rupert was trying to regroup.

Glancing behind, as they rode towards the Royalist ranks, they saw that a company of Roundhead dragoons was pressing forward to attack. Prince Rupert now faced the combined forces of dragoons and cavalry. Back again, in the comparative safety of their own ranks, Jack and his father were able to survey the battlefield and take stock of their position. They saw little of encouragement. To the left the Royalist infantry were locked in mortal combat and seemed to be slowly giving ground to a large body of Scots infantry which opposed them. On the left flank it appeared that, after the victorious charge of Lord Goring's cavalry, the enemy were now gaining ground.

Before Rupert was properly able to reform his squadron, Cromwell's men charged again. The front ranks of the Royalists met the charge resolutely and, for a while along the whole front, they held the line. They duelled horseman to horseman, hacking away at each other with swords. Once again, Jack found himself pressing forward to meet the enemy. Rupert's men were now greatly outnumbered and gradually the enemy wore down their resistance until, in the centre, they broke through. For a few minutes longer the hardened veterans, the cream of Rupert's cavalry, held. Then, slowly at first, they began to give way to the irresistible weight of the Roundhead force. Finally the rout began. Next to Jack one of his comrades shouted to another.

'Tis no use; they've broken through. Watch out behind you.'

A Royalist horseman turned his horse to guard his flank. Another was forced to follow suit. Before long, the line was completely broken. A Roundhead horseman charged towards Jack, who prepared to receive the impact of the blow that was already aimed, but a stray – or perhaps aimed – ball toppled the man from his horse. He fell heavily to the ground at Jack's side. Behind him, more of his fellow Roundheads were thrusting forward over the debris of battle, over the carcasses of fallen horses, over the bodies of friend and foe alike. Under the flailing hooves the wounded were trampled. They tried unavailingly to escape, but fell back with another ghastly wound and died with a prayer on their lips, or an unheeded plea for mercy.

On either side, Jack's comrades were turning, not only to flee, but to meet a foe who now came at them from behind as well as in front. To his left Jack caught a glimpse of the Prince trying to rally his men, but it was too late. Turning his horse Jack rode to rejoin his father who, with the Prince and his aides, now joined in the flight from the field of battle. A muffled cry came from the man riding by his side. He slumped forward, his face turned to one side as he looked at Jack in a mute appeal for aid. In his eyes Jack saw the pain and surprise at having been hit, but those eyes were soon sightless and the man dead when, after his horse had covered a dozen paces, he fell to the ground. Jack rode on. There was no help that he could offer.

Joining his father, Jack urged him to flight. Seeing their leader turn his back on the fray, the Colonel realised that there was nothing but death to be gained by staying and so lost no time in galloping his horse alongside Jack. The flight turned into a rout, as the Roundhead cavalry exultantly chased the Royalists from the field. Jack and his father rode to the west of Wilstrop Wood, which had been behind the Royalist lines when the battle had commenced. The pursuing Roundheads were taking a terrible toll of the Royalists, as they discharged their pistols at the fleeing horsemen, while many rider-less horses raced with those that were mounted. Here and there, Royalist and Roundhead fought running duels, as they rode side by side. Suddenly Colonel Cressley lurched in his saddle and visibly sagged as a ball hit his thigh. Jack raced to his father's side and gathered up the reins, but the Colonel could not keep his seat, so fierce was the pace. He fell heavily to the ground. Jack reined in his mount and leapt from the saddle. Drawing his sword, he prepared to defend himself as he ran back to the aid of his father. Relentlessly the pursuers bore down upon Jack as he stood by his father's side. A Roundhead horseman rode by and dealt Jack such a powerful blow that it crashed through his upraised sword and landed with tremendous force on his helmet. Jack sank to the ground and lay prostrate over the body of his father.

* * *

Wilstrop Wood was somewhat to the north and a little less than a mile from the centre of the battle field. It was from this vantage point, safe as he thought from the battle, that Joseph chose to watch and wait on events, as instructed by his master. Now, hidden in a tree, he watched the rout of Lord Byron's regiment and saw the remainder of Rupert's men in full flight, their leader in their midst. They rode within two or three hundred yards of where Joseph sat hidden, within the branches of a tall tree. Joseph searched in vain for the Colonel or Jack. He fancied that he saw them among a group of riders who followed the Prince, but he could not be sure. Further away, he saw the Royalist infantry being pushed back and, increasingly, turning in flight. With them had gone the Duke of Newcastle, leaving his white coated soldiers to die where they fought.

Joseph witnessed all this from his hiding place, as if in a dream, happening and yet unreal. He knew not what had become of the Colonel and Jack, but he feared the worst. Many would not leave this field alive. He pitied the wounded and wondered if there was anything he could do to help. Then he remembered his master's words, "If the day be lost, stay not to search for me." He remembered the letter he carried and the duties with which he had been charged. With a great mental effort, he pulled himself together and faced the reality of the situation. The day was lost for the King and Joseph must now do his duty. With a heavy heart, he turned his back on the horrid scene of slaughter, shinned down the tree and stumbled through the wood to where he had tethered his horse. Mounting, he cautiously skirted around the edge of the battlefield and headed south.

CHAPTER 15

Evening of 2nd July, 1644
Marston Moor, Yorkshire

Far away, Jack heard his father's voice.

'Jack, Jack, my boy, do you hear me?'

Through the haze of pain he regained consciousness, only to fade away again into grateful oblivion before, once again, returning painfully to the land of the living. The only light that he could see was that which danced before his eyes. He thought he saw stars. Gradually his eyes focussed and he realised that they were stars which he saw and, bending over him, he recognised the figure of his father.

'Thank God you're awake, lad. I thought that you would never come to. That was a savage blow on your head. 'Twas your helmet that saved you. It bears witness to how you were struck.'

Jack tried to sit up. His head ached terribly. He groaned and nursed his head in his hands.

'Come lad, we must be gone from this place. There are all manner of cut throats abroad.'

Gradually Jack's senses returned and, with his father's help, he staggered to his feet.

'But you, father, you were wounded.' He spoke questioningly, as he stood somewhat shakily, looking at his father.

'Yes and damned painful it is too but fortunately the ball only struck a glancing blow. It seems to have glanced off my thigh leaving merely a flesh wound. I have bound it for now with my scarf to stop the bleeding. Had we not been riding so hard, I could have kept my saddle. It was the fall that stunned me when I hit my head. But, come, we must away.'

Supporting one another they staggered off in the direction in which they had been riding, without any clear idea of where they could seek shelter and rest. They had gone less than a mile, when they came upon a fully saddled horse grazing peacefully by the side of the track. One of the many, guessed Jack, which had lost its owner that day. Helping each other they gratefully climbed on to its back and thus made much better progress. Before long they found a signpost, by the help of which they found their way back to York.

York was a sorry sight that night. The streets were filled with injured men and those who were dying in pain and misery from torn flesh and broken bones. It may be said that, perhaps, those who had been carried back to York were luckier than the majority who had been left to die, or have their throats cut by looters, on the battlefield where they had fallen. As badly broken as their bodies, was the morale of the troops who had found the safety of York. Even some of the generals spoke of abandoning the King. Prince Rupert, who had been forced to hide in a bean field to elude his captors, almost alone was steadfast in his determination to save something from the debacle and march to the aid of the King. Even he had to call upon the deepest resources of courage to face up to the total and ignominious defeat of the Royalist forces.

Colonel Cressley and Jack found their lodgings of the night before and, nursing their wounds, counted themselves lucky to be alive. Their rest was not to be for long as, the next day, Prince Rupert led the remnants of his defeated army from the city, anxious to avoid another encounter with the victorious Roundhead army. In the city he left a token garrison whilst, with what was left of his army, he marched to Chester.

* * *

While Colonel Cressley was resting at Skipton castle, some four days before the battle of Marston Moor, Ralph was with General Waller's army at Banbury. Banbury was a town that Ralph had visited with his father and so he felt almost on home ground. The King's army was at Culworth, almost directly between Banbury and Ralph's home at Preston Capes.

The following day, small parties from both armies met in skirmishes around Banbury. Indeed, General Waller drew up his main force on a hill to the south of the town in an attempt to entice the King to a battle, in a position where he would have the advantage. However, the King would have none of this and withdrew north on the road to Daventry, following roughly the east bank of the river Cherwell. General Waller, seeing the Royalists refuse his challenge, followed with his army but on the road to Southam which kept to the west bank of the river.

For two or three miles, to the north of Banbury, the two armies marched almost side by side, divided only by the river and roughly one mile of ground. Ralph was not involved in the ensuing battle which turned out to be a number of disjointed and somewhat indecisive engagements. However, he was able to witness some of the action from the baggage train at the rear of the Roundhead army. The fiercest of the fighting was centred around the bridge over the Cherwell, in the village of Cropredy.

The action of the battle was dispersed and, although the Roundhead forces first scored a victory at the bridge, they were later severely rebuffed and forced to retire to a defensive posture on high ground on the Southam road. This defeat, although not severe and by no means a rout, demoralised many of the soldiers in Waller's ragged army causing many of them to desert. It was only the arrival of Roundhead reinforcements at Buckingham, some fifteen miles away, which prevented King Charles from following up the success at Cropredy with another, perhaps more decisive engagement.

The King withdrew to the west to deal with Essex's army, which was now isolated in Devon and Cornwall. Waller's army retired in confusion to Buckingham. A body of cavalry under the command of Lieutenant General Middleton had been dispatched to the assistance of the Earl of Essex. The rest of Waller's men had been left to garrison the town of Buckingham. Among them was Ralph.

Ralph was glad of the leisure that this respite afforded him. For once, the army to which he had been attached was not immediately threatened by the enemy, nor was it campaigning to bring the Royalists to battle. It was depleted, dispirited and in no shape for battle. Waller knew that to take to the field with these men would be to court disaster. He petitioned Parliament for more and better trained men. The practice of raising troops in one locality was of little use if, when required to fight further afield, they deserted in droves. Matters were often made worse when commanders were not provided with the funds to pay their troops. In many cases, Parliament had been dogged by this difficulty since the early days of the war. Now a 'new model army' was demanded, made of troops recruited by Parliament under one overall commander; properly equipped, trained and paid by Parliament.

It was during this period of relative idleness that, one day whilst walking through the town, Ralph came across Joseph Grimshaw. After the rout at Marston Moor Joseph had been anxious to contact Ralph and, hearing that some of the rebel army had marched south west, he had been concerned that Ralph might have left Buckingham with this detachment and would be even more difficult to find. He was, therefore, much relieved to find that Ralph was amongst those who had been left behind. Recognising Joseph, Ralph bade him follow at a discreet distance to a place where they might safely talk without being overheard or observed.

'What news then, Master Grimshaw?'

'None good, I'm sorry to say, young master. Colonel Cressley and Master Jack were part of Prince Rupert's army which was heavily defeated, barely two weeks since, at Marston Moor near York.'

'So, it's true. There have been rumours of a big battle up north and 'twas said that the Roundheads had the better of the day.'

'Aye and that's the fact of the matter, more's the pity.'

'Were many killed or taken? How fared the Colonel and Jack?' asked Ralph anxiously, the smile now gone from his face.

'Many were killed on both sides, but far more of the Royalists. As for Sir Francis and Jack, I know not; killed or sorely wounded, most likely.' Joseph replied despairingly.

Even now, the shock of what he had seen preyed on his mind. He saw, again and again, the awful rout and slaughter of the Prince's troopers just as clearly as he had seen them on that awful day. He agonised again over his decision to follow his master's orders and leave the field of battle, to hasten with the news to the King. Nevertheless, this he had done. Having delivered to the King news of the battle at Marston Moor, Joseph was now on his way to Hartington Hall to deliver, as instructed, the Colonel's letter to Lady Cressley. Since his route took him via Buckingham, Joseph had decided to call in at that town to see if he might find Ralph, whom he believed to be there. By good luck, he had found Ralph quite easily and was able to tell him of the disaster at Marston Moor and how he had been charged by the Colonel not to delay if the Royalists lost, but to quickly carry the news to the King. It had been only because of the Colonel's specific instructions in this matter, that he had reluctantly left Marston Moor without making a search for Jack and his master.

'Tis possible that one or both of them lived; but I misdoubt it. So many fine men were killed that day and I could see neither Jack, nor Sir Francis, among those who rode by; nor were they at the house in York where we had spent the previous night. I called there on my way south, but I dared not wait. I had my orders. Now I must carry the sad news to Mistress Cressley and her daughter. I care not for the task, but it is one that I must perform.

'So you did not see either the Colonel or Jack?'

'No, I saw neither.'

'Well now, devil take you for being a gloomy fellow. It's possible that both are alive and well.' Ralph spoke with a heartiness that he did not feel.

'Aye, it's possible. We must pray that it is so.' But Joseph shook his head gloomily and plainly did not expect a miracle. Instead, the tears glistened in his eyes as he tortured himself yet again with visions of his master and Jack dying miserably on that field of carnage.

'I might have helped. I might have saved one or both of them.

I dared not go forth while the battle raged, but I could have gone later. 'Twas nearly dark when Rupert's men fled passed the wood in which I hid. I should have gone later.'

'It was dark you say. At what hour did the battle commence?'

'Oh, 'twas late in the day. I do not know the hour, but the light was fading and they were still fighting when I left.'

'Well then, it is quite clear that you could not have hoped to render help. You did not know if they were dead or wounded and you had no idea where they might be found. What! Would you wander on the field of battle, looking for your master in the dark? 'Twere madness to think of it.'

'I could have waited. I might have helped.' Joseph's voice tailed off as, once again, he vainly searched his conscience for an answer that he could not find. It was some comfort to him to have Ralph's support for what he had done and he knew that it was not pity which caused Ralph to speak as he did.

'No, Joseph, you had your instructions. Had you stayed to help you, too, might have been killed. You did what you had to do.'

Ralph spoke with conviction, for he was sure that Joseph had acted correctly, but he could understand his feelings of doubt and remorse and he wondered, if he had been in Joseph's place, whether he might have stayed to search for those whom he served.

Ralph had led Joseph into a wooded area just beyond the town; there, to hear in private, the news that Joseph had brought. They sat together, in the shade of an old oak, sharing their sorrow. Joseph sat shaking his head slowly from side to side, sighing and grieving over the fate of so many fine men. Ralph sat in silence, as the horror of Joseph's story sank in. Ralph grieved too for the loss of two men, neither of whom he had known very well and yet for both of whom he had a high regard. He thought, as indeed he always thought, of Mary. How would she take the news? How would she and her mother face up to life with their men folk both dead? For a long time, they sat together in silence; both completely lost in thought. Taking stock Ralph realised that, although things did look bad and probably Joseph was right in assuming that both Jack and his father were dead, there was no proof and, indeed, there was a possibility, however small, that they both still lived. It was not in Ralph's nature to linger long on gloomy negative thoughts and he thought now of the future. What should he do? Then it occurred to him and, in a flash, he knew exactly what should be done.

'You say that you carry a letter to be delivered to Lady Cressley.'

Joseph nodded glumly.

'Well then, Joseph, last time I asked you to do my bidding you were not too willing. Will you hear what I have to say now and tell me if you are prepared to do as I ask?'

'Aye, that I will, since I have no other to serve now.'

'Well then, will you give me the letter for Lady Cressley? For my part, I will carry the letter to her myself. I can get leave of absence from here for a day or two. The time is opportune and Hartington Hall is scarce two hours ride away. Will you then take a message from me, first to the King and then to the Prince if he is still alive. Try to find out any news of Sir Francis and Jack. If neither the King nor Prince Rupert has any news of them, go back to York and make what enquiries you can. See if any have knowledge of survivors, perhaps wounded or captured. Find out what you can and, if it be God's will, your search may lead you to the Colonel, Jack, or both of them. Will you do that?'

Certainly, it was a plan of action that gave Ralph great pleasure, for it meant that he and Mary might find a precious day or two to spend together. Furthermore, the plan allowed Joseph to relieve his mental anguish by doing something positive about discovering the fate of Colonel Cressley and Jack. It also allowed Ralph to make his situation known to the King and Prince Rupert so that they could make suitable arrangements if, indeed, Colonel Cressley had perished. Ralph knew that there would be little action within Waller's army in Buckingham until it had been reinforced and its morale restored. It would take some weeks for that to be accomplished. Parliament badly needed to recruit and train better soldiers than the disaffected rabble which had shown so poorly at Cropredy Bridge and had deserted, afterwards, in such large numbers. Ralph's work in Buckingham would be light and routine. He felt sure that his captain would not forbid him a day or two away from his quarters.

Satisfied with this plan, Ralph eagerly awaited Joseph's reply.

'Aye, I'll carry your message and do aught I can to find news of Sir Francis and Master Jack.'

The prospect seemed to brighten Joseph's gloomy face and, whilst nothing so cheerful as a smile lighted on his rough hewn features, there was now a sense of purpose in his bearing.

'Give me the letter for Lady Cressley.' Ralph held out his hand to receive the folded paper that Joseph produced from within his grubby tunic. 'Meet me here tomorrow, three hours after sunrise, when I will have the letter for the King.'

Having thus settled the matter, the two men went their separate ways.

* * *

The next day saw Ralph on his way to Hartington Hall. He had written a letter the previous evening to the King or Prince Rupert, giving what information he had to offer on the state of the Roundhead army at Buckingham and requesting instructions as to what he should do if Colonel Cressley had, indeed, been killed. He had written the letter in guarded tones, quoting no names but, nevertheless, making his meaning quite clear. He had sealed the document in the usual way, without his signature and had given it to Joseph when they met that morning as arranged.

Later that day, as he approached Hartington Hall, Ralph felt a mixture of sadness and joy. He was happy indeed to be on his way to see Mary after so long a time, but sad that he should be carrying news which would cause her and her mother so much misery. As he rode and pondered the matter, he decided that there was no good purpose to be served by relating Joseph's worst fears about Sir Francis and Jack. It may well be that both had perished but there was no certainty. There was little point, then, in causing Mary and Lady Cressley such grief whilst matters were uncertain. He resolved, therefore, to say simply that the battle had been lost and there was no knowledge of what had happened to Jack and his father.

Salcey Forest was in full leaf as Ralph rode along the lightly rutted track which bore testimony to the passage of wagons carrying logs back to Hartwell village. It seemed that not all the men were at war. It was still high summer and the sun shone warmly in a mainly blue sky. The buzz of insects and the occasional song of birds were the only sounds to be heard, apart from the tread of his horse on the slightly damp ground. The vegetation, on either side of the track through the forest, shimmered in the heat of the afternoon sun. Arriving at the crossroads, Ralph glanced briefly along the track that lead to his uncle's house and wondered if he should pay a visit during his brief stay in the area. For the present, though, he could hardly wait to see Mary.

Emerging from the forest he saw Hartington Hall nestling among the trees in a slight hollow. Urging his horse forward he galloped the last half mile or so, unwilling to delay his arrival by a fraction longer than he need. Within minutes he was hammering on the front door with an impatience that he could scarcely contain.

The door was opened by Alfred, as it had been on that memorable occasion when the patrol had sought shelter for the night. Alfred did not appear any older. Indeed, to Ralph it was impossible that he could do so since he had always seemed ancient and, certainly, far too old to be carrying out the duties that he performed in the house. Alfred greeted Ralph as Master Snaith, assuming that this was the name by which he now wished to be known although, truth to tell, there were those among the servants who still reckoned that he was Ralph Somers; at least, he had been when he had first called over two years ago.

Alfred showed no surprise at Ralph's coming but, with his usual reserved but courteous manner, ushered Ralph into the Hall.

'The mistress has a visitor at present. I will tell her that you are waiting.'

Alfred's manner was usually formal and unbending. Only occasionally, to Mary whom he had known since she was a baby and of whom he was especially fond, would he allow his feelings to show. It was, therefore, rather a surprise to Ralph when, returning within seconds, Alfred said.

'The mistress will see you now, sir.' And then bending to almost whisper in Ralph's ear, he added in a confidential tone, 'And right glad she'll be to see you, I'll warrant. She's sore in need of a helping hand, I can tell you. That man with her ought to be offering her comfort and aid but, instead, he's trying to persuade her to betray her kinfolk. He be more of a devil, than a true Christian.'

Somewhat taken aback by this announcement, Ralph followed Alfred into the sitting room in a turmoil of expectation. There, he found Mary sitting with a man whom he recognised. It was Dr Murchison who had been a guest of Sir Francis on that, well remembered, evening at the outbreak of war. Ralph remembered how the good doctor's vociferous condemnation of the King's enemies had not been backed with action when the call to arms had sounded.

Alfred had acted with considerable discretion in announcing Ralph's arrival, informing Mary that the gentleman from Preston Capes was waiting upon her. Alfred knew that Master Robert Snaith was, indeed, Master Ralph Somers and had adopted this alias only in the presence of those who supported the rebel cause. Alfred did not pretend to know what the reason was for this subterfuge, but he did know that his mistress was in love with this young man whom he, himself, liked and trusted. Alfred knew, too, that Dr Murchison had met Ralph and knew him by his real name. That the Doctor, in spite of his earlier protestations, was no friend of the Cressley family had now become obvious to Alfred. He had, therefore, decided that it would be more circumspect to avoid mentioning any name at all.

When Ralph entered the room Mary's visitor was no less surprised than she, but their feelings were otherwise quite different. Mary was overjoyed and quite unable to hide her pleasure. Dr Murchison for his part was annoyed and disconcerted by Ralph's arrival and made it quite evident. He saw in Ralph an obvious friend to Mary and one, doubtless, loyal to the crown. He rose abruptly and cleared his throat loudly to cover his confusion.

'Well now, Mistress Cressley, I will leave you to think on these matters and trust to find you more amenable to my suggestions when next I call.'

Giving Ralph a curt nod and bidding them both 'Good day', he strode across the room and left. As soon as he had closed the door behind him Mary rose and threw herself into Ralph's arms, where she burst into a flood of tears.

'That wretched man! He is supposed to be father's friend and this is how he shows his friendship.'

Then, taking a grip on herself, she smiled at Ralph through her tears.

'And, just when I thought myself lost, in you walk, like a knight in shining armour, to rescue a damsel in distress.'

Ralph stemmed the flood of words in a fierce embrace born of love and longing when, for a moment, time stood still and only joy filled their hearts. When, at last, they released each other it was Ralph who spoke.

'Together again, at last! There were times when I thought that I must have dreamed of meeting you and that you were never real. But you are real and more lovely than in my dreams, even though your eyes are filled with tears. What has this man to do with you?' asked Ralph, the anger rising within him as he witnessed her distress.

'Come, sit down and I will tell you all, but first tell me why you are here and on what errand.' Mary guided Ralph to a large couch and sat beside him.

'My story can wait. First tell me why these tears? How has Murchison caused you such hurt?'

Mary sat for a moment in silence as she searched for a point at which to begin her story. A sad smile lit upon her face as she spoke.

'There was a time two years or, as it seems, a lifetime ago

when the whole world was at my feet. I had a lovely home and was part of a happy family. To add to all this, I met a handsome young man, who gave such sparkle and joy to my life, that my heart nigh burst for the love of him. Then, no sooner had he come, than he marched off to war with my father and brother, leaving me to pine at home with my mother. Mother fell ill and, a month since, was buried in Quinton churchyard. Then came this serpent, Murchison, offering sympathy with one breath and with the next telling me that, since the King's cause was now lost, I should pay tribute to the rebels. He is urging me, with warnings and implied threats, to contribute money and provisions to the forces of Parliament. He has thrown in his lot with the rebels and threatens to send Parliament's commissioners to manage the estate and collect the revenues for their army. I know not whether he can do this, nor do I know how to deal with his threats.'

Again, tears welled up into her eyes and her voice choked with sobs.

Ralph's arm closed reassuringly about her and, for a while, he sat lost in thought. It was perhaps harder to sit at home and wait, while your loved ones are in danger, than to go and take your chance on the field of battle. For such people there was neither death nor glory, only the horrid agony of waiting and dreading that awful day, when news would arrive that the one they held dear was no more. There was no effort that they could make, no valiant sacrifice to be offered, which might influence events. Waiting and hoping was their lot and little besides. For a while, Mary had had her mother beside her to share the burden, but now she was alone. What could Ralph do to help in the few days that he had with her? Obviously things were getting on top of her and, doubtless, the death of her mother had been the last straw. Certainly he would spare her the worry about the fate of her father and brother. There would be time enough for that later. Indeed, he would not show her the letter from her father, which would only serve to increase her anxiety. Then, suddenly, he thought of something that he could do to help; something that would remove Mary from the unwelcome attention of Dr Murchison and, at the same time, take her away from the worries of the estate which she now carried alone.

'If you were not here, our worthy Dr Murchison could not pursue his villainous plans. It seems to me that it's about time you had a holiday. While riding here today I determined that I would visit my uncle at Bullshead. If you come with me, I am sure that he and my aunt will be delighted to have you stay for a while. If you prefer, I could ride over tomorrow and see them first. I know that I shall not have to ask them twice. I am sure, that under ordinary circumstances, they would welcome you but doubly so when they hear how things stand with you at Hartington Hall.'

At first, Mary hotly protested that she could not intrude into the home of a family with whom she had no connections. Ralph persisted, persuading her of the advantages of such an arrangement. Truth to tell, Mary was at a very low ebb and, although she was too proud to admit it, she was very much afraid that she would not be able to cope with the continued overtures from Dr Murchison and the veiled threats they carried. So, at last, she agreed that Ralph should try to arrange matters but she insisted that she would go only if the invitation was freely given, particularly by Ralph's aunt who, more than her husband, would have to learn to share her home with Mary.

For the rest of the day they talked endlessly together and, it must be said, that Alfred shared a little in their happiness on seeing his mistress smile and laugh as she hadn't since this young man had last paid a visit. Somers or Snaith, it was plain that it was all the same to Mistress Mary as long as he was by her side.

The next day Ralph arose early and rode the few miles through the forest to his uncle's house. He was received, as always, with a warm welcome and genuine affection. It seemed that the war had passed by this small part of the forest. Uncle Charles was a man of peace. Violence, for any cause, made more problems than it solved and this war was a crime against God and man. Although his sympathies plainly lay with the King, he would have none of it.

Uncle Charles expressed his sadness at the death of his

207

brother, Ralph's father, and wondered whether it had been some time before Ralph, himself, had received the news. Ralph felt that there was some reproach, in that he had not been able to see his aunt and uncle to give them the news in person. He did, indeed, feel somewhat guilty and realised that he ought to have found the time to pay them a visit. He explained that he had been away at the time and that it had been only after some weeks that he had heard of his father's death. He said nothing, of course, of the circumstances surrounding it.

Ralph said little about his own part in the war and he was, indeed, thankful that neither his aunt nor uncle pressed him with any probing questions. He said merely that he served the King and acted, for the most part, on his own initiative answerable to Colonel Cressley. They asked after the health of Sir Francis, as they had always known him, and also of his son Jack. They had heard the sad news of Lady Cressley's death and wondered how Mary now managed. This gave Ralph the opportunity of explaining how things were with Mary and the plight in which he had found her. He told them of the harassment that she was enduring at the hands of Dr Murchison and how she was in need of help and advice. He then went on to tell them the news that Joseph Grimshaw had brought of her father and her brother which he had, as yet, refrained from telling Mary. He explained that, since there was no certainty as to their fate, there was little point in giving her more worry. He went on to explain that Mary needed a complete rest and a change from the worries and cares that now beset her at Hartington Hall. He would like to see her away from the place for a while; removed from Murchison's malign influence.

Aunt Maria was ahead of Ralph when she suggested,

'Why, the poor child must come here. She will be company for me and, in this house, no one will bother her.'

Uncle Charles nodded his agreement.

'I have heard of this Murchison. He is a time serving scoundrel, who flies any colours that are like to serve him best.'

So, it was decided that Mary should pack her bags and come for an indefinite stay with Uncle Charles and Aunt Maria. Only

Alfred, and her maid Amy, should know of her whereabouts.

The next day, Ralph waited for Mary in the library while she finished packing her cases and supervised their loading on to a pack horse. A young lad, scarcely more than a boy, was acting as groom. His father, who had had this job before him, was away fighting with Colonel Cressley for the King. Now he must do the work of a man. Apart from the pack horse, he had saddled Ralph's horse and a horse for his mistress. Soon all would be ready for their departure to Bullshead.

As he waited, Ralph paced up and down in the library lost in thought. A thousand problems occupied his mind. What if Colonel Cressley and Jack were dead? When would he be able to visit Mary again? What should he do with the letter which he had brought from Sir Francis for Lady Cressley? He took it from his pocket and held it in both hands, looking at it as though it would provide an answer. For a moment he was about to tear it up. Then he quickly reminded himself that it was not his to destroy. What then should he do with it? For a moment or two longer he stood in a fever of indecision. He regarded the crowded shelves around him in the library where he waited. Then, of a sudden, he made up his mind. Clambering on a stool he reached down, from the topmost shelf, the dustiest and least used volume that he could see. Opening it, he placed the letter inside, making a mental note of the title printed on the cover. He then replaced the book from whence it came.

At that moment he heard Mary in the hall. Jumping down from the stool he moved it back to its original position. He clapped his hands together to remove the dust and then left the room to join Mary. Together, they mounted the waiting horses and, with a word of farewell to Alfred and Amy and last minutes instructions, they set off for Bullshead farm.

CHAPTER 16

April 1645
Buckingham

"The Winter of Discontent", that is what it had been called. Looking back on it Ralph was not surprised, for it had been neither an encouraging, nor triumphant year, for either Royalist or Roundhead. In spite of their mastery of the north of the country, after the battle of Marston Moor, the armies of Parliament were in disarray. Indeed, after the battle of Cropredy Bridge, Waller's army had virtually disintegrated. While Parliament tried to organise its campaign by committee at Westminster, the arguments continued throughout the army. The Earl of Manchester had been brought before Parliament to explain his lack of enthusiasm, (some called it cowardice), in not pressing his army into battle against the Royalists. In spite of the loss of his army at Lostwithiel, the Earl of Essex was still a force to be reckoned with amongst the ranks of Parliament; but now his health was failing. There was an open breach between the war party and the peace party, while the independent faction was at odds with the Presbyterians.

However, the Royalists could derive little pleasure from the disunity within the Roundhead ranks, for their own unity of purpose was in little better state. After the loss of York, the King was trying desperately to mend the quarrels between his own generals. Goring was answerable to none but the King and spent much of his time in debauchery. The generals in the south west of the country, upon whom the King now most depended, were at each other's throats, whilst in Herefordshire the country folk were in arms against both the King and Parliament. Prince Rupert, while loyal to his uncle, did nothing to lessen the enmity which existed between the King and his advisers.

Sir William Waller had resigned his commission under the Self-Denying Ordinance passed by the Commons, under which no member of Parliament was to command in the armed forces. Ralph had been taking a great deal of interest in the New Model Army and had succeeded in joining its ranks, in the same capacity in which he had served in the rebel army since he had joined. It had suited him, for the latter months of last summer, to remain at Buckingham where he had been able to make infrequent visits to see Mary at Bullshead farm. As he had hoped, Dr Murchison had not dared to take any action openly against the Cressley estate and, not knowing where she had gone, had been unable to harass her further. Mary had settled in so well at Bullshead farm that, in no time, she had become one of the family. Aunt Maria valued her cheerful companionship and soon she became a great favourite with Hugh. He was now old enough to understand his cousin's attachment for this young lady, who brought a great deal of fun and merriment to what Hugh had regarded as a dull household.

It was thus, with an easier mind, that Ralph returned to his unwelcome employment, which he now pursued with more diligence, free from worries about Mary.

One other cloud, soon to be lifted, was the uncertainty about Colonel Cressley and Jack. Some four weeks after their parting Ralph and Joseph met again in Buckingham. They made their covert arrangements to meet elsewhere to talk, but Ralph could tell from the fact that Joseph's face wore an expression, almost approaching a grin, that the news must be good.

When they met in a more secluded spot where they could talk freely, Joseph joyfully reported.

'They both be safe and well, praise be to God. Colonel Cressley has a flesh wound in his thigh but 'tis healing well and will soon be right as nine pence. 'Twas Master Jack's hard head and even harder helmet, that saved him. A blow from a sword would have carried off his head, but for his helmet. As it was he had a sore head for a day or two, but now he's none the worse neither. They both be in Chester with the Prince who was nearly captured himself.'

Slowly the winter passed and blossomed into spring. Ralph had travelled considerably during a season when most persons of good sense stayed put. He spent some time in London and thereafter with the Parliamentary forces in Reading, Abingdon and Andover. Now he was with Cromwell's men outside Oxford. Parliamentary forces were camped around the town with the intention of harassing those within its walls.

Ralph had maintained his contact with Colonel Cressley by the faithful Grimshaw, whom the Colonel preferred to use as his chief courier to Ralph, in spite of his earlier resolve to use different men. Ralph could see arguments for and against this arrangement. Knowing that Joseph was the contact, there was far less difficulty in their finding each other and identification was no longer a problem. However, Ralph was concerned that casual observers might come to recognise Joseph and wonder what Ralph had so regularly to do with him, especially since Joseph turned up in places often quite far apart. However, the work that Ralph did could not be successfully accomplished without some risks. He could only seek to minimise them. The Colonel, too, was suffering from limitations imposed upon his activities because of the reverses suffered by the Royalist armies. He was more often called upon to engage in normal soldiering activities and he had no longer so many men, whom he could rely upon, at his disposal. Joseph Grimshaw was one of the few men working for the Colonel, who seemed able to find his way across country, often through the very lines of the enemy.

Ralph learned from Joseph that the Colonel was, even now, with the Royalist army that occupied Oxford. The rebel army was so close to Oxford and the Royalist pickets on roads leading into the town that, in places, it would be quite possible to observe anyone crossing between the town and the Roundhead army. The situation was not, however, stagnant as with many sieges. Here there was some limited movement into or out of the town, especially at night, since the perimeter was too great for an impenetrable wall to be thrown around it. Indeed, Royalist forces made forays into the surrounding countryside and tried to take advantage of any weaknesses that they could find within the ranks of the besieging forces. So it was that Joseph travelled most often at night time, especially when he had to go into or out of Oxford.

The main force of Cromwell's cavalry was at present stationed at Watlington, some twelve miles south of Oxford. All but a few of his force had left that morning to harry the Royalist forces under the command of the Earl of Northampton at Islip. Ralph, as provisioner to the wagon master, was not expected to ride on such an expedition. He had duties enough at their base camp, maintaining supplies of food and other essentials.

Ralph sat alone in the small cottage, requisitioned by the army to serve as their administrative centre, where Ralph and two others, who served the wagon master, shared a small room for working and sleeping. Now the day's work was done and, for a while, Ralph had the cottage to himself. He took advantage of his solitude to write a little more of the report that he was preparing for Colonel Cressley. Cromwell's cavalry was becoming one of the most feared units in the armies of Parliament. As part of the 'New Model Army', they were a body of highly trained and disciplined soldiers; a far cry from the bunch of amateurs that had taken to the field at Edgehill, or those who had deserted at Cropredy Bridge. This army was comprised of men who had been well drilled in the art of war, who were properly paid, who had no particular local allegiance and who had the will to fight for the cause that they themselves had chosen. Nevertheless, there were those amongst the Royalists who stupidly dismissed this new force as the New Noddle Army, but the more intelligent commanders fighting for the King took them very seriously and urged that the Royalist armies should train and discipline their men in the same way.

Ralph set down all the details of the strength of the forces that he knew to be located around Oxford and their state of readiness to fight. He emphasised the high morale among Cromwell's soldiers, pointing out that most of them had a fanatical zeal and fought more for the cause than for money which, in this case, was regularly paid.

With a sigh of relief he completed the letter, which he felt now contained all the information that he could usefully send to the Colonel. He carefully folded and sealed it with his ring. Then, placing it safely in an inside pocket, he stepped out of the cottage for a breath of air.

The evening was quite mild for April and somewhat humid after rain. The trees had a light covering of green, as the fresh young leaves were breaking forth from the bud. Daffodils were abundant whilst, here and there, some trees were pale pink with early blossom. It was an evening to be relished. Its tranquil calm helped Ralph escape, for a while, from the harsh realities of war and his own unenviable position. He found it difficult to reconcile his naturally frank and straightforward nature with the secretive way of life that he had been forced to adopt. He hated what he was doing and would have much rather served the King astride a horse in a squadron of cavalry. He consoled himself with the thought that the work he did now probably served the King better. Ralph could feel no hatred for the men with whom he worked and for those he pretended to serve. They were, for the most part, good men who offered friendship and goodwill while he, for his part, betrayed their trust. At times he despised himself for the work he was doing and, for the thousandth time, he wondered if the end was worth the means. He tried to avoid making close friends, but it was not in his nature to shun the overtures of friendship so readily offered. Yet again he wished that he, of all people, had not been burdened with this job; but burdened he was and do it he must.

For a while he sat on the fence and enjoyed the peace and quiet of the countryside. With so many men away, there was little to be heard besides the sounds of nature. Only a few remained to occupy the tents pitched nearby. As dusk fell, the lights of the camp fires appeared to burn more brightly and, inside some of the tents, lamps were being lit. Refreshed by this breath of fresh air, Ralph slid from his perch on the fence and sauntered back to the cottage and his bed.

* * *

The following morning Ralph set off on horseback to a village, some two miles distant, where he had business and where he had arranged to meet Joseph Grimshaw. It was two or three hours before noon when he left. The weather was still comparatively mild, with the sun hidden behind a thick layer of cloud. So, in spite of the spring colours, the countryside wore a rather dismal mantel for an April day. However, Ralph did not reflect this sombre mood. He was happy to be out by himself once again. He prided himself that he had his own special way of persuading farmers to part with supplies of corn and fodder but, truth to tell, the country folk were becoming sick of the war and being bled for supplies which they needed for themselves and were beginning to regard each army alike as enemies. Ralph tried to deal fairly and, for the most part, was able to agree a reasonable price for the goods he bought. He hoped that the time would not come when it would be necessary to use force to obtain supplies for the army, but he feared that such times were approaching. Farmers could ill afford to part with produce that could be sold more profitably in the local market town or which they needed for their own use.

Arriving at the village, he set about his business with some measure of success. He identified produce that was available and issued the necessary documents to requisition it in the name of Parliament, arranging for its collection by wagon the next day. His efforts might have yielded greater reward but for the fact that men, also under Cromwell's command, had been abroad in the Oxfordshire countryside rounding up draught horses to deny the Royalists the chance of moving out of Oxford. This had, of course, angered many locals who depended upon these horses for their livelihood. Little wonder then that, as he moved about the village, Ralph was greeted with sullen faces and angry looks. He sensed that, ere long, the grievances felt by these people would erupt in violence.

Riding to the edge of the village, Ralph met Joseph whom he found sitting on a gate by a small orchard of apple trees that were just coming into blossom.

'Give you good morning, Master Somers.' Joseph greeted

Ralph who dismounted to join him by the gate. 'I thought that I would wait on you here. There's little welcome these days for strangers in a village.

'Aye, so I've observed.' agreed Ralph with the glimmer of a smile.

Ralph tethered his horse and seated himself on the gate beside Joseph. He marvelled at the way that this man found his way about the countryside. He certainly had travelled widely and must keep a map of England in his head. He never seemed to get lost and could be relied upon to turn up at any rendezvous at the appointed time. Sometimes he travelled on foot while, at other times, he arrived on horseback but, however he travelled, he had the knack of being quite inconspicuous. He was the sort of man for whom few would cast a backward glance.

'How did you get out of Oxford this morning? Isn't the town tightly sealed? Ralph asked, more than anything out of curiosity.

'Aye, tight enough, but there's always a way through for those who will find it.' replied Joseph casually. He was not a man to volunteer more than he was asked and mostly said less.

'What news of the Colonel?'

'He's out on patrol. He left yesterday for Bletchingdon House just north of Oxford.'

'When will he return?'

'Nay, that I cannot tell you. Maybe in two or three days. I don't know the nature of his business there.'

'Here, then, is something for his return.' Ralph handed his report to Joseph.

The two men exchanged a few further words before going their separate ways.

* * *

At Bletchingdon Hall, Colonel Cressley sat fuming at what he considered to be a waste of time. This type of patrol, or expedition, upon which he was more frequently dispatched these days, thwarted what he considered to be his much more useful task of supplying intelligence to the Royalist command.

During the first year of the war, Colonel Cressley had built up a network of agents working for him in the armies of Parliament throughout the country. He had also secured a band of couriers, in whom he could place absolute trust. The work of both agents and couriers was an inglorious task, but an essential one if the Royalist generals were to have a reliable knowledge of Parliament's forces and their plans. All of them had been handpicked men, loyal to the Royalist cause. A few, like Jim Peabody and Joseph Grimshaw, were men whom he had known for many years and who had worked for him before the war on his estate. Now these were fewer in number. One, at least, had died in the course of his duties whilst others had been taken, in spite of his protests, for other work. Suitable candidates for these jobs were hard to find. Their service required great courage and a strong sense of loyalty to him personally and to the crown. The agents had to be men who had the brains and initiative to work on their own, deciding what information would be of use and finding ways of obtaining it. Theirs' was a battle that lasted every day, while they were in the Colonel's service, with their lives continually at risk.

While these men watched and wrote their reports the couriers ran the gauntlet of patrols, sieges and skirmishes to bring the information back to the Colonel. For his part, he spent many long hours evaluating all this evidence, so that he could present the King with a comprehensive and factual report about their enemy with shrewd deductions about his next move.

This information and the sound advice which accompanied it, had always been welcomed and Colonel Cressley's quiet, well informed comments had been listened to with respect. Now, the King's commanders were at odds with one another. The rancour, which existed between them, allowed little time for useful discussion as in the past. It was apparent to the Colonel that the advice and help, which he had to offer, was now far less valued. Furthermore, perhaps because of a shortage of officers after the losses in the many battles which had been fought during the course of the war, the Colonel was being required more often to take command of a sortie or a patrol which could well have been carried out by a man of inferior rank. Colonel Cressley did not fear to fight, but he knew that he could better serve his royal master by supplying him with information than by wielding his sword.

He sat moodily looking out of the window. He had relieved the garrison occupying the house and had instructions to hold it for the King, as a refuge, in the event of a break out from Oxford. He was also expected to report daily to Oxford but, with Cromwell's troopers marauding in the area, the Colonel felt that his chances of maintaining communications with Oxford were not good. There was a commotion in the passage outside, followed by a knock on the door.

'Enter.'

A man came into the room in some haste.

'A message, sir, from the Earl of Northampton at Islip. He has just repulsed an attack by Cromwell's cavalry. He believes them to be heading this way.'

'Did you see any of them on your ride here?'

'Aye sir. They were re-mustering on the road here from Islip. I rode fast. They can only be a mile or two behind. They will be here shortly, if to come here is their intention.'

The Colonel strode to the door. Throwing it open, he shouted,

'Soames, Taylor, come here at once, if you please.'

Seconds later the two men entered the room. Quickly the Colonel explained the situation. Then to Soames he said,

'Take your men and place half either side of the drive in the shrubbery, hidden from view but ready mounted. Stay hidden until you see a signal from the centre window at the front of the house. After a volley or two of musket fire from our men on the roof and, when a scarlet sash is waved from the window, charge them from the rear. The other half are to guard the courtyard at the rear of the house. Taylor, send half of your men, under the command of a lieutenant, to man the upstairs windows and the roof. The remainder are to be ready mounted, also in the courtyard, but ready to ride out against the enemy if they attack that way. They should also be ready, at my command, to reinforce our men at the front. Send one man out on to the Islip road to watch for the coming of the Roundhead forces. He should remain hidden and find out, if he can, how the enemy intends to deploy his forces and give us what warning he may.'

Both men acknowledged their instructions and quickly left the room. Within minutes there was a stir of men falling to arms; some pounded up the stairs and along the corridors, to take up positions at the windows and on the roof. Scarce ten minutes had elapsed since the arrival of the messenger, before a soldier was back to report that the enemy were forming up for a frontal assault on the house. From the bedroom window Colonel Cressley, with a lieutenant and two soldiers to act as couriers, saw troopers appear at the end of the long drive leading to the building from the road which passed the borders of the estate.

'We'll wait until they are within fifty paces of the house before firing from the windows. When I give the word, signal to Soames for his men to attack from the shrubbery.' said Colonel Cressley to the young lieutenant.

The tension mounted in the rooms, as the occupants watched the strong, well ordered body of cavalry advance steadily up the drive. To these horsemen, the Hall must have seemed deserted and the gardens as silent as the grave. The suddenly, at a command from the Colonel, a volley of musket fire rang out from high up along the front of the building. The phalanx of horsemen seemed to halt momentarily. Here and there horses reared and a few saddles were emptied. At this range the musket was not very accurate and, it was largely because the enemy had been riding in close order, that so many musket balls had found a target. Then, with a howl of fury, the remaining riders spurred forward. A second volley of musket fire did not appear, this time, to check their advance as before, but it served to dispatch a few more riders and horses. Then, on a word from Colonel Cressley, the lieutenant waved his scarlet sash from the window. With Captain Soames at their head, the horsemen waiting in the shrubbery crashed into the rear of the Roundhead cavalry, uttering wild shouts of savage joy as they anticipated the victory which they now saw to be within their grasp. Within seconds the scene at the front of the house was of a seething mass of horsemen, hacking at one another at such close quarters that there was little room for riders to manoeuvre.

So complete was the surprise that it was not long before the Royalist troops were plainly getting the upper hand, but the Roundhead commander, perhaps Cromwell himself, was no beginner at the art of war. He had come with a strong body of cavalry and had held a considerable force in reserve. Even as the Colonel's men seemed to overwhelm the first wave of Roundhead soldiers, a second force of their cavalry was observed, beyond the melee in front of the house, charging to the aid of their comrades.

Quickly, the Colonel instructed the lieutenant to order one more volley of musket fire over the heads of friend and foe fighting below, into the ranks of the advancing cavalry before it joined the battle. Then he gave orders for them to quit the house and follow him to the courtyard at the rear. There he found Taylor and his force, and the other half of Soames' men, ready waiting. Ready too, were the horses of the men who had been with him inside the house. With a message to Taylor to leave a look out at the rear of the house to warn of any further attack from that quarter, the Colonel mounted. Once again he divided his force into two. Placing himself at the head of one body and with Taylor leading the other, they went around either side of the house to attack both flanks and the rear of the second wave of Roundheads.

His blood rising within him, the Colonel spurred his horse towards the scene of battle. Soames and his men scarce had time to regroup before the second column of Roundheads was upon them. This time there was no element of surprise but, occupied as they were in finishing off the first body of cavalry, Soames' men were unable to ready themselves to receive the fury of this new attack. Nevertheless, they fought grimly to hold them. So, it was a cheering sight, when they saw the Colonel on one side and Taylor on the other thrust into the enemy. But these were hardened and disciplined soldiers who neither gave nor expected quarter.

A glancing blow from a pistol ball on his helmet made the Colonel's senses reel. At his side a rebel horseman aimed a wicked blow at his head. He leaned quickly to one side to dodge it and received its full force on his shoulder; fortunately protected by the edge of his breast plate. He countered with a thrust which glanced off the man's armour and caused the Colonel to almost lose his seat. Desperately he fought to regain his balance and evade the further blows that he knew would follow. He looked up fearfully to see his opponent's sword upraised to fall in a cutting blow across his poorly protected rear, as he lay awkwardly across his mount struggling to sit upright. He watched with horrid fascination as the man's face contorted as a sword thrust from the rear burst through his belly spewing forth blood as a lubricant to its passage. He uttered a scream of agony as he slid from his horse.

Saved from this menace, yet another Roundhead trooper faced the Colonel, as he reined his horse round to the right, where one of his men was beset by two of the enemy. A sword thrust sent one crashing to the ground, whilst the other fell with a scream from his saddle, a scarlet gash across his face from a sword cut saved only in part by his helmet. Now there was a lull in the fighting and it seemed for a moment that the Colonel's men had overcome the attack. Then shots were heard at the rear of the house. Before the Colonel had time to investigate, some of the few men who had been left to guard the rear appeared with Roundhead troopers in hot pursuit. Captain Taylor galloped to his side.

'Sir, they have broken through at the rear of the house. There are too many, the men cannot hold them.'

Colonel Cressley was about to lead his men to the rear of the house when he saw yet more Roundhead troopers advancing along the drive towards them. Quickly he made up his mind. Forming up his men, those that were left of his entire force, he led a charge along the drive towards the oncoming horsemen. They met with a fearful clash. Men on both sides were thrust from their saddles by the sheer force of the impact. Once again they hacked at one another, sword to sword. Then behind them, just in front of the building, the Colonel saw those rebel forces which had broken through at the rear of the house, now unhindered, line up to prepare to charge into the rear of his men. For a few seconds he watched his men stand their ground, offering thrust for thrust, but Colonel Cressley was an old enough campaigner to know when the day is lost. He must bow to superior numbers. He gave the order to retreat.

Following his directions, his men disengaged themselves and made off as best they could towards Oxford, followed by the rebels in hot pursuit.

Blood flowed from a wound on the Colonel's arm and from a cut on his face. His head pounded from the shot which he had received on his helmet. With no more than forty of the hundred men with whom he had set out, the Colonel galloped in headlong flight. Ahead of him lay the river Cherwell. Urging his men on, he fell back a little to help the riders at the tail of the strung out posse of horsemen. Here, two of the foremost rebels were either side of one of his men, trying to thrust him from his saddle. Drawing the last of the three pistols that he had loaded, Colonel Cressley aimed carefully. This shot had to count. He fired. Without a sound one of the rebel horsemen collapsed on the neck of his horse and then slid slowly down its flank before falling on to the soft turf. His rider-less horse continued to race along in pursuit of the fleeing Royalists. Freed from one of his attackers, the Colonel's man swung a savage blow at the other pursuer. More by luck than judgement the sword struck the nose guard on the man's helmet and, whilst it did him little injury, the blow was sufficient to unhorse him.

Others from the Roundhead cavalry were determined to continue the harassment of the defeated Royalists and continued relentlessly in pursuit. Now the river loomed ahead. It was too deep to ford, but cross it they must, for here the river followed the course of a large sweeping concave curve which encompassed the riders, both friend and foe. To turn in any direction would lessen what lead they had on their pursuers and the river would still be there to be crossed. Seeing their predicament, Colonel Cressley raced to try to gain the lead. He shouted to his men to ride into the river. With little hesitation, the Colonel's men plunged their horses down the muddy bank into the sluggish water. Almost immediately their horses were swimming. Like many, the Colonel found he was unable to retain his seat and fell into the now muddy water. Clinging to the reins and to the horse's neck, with the remnants of his force he made his way, half swimming, sometimes being dragged by his horse, until he finally waded up the muddy bank on the opposite side of the river, where he floundered in the mud whilst both he and his men struggled up on to dry land.

The rebels, unwilling to pursue their enemy at the cost of a ducking, let them go. They watched with laughter and jeers from the bank as the bedraggled remnants of Colonel Cressley's cavalry clambered up on the other side. One or two of those who had powder and shot left in their pistols fired at the men in the river, but by good fortune none found its mark.

It was a sodden and demoralised body of men that found its way into Oxford that day. In spite of his wounds, his wet clothes and his weariness, Colonel Cressley found time to obtain what help he could for those of his men who were wounded and to ensure that billets were available for them all. Then he went to make his report to his superiors. News of Cromwell's expedition to Islip had already reached the Royalist commanders in Oxford. They were not, therefore, surprised to hear of the encounter with the Roundheads at Bletchingdon. Under the circumstances, it was generally held that Colonel Cressley and his men had acquitted themselves well. However, it was of little comfort to the Colonel to be told this and to hear that he had been outnumbered three to one. Whichever way he looked at it, he had been badly beaten and it sorely rankled.

The Colonel arrived back at his lodgings late in the evening, pale and worn, shivering with an ague. Joseph Grimshaw, who had found his way back into Oxford, laid out dry clothes for his master and helped him into a warm bed. He dressed his wounds, none of which were very serious and were likely to heal if they did not go putrid. Although Joseph did what he could to make him comfortable, the fever gained a hold that night. For three days, the Colonel lay sweating and restless in his bed, aching in every limb. For some of the time his mind wandered and he talked wildly without knowing what he said. At times he became extremely agitated and tried to rise from his bed and would have done so had it not been for Joseph's restraining hands. Joseph watched over him while the fever racked his body and, at times, Joseph feared for his life. At the end of the third day the fever abated and Colonel Cressley fell into a peaceful sleep. After that he became more lucid in his waking moments, but was extremely weak. It was four or five more days before he was able to take a few shaky steps across the room.

During the next fortnight the Colonel began to recover his strength. However, a deep depression pervaded his whole being. In spite of the bright spring weather and the sunshine, which Joseph encouraged him to enjoy, the Colonel brooded over the failure of his recent encounter with the enemy and the many men whom he had lost. Although none blamed him for what had happened, he blamed himself. Now the siege of Oxford had been tightened. Fairfax had taken over from Cromwell and it was even more difficult than before for anyone to leave or enter the city.

The Colonel sat one day, some three weeks after his flight from Bletchingdon Hall, in the room of the house where he lodged. He looked from its windows to the view beyond the town walls. His thoughts turned to home, Hartington Hall, which he had not seen for so long. He thought of his wife, whose death he had learned of last year. He had grieved then, but the sharp edge of grief had been dulled by his being away from home and by the many duties which had occupied his mind. He had managed to obtain leave from the Prince to travel home. There he had felt his grief more keenly and, at the graveside, he had mourned the loss of the woman he had so loved and with whom he had shared so many happy years of his life. Now, still on light duties and, in any case with little to do whilst the town was under siege, he had time on his hands to brood and a great sadness filled his heart. He visualised the emptiness of the life that awaited him when he was able to return home for good. Elizabeth, his constant companion, would no longer be at his side. There would be no one to share his pleasures and sorrows, no one to discuss the running of the estate and no one to share the long winter nights. A sickness filled his soul and he no longer cared whether he lived or died. Better, he thought, to die for the King than to return to such desolation.

Then he thought of Jack and Mary. Were young Ralph Somers to survive the war, he would not be slow to claim Mary and whisk her away to his home at Preston Capes; doubtless with a family shortly to follow. There would be little room in her life for her father. Then, what of Jack? Jack would have the family home and land. That was his inheritance and his right. The Colonel knew that Jack would care for the estate and nurture it. He was a good lad who cared for the important things in life. Yes, Jack would be there and, even if he married, as any man should, there would still be room enough at Hartington Hall for his father, even when a family began to arrive. But, what if Jack were to be killed? No, never! He could not bear the thought.

What then of the estate, if Jack were to perish? It would lie neglected and uncared-for. The Colonel knew from the last visit to see his wife's grave, that those who were left at the Hall were finding it nigh on impossible to keep the place in good order. How could they, when so many were away fighting in this terrible war? Now Mary was no longer living there, so there was no one to offer any real direction to those staff remaining. Colonel Cressley had heard from Ralph, through Joseph Grimshaw, of the problems that Mary had encountered with Murchison and how she was now living with the Somers at Bullshead. They were good people who would protect her. He approved of the arrangement and of Ralph for bringing it about. Hartington Hall was no place for a woman to be on her own save for a few servants, even one like Mary, especially in these terrible times. Fortunately, there was no shortage of money. Of that there was sufficient and some to spare. The Colonel had hidden all his valuables before he left to go to war. They were, with all of his important documents, in a secret compartment behind the oak panelling beside the chimney breast. There they would be safe, even if the Hall were to be taken by the rebels and plundered. That was one hiding place which they would not find. Only he and his wife, Elizabeth, knew its secret. Without that knowledge its very existence would not be suspected, let alone the means to gain entry. Then the thought struck him. Elizabeth was dead. Now, he alone knew how to gain access. In this hiding place was his money and, even more important, those documents and deeds that proved his ownership of the Hall and all its lands, not to speak of the other valuables, jewels and family heirlooms which were also there. What if he had been killed in the fight at Bletchingdon House? What if he had died of the fever which had recently laid him low? What if he should perish during the siege of this city? Jack would have difficulty proving his rights to the Hall and would, certainly, never see all those other things which were his inheritance. This thought greatly agitated the Colonel. He was consumed with a desire to do something to rectify this most unsatisfactory state of affairs. But, what could he do?

The siege grew more severe as each day passed. It was said that siege artillery was on its way. Then Parliament would surely gain the upper hand. Something would have to be done soon.

The Colonel was now reasonably fit again. Although growing stronger bodily, the depression still gripped his mind. For a fortnight, after he had risen from his bed, he felt as weak as a kitten. He had not been fit to resume active service and now he was trapped here in Oxford, like as not to die in its defence. The problem of letting Jack know the secret of the hiding place in Hartington Hall still nagged away in his mind. Jack was now with Prince Rupert somewhere up north, Chester he believed. Whilst the Colonel realised that the attack of depression, from which he suffered, was likely to pass and that many of his fears had been aggravated by it, yet he knew that his concern over the secret to his hiding place was valid. He had no fear of dying and, although he had no longer any wish to die and took a more cheerful view of the future, he still saw his death in battle as at least possible. To die for the cause that he believed in was not such a bad thing but, before that fatal day, he must find a way of letting Jack know the secret of that panelled room in their family home.

***

That evening he was to dine with the Governor of Oxford, William Legge. Still a little shaky, Colonel Cressley set forth to join the Governor in his lodgings near the castle. Even as he walked through the narrow streets, his mind was still wrestling with the problem of how to let Jack have this vital information.

The morale in Oxford was high. So far the siege had done little hurt to the buildings or the inhabitants of the town. Indeed, the enemy had suffered more casualties than those behind the walls and fortifications that had been thrown up at strategic points around the town boundaries. However, food was beginning to get a little scarcer and, now that Fairfax and Browne had joined forces with Cromwell, the noose was beginning to tighten. The Colonel doubted whether any more substantial amounts of provisions could be brought in.

The streets of the city were full of soldiers as the Colonel made his way to where the castle stood proudly on its ancient mound. With the soldiers was the usual throng of camp followers which came with any army; prostitutes, women, children, itinerants etc. Around the Colonel, as he walked through the streets, was evidence of the debauchery that followed in the wake of this sort of rabble. This was the garbage of war that one had to accept. He hurried past the gibbet, where hung the body of a man captured but two days since. He had been found spying for the rebel cause. As the Colonel passed he watched the corpse swing mournfully in the wind. He saw the face contorted in the agony of death, the tongue protruding and the eyes bulging. He shuddered. How many of his agents had met this fate? One, he knew, had died in a like manner. Others had vanished; their fate unknown. He thought of Ralph. Dear God, was it fair to ask a man to put himself at such risk?

Thrusting these gloomy thoughts from his mind he found that, once again, his head was filled with concern about Jack and his ignorance of that vital secret.

A drunken soldier, with his arm around a woman, lurched along the street and collided with the Colonel. The soldier stifled a curse as he recognised the Colonel's rank and instead mumbled an apology, then staggered on his way.

Coming to the Governor's house, the Colonel was soon admitted and, ere long, found himself seated with the Governor, his lady and a small number of guests. There were some polite enquiries about the Colonel's health and then the conversation fell naturally to a discussion of the military situation.

'I'll warrant that the King will not let us linger long bottled up like this.' declared a red faced officer who sat opposite Colonel Cressley. 'What say you Cressley?'

'The King will not want to lose Oxford, but he will expect us to fend for ourselves for a week or two yet. He has work to do up north.'

'We can defend the city for longer than that, or my name is not William Legge. These rebels will have to sit many a long week at our gates, ere they see inside our city bounds. Eh, Smeaton?'

'Our walls and fortifications may not stand for long when they bring their siege artillery to play.' replied Captain Smeaton gravely.

'Come now, Smeaton. What sort of talk is that?' asked Legge gruffly.

''Tis the plain truth, I fear sir.' said another guest in support of Smeaton. 'I fear that the siege is not yet properly invested. We shall, no doubt, stand for a few weeks, but our soldiers cannot expect to find much protection within our fortifications when the enemy starts to use his artillery.'

This talk plainly disconcerted some of those present, especially one or two of the ladies for whom, so far, the worst realities of the war had been a limitation of some of their pleasures and the occasional absence of their men-folk. Sir Francis attempted to change the subject.

'Does the King know of our circumstances, Governor?'

'Not the strength of the rebels now outside the city.'

'Could not a courier be sent, at least to inform the King of this greater threat?' asked Smeaton.

'Aye, a man might get through even now. Cressley, you have

some knowledge of these matters, I believe. Have you not some men who could carry messages for the King?' asked Legge.

'Yes, it could be done. The watch on the city has been greatly tightened but, yes, a good man could find his way through.'

'Then we'll do as Smeaton suggests and acquaint His Majesty with the situation. Bring me your man tomorrow and I will have a message for him to take to the King. What say you Cressley; will you do it?'

Sir Francis' thoughts were elsewhere. With the King, rode his son Jack. A messenger to the King might well also carry a message to Jack. Yes, that would be a way of solving his problem of telling Jack the secrets of the hiding place at Hartington Hall.

'Eh, what's that? Oh, yes sir; by all means. It were best if the attempt was made after dark. The chances of success will be much greater. So, shall we say at 9 o'clock in the evening? Will that suit you?'

The evening passed very pleasantly. The Colonel, relieved that he had at last found a way of contacting Jack, felt the burden of gloom that had oppressed him for the past three weeks begin to lift. This, together with the soothing influence of one or two glasses of good wine, left Sir Francis with a feeling of ease and contentment that he had not felt for a long time. He began to feel that, at last, he was shaking off this wretched illness which had brought him so low and robbed him of so much strength and vigour. It was not all that late when he arrived back at his lodgings where, by candlelight, he sat down straight away to write his letter to Jack. It must be carefully worded so that none but Jack would know of where and what he was writing. The Colonel was very much aware that this letter and the one to be sent by the Governor, may well end up in the hands of the Roundhead commanders. He must ensure that they could learn nothing from it that would lead them to Hartington Hall. Folding the letter, he took his seal from the drawer of his desk and, heating the wax in the candle flame, sealed the letter.

The number of men that Colonel Cressley had at his disposal to act as couriers was now quite few. Mostly, Colonel Cressley relied increasingly on older men. He had lost some of the younger ones who had, in the past, taken his messages. Apart from the fact that the Colonel now had a very restricted choice of younger men, he had found that the older men often acted with more mature judgement in a crisis and, because of their age, were not regarded with such suspicion.

However, the situation in Oxford was somewhat different. Normally, any of the Colonel's couriers could travel freely and, unless something that he did gave rise to suspicion, he would not be stopped and questioned. Now no one, young or old, rich or poor, could travel into or out of Oxford. So anyone who was to successfully get through the rebel lines must do so by stealth and cunning, ready to ride hard and, if necessary, to fight. This work called for a fit young man of action. One such man was Henry Savage. He was a man of many parts who had, in the past, shown himself able to fight his way out of tight corners. Of all the men under his command, it was Henry Savage whom Colonel Cressley thought would have the best chance of success. He was unswervingly loyal to the King's cause. He was young and agile. He had the cunning of a fox. He could ride like a demon and, furthermore, he could look after himself in a fight. Nevertheless, the Colonel did not underestimate the danger that this man might encounter. The Roundheads would surely be vigilant for anyone trying to sneak through their lines. He would need all his skill and a great deal of luck, if he were to reach the King.

It was, therefore. with Henry Savage that the Colonel arrived at the Governor's house the next evening at dusk. It was arranged that he should slip out of the city under cover of darkness when, with stealth and good luck, he might escape detection.

The Governor handed the letter for the King to Savage and wished him good luck and God's speed. Taking the Colonel to one side, he confided in him that the letter informed His Majesty of the degree of the siege and of the apparent strength of the rebel armies surrounding Oxford. Of the state of the city and its defenders, it made only the comment that morale was high. Like the Colonel, William Legge recognised that Savage's chances of success were limited and any messages must therefore be guarded in its contents. He asked the Colonel to ensure that Savage told more to the King of the urgency of their plight than was in the letter.

Leaving the Governor's house, the Colonel walked with Henry Savage to a small gate in the fortifications adjacent to the castle through which, it was judged, that he had the best chance of passing unseen. Sir Francis impressed upon Henry that it was necessary for him to embroider the message verbally to convince the King that, if not relieved soon, Oxford is likely to fall within a few weeks; less if siege artillery was brought to bear. As luck would have it, the night was a dark one. The only light was from the windows of the houses and the doorways of the taverns and, here and there, from the flaming torches set up in brackets on the walls by the watchmen. The light reflected back from the cobbled streets, wet with rain. In the dark shadows, vague noises betrayed the presence of nocturnal prowlers. Now and then figures scurried by, anxious to gain the safety of their lodgings, while occasionally they were passed by a far from furtive group of revellers proceeding merrily to the next ale house. Oxford was not a safe place to be abroad alone after dark, especially these days.

Having impressed Henry Savage with the need for a verbal accompaniment to the Governor's message, the two men walked for the most part in silence. As they neared the gate the Colonel asked Savage.

'Do you know my son, Jack? He is serving with Prince Rupert's cavalry.'

'Aye, sir. I met him at the siege and fall of Bristol. He is a fine man sir. I would say a credit to you.'

'He serves the cause well and does me great credit. I have a letter here which contains information for his eyes only. Will you see it safely into his hands. Prince Rupert is now with the King. Jack should not be hard to find.'

'I will seek him sir and, if I can find him, he shall have your letter.' So saying, Henry Savage took the letter and placed it safely in his pocket with the other.

At the gate, the Colonel handed to the officer of the watch

the Governor's authority for Henry Savage to pass through the Royalist picket.

Colonel Cressley shook Henry Savage by the hand. 'It is a perilous venture you undertake Henry. God go with you and give you safe deliverance.'

With those final words, the Colonel watched Savage jump astride the mount which had been saddled for him by soldiers at the gate. At an order from the officer and a sign from a man on the wall that all was clear, the gate was quickly opened. Within seconds the gate was shut fast again and Colonel Cressley stood alone.

CHAPTER 17

May 1645
Bletchingdon House, Oxfordshire

It was well over a month since Ralph had seen Joseph Grimshaw. That was some few days before Cromwell's cavalry had taken Bletchingdon House. Ralph's anxiety on hearing the news of the battle for the house had reached fever pitch, due to the absence of any news of the fate of Colonel Cressley whom he had known, from Joseph, to be one of the defenders in the battle for the mansion. The first news of the skirmish had been an account of a complete defeat of the Royalists, with the defending garrison killed almost to a man. Ralph tried to make some discreet enquiries about how many had really been killed, who was there and how many escaped. His enquiries had made those he asked curious to know the reason for his interest in such detail. Ralph had had, therefore, to moderate his enquiries and excuse his interest by saying that he had known a family who had served in the house just before the outbreak of war. On the whole Ralph considered that, in this case, no news was good news since, in all that he had been able to find out about the dead and injured, there had been no mention of a Colonel. The highest rank had been Captain Taylor who had died of his wounds some two days after the battle.

Now, by a quirk of fate, Ralph found himself billeted at Bletchingdon House which was currently garrisoned by a troop of Fairfax's dragoons. Since his last meeting with Grimshaw, Ralph had been within ten miles of Oxford helping to provision the armies of Parliament. The country folk were now more hostile than ever and, as Ralph had feared would be the case, persuasion was no longer of any use. Compulsion, amounting to plunder, was the order of the day although some pretence at legality was made with a token payment.

Ralph yearned for an end to this war and to this kind of life. He began to feel that he no longer cared who won or lost, if only peace could be restored to the land. He had seen little enough fighting, but he had known both sides and knew them to be for the most part honest, decent men, caught up in an ugly war about which many had no strong feelings. For the most part they fought for the side that they were on, simply because their fellows did or the squire had enlisted their services. Only Cromwell's men were different. They were often fanatics. To them the war was a religious crusade against popery, against bishops and against all the paraphernalia of the Roman Catholic faith. There were those who wanted equality for all and an end to the aristocracy and ruling classes which dominated. Many were fighting for their vision of a new world, where they were free to pray as they wished; to be Presbyterian, Protestant, Puritan, Baptist, Seeker or any other. Ralph did not begrudge them the freedom to pray as they wished, but he despised them for their self-righteousness, their arrogance and their hypocrisy. At the same time he feared them and their generals, Cromwell in particular, for he knew that it was such zeal which won wars.

He lay moodily on his bed in one of the rooms near the kitchen at the back of the house. His companions lay in their beds snoring. From the kitchen came the sound of the cooks preparing the morning meal. Soon the whole house would be astir. He got out of bed and looked out of the window to see what sort of day it was. At least the rain of the last two days had stopped. What a wretched summer it had been so far. But now, for once, it looked as though the sun might break through to brighten up the day. Quickly he pulled on his stockings and breeches, put on a shirt and leather tunic, buckled his shoes and stepped out into the mild fresh morning air. He strolled along the quiet country lane for a mile or two, enjoying the peace and freshness of the countryside on that May morning. It was with no more than a little reluctance that he retraced his steps back to the house and the trappings of war that he hated.

As he approached the drive leading to the house he heard the sound of voices, talking and laughing. Stepping into the concealment of the shrubbery, which had some three or four weeks ago hidden Colonel Cressley's horsemen, he waited for the owners of the voices to show themselves. As it soon appeared there were three men on horseback, obviously in no great hurry for their mounts merely ambled along the drive. It was, however, only two of the three riders who conversed so cheerfully, the third said nothing and had little to laugh about for he, being a prisoner, was tied to his mount. From his place of concealment Ralph watched the three men ride past. He regarded the prisoner with particular interest, although he had no idea who he was and had never seen him before.

When they had passed, Ralph followed at a distance as they rode around to the back of the house. He watched the two soldiers roughly drag their prisoner off the horse and thrust him forward, hands tied behind his back, into the house. A few moments later the two soldiers, having delivered the prisoner to their officer and returned were, still talking and laughing as they made their way to the kitchen. Ralph followed them in and, like them, helped himself to a slice of newly baked bread. He took a slice of meat and drew a mug of ale from the cask which had been set on the bench. Then he sat down at the long table, beside the two men, to eat his breakfast.

Like so many kitchens in large country houses, this was a barn of a place with a fireplace over which was a roasting spit, while at the side of, and part of the fireplace, stood a large oven. From the ceiling, suspended from hooks, were sides of bacon and other cured and smoked meats. On the shelves covering the high walls were all manner of pots and pans, as well as jugs, mixing bowls etc., in what had been once well burnished copper. Now they looked well used and none too clean. At one end of the room was a huge table, where the cooks were at work. Whilst by the fire was the table at which Ralph and the other soldiers sat for their meals. Since Ralph's work had much to do with provisioning the soldiers and obtaining supplies for the kitchen, he was amongst the privileged few who had their meals cooked for them. The ordinary soldiers were generally provided with food which they themselves must cook, as they wished, over their open camp fires. The cooks were here mainly to provide meals for the officers and for a few of the administrative staff. Plainly, the two soldiers had been instructed to report to the kitchen for a meal since they were away from the posts at which they would normally prepare their own food.

'I see that you had better luck today than some who go fishing.' Ralph remarked casually to the two men.

For a moment they looked at him in bewilderment. Then the face of one creased into a smile as he realised what Ralph was talking about.

'Aye, we made a catch today, leastways our patrol did. We found the varmint sneaking through our lines north of Oxford. Said he was one of us, he did, but he didn't know the password. Soon found him out. If he's for Parliament, then I'm King Charles.'

They both guffawed hugely with laughter at this pronouncement.

'What have you brought him here for?'

'He's got to be questioned, ain't he? Questioned and, if they don't get the right answers, hung. Mind you, they'll make sure that he tells them all he knows first.'

Again they laughed loudly at the prospect.

For a while Ralph sat thinking what he could do to help the fellow. He wondered if, like himself, he was working for the Royalist cause or, perhaps, he was an innocent bystander caught up in the turmoil of war. If he had been trying to pass through the Roundhead siege lines around Oxford, it may be that he was a courier. If that were the case, his interrogators would have the message by now. He would then be clearly a Royalist and likely to remain a prisoner for the rest of the war, unless he could be persuaded to change sides. If he carried the message in his head and could provide a good reason for his passing through the siege lines, he might save his skin; but it seemed unlikely.

Ralph needed to know more, so he decided to take a walk through the corridors at the rear of the building, near where he knew the prisoner was being held. He might be able to find out what was going on. Nodding to the two soldiers, he left the table and walked across the kitchen to the door leading into the corridor that traversed the width of the house at the rear. Turning left, for it was that side of the rear of the house to which the prisoner had been taken, Ralph walked slowly along the passage, stopping from time to time to listen for the sound of voices. Soon he heard a loud, hectoring voice which rang out in a demanding tone. The words were indistinct. Following the direction of the sound, Ralph came to a closed door on the other side of which, it soon became clear, the interrogation was taking place.

From within came the sounds of a scuffle with several loud thuds, the cries of someone in pain, followed by a silence broken only by a groan. Then, of a sudden, the voice of the interrogator rang out again.

'For the last time man, tell me who sent you and who wrote this letter.'

The voice was harsh and demanding. It told of complete authority, coupled with a ruthless determination. For a moment there was silence again, then;

'Well, if needs must, we will get the truth from you by harder means but, mark you, the truth we shall have and, before we have finished with you, death will seem a very sweet thing to embrace. Take him to the stables. Hang him by his wrists from a beam. We'll see him again this evening. There's time a'plenty.'

Ralph scarce had time to hide in a doorway before the door crashed open and two soldiers dragged the prisoner outside. One of his eyes was swollen and closed, blood ran from his mouth and a livid red weal ran across his face. He was dragged along the corridor. Staying in his hiding place, Ralph listened to the two officers who remained in the room discussing the prisoner and his reluctance to talk.

'He's a stubborn fellow.'

'Aye, but he'll talk in the end. You see if I'm not right.'

'I'm not so sure. He's a hard man. He'll maybe die first.'

'He'll die last, when he's told us who wrote this letter.'

'Well, if he doesn't tell us, the letter will be of little use. It's hard to make top nor tail of it, but there could be something worth the finding if only we knew to what place these instructions belonged.'

'What of the letter to the King?'

'It tells us nothing that we don't already know, but it might bring the King quickly back to Oxford if he were to read it. It's the other letter that interests me. We must find out who sent it.'

'We'll find out, all in good time.'

The two fell silent and Ralph retreated back down the corridor to the kitchen and, through it, back to the room that served as his office. He had work to do and would soon be missed. He also needed time to think over the possibility of perhaps helping the prisoner to escape. No obvious plan came to mind by which he could do anything immediately. It was something that needed careful consideration.

As he copied lists of figures and made out purchase orders, his mind dwelt on how he could release this unfortunate man from his predicament. He had his own safety to think of, for little would be served by exposing himself in any bodged attempt to help. Harsh as it was to contemplate, Ralph supposed that the work he did for the Royalists was perhaps of more value than the life of this man, not to mention his own. His plan must be fool proof and ensure that he was, himself, beyond suspicion. Finally, he settled on a course of action which he believed could well be successful and yet, unless caught in the act, would place him beyond suspicion.

* * *

It was an hour later, when Ralph sauntered out into the courtyard. He walked casually past the sentry standing outside the stable in which the prisoner was held. Ralph had been in the stables several times. One of them was in use as a temporary store for the regiment's provisions. There were five stables in all, making one long building, all under one roof. Ralph entered the stable at the opposite end of the building to where the prisoner was held. He was fairly certain that no one had noticed him. He really had no good reason to enter this part of the stable block, although neither was there any reason why he should not be there. The courtyard between the stables and the house was a busy place with many people coming and going. In acting naturally, he believed that he would have attracted little attention to himself.

Along the top of the building ran a beam some four feet from the apex of the thatched roof. The beam was some ten feet from the floor. It was almost certainly this beam from which they would have hung the prisoner. Each stable was divided off, almost to the height of this beam but, above that, they opened up to one another. Ralph had previously noticed a ladder which had been propped against the wall. He moved it a few feet so that he could climb up on to the beam. Seizing one of the coils of rope which hung from pegs on the wall, Ralph climbed the ladder and sat astride the beam. Then, pulling himself forward, he passed into the next stable. Slowly he progressed along the beam, from one stable to the next, until he reached the one in which the prisoner was held. It had taken him some minutes to reach the end stable. During this time he was agonisingly aware of his predicament, should someone enter one of the stables he was crossing to find him exposed on the beam above. The journey of fifty feet had seemed to take a lifetime. Now he was just inside the end stable. As he had guessed, a rope slung over the beam supported the man, who was tied by the wrists and hung at full stretch. His hands were about two feet from the beam and his feet were less than two feet from the floor. A yard or two away was a box on which his captors had stood him while they tied the rope, after which they had kicked away the box from under him so that his full weight was taken by his arms and wrists. The rope was secured at the other end to an iron circlet fastened to the stable wall.

Quietly Ralph edged forward. Silent as he was, his coming had been heard by the unhappy man below. The expression of suffering on his uplifted face gave way to an expression of surprise and hope. He was about to speak when Ralph put a finger to his lips in case any exclamation of surprise should be heard by the guard outside the door.

Ralph cast his eyes around the stable. A ladder, which might have helped him get down from the beam, lay uselessly on its side against the wall. Unslinging the coil of rope, Ralph fastened one end securely around the beam and allowed the remainder to fall to the floor. Quickly he shinned down the rope.

Softly he spoke to the man.

'I will loosen the rope around your feet. Then I'll put the box under you so that you can stand on it.'

Quickly he removed the rope that bound the prisoner's feet together. Then he placed the box under his feet. With a sigh of relief the man took the weight off his arms. Next, Ralph loosened the now slack rope in the iron ring so that the prisoner could lower his arms. He would have fallen from the box, had not Ralph stepped quickly forward to support him.

'For your life's sake make as little noise as possible, there is a sentry outside the door.'

He next freed the man's wrists.

'I will re-tie the rope in position in the iron ring, so that it will be thought that you freed yourself. Give me a quarter of an hour to get out of here and then make your escape. I wish you luck.' Ralph spoke softly.

'My thanks to you friend!' replied the man. 'Can I know your name?'

'No names. It's better that way. Fare thee well.'

Ralph picked up the box and put it back where he had found it lying. Then, grasping the rope by which he had climbed down, and using his feet against the dividing wall between the stables to aid his ascent, he regained the beam in seconds. Undoing the rope, he quickly coiled it and slung it over his shoulder. With a final wave to the erstwhile captive, he started back along the beam to the opposite end of the building. As he approached the fourth stable, he heard the door of the fifth open and horses being led in. Ralph considered jumping down on to bags of grain, in the fourth stable, but knew that the door was locked so he would find no exit that way. All he could do then was wait and hope that the soldiers would quickly see their horses fed and watered and then leave. It was not a job that they were likely to prolong but Ralph feared that, if he were delayed for much longer, the prisoner would try to make good his escape. When that happened, Ralph wanted to be somewhere other than inside the stable block.

For what seemed an eternity, Ralph sat on the beam in a fever of anxiety waiting for the men in the next stable to leave. He listened to their movements and overheard their conversation, expecting all the time that someone would wonder why the ladder was propped near the beam. At last he heard one of the soldiers open the door and call to his companions to make haste. Within a minute they were gone and Ralph was able to slide into the stable and clamber down the ladder which fortunately no one had noticed. Hindered by the horses, Ralph replaced the ladder where he had found it and hung the coil of rope back on the hook from which he had taken it. Then, again without any hint of furtive behaviour, he opened the stable door, slammed it behind him and without glancing to his right or left strolled casually across the yard and made his way back to the small room that was presently his office.

Fortunately he was alone. From his chair he could look out over the courtyard to the stables opposite. He sat for some ten minutes with mounting excitement, his eyes riveted on the stable where the sentry stood. He tried to imagine the man, weakened by pain, but ready to make a desperate attempt to escape. Ralph wished that in some way he could offer further aid, but he had his own position to safeguard. He had done all that he could. He wondered whether it would be thought that the man had escaped due to his own efforts. It was just possible that an athletic person could have swung his legs up and over the beam where, using his teeth, he might have been able to loosen the bonds around his wrists. After that, it would have been a comparatively simple matter to lower himself to the floor. Well, the die was cast, there was no going back. In any case, thought Ralph, he would be no more suspect than any other, especially since he was now nowhere near the stable. Ralph was glad that he had had little to say to the man. If he were recaptured, there was no way in which Ralph could be incriminated.

As he sat watching the stable, Ralph saw the sentry turn and listen, as if he had heard something inside. Then, pike at the ready, the man entered. The door closed behind him and, for at least a minute, nothing happened. Then the stable door opened and the prisoner emerged, wearing the helmet and uniform of the sentry and carrying his pike. Adopting the same ploy as Ralph, he strode boldly into the yard and turned into the stable next door. Ralph guessed his next move, for in the stable were horses and saddles.

Confident now that the man would make good his escape, Ralph waited expectantly for him to lead out a horse, mount and ride casually out of the courtyard. He would almost certainly go unchallenged. Then, to his horror, Ralph saw an officer and two soldiers walking purposefully across the yard. Where they were going, he could not tell. It did not appear to be towards the stable where the prisoner was supposed to be confined. However, although he had not seen them, Ralph identified one of the officers who had interrogated the prisoner by his voice and this, Ralph was certain, was the lieutenant who had assisted the captain in the interrogation. Surely he would notice the absence of the sentry. Ralph held his breath. The three men were deep in conversation, so it was just possible that the officer would not notice that there was no sentry. It also occurred to Ralph that the prisoner might choose this moment to lead his horse from the stable.

The three men continued across the yard, completely unaware of anything amiss. Then the officer looked across at the stable; just a casual glance. Ralph saw him stop abruptly, pause for a second and then, bidding the two soldiers with him to follow, he sprinted across to the stable door. Throwing it open, he strode inside. In a trice he was out again giving orders to the two men with him. One ran across to the house to raise the alarm and fetch help.

All this Ralph watched from the window of the office where he now stood in a turmoil of indecision. What could he do to help? A thousand thoughts ran through his mind. Then he leapt into action. He ran quickly along the corridor. In his head was a wild idea to tell the officer that he had seen a man ride away in unusual haste. Fortunately, he paused to think of the stupidity of such an action. Whatever would the officer think of being offered the unrequited, inconsequential information that a man had ridden hastily out of the courtyard. Ralph fancied that this might bring suspicion on himself almost as quickly as being found inside the stable.

Stopping just inside the doorway into the yard, Ralph waited and watched. The prisoner had evidently heard that his escape had been discovered. He burst forth from the stable already mounted. Tucked under his arm, like a lance, was the pike that he had taken from the sentry. With a vicious thrust, backed by the impetus of the careering horse and not a little by the hate he felt for the man who had caused him such pain, he felled the officer who was stupid enough to stand in his path. The officer died instantly from a fatal wound in his chest. The soldier who remained with him valiantly tried to seize the reins, but staggered back and fell as he sought to avoid the deadly tip of the pike.

Spurring his horse like a madman the rider clattered over the flagstones of the courtyard. Once again, Ralph thought that freedom was within his grasp. Yet again, misfortune struck. Around the side of the house came the soldier with the help for which he had been sent. In charge of the party was the captain, whom Ralph identified as the senior of the two men who had questioned the prisoner earlier that day.

As they entered the courtyard, they had only seconds to assess the scene before they were forced to scatter to avoid being run down and skewered by the pike which was being expertly wielded by the escaping prisoner. Quickly, the captain jumped aside to let the rider pass. Then, drawing his flintlock pistol from his belt, he took careful aim at the fleeing rider and squeezed the trigger.

The ball hit the man full in the back. In a convulsion of pain his body arched. The pike fell from his hand and clattered to the ground. His shoulders jerked back causing his left arm to pull at the reins. The horse reared, throwing the rider heavily to the ground.

In a moment the group of soldiers was upon him, but he was beyond further flight. Ralph, scarcely knowing what he did, ran to where the man lay surrounded by soldiers. He was still conscious. From his mouth came a trickle of blood. As Ralph joined the group he found a soldier cradling the man's head, while the captain knelt by his side.

'Tell me man. Who sent you? Who wrote that letter?' asked the captain in urgent tones.

The man regarded him with eyes that blazed hatred and contempt.

'May you rot in Hell.' The words were spat forth with such venom that the officer was visibly shaken by the loathing thus conveyed. It was clear that life was ebbing fast away. He coughed and blood flowed freely from his mouth.

'You are dying. Will you take your secret to the grave?' The tone employed by the officer was now more of a supplicant than an interrogator.

'I'll tell you nothing….' started the prisoner. His eyes caught sight of Ralph. He paused, made to speak again but, with a final convulsion, his head fell back and he lay quite still. His spirit succeeded in the flight for which his body had striven.

They carried him back to the stable to lie in peace where he had hung in pain. Ralph followed in a daze. Was he to blame? He felt that he had done all he could have. At least the man had died fighting. With a heavy heart, Ralph walked back to the quiet of his room.

CHAPTER 18

June 1645
Oxford

On the 30th May 1645, Prince Rupert laid siege to Leicester and sacked it. On 5th June, under orders from the Parliamentary Committee at Westminster, which feared the King's threat to the east of the country, Fairfax raised the siege of Oxford. With his army he marched to Newport Pagnell. His purpose was to seek out the Royalist army and bring it to battle.

Needless to say, there was great rejoicing by the citizens of Oxford when the siege ended and life was able to return to near normal. It was an especial relief to the ladies of the King's court which had stayed at Oxford. The threat of personal danger, not to mention the pinch of hunger which they had begun to feel, had brought home to them the realities of war to which they were totally unaccustomed. Among those who joined in the general rejoicing was Colonel Cressley, who by now had fairly well shaken off his recent illness. Such a turn of events was enough to banish the last gloomy thought from his mind. Soon he would be able to re-join the King and, once again, get to grips with that all important task of organising the King's intelligence service. Perhaps His Majesty would once again encourage him to actively pursue this vital task. For, without such information, the King would be like a blind man fighting for his life against one who had all his faculties.

It was four days, after the siege had been raised, before the Colonel left Oxford. The Governor prevailed upon him to remain for a while to help with the reinvestment of the city's outer defences. The Colonel did this with some reluctance, for he was impatient to be back with the army. It was, therefore, with more than a little relief when, on the 9th June, he shook the dust of Oxford from his heels and headed for the King at Leicester.

He learned from a courier, whom he met riding to Oxford with a message for the Governor, that the King had left Leicester where the Colonel had been told that he would find him. Now, the Royalist army was fortifying Borough Hill only a mile or two from the small town of Daventry. Hearing this, the Colonel rode straight away for Daventry to find the King and receive his instructions. By ill luck he missed his son, Jack, who had been sent in charge of a strong escort of soldiers guarding a wagon train of provisions to restock the depleted larders at Oxford. They must have taken a different route to the one ridden by Colonel Cressley, otherwise the two could not have failed to meet.

The Colonel had heard that the King had been distracted by disputes within the Royalist leadership. However, although he received the Colonel with great courtesy and a genuine welcome, it seemed that he was in no mood to listen to the Colonel's plans for strengthening his intelligence network; either throughout the armies of Parliament or, of even greater importance, in the city of London – the seat of the rebel government.

Although the King was not hostile to Colonel Cressley's plans, he was clearly agitated. As they spoke, a member of staff approached the King. The Colonel did not hear what was said, but the King was visibly angered by what he had been told. With growing impatience, he said to Colonel Cressley, 'I have always appreciated the intelligence which you regularly bring me. However, now I need you to urgently go and seek the information which I must have as soon as possible. Go yourself, with a patrol, seek out the enemy and find for me, if you are able, his strengths and weaknesses and what moves Fairfax is making now.'

Having Colonel Cressley's attempts to impress him with the importance of reliable information, the King dismissed him. With such specific instructions the Colonel could not argue and, therefore, withdrew to carry out the King's command. With the few men who had accompanied him from Oxford, including

Joseph Grimshaw, he found quarters for the night under canvas and made preparations to set forth early the next day. From the further detachment of men now assigned to his command, the Colonel was able to make ready a strong cavalry patrol to travel south in search of the enemy's position.

It was not far off being the longest day so it was still quite light when, the work of the day done, the Colonel sat at the entrance to his tent looking out over the rolling countryside. Northamptonshire, his own county, which he thought as fair, in its own way, as any that he had seen on his travels with the King's army. How beautiful it looked on this summer's evening. So far it had been a poor summer. The weather had been cold and wet but, tonight, the air was soft and clean after the rain. He sat for a while at peace. His own home was not far away. Perhaps tomorrow his patrol might take him in that direction.

As he sat at ease, his thoughts returned inevitably to the vexatious business of the best method for providing the King with the information which he needed. The Colonel's face twisted into a wry smile at the thought that tomorrow he was to go in search of information that was not going to be easy to obtain and yet, a year ago, it would have been available for the asking, by virtue of his well-placed agents and the time he was able to spend on the analysis of their reports. Well, what a pity, when he still had a number of men left upon whom he could rely. If it was the strength of the enemy that His Majesty wished to know, or the quality of its soldiers; if he required to know what ordnance the rebels could field, the number of their cavalry or their readiness to fight, then it would have been these men working for Colonel Cressley who could have supplied the answers. Such information would be far more accurate and detailed than any report the Colonel could provide by scouting around the countryside in a vain attempt to size up the enemy.

It had been many weeks since Colonel Cressley had been able to make contact with any of his agents. His confinement in the city of Oxford, together with his illness, had not permitted him the opportunity of obtaining and using the information that had doubtless been gathered. However, on reflection, there was one man who would be well informed about the army of General Fairfax and that was young Ralph Somers. It was not the Colonel's usual practice to communicate, himself, with his agents. They knew what sort of report the Colonel expected and so he was content to leave them to use their discretion in deciding if any other information was worth the telling. However, on this occasion, there were specific items of information which the King would need if he were to make a decision as to whether he should engage the enemy or wait for reinforcements. The Colonel decided there and then that he would write to Ralph Somers. Joseph Grimshaw could set out the next day on his own search for the Roundhead army and, specifically, the intended recipient of the Colonel's letter.

At the entrance to his tent there was enough light still for Colonel Cressley to see to put pen to paper. He called to Joseph who quickly supplied the necessary materials. Had the letter been much longer a candle would have been needed for its completion but, as the dusk deepened and the sky turned from a pale to a darker blue, the Colonel folded and sealed his letter. With a grunt of satisfaction he sat back in his chair, content to enjoy the sunset, let his mind wander and contemplate any thoughts that might enter.

Sir Francis was not left in solitude for long however. A fellow officer paused by his tent to look more closely at the figure seated at the entrance to make sure that his eyes did not deceive him.

'Why, Francis, I thought it was you. I'm glad to see that you're back again. Where have you been?'

Colonel Cressley explained that his long absence from the King's army had been due to his recent illness which, in turn, had led him to be trapped in Oxford during the siege. He invited the officer to join him in a glass of wine. Colonel Leveson, for that was the name of his visitor, was a fellow officer of whom Sir Francis had seen a great deal during the past two or three years. They had taken to one another and had often sought each other out to relax of an evening together. This evening, of all evenings, when he needed someone to cheer him, Sir Francis was especially glad to see his old friend.

'Well, Thomas, this is a pleasant surprise. I've only just arrived today. I thought that I would never see the back of Oxford, but here I am for better or for worse. How are you and what news have you? More than I have to tell, I'll warrant.'

Colonel Cressley was happy to sit and listen to his old friend recounting the events of the past two months. Events that, had it not been for his illness, he might have witnessed at first hand.

'What news have you brought the King?'

'Little enough, I'm afraid.' replied Sir Francis sadly.

Colonel Leveson shook his head thoughtfully.

'We know nothing of the enemy and his movements these days. Why, we're not even sure exactly where he is at present.'

'Somewhere to the south, I believe.' volunteered Sir Francis.

Colonel Leveson looked at Sir Francis in disbelief. This is not the way it had been a year ago. Such a question would have brought forth a guarded answer, which impressed one with the obvious fund of knowledge that the Colonel had about the enemy and left one with the distinct impression that Colonel Cressley knew a great deal more than he said. Now, however, it was apparent from the Colonel's rather vague reply that he told all he knew when he said that the enemy was 'somewhere in the south'.

'Aye, and Cromwell's bunch of fanatics somewhere to the east. Where is that detailed knowledge which you used to have of the enemy forces? When are you going to tell us, as you used to, where we may find him and in what strength?' asked Leveson urgently.

'Not as often as I used to Thomas.' The Colonel shook his head as he replied. 'The King has lost so many good officers, that he now values my services more in the field, although I still try to collect and collate intelligence when I have the time.'

'But, we cannot fight blind. 'Tis well known that Fairfax knows more from Sir Samuel Luke about our army than does the King himself.'

'I know, I know, old friend. I have the agents and, given time, I could arrange for their news to be collected and sifted through to find out what the enemy intends. His Majesty, however, has commanded that tomorrow, I must ride south, with a strong band of men, in an endeavour to discover for the King some of the information that, otherwise, would have already been in my possession.'

'What are the King's plans?' asked Sir Francis, changing the subject which he found so depressing. 'Does he intend to engage the enemy when he finds him? Have you any idea?'

'If the enemy be massing strongly he will not fight; that is, not until Goring joins us. Langdale's men are in a mutinous state. We are not fit for another major battle like Marston Moor. We must ensure that we are strong enough before we meet the enemy in such an engagement. Another disaster like Marston Moor could be the end of the King's struggle against Parliament.'

'Well, if God rides with me tomorrow, I'll have the news that His Majesty seeks,' Sir Francis spoke with great feeling.

Joseph brought a lantern as the deep blue of the sky changed slowly to a black velvet, relieved only by the brilliance of the stars with which it was strewn. For a long time the two friends sat talking. Today's war forgotten, they re-lived together the battles of yesterday.

* * *

The next morning, the 11th June, the skies were leaden and rain tumbled from the heavens in a never ending torrent. To add to the misery of the soldiers camped on Borough Hill, the weather was unseasonably cold as well as wet. Nevertheless, it was before eight o'clock when Colonel Cressley set forth at the head of his patrol travelling to the south of Daventry.

Before his departure, he had given to Joseph Grimshaw the letter he had written to Ralph Somers. It was left for Joseph to clear up after the Colonel had gone and then to leave with the letter for Ralph Somers. Colonel Cressley had impressed upon Joseph the urgency of his mission and the need to seek out Ralph Somers as soon as possible and obtain from him an early reply to the Colonel's questions.

The last reports of Fairfax's army had been that it was in the area of Newport Pagnell. Knowing that, rather than set off due south, Colonel Cressley decided that he would ride first south west and then move across to the east, hoping to cut across the track of the Roundhead army which he believed would be marching north. So the Colonel set off along the road to Charwelton; the very road that he had followed in the opposite direction the day before on the last stages of his journey from Oxford. At Charwelton he took the road that led south east.

After less than half an hour's riding from Daventry, the patrol came by a small village where Colonel Cressley asked an old man, whom they passed on their road, whether he had seen any sign of Roundhead troops. It was apparent that the old chap, as well as one or two other villagers who joined him, had seen no other soldiers than the Colonel's patrol which they now regarded with some suspicion. Their village lay slightly to the north of the road which the patrol now followed. From where the Colonel sat on his horse he could see Fawsley deer park in the valley below. Past a cottage at the side of the road and beyond the church some quarter of a mile distant, Colonel Cressley could see a neat little manor house nestling into the side of the hill. Upon learning that the village was Preston Capes, Sir Francis immediately thought of Ralph Somers. So this was his village and that was the house of which he was now master. In that house, if Ralph were to be spared ill fortune, Mary would soon become mistress. It was no match, he thought, for Hartington Hall but Mary could be happy in such a place and the Colonel prayed that it would be so.

If the reports of Parliament's forces were true and they were advancing north to seek the King's army, the Colonel had no wish to run headlong into them. He therefore sent out scouts in pairs; one pair in the direction that the patrol was heading and a pair to ride about one mile to either side. One man in each pair was to report back at regular intervals.

From Preston Capes, the Colonel proceeded roughly east along the road leading to Cold Higham, past the tiny village of Maidford. As they went, they made enquiries of the villagers for any sign of rebel soldiers but none had been seen. Near Cold

Higham they joined the ancient drover's road from Northampton known as the Banbury Lane. Less than a mile to the east they came upon the Watling Street which they followed south to Towcester. It was about midmorning when they arrived at this small town. Enquiries there met with more success. Travellers passing through the town had spoken of a large army under General Fairfax camped around Stony Stratford. The latest information suggested that it was preparing to march north.

An itinerant tinker was able to verify this news. He travelled on an old cart with the tools of his trade heaped on the back amongst a pile of pots, pans and other hardware. Pulling the cart was an old horse; as mangy and scruffy as its owner. The tinker was a sly looking fellow, who was either too fond of the clothes that he wore or too mean to part with them, although they had long outlived their useful life. He answered the Colonel's questions in ingratiating tones. It seemed at first that he had nothing to tell.

'I see little except the pots I mend, your honour. In these hard times it isn't wise for a man to see too much and far less to talk about it. May I make so bold as to show your honour some of the fine pots that I have for sale. This is an excellent iron pot. It will last you a life time. If you are seen buying something, your honour, folk will have no cause to wonder what we talk about.'

The implication was quite clear, so the Colonel paid up and acquired an iron pot of doubtful quality which he did not want. At the same time, however, he did receive news first hand of the rebel army from the lips of one who had been amongst them the day before.

As they rode along, Colonel Cressley marvelled at the straightness of this ancient highway. He had used it several times before, but he never ceased to wonder at the skill of its builders. He remembered that it was centuries old; built by the Romans who had lived in Britain, heaven knows how many years ago. He had heard that they were a very martial race of people who had conquered the native Britons. He tried to imagine them riding, or marching, along that long straight road, just as he and his patrol were riding today and he reflected how little times had changed. Apart from the pistols that he and some of his men carried in their belts, the Colonel doubted that their arms were very different. He remembered hearing that they threw javelin and used shields for protection, but they also carried swords.

His thoughts were interrupted by the hasty return of one of his scouts. The patrol had just passed Paulerspury and now they approached Whittlebury forest. On either side trees were more in evidence, although they had not yet come to the thickest part of the forest which was some three or more miles ahead.

'There's a body of men with wagons and heavy artillery about a mile ahead, sir.' reported the scout. 'They are moving north towards us. We think that they must be part of the rebel army that is said to be coming this way. There are about fifty men, sir.'

Immediately, Colonel Cressley looked about him for a good place to set an ambush. He called his four officers to him. To Captain Richards he gave some ten horsemen with instructions to make a wide circle to the east and come up behind the enemy. If they were accompanying wagons, the Captain would have ample time to complete this manoeuvre. With the remainder of his force, he concealed himself just below the crest of the small hill which they were approaching, beyond which the scout had reported sighting the enemy. Captain Richards had instructions not to attack the enemy's rear until he saw that the van had been engaged by Colonel Cressley.

The Colonel decided to adopt the same demoralising tactics chosen by Cromwell at Bletchingdon House, although he realised that he didn't have the advantage of such superior numbers. Nevertheless, he did have the advantage of surprise. He divided the men who remained with him into two. He took command of one half himself, setting a lieutenant in command of the other half, with instructions not to attack until both the Colonel and Captain Richards were well engaged.

The bulk of the forest lay away to the south and the west. The trees were scattered in a sort of parkland, with clumps of trees and bushes here and there, big enough to conceal Colonel

Cressley and his men. For a quarter of an hour they waited. The men were tense with the nervous excitement which comes with the expectation of battle. The wondering about what lies in store, the tightness in the stomach, the dryness in the throat; all served to heighten the tension felt by that band of Royalists waiting in eager anticipation. They sat astride their horses, some in concealment behind the cover just below the crest of the hill, others some twenty yards distance behind. Their horses snorted, pawed the ground and tossed their heads aware, as it seemed like their riders, of the action that lay ahead.

After what seemed an eternity to those waiting men, there came the first sound of the approaching troops. From a vantage point, the Colonel could see that it was a wagon train guarded by a small force of infantry. In the train were at least two pieces of ordnance. It was these two heavy guns, more than the wagons, which accounted for the slow progress of the troop. A team of four horses hauled each gun, while men with thick staffs of wood strove to lever it free from the mud into which it now and then sank. It was hard work for both men and horses. The recent rain, which had now eased to a slow drizzle, had so softened the ground that, had it not been for the solid foundation laid so many years before, the guns might have sunk irretrievably into the mire. As for the wagons, which were also heavily laden, the Colonel could only guess that these contained food and other supplies. The soldiers plodded on in silence, doubtless depressed by the soaking from the weather and the slow tedious progress. Every now and then, they must halt to allow the wagons and artillery to keep pace with them.

The Colonel let them approach unmolested until they were within thirty paces of where he lay hidden. Then, with a flourish of his sword, he gave the signal for the first group of horsemen to attack. The officer in charge of the troops guarding the wagon train, who was the only mounted soldier, had no time to order his men into any sort of defensive posture. He scarce had time to draw his sword before Colonel Cressley was upon him. Deftly avoiding the wild scything blow which the officer aimed at him, the Colonel thrust his sword neatly below the man's corselet and turned him in his saddle as the impetus of his charge took him past. Dragging his sword from his vitals he watched him fall heavily to the ground.

The pike-men guarding the wagons were better placed to resist the charge. They could seek cover from the charging horsemen behind the wagons and from there they could wield their long pikes. Colonel Cressley caught a glimpse of one of his men being thrust from his mount by this effective weapon. With a swing of his sword the Colonel turned aside the pike now being thrust viciously at his chest. The frightened man was not quick enough to dodge the flashing blade that slashed across the side of his head. He fell screaming to the ground.

The noise of battle was now loud around him and the Colonel saw with satisfaction that Captain Richards had engaged the rear of the train, benefiting also from complete surprise. A Roundhead musketeer ahead of the Colonel had, by now, found time to light his match and was taking aim at one of the horsemen who was engaged in defending himself against the effort of a pike-man. Drawing one of his pistols, the Colonel aimed at the musketeer. The ball hit him just as he pulled the trigger to set match to powder. The musket fell from his grasp as he slumped forward. As the weapon fell from its rest, it discharged itself harmlessly into the sky.

Now the third line of attack could be seen bearing down on the melee. Colonel Cressley saw that some of the rebel soldiers were throwing down their weapons and asking for quarter, but others fought on and died bravely where they stood. Within ten minutes of the first charge, the action was over and the Royalists were herding up between twenty and thirty prisoners. They were also counting their own dead and wounded which, fortunately, amounted to only four dead and only four more with serious wounds. It had been a very short and very bloody battle.

Colonel Cressley called for a length of rope which he fashioned in a hangman's noose. This was thrown over a stout branch of a tree and fastened to a wagon. Then, turning to the prisoners, he said.

'I have some questions and you have the answers. Either you talk or you hang.'

To his sergeant at arms he gave instructions for each man to be brought before him separately. To each man he addressed the same questions. Where have you come from? Who do you serve? Where are you going? Where is the rest of the army?

There were none who wished to try the Colonel's alternative to talking, although there were those who tried to mislead the Colonel with false information. A well placed thump with the butt of a musket prompted a more acceptable reply. Finally, by a consensus of answers thus obtained, the Colonel was able to deduce a great deal about the enemy's strength and their direction of march. All of this intelligence he committed to paper and entrusted the letter to an officer who served as an aide to the King. In this letter he also informed the King of his intention to use the information, thus gained of the enemy's whereabouts, to try to confirm the actual position of the main rebel force and the direction in which they marched.

While Colonel Cressley wrote his letter, the officers in his patrol attended to his orders in respect of the wagons, the prisoners and the wounded. One wagon was emptied to carry four of his men who had been wounded so badly that they were unable to walk. They also packed some of the more useful supplies that they found. The other two wagons were emptied and their contents examined. Such items that were less useful and would be a burden to carry were destroyed. One of the wagons was then free to carry the two seriously wounded soldiers from the Roundhead force. Apart from sufficient horses to pull the wagons, the rest were driven away. The Roundheads were disarmed and their weapons loaded into the wagon carrying the Royalist wounded. The two big guns were spiked with nails and the wheels removed and broken. Then, as the Royalist patrol prepared to continue on its way the uninjured prisoners, and those with only minor injuries, were released to make whatever progress they could to wherever they wished to go.

The Colonel led his patrol on along the Watling Street. By now it was late in the afternoon. He decided to make a cautious approach towards Stony Stratford to see whether the

Roundhead army had camped there or if they had now departed. Carefully he encircled the town to the west. He sent out scouts to ensure that he would not be surprised by any contingents of the army moving north. It soon became apparent that the Roundhead forces had gone and the town once again left to its inhabitants. It was now within an hour or so of dusk. Riding to the west a little to ensure that he would be away from the likely route of any further Roundhead movements, he followed the practice of so many patrolling bands during this war and sought accommodation for the night in a largish house in the first village that he came to. Here, he and his men forced themselves on an unwilling host. Perhaps in remembrance of that patrol which had visited his own house, as he had heard, or possibly because it was not in the Colonel's nature to do otherwise, he gave his men strict orders to behave correctly. Whilst they sought shelter in the stables, he and his officers troubled his host for beds in the house.

The owner of the house was an elderly man living with his wife and a few servants. After initial protests he recognised that the Colonel was acting out of necessity and not without some courtesy and restraint, so he decided that it were best if he acceded to the visitors' modest requests. Indeed, with the food purloined from the Roundhead wagon train, there was little need for the old man to provide much more than a roof over their heads for the night. When he realised that there would be little hurt to his person, his pocket or his property, he entertained the Colonel and his officers with considerable good will.

The Colonel and his men were up and away early the next morning, giving their host scarce time to dress and bid them farewell. Colonel Cressley was almost a happy man as he rode along at the head of his patrol. With yesterday's success behind him, he now found himself riding through that part of England which he loved best. This was almost home territory and he knew it well.

Retracing their steps somewhat, the patrol turned east. As they crossed the Northampton road from Stony Stratford, they found that whatever surface there had been on the road before was now churned up into a sea of mud; evidence clearly of the passage of a large body of men, horses and equipment. It seemed clear to the Colonel that this was the route chosen by the bulk of the rebel army. However, to ensure that no part of that force had headed north east, he led his patrol towards Castlethorpe; riding across the flat pasture land of the Tove valley. They crossed the river by the mill and climbed the gentle hill to the village. None in the village had seen any part of the rebel army pass in their direction. Deeming it prudent to avoid the route chosen by the rebels, Colonel Cressley led his patrol roughly north west and parallel to the Northampton road, but on the other side of the shallow Tove valley. Finally, they reached the small village of Ashton. Here the folk were full of talk of the endless procession of soldiers that had passed, to the west of their village on the Northampton road, only the day before. It seemed certain that the whole of Fairfax's army had marched by that route. The villagers, many of whom had walked the mile or so to watch, described men on horseback, soldiers with muskets, others with pikes, wagons drawn by teams of horses and other horses hauling great guns. The Colonel led his patrol back to the Northampton road where he saw that the lanes had been churned into great swathes of mud.

With orders now for his scouts to keep a sharp look out both in the van and in the rear, Colonel Cressley moved his patrol north along the road in the direction of Northampton. They had progressed barely a mile, nearing the village of Roade, when one of the scouts, detailed to watch the road behind them, gave warning of a body of horsemen following the road which the Royalist patrol now travelled and were likely soon to overtake them.

There was little time to lose. The scout had reported the approaching cavalry to be some thirty in number. Once again the Colonel divided his men into three equal groups. One he sent to take cover along a lane off to the left that led to Blisworth. The second group was to ride on some hundred paces where they would be out of sight, while he waited with the remainder of his men concealed amongst the trees that bordered the road at that point. The orders were for the three groups to attack in succession; the Colonel first, the group in the side lane second and, finally, the group that had ridden ahead.

Unlike yesterday, they had not long to wait. This was not a slow moving wagon train but a group of mobile, well-armed cavalry. They would not be such easy meat. However, the Colonel had surprise again on his side and some advantage in numbers. Waiting until the troop of horsemen had almost passed by where the Colonel and his men lay hidden, the Colonel led his men to attack them from the side and slightly from the rear. Few had time to turn their mounts before the Royalists were upon them. Scarcely had the rebel commander rallied his men to meet this threat from behind and to his right, than the second group of Colonel Cressley's patrol crashed into the Roundheads on their left. Now they were forced to meet an enemy from both sides. The attention of the whole group was therefore directed to protecting their flanks and rear. Riders in the van turned to give assistance to their comrades behind them in the middle of their troop. So, yet again, they were facing the wrong way when they were assaulted in the van by Colonel Cressley's third group.

Within minutes the Royalists had the upper hand. In the midst of the fighting Colonel Cressley sustained a stinging sword cut across his left forearm. The blood spurted and, at the same time, his mount reared. Unable to retain his seat, he was thrown to the ground. Fortunately the soft mud saved him from any great harm. Sword still in his hand, he scrambled to his feet. The blood was flowing freely from his wound. His horse bolted. Standing vulnerably amongst bucking and rearing horses, ridden by friend and foe, the Colonel sought refuge at the side of the road, there to stem the bleeding in his arm with a rough bandage before re-joining the fight. As he scrambled clear of the flailing hooves, he caught his foot in the branch of a fallen tree. A sharp pain shot through his leg as his foot, unable to turn, caused his knee to be twisted. He fell heavily, his foot held fast where it had been caught. He lay winded and in pain, unable to free himself, blood pouring from his wound. He heard the final shout of victory from his men, as the last few men of the Roundhead patrol turned and fled for their lives. A passing horse caught him a glancing blow on his head with its hoof as it rushed by, mercifully rendering the Colonel unconscious.

* * *

He came to, to find himself lying on his coat not far from where he had fallen. His men were standing or sitting nearby, some anxiously looking in his direction. Captain Richards was bending over him as he bound his wound tightly to staunch the flow of blood.

'Lie still sir, I beg you. Do not try to move for a moment. You have lost much blood. I must stop the bleeding.'

Captain Richards regarded him with some concern as he tightened the bandage around his arm.

'The enemy, Captain? What of the enemy?' asked the Colonel weakly.

'Routed sir. Many killed, surprisingly hardly any wounded and the rest fled.'

'And our own men?

'Seven dead, I'm afraid sir, and several wounded, but only one or two seriously,' replied the Captain gravely.

'Have all the wounded put into our wagon with the wounded of yesterday. We had better take the worst of the rebel wounded as well. We cannot leave them here to die by the roadside.'

'I will attend to it immediately.'

'My horse' Colonel Cressley looked around anxiously. 'He bolted.'

'He didn't go far sir. See, he's over there quietly grazing. Can you mount sir, if we bring him over to you? I think we should move away from here. A stronger force may pass this way soon.'

The Colonel nodded his agreement. He tried to stand.

With a cry of pain, he was forced to cling to the Captain for support. Rolling up the leg of his breeches, he was dismayed to see that his knee was swollen and discoloured. He looked around at the rest of the patrol. Many were nursing minor wounds while one or two others, more badly wounded, were being loaded into the wagon. Plainly, his men were not fit to ride much further and yet, to stay here on this highway, so much in use by the Roundhead army, would be courting disaster. The solution was obvious and had been in the Colonel's mind even before the recent skirmish. They were less than three miles from Hartington Hall. There, they would find food and shelter and a place to lick their wounds until they were ready to ride again. He told the Captain of his plan and gave him directions. Gently, the Colonel was lifted into his saddle and was supported, as he rode, by two horsemen on either side. Leaving the scene of their most recent bloody, but victorious encounter the patrol made its way to Hartington Hall, leaving the dead for the country folk to bury.

It was a sorry party that entered the courtyard of Hartington Hall and it was a strange homecoming for Colonel Cressley. Half fainting and dizzy from loss of blood, he was lifted from his horse. Having given instructions to Captain Richards to ensure the welfare of his men, the Colonel allowed himself to be carried upstairs guided by the surprised and anxious Alfred who was much upset to see his master in such a sorry state. In bed, he gave way to the waves of exhaustion which swept through his body and, in spite of his wounds, soon fell into a deep sleep.

The next morning Colonel Cressley was awoken when his Captain peered around the door to see if he still slept. He was anxious to receive the Colonel's orders. Startled at having overslept, Colonel Cressley tried to get out of bed but his knee, now the size of a balloon, would not bend without much pain and would certainly not bear his weight.

'Sir, you cannot ride today in this state. You must rest to give the swelling in your knee a chance to heal.'

Captain Richards was anxious, not only for the Colonel, but also for himself and those of the patrol who were uninjured and ready to ride. In this state the Colonel would be a liability to his men.

'Yes, damn it, you're right.' he agreed, with profound annoyance at the realisation that he had little choice but to do as the Captain suggested. Quickly accepting the inevitable, his mind turned to the arrangements that must be made.

'What is the state of the men?'

'There are fifteen who are fit to ride. I sent one man yesterday, after we arrived, to inform His Majesty of our situation and convey to him what news we had of the enemy. Six of our men are not fit to leave, but they should be ready to ride again within a few days if their wounds do not poison. Two men died through the night and I fear that three more will take much longer to recover. There are but two of the enemy who are badly wounded, but likely to live.'

'Tis no worse than I expected. Battles cannot be fought without casualties, more's the pity. You had better take the patrol back to re-join the King at Daventry. If a battle is to be fought, he will need all the men he can find. I doubt that he will seek to fight until he is joined by Goring, but his hand may be forced. Since needs must, I will remain here with the wounded and re-join His Majesty as soon as I may. Pray, present my compliments to His Majesty and beg him to excuse my absence until I am able to ride once again.'

So it was arranged. Later that morning Captain Richards rode off at the head of the victorious, if somewhat depleted patrol. Hearing the column ride away, the Colonel reflected that they had achieved something for the King during the past two days. They had been able to report the whereabouts and size of the enemy forces. They had also caused the death of a few Roundhead soldiers and the destruction of some of their supplies. He felt a great deal of impatience about his wounded knee which, he guessed, would be several days in the mending. The wound in his arm throbbed damnably but it was a clean cut and doubtless would soon heal.

Colonel Cressley was forced to admit to himself that it was certainly some compensation, if one had to be wounded, to be wounded on his own doorstep. Then it occurred to him that he could see Mary. The thought cheered him greatly. Calling for Alfred, he asked for a message to be sent to Bullshead Farm, telling Mary of her father's presence at Hartington Hall and asking her to visit him.

CHAPTER 19

June 1645
Cosgrove, South Northamptonshire

Two days before, while Colonel Cressley was skirmishing among the oaks of Whittlebury Forest, Ralph was one of the multitude of Fairfax's army which struggled north through the rain and the mud from their camp at Cosgrove, just to the north of Stony Stratford. However, more fortunate than the infantry men, Ralph rode horseback and yet, unconstrained like the cavalrymen who must ride in column, he was able to ride as he pleased.

Having arrived at Cosgrove only two days earlier, Ralph had scarcely had time to realise that it was not many miles to Bullshead farm and to Mary. In any case, until today, he had been fully taken up with his army duties. Now, however, under orders simply to march north with the army, General Fairfax himself would not have prevented Ralph from calling at his uncle's house.

The weather was miserable, but Ralph cared nought for the rain as he left the main body of the army plodding northwards and rode north east. After some five or six miles, he entered the sombre confines of Salcey Forest. The trees, dark and forbidding on that grey day, moved little in the lethargic breeze but dripped noisily, disturbing the silence of that dank woodland, as Ralph rode on his lonely way.

His uncle's house seemed to have shrunk into the forest for shelter against the incessant rain. Ralph slid from his saddle and stood before the door, dripping wet. The door was soon opened in response to his knocking and, within seconds, he found himself in front of a glowing fire in the kitchen hearth. Mary was soon by his side. She was breathless with surprise and joy as she took his sodden cloak and hung it by the fire to dry. Uncle

Charles was away on business in Northampton and, with him, he had taken Hugh but Aunt Maria was there, pleased as always, to see her nephew. Having stayed to welcome him and provide him with food and drink, she withdrew to leave the young couple together.

'How are you, my darling Mary?' asked Ralph, holding her by both hands and surveying her at arm's length.

'Happier, now that you have come.' She declared with a smile; such a smile.

Once again, Ralph hugged her to him and smothered her with kisses. Then they sat down together happily chatting.

'You have arrived only just in time to catch me here,' said Mary.

Ralph looked at her in surprise.

'Why, where are you going?'

'Your Aunt has a sister in Oundle who is ill. Both her son and her husband have been away fighting in this wretched war for Parliament. First her husband was killed and now her son as well. You can imagine what misery she must be suffering. Aunt Maria has said that she must go to help and I have offered to go with her. The two of us leave early tomorrow.

'Poor woman!' It was all that Ralph could think to say, but it was heartfelt and sincere. Enemies her menfolk may have been but, before all else, they were human beings.

'Well then, it was a lucky chance that I called today. Will you be gone long do you think?'

'For two or three weeks, I suppose.'

'Are you happy here?'

'Only one thing could make me happier and that is to have you by my side. Your aunt and uncle have been wonderful. They treat me just like one of the family. We get on famously. I think that Hugh likes me as well, but he's far too proud to admit it. I really am so happy here that those days at Hartington Hall seem like a bad dream.'

'I'm truly glad to hear it. It helps me to know that you are among friends, cared for and with someone to share your worries.' Ralph smiled happily. He was indeed glad to know that she was safe in this secluded spot which the war seemed to have passed by. At Hartington Hall, alone in a county predominantly for Parliament, she may not remain safe for much longer.

They walked arm in arm into the drawing room. Now that Ralph's clothes were dry, it was too warm to sit in front of a fire.

'What brings you here?' asked Mary.

'The Roundhead army is moving north in pursuit of the King. We were passing so near, that I just had to call on you. I doubt that I'll be missed if I do not stay too long. Just four or five miles to the west a whole army is marching by. Thank goodness that this place is well away from its path, though I doubt that they would have the time to do more than scavenge for food.'

'How much longer must you play this risky game? My father asks too much of you.'

'Yes, perhaps, I like it not; you may be sure, but I serve the King better this way than as a soldier. I hate most the double dealing. I am a traitor to the men that I call friends but, for all that, I am loyal to the King. Many soldiers in the armies of Parliament, are mostly decent men embroiled, often unwillingly, in this ghastly war. Surely it must all end soon. As for your father; he has a job to do and must use what people he can.'

'Talking of your father,' continued Ralph, 'I should have heard from him by now. During the siege of Oxford, he had difficulty in getting his agents through the rebel lines. Now the siege is lifted, I expect that he will contact me ere long. If I do not hear soon, I shall have to try to get word to him myself. The Roundhead army is, I believe, seeking to bring the King to battle. The King should know of this and know also its strength, before he decides whether or not to meet its challenge.'

Ralph paused to consider how he could communicate with the Colonel, if the Colonel could not seek him out in the usual way. But, this was a problem for another time. There were better things to think about now. They had so much to say to each other that, inevitably, Ralph spent far longer with Mary than he had intended. He was not obliged to ride with any column, but he was expected to report within a certain hour and he had no idea where he would find his captain.

'I must leave dearest. If I do not, it will be dark ere I find where my comrades have camped for the night and my captain will want to know the reason for my absence.'

'Oh Ralph, I fear for you so when I think of what danger you run.' Mary's eyes reflected the anxiety her words expressed.

'You mustn't worry dearest. All will turn out well. Just you wait and see.'

The words were reassuring, as was the manner in which he put his arm around her shoulder, but he did not feel the reassurance that he attempted to give. The war seemed endless and danger seemed always to lurk unseen, waiting to catch him out, perhaps when he least expected it. He did not fear death, but he desperately wanted to live and to live with Mary as her husband. She nestled into the protective comfort of his strong arms and rested her head on his chest underneath his chin.

'Dearest Ralph, when will this awful fighting end?'

'Soon, my darling, soon and when it does, God willing, I shall be back to claim you for my own. You will marry me, will you not? I love you dearly, but surely you must know that by now.'

'Of course I'll marry you, because I love you and have done so since the day I first saw you.'

The bargain was sealed with a kiss and an embrace which told more than words can say. For a while longer they sat together, but the minutes flew by and Ralph knew that he must leave. Tearing himself away from the woman he loved best in the whole world, he bid farewell to her and to his aunt. Then, with great reluctance, he left the house and set off to re-join the army on its northward march.

He found his company where they had halted for the night, with the greater part of General Fairfax's army, near the village of Wootton, some three miles south of Northampton. That night, Ralph, in common with the great multitude of the army, slept rough. He managed to find shelter under the cover of a wagon and, in doing so, faired a great deal better than many of the common soldiers.

The next day, Fairfax's army moved only a few miles. The Royalist army was, apparently, strongly entrenched on Borough Hill just outside Daventry. Ralph was, by now, desperately anxious to inform the Royalist command of the enemy's position and strength and to find out why he had not heard from Colonel Cressley.

Skirting to the south west of Northampton, General Fairfax lead his army towards the position held by the Royalists. Passing by Hunsbury Hill and the old, so called, 'Danes' Camp', they followed the south bank of the River Nene until they came to the village of Kislingbury, where it was decided that they should make camp.

More fortunate than on the previous night, Ralph was found quarters in a small cottage. Here, he was soon hard at work accounting for supplies arriving by wagon. With his captain, he was busy until well into the afternoon, compiling lists and checking the availability of equipment needed for the expected battle. They had almost completed their task when the captain gave Ralph an order for further supplies and instructed him to take it to a Colonel Scotford, the officer commanding the regiment, to be signed. The headquarters, where the Colonel was to be found, had been set up in a rather large building constructed, like many others, of the ruddy brown Northamptonshire sandstone and covered by a thatched roof.

Having had the orders signed by Colonel Scotford, Ralph was about to leave when he was almost bowled over by an officer who was obviously in a great hurry and expected to be yielded right of way. Just managing to keep his balance, Ralph was about to apologise when the officer rounded on him in the most officious manner.

'Out of my way, fellow. What are you doing skulking in doorways? What is your business here?'

'I was not skulking, sir. and my business was with Colonel Scotford.' Ralph replied evenly, not wishing to give any provocation but, at the same time, determined not to be intimidated. The officer eyed him distastefully and then his expression changed.

'But, wait, I know you. I crossed swords with you two years and more ago. Aye, sir, and you had the better of me on that occasion. What are you doing here? Are you a turncoat?' he asked with a sneer, 'Or are you a spy?'

Ralph's heart began to thump. When he had first seen the man's face he had thought it somewhat familiar. Now he remembered. This was the officer then Lieutenant Burns, with whom he had fought during the attack on Wormleighton Manor, as the officer had remembered, the evening before the battle of Edgehill. Bringing all his powers of dissimulation into play, he answered in a voice which surprised him with its even tones, although, as he spoke, his heart was pounding so violently that he thought it would leap out of place.

'You must be mistaken sir. I am but a clerk to the Wagon Master. I do not believe that we have ever met before.'

'I never forget a face; especially one belonging to a man with whom I have a score to settle. Come man, admit it. You were with Rupert's men before Edgehill. I was held prisoner three months ere I could free myself and you're the man I have to thank for it.'

'Not I, sir. I must have a double.' Ralph tried to make a joke of it. Fortunately, it was the Colonel who came to the rescue.

'What, Snaith, will you prattle all day in the doorway? You have my orders. See that they are carried out.'

For a moment Ralph thought that the Captain, now promoted from lieutenant when they had last met, would appeal to the Colonel and accuse Ralph in front of him. However, Ralph must have sown the seeds of doubt in his mind for he contented himself with a muttered remark and a scowl.

'I never forget a face.' he declared, angrily staring at Ralph, before he turned sharply away and left.

The incident caused Ralph some anxiety as he mulled it over in his mind. Plainly the man had recognised him and was certain of it, but he could prove nothing and would probably be forced to the conclusion that it was, as Ralph had suggested, a case of mistaken identity. The thought which gave him most consolation was that, in all probability, they would never meet again.

Having obtained the Colonel's signature on the documents for his captain, he was about to leave when the Colonel bade him wait while he wrote a message that Ralph was to take to an officer billeted a mile or two distant. As Ralph waited, two captains entered to receive their instructions. These were given and, as they were about to leave, the Colonel said,

'Test well their defences. Remember, we are ordered to bring them to battle. General Cromwell will arrive soon with his 'Ironsides' and, God willing, then we shall attack.

His face impassive, Ralph heard the news with an excitement that was betrayed, perhaps, by his eyes alone. Here was intelligence that must be taken to the King. The only problem was how to do so. Taking the message, which the Colonel handed him, he left the cottage in which the headquarters had been established to return to his captain with the documents which he awaited. There he requested leave of absence to deliver the message given him by the Colonel. This was readily given, leaving Ralph free to depart on horseback. His errand took him to the small village of Nether Heyford, some two or three miles west of Kislingbury. As he rode he wondered how best the vital information he had come by could be transmitted to the Royalist camp.

At a small cottage, just beyond Nether Heyford, he found the encampment of a small outpost of Roundhead forces. Here he delivered his message and, since there was no reply, he was, for a while, a free man. Now astride his horse, almost his own master and within six miles of the King's army he wondered what his next move should be. There were still four or five hours of daylight left. He could easily ride to Daventry and be back before nightfall. So he made up his mind. He turned his horse towards Flore. From here it was but ten minutes ride to Weedon where he crossed the Watling Street and followed the road towards Daventry.

As he went Ralph kept his eyes and ears well open for what might be ahead of him. He was anxious not to run into patrols from either army, but rather he wished to deliver himself to the troops guarding the outer defences of Borough Hill without incident. When he came nearer, he could see some of the fortifications thrown up by the defenders. Since he had no desire to be hit by a musket ball, fired by a sentry who might think that he was trying to pass unobserved, Ralph chose to ride over open ground. He hoped that, if he rode where his approach could be seen and where it could be noted that he was unarmed, he would be merely challenged.

As he rode forward he became tense with anticipation. Surely he must soon be challenged or, perhaps, if the sentries were a little on edge they might shoot first. Ralph doubted this and hoped that, since his approached was unhurried and in clear view, a challenge was more likely.

Suddenly, emerging from the cover of some bushes, which lay twenty paces ahead, four men appeared standing in his path. One levelled a musket at him while another, sword in hand, called upon him to dismount. This he did. A quick search revealed that he carried no weapons and the manner of his coming assured them that he was not overtly hostile. Nevertheless, they still regarded him with suspicion.

'What brings you here?' demanded the Ensign in charge of the small picket.

'I have urgent information for Colonel Cressley. It is a message of great importance.' Ralph tried to impress them with the need for urgent action.

'Yes, well, perhaps you have and perhaps you haven't. What is this message of such great importance?'

'That is for Colonel Cressley to hear and not for you.'

The man considered this for a moment and then, turning to the others, declared.

'I'd best let the lieutenant sort this one out. Saunders, you and Griffiths stay here until I return. Keep a good watch while I'm gone. Alderson, Lindsay, come with me to escort this man to our lieutenant'

They were now at the foot of Borough Hill. With the three soldiers keeping a close watch on Ralph, they began the climb up the grassy slopes. As they went, they passed through the several fortifications raised by the Royalists who occupied the Hill in large numbers. They had taken advantage of every natural form of protection and, where these did not exist, they had thrown up earth works and ramparts. Not far from the broad summit, they came upon a tent pitched on a relatively level piece of ground. The Ensign ordered Ralph and the soldiers to wait outside.

'Wait here with him. I'll go and see the lieutenant.'

A minute or two later, Ralph was motioned to enter. He found himself in the company of a rather officious young man.

'Now fellow, state your business and I trust that, for your sake, you are not wasting our time.' As he spoke, he gave Ralph scarce a glance.

'My business, sir, is not with you but with Colonel Cressley.' replied Ralph with growing impatience.

'What business have you with Colonel Cressley that makes you think he will see you?' asked the officer with little attempt to disguise the disinterest with which he viewed Ralph's visit.

'The business, I repeat sir, is none of yours but with Colonel Cressley who will see me because he is my father in law.' replied Ralph angrily, feeling that such a statement, whilst not yet true, would produce the desired effect.

The young officer's attitude changed immediately.

'Your pardon, sir. Had you told me sooner I would, of course, not have hindered you. Pray take a chair.' He motioned Ralph to a seat. Then to the Ensign

'Tell Alderson and Lindsay to return to their posts and then go yourself to find Colonel Cressley. Present my compliments to the Colonel and inform him that his son in law awaits him in my tent.'

The man gone, Ralph was left to wait in the presence of the somewhat discomfited young lieutenant who tried unsuccessfully to make conversation.

'Is it long since you saw your father in law?'

'Long enough.'

'Have you ridden far today?'

'Less than a dozen miles.'

So the conversation continued; the young man trying to ingratiate himself with a relative of the Colonel, while Ralph refused to encourage a man to whom he had taken a dislike.

They were rescued from this predicament by the entry of another officer. Ralph glanced at the man as he entered and, taking a second look, could scarce believe his eyes.

'Jack.' He cried and leapt up from his seat to grasp him by the hand.

'Why, by all that's wonderful, it's Ralph Somers. Whatever are you doing here?'

They shook hands warmly, each overcome by the surprise of seeing the other. Although, as Ralph reflected later, why should he not have met Jack with the Royalist forces? How much did Jack know about his work for Sir Francis?

'It's your father whom I came here to see.' explained Ralph. Then, anxiously looking at Jack, he asked, 'Your father has told you how I serve him?'

'Yes and no. He tells me little about his work and I needs must add two and two together to make ten. So, what he has not told me, I have guessed.'

'Can I see him now? It is a matter of great urgency.'

'I fear that you cannot, for he is not here. I am told that he left some three days ago at the head of a patrol. He had orders from His Majesty to carry out a reconnaissance to determine the enemy's position and his strength. Like you, I am anxious to see my father but for a different reason. We have not met for over two months. He has arrived recently from Oxford, where he was confined during the siege. While he rode here to join the King, I rode on escort duty in the opposite direction towards Oxford. I cannot imagine how it came about that we did not meet, but somehow we missed each other.'

Ralph's face registered disappointment at not being able to communicate his information directly to Colonel Cressley. However, he realised that there were others who would be glad to hear his news.

'I bring information that should reach the ears of the King and his staff officers as soon as possible. Is there somewhere we may talk?' Ralph glanced at the young lieutenant who was listening to their conversation with ill-concealed interest.

'Come with me.' Jack led Ralph out of the tent and further up the hill. Out in the open they could speak freely.

'Where have you come from today?' asked Jack.

'I have ridden over from Kislingbury, where General Fairfax's army is camped.'

Jack regarded him with a look of surprise mixed with admiration.

'You have ridden here; just like that. How do you propose to return? You run a very great risk.'

'The information was worth the risk. I had expected to hear, before now, from the ubiquitous Joseph Grimshaw but he has not put in an appearance for some time now. It must be seven or eight weeks since I saw him last. How fares he, do you know?'

I know little of his activities, save that he serves my father. I believe that he was here in camp until recently. Certainly, I haven't seen him today, or yesterday, as far as I can remember. But what is this news that you bring? Can you tell me?'

'The news is that the rebel armies are assembling in strength, under orders to bring the King's army to battle. They intend to do this as soon as possible after the arrival of General Cromwell and his Ironsides, who are expected this evening.'

'My God, that is news indeed and must be taken directly to the right quarters.'

Jack led Ralph through groups of men, passed pieces of ordnance, to a large tent near the top of the broad hill. This appeared to be some sort of command post. There they found Colonel Leveson who was the senior officer on duty at the time. He received Ralph with great courtesy. He listened to his report, asked him a number of questions to clarify the Roundheads strength and readiness for battle and thanked him for taking such risks to bring his news to the Royalist command.

'What will you do now?' asked Colonel Leveson.

'Go back to my post with General Fairfax's army at Kislingbury.'

'You won't know that Colonel Cressley is not as free as he used to be to collect intelligence for our generals. He has not been forbidden to do so, but he is given little time and encouragement. The King is short of such capable officers and wishes to use Sir Francis for many other tasks, where he has talents above and beyond so many other officers. I believe that His Majesty is ill advised in this by those around him who do not properly understand the value of the service that Sir Francis has rendered. It's a misfortune to our cause that there is so much jealousy and discord amongst the King's advisers. Colonel Cressley feels strongly that the King is wasting this most useful asset and indeed, on this occasion, he could have had from you the information that he seeks at this very moment. I agree with him and wish that he had a freer hand in this matter.'

'I'm sorry to hear that, sir, for I feel that my efforts haven't been entirely useless. However, until I am specifically commanded to relinquish my duties, I must continue as ordered. Please tell Sir Francis, on his return, that I await his instructions.'

There was a pause, during which Ralph wondered if Colonel Leveson might have further to say, but plainly he felt that he had probably said too much and there was no purpose to be served in making Ralph feel that the perilous work he did was not appreciated.

'Well, sir, with your permission I will withdraw and ride back to Kislingbury.'

'Yes, of course. My thanks, once again, for the news that you have brought. I shall ensure that it is swiftly conveyed to those best able to use it. I am sure that, very soon, wiser counsels will prevail with the King and that, once again, your reports and those of the Colonel's other agents will receive the consideration that they deserve. Captain Cressley will see you back through the picket lines and safely on your way.'

With that Ralph and Jack left the Colonel's tent. They had scarcely walked a dozen paces when they heard someone behind them calling Jack.

'There you are Jack. You were going to meet me after duty. Where did you get to?

The speaker was a young man in his early twenties, finely dressed and wearing a ruddy complexion to match the colour of his tunic.

'Thomas! Oh do forgive me; I quite forgot. I'm sorry. Never mind; you've found me now. My mind has been on other matters for the past half hour.' Jack saw that the young man was looking questioningly at Ralph.

'By the way, let me introduce you to a very good friend of mine. He serves my father and the King's cause. Thomas, this is Master Ralph Somers. Ralph, this is my cousin, Master Thomas Cressley.'

The two men bowed and shook hands as they expressed their mutual pleasure at making the other's acquaintance. Thomas was a complete extrovert; a good natured, gay, pleasure loving young man with an eye for a good woman, a good wine and a good time. For all that, when the need arose, he was able to acquit himself with considerable courage and competence on the field of battle. Jack and he had, more than once, owed each other their lives when they had fought side by side.

'Well, come on both of you, back to my tent. I can't offer you an exciting evening, but I do have a bottle of wine or two that we can share.'

'Sorry, Thomas, but Ralph is not staying and I must escort him through our defences.'

'Not staying, but where is there to go?' Thomas asked in amazement, as if they had just entered a tavern and Jack proposed to leave as the drinks were being poured out.

'You can say that Ralph is on special duties.'

'Well, if you say so. Can I escort him with you? Or are his duties too special for prying eyes like mine?' Thomas surveyed them both with an infectious grin.

'Oh, come on then and stop acting the fool.' replied Jack grabbing his arm.

The three of them returned down the hill which Ralph had been brought up some half hour since. They passed through groups of soldiers who still laboured to improve their defences against the half expected attack. The musketeers looked to their weapons and practised their elaborate drill, while the pike-men polished and sharpened the steel blade on the tips of their long shafts. Others simply rested and waited.

Finally, the three men came to the furthest outpost, which was the one that Ralph had first encountered and where his horse remained tethered. Since it was, after some awful weather, a relatively pleasant evening and none was anxious to part, Jack and Thomas continued their walk with Ralph for a short distance further. As they walked, they talked of all the things that had been happening during the last two or more years. Thomas soon had a pretty good idea of what Ralph's special duties were, although Ralph said nothing about that side of his life. He learned, too, that Ralph hoped one day soon to become Jack's brother in law.

'He isn't talking about that freckled faced virago of a sister of yours, is he Jack? The last time I stayed with you, she fought me like a tiger.' He grimaced at the memory. 'No, it can't be her, can it; but then you have only one sister, haven't you?' he added with an impish grin.

'That was nearly eight years ago, you idiot. She has grown a little since then. Mind you, I find it hard to know what Ralph sees in her.' Jack smiled at Ralph. 'Cheer up, Ralph. It won't be long before you're wedded and bedded. I wonder if you'll be so starry eyed then.'

It was a now a sunny, warm June evening and all three were enjoying each other's company. Ralph had always liked Jack with his rather shy, no nonsense but friendly manner and this other fellow; brash, boastful and so full of fun was just the man to stop Jack taking himself too seriously; a tonic for anyone, at least, in small doses.

Ralph led his horse as the two men walked by his side. Their path took them from the open ground at the foot of Borough Hill into a leafy lane which would take Ralph back to Weedon and Nether Heyford. He was in no hurry and had decided to take a roundabout route back to Kislingbury. He did not want it to be noted that he was returning from the direction of Daventry.

The three men ambled along deep in conversation, interrupted by gusts of laughter. It came then as a complete surprise when four men emerged from the cover of the trees to block their path. The officer spoke as they did so. Ralph's heart sank with a thud to his boots, for the man who confronted him was none other than Captain Burns.

'So, I was right after all. You are a damned spy and I've caught you red handed. Well, we have ways to deal with spies and you will soon learn all about them. Take him.' he nodded to his three soldiers.

'You'll have to take us too.' said Jack grimly, as he and Thomas drew their swords and prepared to defend themselves.

Ralph was unarmed. It was part of his plan never to carry a weapon. He had always pretended to have no knowledge of sword play, nor any ability to use other weapons. His work did not need such skills.

One soldier and the Captain turned their attention to Jack and Thomas while the other two made for Ralph. Jack immediately placed himself between Ralph and the two men, attacking them both as best he could, while Thomas tried to deal with the other two.

As soon as he had recovered from the shock of the encounter, Ralph had been casting his eyes around for any likely weapon and, as luck would have it, he saw some four or five yards away a stake, some six feet long and about the thickness of a man's wrist. A quick dive and it was in his grasp. Like a tiger, he leapt at one of the two soldiers who fell back under the ferocity of his attack. Dodging the lunging point of his opponent's sword Ralph, with the benefit of the length of his newly acquired weapon, dealt his adversary a crashing blow on his helmet. The force of the blow broke the staff in two but knocked the soldier senseless to the ground. Quickly he seized the man's sword.

Rushing forward to where Jack and Thomas were hotly engaged with the other three men, Ralph thrust himself in front of the Captain.

''Leave this one to me Jack, he's mine.' Then, addressing the officer. 'Now sir, we have some business to finish, I believe.'

Even as he spoke Ralph realised the stupidity of his bravado, but this was his fight and he was damned if he was going to hide behind someone else. Folly it was, however, for while Ralph had been wielding his pen over the last two and a half years, this man had been wielding his sword. Now, Ralph must back up those braggart words with action. He attacked the man with a cool, clear mind; his anger held at bay, his eyes watchful and his pounding heart just under control. But equally cool and calculating were those eyes of his opponent.

Ralph attacked vigorously but found himself up against a wall of steel. As his attack flagged the Captain went over to the offensive, seeking to penetrate Ralph's guard. Not daring to take his eyes off that flickering blade for a split second, Ralph could not see what obstacles lay behind him as he was forced to retreat under such a merciless attack. His foot stepped on a piece of wood. He stumbled and fell. In a second the Captain was upon him. He thrust his sword hard to penetrate the vital parts of Ralph's unprotected body, but buried the point instead in the soft turf as Ralph rolled over to avoid the lethal blade.

Regaining his feet, Ralph received a fresh onslaught from the Captain who, unable to dispatch this brash young man, was showing signs of increasing anger. Ralph backed away under the overhanging branches of a large elm tree, until he found himself up against its huge trunk and unable to retreat further. The officer, seeing Ralph's disadvantage, thrust viciously at him aiming to pin him to the tree. With an agility born of desperation, Ralph arched his body to allow the sword thrust to shave his tunic and bury its point in the bark of the tree.

In a flash, Ralph saw his chance. At the same time, his adversary was aware of his peril as he sought to withdraw his sword from the tree. A good tug was all that was required but, in the brief moment that it took the Captain to free his sword, Ralph lunged, passing the sword through the man's stomach just below his ribs. The horror and the pain lit clearly on the man's face as Ralph withdrew the blade from his body. The Captain dropped his sword, while his hands clutched frantically at the wound. He staggered back and, without a sound, fell to the ground where he lay still.

Ralph stood, himself transfixed with revulsion, gazing at the prostrate body. Then, collecting his wits, he gazed around to see that both Jack and Thomas were despatching the two remaining soldiers.

'You skewered the knave then.' observed Thomas. 'Damned good fight you put up, I'll warrant.'

Jack, ever awake to the finer feelings in a man, put his hand on Ralph's shoulder.

'You'll get hardened to it. Remember, it was your life or his. There was no half way.'

'Yes, yes, I suppose I had to kill him, but what a way ....., my God....' Ralph couldn't find the words to express his contempt and loathing for a war which had brought him, like so many others, to such depravity that he must kill his fellow man. Never before, had he killed a man in single combat like this and, never before, had the bestiality of war so forcefully struck him.

The three men stood for a moment; the two hardened soldiers in silent sympathy for one who had fought his war with equal courage but, in another way, so that pain and killing had always been remote. Now he had an intimate acquaintance with death, for he had been its instrument and its agent when he had ended the life of a man whom he had, albeit briefly, known.

As they stood there surveying their lethal handiwork, they heard a sound behind them and, turning, saw that the fourth soldier whom Ralph had felled had recovered consciousness. While their backs had been turned, he had crept over to Ralph's horse and was now urging it to a gallop. They watched, helplessly, as he made good his escape. There was nothing that they could do save watch him disappear around the bend in the narrow lane. This occurrence jolted Ralph out of his mood of anger and anguish and brought him back to the realities of his own position.

'Well, one thing is quite certain. I cannot return to my post at Kislingbury. Even if none of these fellows had escaped, I could not be sure how much they had told others, although I fancy that Burns, the Captain I just fought, kept this very much to himself. Ralph told Jack and Thomas how the Captain had accosted him in Kislingbury and accused him of spying. Now, Ralph wished that he had kept a better lookout on his ride to Daventry, but all his attention had been towards any dangers in front of him, not behind. Otherwise he might just have noticed that he was being followed.

'Had none of the four escaped, I might have risked returning to my post. Now, I cannot.'

'Well, cheer up. The rebel's loss is our gain. I don't doubt that our Colonel will find you a horse and weapons so that you may ride with us.' Thomas spoke with a cheerful smile. 'What do you say, Jack?'

'The obvious answer!' replied Jack. 'Come on then; let's go back.'

CHAPTER 20

June 1645
Borough Hill, Daventry, Northamptonshire

It was nearly midday on the 11th June before Joseph Grimshaw set off on his mission to find Ralph Somers among the hosts of the Roundhead army. He had had to clear up after the Colonel's departure and carry a message to an officer serving on Prince Rupert's staff. The officer, being in conference with his Royal Highness, had been unable to receive the message that Joseph Grimshaw brought and, since Joseph had strict instructions to deliver it into the hands of this one officer and none other, he had no alternative but to wait.

When he did finally quit the Royalist stronghold on Borough Hill, it was to travel south to Weedon and along the Watling Street. The Roundhead army had last been reported in the vicinity of Newport Pagnell. So, it seemed to Joseph's uncomplicated mind that it was there where he should commence his enquiries. Should the army be travelling north, well, he would meet it all the sooner. His task was rather like looking for a needle in a haystack; but he had found Ralph before and he would find him again.

Joseph was not a man to let difficulties worry him. He was by no means a cheerful fellow but he was, by nature, contented and this contentment probably sprang from the fact that he took the world as he found it, never allowing events to fluster or stampede him. If Ralph was with the rebel army, Joseph would find him; maybe not today, maybe not tomorrow, but sometime.

For three hours he rode slowly south, stopping for more than an hour to sit by the side of the road and make lunch from the bread and meat that he carried in his pack. If Joseph took his work seriously, so too did he take seriously the care of his own creature comforts. The afternoon was well advanced when he came to Towcester. He stopped to strike up a conversation with some of the folk he met in the High Street of this small town. They had seen few soldiers recently, save for a Cavalier patrol which had ridden through earlier that afternoon. From the description he was given, Joseph soon identified the patrol as the one led by Colonel Cressley. He wondered how far ahead it would have got by now.

Remounting his old mare, he set forth at an ambling pace to follow the Watling Street south out of the town. He rode past the last of the straggling cottages which stood either side of the ancient highway. A mile further on he met a very dishevelled figure approaching on foot. Although he had lost his helmet and his sword was gone from its scabbard it was, nevertheless, apparent from the clothes the man wore that he was a soldier. He was covered in mud as though he had fallen several times and, from a gash on his forehead, blood flowed into his eyes. As he alternated between running and walking, he cast anxious glances over his shoulder as if he feared pursuit.

'Hey, fellow, what ails thee?' cried Joseph.

The soldier seemed pleased to see a friendly face.

'They Cavalier ruffians, King's men. About a mile back, it was just as we approached the crest of a hill they attacked our wagon train, killing and looting. I only just escaped with my life.' He gasped for breath, still glancing southwards along the lane as he stopped to speak to Joseph.

'Do you say so? Were many killed?' asked Joseph.

'Aye, many were killed and more will die of their wounds, but how many I cannot say. They took us by surprise. We had no time to arm and prepare ourselves. When I saw that it was useless to fight, I fled. One of them chased me some way on horseback but I dodged him in some trees.'

'You were journeying south then?' From Joseph's lips it hardly sounded like a question, but it got the answer he desired.

'No, we travelled north from Stony Stratford with the rest of the army.'

'Oh, has the army passed this way today then?'

'No. Only part of the army will choose this way since it's a better road for heavy wagons and large guns. Most have travelled north along the lanes to the east leading to Northampton.'

The conversation with Joseph seemed to calm the man who, while standing talking, could see that none followed him.

'Someone tried to cut your hair, I see. It's a nasty wound.'

'Aye, I wish I had the fellow who did it.' The soldier replied with a show of ferocity.

'Where will you go now?'

'I don't know. I suppose that I must try to find the rest of the army. It's said that General Fairfax is moving to meet the King's army near Daventry. What is the town ahead?'

'Why, that's Towcester.'

'I'll try for food and shelter there tonight then.' declared the soldier and, with that, the two men parted.

Joseph pondered as he continued south. If the Roundhead army was travelling north, why then, it was unnecessary effort on his part to travel south to meet it. Better to wait on its coming. However, if the greater part of the army was making for Northampton, then his path lay to the east. Joseph decided that it was pointless to travel further that day. So, although it was as yet only late afternoon, he found lodgings in the next village and spent the rest of the day comfortably doing very little.

The next day, having breakfasted and bought himself food for his lunch, Joseph set forth along the lanes leading east, hoping to find news of the rebel army's progress. Unbeknown to Joseph, Colonel Cressley was only two miles away, questioning the villagers of Ashton, while Joseph had been seeking information from those whom he met on his journey.

Heartened by the news that he was less than an hour or two's ride from the Roundhead army, Joseph took the road towards Northampton. Before he got to the town he came to the village of Wootton and needed no telling that a vast number of men had camped there the previous night. It appeared that they had left only a few hours earlier. Now he was hot on the trail and, indeed, was so close to the main body of the army that he was getting caught up with the stragglers.

It was the afternoon when he came to Kislingbury, which had swollen to many times its normal size with the multitudes of the Roundhead army. The village and the surrounding countryside were full of wagons, ordnance, and all the accoutrements of war, with the inevitable hotchpotch of camp followers. Joseph had found the army; now all he had to do was find Ralph.

For an hour or two he sat on the old bridge over the placid River Nene. He watched the traffic bustling back and forth over the river and hoped that, by placing himself where all could see him, Ralph might chance by and catch his eye. When, after a while, there was no sign of Ralph, Joseph decided to find a quieter place. The churchyard had often been their meeting place in other towns and villages. This was for two good reasons. Every town or village had one, so no prior knowledge of the place was necessary and, usually, it was set apart from the hustle and bustle of life in the rest of the town; a quiet retreat, where two people could talk privately and probably unnoticed. With this in mind, Joseph spent a further hour sitting on a tombstone where he was, at least, able to enjoy the summer's evening in peace. Few people passed by and none spared him a second glance. Even the parish priest, concerned at any excesses from the puritan element in the army, was too preoccupied with his own problems to notice Joseph. He was well aware that the Roundhead army had, within its ranks, zealots and fanatics from many different sects. Such bigots were only too ready to smash any object which they regarded as idolatrous, paint over religious murals and destroy anything without consideration of its artistic value, if they thought it to be papist.

Joseph rested in the quiet of that small churchyard, enjoying the warm rays of the late evening summer sun. It was a pleasant evening after so much rain. But, soon the warmth of the sun began to fade as it sank lower in the sky. Within an hour or so the sun would have set and, where the birds earlier had mastery of the sky; bats and perhaps an owl or two would hold dominion.

With a sigh, Joseph roused himself and set off to find refreshment in a nearby tavern. It was, as he had expected and indeed hoped for, full of soldiers. Picking his way through the smoky gloom he found a place at the long table. He ordered a mug of ale and a pasty from one of the young serving girls, who scurried back and forth, bringing food and drink from the overworked kitchen to the demanding clientele of the noisy room. The air was heavy with a mixture of odours. There was the appetising smell of food, the unsavoury smell of stale sweat on the unwashed bodies of soldiers, the smell of ale and, within that cocktail, the pungent smell of tobacco. These were all too familiar smells to Joseph, whose work led him to frequent such places almost on a daily basis when he was acting as courier for the Colonel. He sat in silence, listening to the talk about him without inviting conversation. He watched men come and go through the small door which led to the muddy village street. He watched many about him getting drunker as the evening wore on. He watched the serving girls unused to the rough soldiers, first with giggles and then with slaps, fend-off the crude advances of the men they served.

Scarcely fifteen minutes had passed, while Joseph sat there eating, drinking, listening and watching, when he saw a man enter and stand in the doorway, looking around the ill lit room, as if searching for someone. Of a sudden the man saw one whom he recognised and pushed through the throng to join him.

'George, have you seen Allen Davis? It was he who rode out with Captain Burns some few hours ago and two other lads. It's said that they were following one of our men what they reckoned might be spying and passing information to they Royalists. It seems they caught him right in the act. Leastways, that's what Allen says. There was some kind of a fight. The Captain was killed and so was Harry Rickerby and Vincent Jones. Allen was knocked clean out but when he came round he was able to sneak up to a horse, jump on and escape back here. Guess who was the spy?'

'General Fairfax.' came the reply from George Rollins who, being more than half drunk, collapsed helpless with laughter at his own wit.

'You daft fool. No, it was young Bob Snaith; him as works for the Wagon Master.'

'Never!' said George Rollins, looking incredulously at the other man who swelled visibly with importance at being the bearer of such momentous tidings. Others, who had heard also looked up in surprise, but their surprise could not match that of Joseph Grimshaw who strove to keep his feelings under control. Although Ralph Somers was always Master Ralph to Joseph, he had been well aware that the name he was known by in the Roundhead army was indeed Bob Snaith.

'Be you sure of this, Tom Appleby?' said one man in menacing tones. 'Bob Snaith's a good lad. He'd not do a thing like that.'

'Well, that's what I were told at any rate.' replied Tom emphatically.

Joseph noticed that suddenly the talking had stopped as men turned to hear what was being said. At that moment another soldier appeared framed in the doorway.

'Why,' said one of the men, 'It's Allen Davis hisself.'

One or two, who knew Allen Davis, jumped up and ushered him to a seat, plying him with questions, while another offered him a drink. 'Is it true what Tom is telling us about Bob Snaith?'

'If you've heard that he be a dirty spy then, by God, it's true enough; rot him! 'Twas he what raised this upon my head.' replied Allen fiercely, indicating an angry looking contusion on his head where the hair around was matted with congealed blood.

'How did you find him out?' asked one of the soldiers.

'It were that Captain Burns what recognised him. He didn't tell us much. He ain't the sort to talk ower much to the likes of us. He just said that we was to come with him while he followed Bob. He reckoned that when he'd seen him last, he'd been with the King's men. He wanted to know what he were up to. We saw him leave on horseback to deliver a message for the Colonel. After that he set off to where the King's army is camping near Daventry. We followed him right up to where he met their picket lines.'

'What did you do?'

'Waited; what else? The Captain reckoned as Bob would come back. We hid our horses and lay in wait for him. Sure enough, after about half an hour he came back; large as life, with two of his mates.'

'What then?'

'Well, Captain Burns challenged him with being a spy and tells him as how we was going to take him prisoner. There were four of us, so the Captain reckoned that we could deal with three of them, especially since Bob was unarmed. As we went for him, his two mates took us on. Bob hadn't got a sword. He always told us that he wouldn't know how to use one. Well, he picked up a stake and flew at me; knocked me down and out. I came round to see him fighting with the Captain. It was my sword that he was using; him as said he couldn't use a sword. Well, he used one alright then. Captain Burns was always a fair hand with a sword, but Bob had the better of him today and ran him through. His two mates had done for Vincent and Henry. They must have forgotten about me so, while they were talking, I sidled over to Bob's horse, jumped on and rode away like hell. I reckoned as I'd done enough for one day and I didn't fancy sorting out the three of them.'

With that rather lame attempt at bravado, Allen Davis ended his tale and emptied a mug of ale to refresh his throat after so much talking.

'Well, I'd never have believed it of Bob Snaith. Him of all people!' said one of the group who had listened to the story Allen Davis had told.

The news seemed to have a sobering effect on many of the soldiers in the tavern. Those, who had known Bob Snaith, found it hard to believe and sat in silence contemplating the news. Many, however, had never even heard of Bob Snaith and cared nothing about him. There were always spies. What was one more, or less? Gradually, the hubbub began to fill the tavern once again and, within five minutes, the atmosphere was back to normal.

Sitting in silence, Joseph contemplated the news he had just overheard. He realised again the wisdom of keeping one's counsel, especially in this kind of work. Often, on past occasions when seeking Ralph, Joseph had been tempted to make enquiries of soldiers whom he met on the streets, or in taverns, to see if any knew the whereabouts of Bob Snaith. However, he had never done so, preferring not to let it be known that there was any connection between them. What if he had asked for Bob Snaith in the tavern that evening? What might have been the repercussions when news of Ralph's defection had arrived?

Joseph gave a slight shudder at the thought of what might have been. He rose and left to seek a place for the night in the large communal bedroom upstairs. He lay in silence on a straw mattress listening to the noises around him; the snoring and snuffling of others asleep, whispered conversation, others coming late to bed and, above it all, the gusts of merriment wafting up from the room below. What must he do now? He had the Colonel's letter to deliver but it seemed likely now that, by the time he was able to deliver it, Ralph and the Colonel would have already met. Well, Joseph's place was with the Colonel and, in all probability, that is where Ralph would be. So the sooner he got himself back within the ranks of the Royalist army, the better. Having thus resolved what he must do next, Joseph once again fell to musing on what a narrow escape Ralph had had. But, it had been a long day if not a tiring one and so, with these thoughts going round in his head, Joseph fell asleep.

The next day, after breaking his fast, Joseph fetched his mare from the stables, paid his bill and set off. He was not the only one leaving the village, for it seemed that the whole Parliamentary army was about to decamp. They, it seemed, were marching north and so left in the direction of Harpole. Joseph rode off west, towards Weedon, with a view to approaching the Royalists at Daventry from the south. If the two armies were to meet, Joseph preferred not to be between them at the time. He was not at all sure that he would find the King's army still camped at Borough Hill, but the only sensible thing was to go there and, if need be, follow the army from there. In spite of the

288

need to find Ralph, the Colonel, or both, Joseph made no attempt to urge his mare beyond her normal speed. He did not like to hurry and neither did his horse. Both felt that the days for rushing about were long gone. Indeed, rather than try to catch up with events, Joseph much preferred it when events caught up with him and saved him further effort.

So it was, while he was riding gently along enjoying the sights, sounds and scents of the countryside in June, that Joseph heard a horseman coming up behind him. By now, he was in wooded countryside near the small village of Flore. Quickly turning his horse off the track, he waited in hiding to see who it was approaching. It was a lone soldier on horseback whom it seemed to Joseph, by the way the rider rode cautiously and strained to see what lay ahead, that he was perhaps scouting for a larger body of horsemen. Joseph stayed in hiding and let the man pass. He had guessed correctly since, within minutes, a troop of cavalry came into view. To his surprise and delight he soon recognised some of the men from Colonel Cressley's patrol and, in particular, he recognised Captain Richards at their head. His pleasure turned to consternation when he realised that the Colonel was not with his men.

Emerging from his concealment, Joseph hailed the Captain. Captain Richards, recognising Joseph, halted his patrol.

'Why, Master Grimshaw, what business brings you here? Perhaps, like us, you are seeking to evade the Roundhead army which seems to infest this part of the country in very large numbers.'

'Aye, I left them a mile or two back. Now I ride to Daventry to join the King's army. But, tell me sir, where is my master, why does he not ride with you?'

'Colonel Cressley was wounded in a skirmish with a small Roundhead force that we encountered yesterday.'

Seeing Joseph's genuine dismay, the Captain smiled reassuringly. 'Don't worry, his injury though painful will scarce prove fatal. He twisted his knee in a fall and will need to rest for a day or two ere he walks or takes again to a horse.'

'Where is he now, sir?'

'He is in his own home. It chanced that our encounter with the Roundhead troopers was less than two miles from Hartington Hall. There he'll stay until he is fit enough to re-join the King.'

For once Joseph's mind worked fast as an idea occurred to him.

'My place is with the Colonel, but I have a letter which he gave me before he left, to take to one of his agents within the Roundhead army. That man was forced to flee from their ranks in peril of his life when his purpose within their army was discovered. He has now rejoined the King's army. If I ride to Daventry to seek Master Somers – for I can now tell you that that is his name – I shall be going in the opposite direction to Hartington Hall which is where my journey must end. Will you be good enough to take the Colonel's letter and deliver it to Master Somers in my place? When he cannot find the Colonel it is certain that he will seek out the Colonel's son, Jack, for news of his father.'

Joseph looked anxiously at the Captain. He wondered if he might consider it beneath him to aid a servant by turning messenger, but Captain Richards was made of better stuff than that. He realised that Joseph would be of more use at Hartington Hall, than at a loose end within the army. So he was happy to help if he was required to do no more than deliver a letter. Joseph fished inside his tunic and held out the letter which Captain Richards accepted.

'I'll be glad to take the letter and see it safely in the hands of this Master Somers. You say that he is known to the Colonel's son Jack?' The Captain glanced at the letter. 'It bears no address.'

'No, nor signature neither. It's the way the Colonel works. The seal tells all to those who know, whilst others cannot tell to whom it goes or from whence it came. Yes, Master Somers is well known to Master Jack Cressley. The one will lead you to the other. I thank you, sir, for your help.'

Joseph turned his mare and, bidding the Captain 'Good day', set off back the way he had come. Those who knew him well might have noticed, as certainly did his mare, that he urged her to a somewhat faster pace than usual.

Leaving Joseph Grimshaw to seek the Colonel at Hartington Hall, Captain Richards lost no time in leading his patrol towards Daventry. The countryside, which they had ridden through earlier that morning, had been swarming with Roundhead troops. Unlike yesterday, the troops which they encountered were in such numbers that there was no question of attempting any attack. Rather, it was Captain Richards desire to avoid any contact with the enemy. His orders from the Colonel had been to lead the remainder of the patrol safely back to the Royalist army. Apart from one brief skirmish, when they had surprised some infantry marching north and a few shots were exchanged, they successfully eluded the rebel forces. It was, therefore, with relief that the Captain approached Borough Hill.

His relief turned to dismay when he found that the army had decamped. It was not difficult to follow their tracks and, since his patrol was able to make better time than an army on the march, it was still before noon when Captain Richards came upon the main force just beyond the village of West Haddon. In the absence of Colonel Cressley, the Captain reported to the Prince's staff officers and handed over the letter written by the Colonel explaining his absence. The Captain amplified this written report with a verbal report of what he had seen of the rebel army that morning.

Having thus discharged his duty, Captain Richards enquired of Colonel Leveson if he knew a master Ralph Somers. As predicted by Joseph Grimshaw, Ralph was with Jack Cressley and so the letter that the Captain carried for Joseph was safely delivered.

The instructions and information contained in the letter had little relevance now, in view of the dramatic turn of events which had resulted in Ralph's desertion from the Roundhead ranks.

After his encounter with Captain Burns and his soldiers, Ralph had returned with Jack and his cousin Thomas to Borough Hill. In doing so he had experienced an overwhelming sense of relief, knowing that the past two and half years of subterfuge and secrecy were now at an end. In future, come what may, he could live without constant fear, make real friends and fight openly for the cause that he generally supported. There was no going back and Ralph was delighted.

Ralph and his two newly acquired comrades had arrived back on Borough Hill to the sounds of battle on the far side. They discovered that a surprise attack by some of General Fairfax's cavalry had been thought, perhaps, to be the commencement of a more serious onslaught. However, the failing light had put an end to any more serious engagement that day. While Jack and Thomas had been ordered to re-join their regiment, Ralph had been able to relax for the rest of the day under the cover of a tent, with a bed to lie on. The next day, furnished with a horse, armour and weapons, Ralph, after his prolonged absence, once again took up his former position within the ranks of Prince Rupert's cavalry.

All that night, while Ralph slept, the greater part of the Royalist army had been on the alert. When he awoke, soon after sunrise on the following morning, Ralph learned that it had been decided to march north to avoid any encounter with the Roundhead forces. The plan was that the King's army should fall back on Leicester; there to await the expected reinforcements which Lord Goring was said to be bringing. So it was that the army was now riding and marching north in a well ordered retreat from the advancing forces of Parliament.

They followed a route that took them through the west of the Northamptonshire uplands, in the opposite direction to the path which they had taken when they, the King and his army, had ridden to Daventry following the sack of Leicester at the end of May. This took them through the villages of West Haddon and Welford to the small town of Market Harborough, where the army camped for the night of 13th June. King Charles spent the night at Lubenham, while Prince Rupert quartered in Market Harborough with the bulk of the army. Ralph considered himself lucky to be able to share, with his new comrades, the shelter afforded by the outbuildings of a farm close to the town. The rest of the army was scattered in small contingents around the town, finding shelter where it was offered or, for the most part, passing the night in the open. So, in the company of Jack and Thomas, Ralph slept well for as long as he was allowed, little knowing or dreaming of the battle that was to follow the next day which would prove so fateful and fatal to the King's cause.

CHAPTER 21

14th June 1645
Market Harborough, Leicestershire

Ralph was awoken early next morning with the news that a hastily convened council of war, with the King and his generals, had decided that the army should stand and fight. During the night, Royalist troops quartered as far south as Guilsborough had been harried by some of Ireton's soldiers. It now became apparent that, owing to the rapid manoeuvring of the Parliamentary forces, an orderly retreat by the King's army to Leicester was not possible. Prince Rupert, who normally allowed his heart to rule his head had, on this occasion, advised the King that a battle should be avoided until the army had been reinforced. This was a pointer to lesser generals that the odds were very much against the Royalists. Even now, argued Rupert, it would be better to risk some loss in retreat than a total loss in battle. The arguments had raged back and forth during the night and now the die was cast. The King's army would turn and fight.

So it was that, before first light, at a time when the days were at their longest, Ralph found himself mounted and riding with Prince Rupert's cavalry back over some of the ground which they had covered yesterday. They rode back through East Farndon to Clipston. It had been light for some two hours when the army was drawn up in battle order on a ridge just south of Clipston. There they rested for a while, awaiting the progress north of the Roundhead army. The Scoutmaster was sent forward to determine the position of the enemy. The first report was that there was no sight of him. Prince Rupert rode out and sighted a Roundhead cavalry force that was apparently retreating. Consequently, abandoning the excellent position which he had chosen to receive the enemy attack the Prince, together with the King, led the army south west to take up a position facing the enemy forces, which had drawn up in order of battle just north of Naseby. It was after this manoeuvre, which caused both armies to move to the west of the Clipston to Naseby road, that Prince Rupert and the King's cheif adviser, decided to face the rebel army at the top of the gentle slope of Dust Hill. This, decided the Prince, would be the ground over which he would lead the army to the attack.

All this was a new and fascinating experience for Ralph. To say that he was afraid would be to tell only half of what he felt at that time. Certainly, he was afraid, but his fear was suppressed to a certain extent by excitement. There was, too, a sense of elation and a feeling of pride at being part of such a large and grand army. During his short spell in the ranks of Prince Rupert's cavalry, he had been involved in one or two skirmishes and had also seen the battle of Edgehill from a distance. Now, he was to take part in a major conflict between the King and his enemies. He had known violence and detested it. Yet his whole being thrilled at the thought of what the day might bring. So, while a mixture of fear and excitement dominated, he was aware of that still small voice of reason which spoke of the horrors which result from battle, the pain, the injury and death; but he was young and young men's minds do not dwell on such fears, but think rather of the glory that a battle and victory can bring.

The King and Prince Rupert were anxious now to bring the rebels to battle as soon as possible. They hoped to make what advantage they could of surprise and speed and let that serve to compensate for their lack of numbers. So it was that Ralph had little time to contemplate the battle before it commenced. No sooner had Prince Rupert decided upon the ground over which his cavalry should attack than the ranks were formed and, with the Prince at their head, the pride of the Royalist army moved forward to engage the Roundhead cavalry under Sir Henry Ireton. As they rode down the slope of Dust Hill to meet the enemy, the Royalist horsemen came under fire from Colonel Okey's dragoons; mounted infantry with muskets. His men had been placed behind an ancient hedge which separated the lordships of Sulby and Naseby. It ran parallel to the line of advance of the two opposing armies traversing, on the westward flank, the ground over which Prince Rupert now led his charge. Ralph heard the balls singing passed his head, but the fusillade had little effect on the Royalist charge and did nothing to stop its impetus.

Just before the Royalist cavalry commenced its charge, the enemy retreated below the crest of the ridge which they had chosen and were out of sight until the charge was underway. Then they emerged, once more, from the cover of the ridge as they began to move against the Royalist cavalry in a counter charge.

The ground over which the two opposing forces rode to meet one another was not as smooth as it had first appeared and the ranks of both sides became broken. While yet a hundred paces apart, as if by mutual consent, both sides paused to reorder their lines. Then suddenly, with renewed vigour, the two sides hurled themselves at one another in a final charge.

While Prince Rupert led his cavalry into action, Lord Astley advanced in the centre with his infantry, flanked on his left by Lord Langdale who rode into battle at the head of his cavalry.

From the thrill of anticipation, as he awaited the order to move forward, to the excitement of the charge, Ralph found himself plunged into the horrible reality of battle. Around him men fought desperately for their lives. Men swore, others cried in fear and some screamed in pain until death and oblivion brought an end to their sufferings. Horses fell wounded or reared in fright, pitching their riders to the ground. Men's faces, one moment alight with savage triumph, contorted suddenly with pain and horror as a weapon or a ball found its mark on their bodies. Eyes glazed, mouths voicing their agony, Roundhead and Cavalier fell bleeding or lifeless to the now muddied turf of Naseby field. The dead, with the dying, lay helpless beneath the pounding hooves of the Royalist horses as they pursued their savage, relentless charge.

Ralph, inflamed with the madness of battle, swung his sword

with a horrid venom at the first of the enemy whom he encountered. The blade struck but a glancing blow on the man's armour and Ralph was forced to swerve in his saddle to avoid the counter blow which his assailant dealt. The impetus of the charge carried him on to a new opponent who came at him with such a cry of hatred and fury that Ralph recoiled as if from a blow. Such vicious energy was in the sword cut which the man aimed at Ralph that, when Ralph turned the sword of his opponent with his own blade, the man all but fell from his saddle. Now, side by side, Ralph dealt a measured blow at the man's head just below the rim of his helmet. His sword bit deep through the metal guard and into the flesh and bone beneath. The man reeled back with a frightful scream. His ability to defend himself, now lost in a frenzy of pain, left his side defenceless to a thrust from Ralph's sword which pushed him from the saddle.

Suddenly the ranks of the Roundhead cavalry were broken and the Royalists were through. Beside Ralph, Jack sat astride his horse wielding his sword like a demon while, a little beyond them both, Thomas strove to retain his seat. He had passed his sword through the body of an enemy trooper who fell to the ground threatening to drag Thomas with him. Desperately, he tugged at his sword and, finally, was able to release himself from this dead weight.

'They run.'

The exultant cry came from the troopers of Rupert's cavalry as they spurred their horses on in a frenzied pursuit of the terror stricken rebels. Taking a pistol from his belt, Ralph aimed at one of a handful of the enemy who, unlike their fellows, bravely stood their ground and prepared to fight to the last rather than run. Seeing his danger, the man threw himself low behind his horse's neck as Ralph fired. The ball whistled harmlessly over his head. Before Ralph could return the pistol to his belt and withdraw his sword, the man was upon him. Ralph was unable to avoid the cutting blow from his opponent's sword, which sliced through the leather of his tunic and sank into the flesh of his left arm, just below his shoulder, until it met the bone. It was not far from the wound he had received in the skirmish at Blisworth; although that had now healed and caused him little pain. Blood spurted from this new wound and Ralph reeled in the saddle as pain seared through his arm. Before the rebel horseman could press home his advantage, Ralph watched helplessly with a mixture of horror and relief as the man, with sword upraised to strike again, lurched and fell from his saddle as the ball from a pistol took away the lower half of his face and jaw. Recovering himself, Ralph spurred his horse forward to ride after his comrades who galloped in reckless pursuit of Ireton's routed cavalry.

Soon they were close to Naseby village and saw, ahead, the baggage train of the rebel army. Ralph saw Prince Rupert rein in his horse and call upon the soldiers defending the wagons to yield. To Ralph's amazement an officer came forward to address the Prince. The man had obviously failed to recognise the enemy. Quickly, realising his mistake, he dived for cover behind one of the wagons and, in response to the Prince's demand for surrender, answered with a volley of musket fire which found its mark in several of the Royalist troopers.

Angered at this, a number of riders near to Ralph, led by Thomas, charged at the small group of musketeers. Unable to reload in time, the musketeers seized the barrels of their weapons and began to club at the horsemen while other rebel soldiers ran to their aid wielding swords.

In the melee that followed, Jack rode to assist Thomas who was beset by three musketeers. Running up behind him, a pike-man thrust at Jack catching him in the thigh below his armour. Within a second he was unhorsed and lying on the ground, winded and bleeding. Leaping from his horse, sword in hand, Ralph charged into the affray. He had a glimpse of the pike-man's face. It was a mask of savage joy as he prepared to thrust again at Jack's defenceless body. The expression changed from joy to surprise, then fear and finally to pain, as Ralph's sword thrust entered his body. Dodging the vicious swing of a musket, Ralph thrust again and yet another of the group fell with a choking cry on to the soft grass.

Quickly Ralph helped Jack to his feet.

'Can you walk?' he yelled.

Jack nodded and grimaced with pain as he strove to support himself upright on his feet. Half carrying Jack with his wounded left arm, he gritted his teeth as the pain shot through his shoulder. Jack lent heavily upon him as the two stumbled towards the waiting horses. As he did so he was confronted by another of the rebels, sword upraised and about to strike. Swiftly Ralph raised his sword to parry the blow. The expected blow did not fall. Instead Ralph heard a familiar voice as the man lowered his sword and, as if he could scarce believe his eyes, spoke in tones of bewilderment and disbelief.

'Why, it's Bob Snaith. What do you with the King's men?'

Ralph, equally taken aback, answered with a mixture of anger and surprise at this confrontation.

'Bill, Bill Sheppard. Go your ways. I'll not fight with you.'

The man who now confronted Ralph was one of the few friends that Ralph had made. The expressions on the faces of the two men bore testimony to the horror, the stupidity and pathos of war. Bill looked at Ralph with a mixture of dismay and disbelief while Ralph, ashamed at the betrayal of friendship, sought to avoid the questioning gaze on Bill's honest face. But, his gaze demanded an answer. Once again the question was on his lips.

'Bob, why be you with the King's men? Is it true then? They did say you was a spy. I said they was talking daft; you weren't no spy. But here you be, riding with the .....'

A cry of pain cut short Bill's attempt to find a reason for his friend's presence in the ranks of the enemy troopers. A pistol ball struck him full in the chest as one of the Royalist horsemen, seeing Ralph and Jack confronted by one of the enemy, came to their aid. Bill fell back heavily on the ground. Ralph watched in horror as, raising himself a little on his elbows, he looked at Ralph with an expression of pain and sadness as, in that moment, he realised the truth.

'Tis true then, what they did say. You are a spy. You be one of....', but the effort was too great. His breath failed and the rest of his words remained unspoken, but understood, as the sight faded from his eyes. He fell back on the grass and lay still.

Stupefied by the death of this man, whom he had once called friend, Ralph stood transfixed, staring down at his lifeless body. This then was the end product of war; death, shame and sorrow. Where, then, was the glory of which men had spoken? Who could now claim victory? Sickened and shocked by what had happened, Ralph seemed oblivious of the horror and carnage about him. He was brought to his senses by a shout from Thomas.

'Ralph, look out man. Over here, quickly.'

Another of the soldiers guarding the baggage train had leapt out from behind a wagon and was rushing, sword in hand, towards Ralph and Jack. Before Ralph could move two paces, supporting the half fainting Jack, the man was upon him. Parrying the cutting blow from his assailant's weapon, Ralph planted the flat of his boot in the man's stomach and sent him sprawling backwards on to the muddied grass. Half carrying and half dragging Jack, Ralph covered the dozen paces which separated him from Thomas who was holding the reins of their horses. Thomas quickly realised that Jack was in no fit state to ride unaided. Reaching down he grabbed Jack's arm and, with Ralph's help, pulled him up in front of him. As Ralph helped Jack to mount, he saw the fearful gash that the pike had made in Jack's thigh. Turning now to his own horse, Ralph swiftly mounted. Quickly they galloped away from the dangerous proximity of the Roundhead baggage train. As they did so, Ralph became aware again of the nagging hurt of his wounded arm.

Making what haste they could, the trio re-joined the small force of Royalist horsemen which comprised the more disciplined element of Prince Rupert's cavalry. The remainder were now strung out, far beyond Naseby field, chasing some of the panic stricken troopers of Ireton's cavalry over the Northamptonshire countryside. Prince Rupert strove desperately to rally his men and lead them back to the battle where their presence was sorely needed. Once again his cavalry had routed the opposing enemy cavalry and, once again, they had thrown away their advantage. Difficult as it is for a cavalry commander to control his men in the heat of battle, once a charge has struck home, it was the indiscipline of the Royalist cavalry that made it impossible for Prince Rupert to return with an effective fighting force to aid the beleaguered Royalist army, now slowly losing the battle on Naseby field.

Some of the Royalist cavalry regrouped and, led by the Prince, returned to the field of battle. Surveying the scene, it was soon apparent to Prince Rupert that the battle was lost to the Royalists. After some initial success for Lord Astley's infantry, they were now beset on three sides and were slowly being hewn down. Cromwell's first line of cavalry had charged the Royalist left flank under Lord Langdale. His second line had charged into the left flank of Astley's men. Not all of Ireton's cavalry had been routed and they now attacked the right wing of the Royalist troops. Even some of Colonel Okey's dragoons had abandoned their position, along the Sulby hedge, to mount their horses and join in the massacre of what was left of the King's army.

Bitterly, Prince Rupert thought of that first crushing charge which had swept Ireton's cavalry from the field. He thought of those of his troopers who, even now, pursued a handful of the enemy towards Daventry. Had they the discipline of Cromwell's 'Ironsides', there would have been a strong enough force left for him yet to swing the battle in favour of the King. But, not now; the chance was gone.

However, action was needed, for the elements of Ireton's cavalry were reforming to present a threat to Prince Rupert and his small band. Turning his back on the struggling mass, some three hundred paces to the east of where he surveyed the scene of carnage, Rupert led his men west of the field, where Astley's men fought and died, and finally re-joined the King,

Ralph watched anxiously as Thomas held Jack and strove to maintain pace with the others and yet remain seated. As they rode, they ran the gauntlet of musket fire. Stragglers were isolated and cut down. Finally, they reached the comparative safety of the northern edge of the field, by the farm where they had commenced their charge. There they joined the King and his Life Guard and the small reserve which he had tried to lead to a counter attack. In this attempt he had been stopped by his own staff who thought such an action would be futile and probably lead to his death or capture.

Ralph could see that the enemy was forming up to mount an attack on what was left of the King's army in their position, now to the north of where the main battle was coming slowly to its inevitable conclusion. In obedience to Prince Rupert's command, Ralph fell into line to receive the enemy's charge. With Jack mounted behind him, Thomas had little choice but to fall back. Ralph's arm and shoulder hurt damnably now but, in spite of the pain, his sword arm was still intact. There were pitifully few of Rupert's men left who were prepared to stand and fight. In spite of the pleas and threats of their commanders, the troopers melted away. Finally, a volley of musket fire decided the issue. Now, utterly broken, even the brave few turned and joined their King in flight from the field, where the fate of the King had been sealed.

Realising that the King's army had been beaten, Ralph also turned his horse and galloped over to where Thomas sat astride his mount supporting Jack who was barely conscious.

'Come. Let's away from here. The battle is over and we have lost. If we stay, we shall surely die.' Then, to Jack. 'Can you keep your seat Jack?'

Ralph looked anxiously at Jack who, half fainting with pain, strove grimly to remain seated in front of Thomas. With the ghost of a smile, in spite of the pain, he indicated that he would be alright.

So, the three rode from the field of battle. Not far behind them rode the vengeful rebel horsemen, whose comrades Rupert's cavalry had hounded a short time before. Making what speed they could, travelling north, they soon came upon a wood. Leaving the main body of the fleeing Royalists who, although well scattered, were mostly heading towards Market Harborough, Ralph and his two companions entered the wood where, among its trees, they found sanctuary from those who pursued them. A hundred yards or more, along a riding into the wood, they turned in amongst the close thickness of the trees to a small clearing where they were completely hidden.

Ralph slid from his saddle feeling sick and exhausted. The pain in his arm was like fire. Thomas held Jack in front of him. Had he not done so, Jack would surely have fallen. Thomas eased himself and Jack in the saddle to a more comfortable position.

Thomas saw Ralph's left arm hanging limply and the ugly red gash just below the shoulder from which blood still flowed, soaking his tunic.

'Are you alright?'

Ralph nodded. 'I can manage. But, we'd best not stay long here.'

'No,' agreed Thomas, 'we must soon find rest and shelter. We're in no shape to fight or survive a chase. Most of what's left of our army will be riding back to Market Harborough and it's in that direction that the rebels will pursue them. My aunt lives in West Haddon. That's south west from here. If we ride first to the west, and then turn south, we should keep clear of any of the enemy. Once in West Haddon, my aunt's house will provide a safe place to rest and lick our wounds.'

So it was decided. Making use of the shelter which the trees provided, they went back to the riding and continued west along it until they came again into open meadow land where they turned south on a circuitous route for West Haddon.

They arrived later to find the house locked and empty. Neighbours told them that the aunt had died about a month ago and the house had been sold. Denied shelter here, in spite of their wounds, they rode on to Ralph's home in Preston Capes where they arrived, after a slow and painful journey, in a state of complete exhaustion.

CHAPTER 22

16 June 1645
Hartington Hall

Colonel Cressley sat in a chair in his comfortably furnished living room, looking out of the window. The view on that fine summer's afternoon, looking beyond his well laid-out, but now ill kept, garden was magnificent; but the Colonel did not see it. His vacant gaze told of a man whose mind was far away on other matters. Truth to tell, he was bored, bored to tears. There were so many things to be done and he had so many plans, but he must rest. The longer he rested, the sooner his knee would heal and allow him to be on his feet again. So, for five days, he had rested and slowly the swelling had subsided and the pain eased. He had tried standing and could now do so with only a little pain. How much longer, he wondered, before he could be up and about as normal. It was no good trying to hurry things. That would only result in the knee becoming worse. Impatient as he was, he knew that he would just have to wait and let the knee mend in its own good time. A few more days and then perhaps he would be able to ride back to join the King.

During the time that he had been confined to a chair, the Colonel had heard nothing of the Royalist army. He had been relieved and pleased when Joseph Grimshaw arrived some five days ago. However, since Joseph had left the Royalist camp, only hours after the Colonel, there was nothing that Joseph could tell him which he did not already know about the military situation. Joseph added a little to his knowledge of the Roundhead army's movement north, towards Daventry, on the day that he met Captain Richards; that is on the day that he had arrived at Hartington Hall. However, the news of Ralph's discovery as a spy in the rebel camp had been a disappointment to the Colonel, although he was greatly relieved to hear that Ralph had made good his escape, unscathed, to join the Royalist army. He had been very lucky. It could have ended very differently. Nevertheless, it was a pity that this source of information had now dried up. Ralph had done a wonderful job and deserved to be free at last of this perilous work which he had undertaken. The Colonel could only feel thankful that this episode had been concluded in such a satisfactory way.

As for the present whereabouts of the King and his army, Colonel Cressley had no idea. There had been a rumour abroad, which had reached the ears of the few servants left at Hartington Hall, that a battle had been fought somewhere in the north of the county which had gone badly for the King, but there were always rumours and one never knew how much credence to give them. It may well have been a pitched battle between the two armies, but the Colonel was inclined to doubt it since he knew that the Royalists were in no real state to take on the might of the New Model army of Parliament until they were reinforced. Perhaps it was some skirmish between the two sides when Fairfax tested the defences at Borough Hill.

Also resting and recovering from their wounds at Hartington Hall were three of the Colonel's men and, now, just one of the enemy troopers; the other had died from his wounds. The Roundhead soldier still living was in a bad way, but with care he might pull through. The women of the household had nursed them all as best they could and it was largely thanks to their care and attention that more soldiers had not died. Like the Colonel, his own men were well on the way to recovery and would soon be fit to ride again.

For once the sun was shining and it was all that a summer's day should be. The warm breeze gently moved the drapes at the open window. Thank goodness for some warm and dry weather at last. What a miserable summer it had been until now. Easing himself out of his chair the Colonel hobbled around the room. It wouldn't do to sit too long and let the damned knee set. A little exercise and a lot of rest was the only cure. He stifled a cry as, setting his full weight upon his injured leg, a stab of pain shot through his knee.

Persevering, he limped out of the room using a walking stick. At the back of the house, in a room looking out on to the courtyard, were quartered those soldiers whose wounds had compelled them to stay behind with the Colonel.

'Good morning sir. I see that your leg is improving.'

It was a young man who spoke, little more than a boy. His arm was in a sling. Across the room sat an older man with a bandage around his head, whilst a third man lay on his bed resting an injured foot. A fourth man, the Roundhead soldier, lay quietly on another bed staring at the ceiling.

The Colonel wished them all good morning.

'Yes, thank you Jenkins, the knee is getting better by the day as, I trust, is your arm.'

'Oh, almost better now, thank you sir.'

The Colonel sat chatting to them for a while. Truth to tell, he was glad of the company. He hobbled over to the wounded Roundhead. His head was bandaged and around the upper part of his right leg was another blood soaked bandage.

'How's the enemy today?' he asked, in not unkindly tones.

The man looked at the Colonel as if in a daze, as though he had not heard the question.

'Water.' He croaked feebly.

The soldier with the bandaged head got up and, filling a cup from a nearby bucket of fresh water, gently helped the man to a few sips.

'He don't seem to know what's going on at all, sir. It must have been the bang on his head. He's been bleeding a lot and he be very weak. Them women have looked to him. They have to all of us. If it weren't for them, some of us wouldn't be here now. He wouldn't. That's certain sure.'

The Colonel felt that there was little more to be said. He decided to get a bit more exercise.

'Glad to know that you're on the mend. I'll see you all tomorrow.'

As he shut the door, he reflected again on the folly that was war. One minute men were trying to kill each other, the next they were doing all they could to make sure each other lived.

What a terrible war this was; Englishman against Englishman. When you came face to face with the enemy, wounded and beaten, it was hard to feel the same enmity that you felt on the field of battle. Many of these men fought for whom they happened to serve when the war had started. Many, of course, had chosen sides but in most cases the choice had been made for them. Well, he was glad that his men were helping the rebel soldier and hoped that he would live.

Colonel Cressley stumped along to the kitchen. His leg must be much improved for, having given it a little exercise, it was much less painful. On his way, he met Alfred who had just emerged from the pantry.

'I see that you be better on that leg now, master.'

'Yes, Alfred. It's definitely improving.'

'Twas a pity that Mistress Mary weren't able to come and care for you, sir. 'T'would have made a big difference.'

'Indeed it would.' replied the Colonel with feeling. It had been a great disappointment to find that Mary was away from Bullshead farm, paradoxically to nurse the wife of a Roundhead family. Well, there was nothing to be done about it, but how he would love to see her.

'How long is she to be away? Did they say?'

'Well, they weren't sure, but they reckoned 'twould be three weeks or more.'

'Ah well, Mary is not one to be missing when help is needed. The Somers have been very good to her. When I can, I must ride over to Bullshead to thank Charles Somers for all that he and his wife have done.'

Then, changing the subject, the Colonel asked, 'Are you able to manage this house without Mistress Mary, Alfred?'

He knew that Alfred was too old to do very much and, with so little help, it must be quite a burden for him to merely look after the day to day running of the house. Certainly, he would not be able to do much outside the house in the garden and the estate. Things were going to rack and ruin out there, more than in the house, but it couldn't be helped.

'Ah, we manage master, but I'll be right glad when we git

some o they young chaps back from the war. The women folk do what they can, but 'tis the land, do you see, what needs attention. I can look arter the house, with the help of Amy and Mabel and that other young wench what comes in from the village, but I can't do no more.' replied Alfred sorrowfully.

'I know, Alfred, I know. It's the damned war. The whole country is going to ruin, but you're doing the best you can. I wonder if I'll ever see things to rights again. I wish Jack were home. When I'm gone, all this will be his. Let's hope that it will be worth having.'

The Colonel hobbled off back to the living room where he, thankfully, took the weight off his knee and resumed the comfort of his chair. His knee was aching again but it had stood up well to a bit of walking.

He sat musing for a while on past events. When would this wretched war end? At first it had seemed that one battle with the rebels might put an end to the matter but, after Edgehill, it had become apparent that their support ran deeper than had first been thought. It soon became clear that the war could go on for quite some time yet. The forces of Parliament were well organised. They had men of talent leading them; men like Cromwell and Fairfax, especially Cromwell whose generalship and ability to inspire men as a leader had been proven. No, he could see no hope of an early conclusion.

Colonel Cressley looked out of the window at the beautiful rolling countryside, the rich greens of the meadowlands in the middle distance and the darker greens of the forest beyond. The sun was still shining; not yet near its zenith, but with all the warmth and promise of a golden summer's day. To think that, on such a day, men all over England were armed and fighting one another while their country suffered from ruin and neglect. Surely there must be an end to it soon.

Sir Francis' thoughts turned to his late wife, Elizabeth. Although it had been a bitter blow indeed when the news had reached him of her death, he had had little opportunity so far to miss her. Being away from home, with most of his waking hours taken up with work, he had been too busy to take in the full meaning of his loss. He thought often of all of his family and missed them but until now, although he knew Elizabeth to be dead, she had seemed no further away from him than she had ever been after the war had taken him away from his home. Now he was back at Hartington Hall and she should be with him, as she had always been. It was here and now that he missed her, more than ever before. He yearned to see her sitting in her own chair on the other side of the hearth, able to listen to and discuss the worries and anxieties which filled his mind. He wanted to talk to her about the estate, about his fears and hopes for the future, about Mary and Ralph and about Jack in whose hands lay the future of the Cressley family. But, alas, she was not there and, hard as it was to believe, she would never again sit there and offer him that quiet comfort which he had so valued in the past.

As he thought sadly of the loneliness which the future held for him without Elizabeth, the tears welled in his eyes. Then, almost savagely shrugging aside these thoughts, he braced himself and refused to wallow in self-pity. What was gone was gone and all the tears in the world would not bring back the past. So now he must think of the future, which would be here at Hartington Hall with his children Mary and Jack, especially Jack. Mary would be off at the very first opportunity to Preston Capes with her Ralph. God send that it would happen for them both very soon. But, it was here, with Jack, that he would spend his old age, that is unless the war dealt another blow.

So far, they had both been lucky. Both he and Jack had survived their many skirmishes relatively unscathed. He thought again of the possibility of being killed and the consequences for Jack. He had never heard what happened to Henry Savage and whether his letter to Jack had been delivered. That Henry had been taken or killed was certain, for he had never reached the King and had not returned or been seen since. The Colonel was not unduly worried about the contents of his letter, which had been couched in such terms that only Jack would understand about the family valuables to which it referred and where they were to be found. But, he still did not know if Jack had received the letter. He would not feel easy until he had spoken to Jack and made certain that he knew how to gain access to all those important things that one day would be his. There were papers, gold, money, valuable jewellery and family heirlooms, not to mention the deeds to the house and lands and, of course, his will. It would be a good idea, while he had time on his hands, to check everything and make sure that it was all in order. He ought perhaps to write a new will now that Elizabeth was dead.

Stiffly, the Colonel rose from his chair. The years were telling on him now. He limped over to the door and turned the key in the lock. Then he walked over to the recess at the side of the fireplace, opposite the window.

Dark oak panels covered the walls, typical of the Elizabethan style to be found in some of the richer homes. Many of these panels were ornately carved around the edges. The fireplace, in particular, was a masterpiece of the woodcarver's art. It was lavishly decorated with the most exquisite carvings of many different designs. These carvings were of rural scenes; animals, birds and flowers. There was one that Sir Francis particularly liked, of an eagle in flight carrying, in its talons, a small creature which he had always taken to be a lamb. It was from this design that Sir Francis had made the seals with which he secured his correspondence. He had also had made a number of seals with variations of this, and other designs, to distinguish the agents whom he had organised into a comprehensive spy network at the outset of the war.

The fireplace protruded some three or four feet into the room. In the recess either side of it the panels, each about two feet square, were less richly decorated. The join between each panel was covered by beading and, at every corner, there was a rose carved from wood. The Colonel directed his attention to the back of the recess on the right hand side of the fireplace. Here he grasped, with his left hand, a rose some two feet from the inside corner with the fireplace and some six feet from the floor, while at the same time pressing on a rose further down and to the right. As he pressed, the rose in his left hand pulled out of the wall on a rod which passed through the wall. Pressure on the lower rose had released a catch securing the rod, leaving it free to be withdrawn by some four inches. Withdrawal of the rod had activated a mechanism inside the wall. With scarcely a sound, one of the panels to the left of the Colonel, on the right hand side of the fireplace near to the back of the recess, swung outwards on substantial hinges strong enough to carry the weight of the panel and a piece of masonry attached to it. So cunningly had this been constructed that, since every join between each panel and its neighbour was covered by beading, it was impossible to tell that this particular panel was hinged and formed the door to a compartment, built partly into the fireplace and partly into the rear wall of the room. All the roses looked exactly alike so there was nothing to distinguish the two roses by which the mechanism was operated. The piece of masonry which backed the panel was sufficiently large to ensure that no hollow sound could be detected by tapping the wall. The bottom rose had to be pressed to release the top rose and allow the rod to be withdrawn, thus limiting the possibility of accidental discovery of the secret chamber.

Inside the opening was a small vault, some two feet deep towards the back wall and, perhaps, eighteen inches wide towards the fireplace. It was the height of the two feet square panel, which formed the door. The thickness of the walls surrounding the fireplace and the back of the room had been used to accommodate this vault. The massive masonry surrounding the large fireplace was one of the few places in the house where a small vault could be accommodated. It was not intended as a priest hole, or to conceal a person, but simply as a safe storage for valuables. Inside there were some bags of gold coins, some jewelled ornaments, silver plate and goblets. There were also some documents which were either rolled and tied with red ribbon or stacked in a neat pile.

Ignoring the money bags, the contents of which were already known to the Colonel, he took out a roll of paper. This was a document that he had had drawn up some years ago by a clerk in Northampton who was well versed in matters of law. This was Colonel Cressley's will and dealt with the disposition of his estate and possessions upon his death.

Unrolling the document which, in fact, was of parchment not paper and was covered with writing in a thin spidery hand, he sat down at the nearby table to examine its contents. He noted that provision had been made for his wife, had she outlived him, to be accommodated at Hartington Hall for the rest of her days. Sir Francis satisfied himself that her death in no way invalidated the will as it stood. Reading further he noted that, upon his death, the estate would go to his son Jack. That was exactly how it should be. There was a provision that, should Mary marry after her father's death, a dowry would be provided by the estate, while other provisions had been made for her support should she remain single.

The Colonel spent some time going through this document to ensure that it was in good order. It seemed that, after all, the will was sufficient as it stood and, in spite of Elizabeth's death, needed no altering. It made several bequests to certain members of his household and to one or two of the tenants on his estate, but the bulk of his wealth would pass to Jack.

Taking out other documents stored in the chamber he began to read through some of these. There were several letters relating to private matters, of some importance, which he had dealt with over the years. In reading them, Sir Francis was transported in memory back to the days of his youth and early manhood. He remembered how, as a young man upon the death of his father, he had been the third generation of the Cressley family to inherit Hartington Hall. He turned to another letter which reminded him of his first meeting with Elizabeth, of their marriage and, later, the birth of their three children; including their little girl who had survived for only six months.

The years fell away and the memories came flooding back, each reminiscence prompting a host of otherwise forgotten memories of events so long ago. There were sad memories and happy ones but, on the whole, thought the Colonel, he had had a happy life, a loving and lovely wife, a good home and two fine surviving children. Really, he had little to complain of.

So absorbed was he with his letters and his memories that he quite failed to hear the commotion in the hall outside the living room door. He failed to hear, that is, until it was forcefully brought to his attention by a loud banging on the living room door.

With a twinge of pain from his knee, the Colonel rose from his seat at the table and crossed to the door. Turning the key, he opened the door by only a few inches so that the open door to the vault could not be seen. He found himself confronted by a very anxious Alfred and a distraught young woman. The woman, she was no more than a girl of sixteen, he quickly recognised as Lucy Jenkins his gamekeeper's daughter.

'Oh sir, you must come and help him. He's wounded and the soldiers they be after him. 'Tis awful. They'll kill him for certain if they get him. Father's taken him into the cottage. Oh sir, please come quickly.'

The Colonel, standing in the doorway, looked enquiringly at Alfred.

'She be like a wild thing sir. I can't make neither sense nor reason of what she says, but plainly there be something sadly amiss.'

Shutting the door behind him, the Colonel led the girl to a seat in the hall.

'Now calm yourself. Who is it that is injured?' asked the Colonel quietly,

'A soldier, sir, a gentleman. They'll get him, sir, if you don't hurry. I told....'

'Now wait a minute.' The Colonel cut her short. 'Who is after him?'

'Those Roundhead soldiers. There have been a number of them about after that big battle.' She seemed a little calmer.

'And you say that he is wounded and that your father has taken him into his cottage?'

'Yes sir. My dad sent me to fetch you. I slipped out of the back of the cottage, while one of the rebel soldiers went off to call some of his mates who were riding by. That left only one of them to watch the cottage. The gentleman, he be a King's man, gave me a letter for you.' Reaching into the folds of her skirt, she drew forth a letter from a pocket and handed it to the Colonel.

'For me?' asked the Colonel with some surprise. 'Did he say where it came from?'

'He said that he had ridden from Preston Capes sir, just beyond Towcester.'

Suddenly the truth dawned on Colonel Cressley.

'By God, it must be Ralph,' he said to himself, although the words were spoken out loud; then to the girl. 'And the rebel soldiers, do they know where he is?'

'Yes sir. As I ran away, one of the two who were chasing the gentleman went to fetch his mates. My dad wouldn't let them into the house to get the gentleman. He's got his gun to them but he can't hold them all off. Oh sir, they'll kill him. Please hurry sir.'

Sir Francis glanced at the letter which he held in his hands. Turning it over, he saw that, indeed, the letter bore Ralph's seal. His mind raced as he tried to fathom what this could all be about. Oh dear, he must be getting old. Quickly he opened and unfolded the letter. Yes, it was undoubtedly Ralph's hand. He began to read.

> *"To Colonel Sir Francis Cressley.*
>
> *Sir,*
>
> *You will have heard of the great battle fought between His Majesty's army and the army of Parliament at Naseby and will, doubtless, know that the day was given to our enemies. The King is fled with the little that is left of his army. During the battle your son, Jack, was sorely injured but, thank God, his wound is now healing. With rest and care he should, in time, be restored to full health and strength.*
>
> *I have to tell you that my purpose in the rebel army has been discovered and it was only by God's grace that I escaped with my life.........'*

'Oh sir, please hurry. It may soon be too late.'

The girl's anxious pleading broke into the Colonel's concentration, causing him to stop reading the letter as he began to realise the urgency of the situation. His hand went to his brow. He needed time to think, but there was no time. It was action that was needed now.

'Alfred, go and raise my men. Get horses saddled and muster

all who can ride. I want every able bodied man to arm himself with what he can and be ready to ride against these rebels in five minutes or sooner.'

Swiftly he turned and strode back into the living room. If his knee pained him, he did not show it. Now that he had grasped the situation, he acted purposefully in the realisation that this was a matter of life or death. Gathering up his documents from the table, he replaced them in the chamber by the fireplace and, on top of them, put the letter that he had just received. Then he gently pushed the door closed. As he did so the rod holding the top rose slid back into the wall. The bottom rose moved slightly as, with a click, the door locked into place. The secret chamber had now vanished without trace and even the most minute examination, by one who knew where to look, would fail to reveal any trace of a door.

Immediately, the Colonel went to another room at the back of the house, where he buckled on a sword. Taking two flintlock pistols from a shelf, he loaded and primed them both. With these in his belt he hurried out into the courtyard. Already his men were there looking to their horses. Alfred, too, was scurrying around as if twenty years younger. With him was Joseph Grimshaw who hurried to the Colonel's side to see what was to be done. There were no young men about the estate, but Alfred had pressed into service two older men who were within hailing distance which, together with the three recovering soldiers, completed Colonel Cressley's less than adequate fighting forces.

Alfred led the Colonel's horse out and helped him mount. Joseph Grimshaw was already mounted and armed with a pitchfork. Fighting had never been his trade so a pitchfork would serve as well as any other weapon if fight he must. There were times when the least likely of men must fight and this was such an occasion.

Alfred spoke to the Colonel as, with some difficulty, he helped him astride his mount.

'I've saddled the old chestnut mare, Sir Francis. I'll ride along with you sir.' He turned to bring the mare from the stable.

'No Alfred, your place is here at the Hall. Look after the

women folk.' answered the Colonel gently.

Alfred looked somewhat rebellious, but he knew better than to argue. He watched the small party of horsemen ride out of the courtyard and up the gently rising ground to the north-west of the Hall. As Alfred watched them go he saw smoke rising from just beyond the crest of the hill.

Back in the saddle, with the weight off his knee, Colonel Cressley felt much less pain, although some of the muscles in his legs and knees, which he was forced to use to control his horse reminded him of his damaged joint. As he rode, the Colonel also saw the pall of smoke rising from some unseen conflagration ahead. He knew, from its position that it must be from the gamekeeper's cottage and wondered anxiously if they would be able to save whoever was trapped inside. Another two hundred yards and the party of horsemen topped the gently rising ground. The Colonel's worst fears were confirmed. There lay the gamekeeper's cottage, with flames and smoke billowing from the door and an upstairs window at the back, making any escape impossible from that side of the building. At the front, taking cover from the gamekeeper's gun by hiding behind a low stone wall, were some half dozen Roundhead soldiers. They seemed content to wait, sheltered by the wall, until the fire forced the occupants of the cottage to make their escape by the only route left open to them, through the front door, when they could pick them off at leisure. Plainly, the soldier who had gone for help had found his companions.

Back at the Hall, the gamekeeper's daughter had also seen the smoke rising in the distance and knew only too well from whence it came. Leaving the room, before Amy could stop her, she ran out of the house and started up the hill after Colonel Cressley and his men.

The Colonel knew that the odds were against him and he could only hope that a swift and determined assault would give him the upper hand. In any case there was little time for strategy. If rescue did not come immediately those inside the cottage would certainly perish. He glanced behind him at his "troops". The three wounded soldiers were not yet fully recovered and fit for active service. Then there was Joseph Grimshaw, who fought only out of necessity, and the two elderly men from cottages nearby who brandished bill hooks. Even he, their leader, had difficulty in keeping his saddle because of the pain from his wounded knee, where muscles were being used that had not been exercised since his accident. If ever luck was needed, it was now. Drawing his sword he gave the signal to charge.

It seemed that luck was, after all, on their side for the rebel soldiers were so intent on watching the fire and the fate of those inside the burning cottage, that they failed to notice the Colonel and his men bearing down upon them until it was too late. When they did hear the thunder of hooves, there was no time to get to their own horses. In desperation and some panic they ran for their mounts which were tethered some distance from the blaze. They were not half way to them when the Colonel and his men were among them. Colonel Cressley's sword hissed as it swung through the air in a scything blow which caught one of the rebels on the neck. The collar of his leather tunic, thick as it was, did little to protect him from the cut of that sharp blade. With a scream he fell to the ground, his life's blood pumping into the earth from a severed jugular vein. One of the Colonel's men was wielding his bill hook with considerable effect. The soldier he was attacking was unable to get in close enough to use his sword. With a tremendous blow the hook bit deeply into the man's chest. Another rebel, seeing his comrade fall and himself threatened, drew a pistol and discharged it at the rider as he bore down upon him. The Colonel's man was a dozen yards from the rebel, his billhook raised for another vicious swing, when the ball hit him in his chest. He seemed to rise from his seat and fall from the rear of his mount to hit the ground with a sickening thud.

Within three minutes, five of the rebel soldiers lay dead. The sixth ran for his life, which he failed to save, as the Colonel signalled to one of his men to run him down. With the rest of his band of men, the Colonel now turned his attention to the blazing cottage. Quickly he dismounted and ran towards the building. Although smoke was now issuing in black clouds from the front upstairs window, the seat of the fire appeared to be at the back. At the window of the smoke-filled downstairs room

317

appeared the figure of Tom Jenkins the gamekeeper. Half blinded and choking from the smoke, he wrestled to open the window which was obviously stuck.

Trying the door Colonel Cressley found, as he had expected, that it was either bolted or barricaded on the inside. Seizing a shovel which was leaning against the wall, he smashed the glass and battered at the window frame until there was room enough for the Colonel to climb through. The gamekeeper was still conscious, but choking and unable to see from eyes that were reddened by the smoke. He had lost his bearings and was staggering around helplessly, coughing and spluttering from the thick acrid fumes which filled the room. In spite of the dreadful pain from his knee, the Colonel dragged a heavy chest away from the door. He drew back the bolt and swung the door open. Then, grabbing the gamekeeper, who by now could scarcely stand, he half carried and half dragged him out into the fresh air where he let him collapse on the grass.

'Where is the soldier who was taking refuge inside? demanded the Colonel of the gamekeeper urgently.

'We hid him in the cellar under the trap door. He was pretty far gone, but we might have saved him. Those fiends knew that we had him somewhere inside. They wanted to search the place, but I told them to clear off and leave us be. That's when they set fire to the back of the cottage and waited for us to come out, like rats, at the front.'

The Colonel turned to go back into the cottage but, suddenly, fanned by the draught from the broken window and the open door, with the stair well acting as a chimney, the flames took hold and within seconds the room was a blazing inferno.

Distraught at his impotence in the face of the fire, the Colonel could only watch in anguish and despair as he thought of Ralph trapped in the cellar.

The gamekeeper had by now managed to clear some of the smoke from his lungs and, although his eyes were still red and streaming with tears, he could see again. He struggled to his feet and ran towards the cottage, calling to the Colonel as he ran past him.

'My wife, Betty, she's upstairs and that soldier fellow be still in the house,' he gasped, barely able to get the words out.

At that moment there was a crash of breaking glass from the upstairs window. The group of men looked up to see a woman trying to make her escape through the window which, like the one downstairs, would not open. In desperation she had smashed the glass with a chair. As she battered the window frame with the chair to force it open, the onlookers on the ground could see the flames behind her. The back of the house was now well alight and the flames had spread to the front, so that the house was completely ablaze. Some of the men were trying to extinguish the flames with buckets of water from the well. With only a couple of buckets and the need to refill them from the well, the attempt was futile. The fire had now reached the thatch. The huge clouds of black smoke hiding red flames seemed to fill the sky over the cottage. The men looked up in horror at the desperate figure at the window.

'A ladder.' shouted Colonel Cressley. 'We must find a ladder.'

He knew that they would have to act very quickly if there was to be any hope of rescuing the woman, not to mention Ralph, of whom there was no sign. In any case, they could not just stand by and watch her burn to death.

'Round the back!' shouted one of the men from the estate. 'He's got a ladder round the back.'

As they rushed to find it, the daughter arrived on the scene. Breathlessly she hugged her father who pointed frantically at the upstairs window.

The girl screamed in horror as she caught sight of her mother still desperately trying to open the window. Leaving her father she dashed towards the open door of the cottage. Too late the warning cries. Before anyone could stop her, the girl vanished into the dark smoke through which could be faintly seen a dull red glow.

Suddenly there was another crash from the upstairs window as, at last, the woman had managed to force the window open and half knock the frame from the masonry which held it.

319

Throwing what remained of the chair down, careless of the glass and splinters, she strove with her bare hands to push the remnants of the window frame from its place, so that she might make room enough to climb through. Behind, the flames leapt forward seeking to consume her, fanned by the draught from the window. Spellbound by the horror of this waking nightmare, the men below watched the drama reach its awful climax. The men who had gone for the ladder now came running to prop it against the wall, but too late. Her clothes and hair alight, the woman tried to throw herself from the window, but the flames claimed her. She fell back into the room behind her with a final hideous scream. Both she and her daughter were now beyond rescue. As if in triumph at their victory, the flames shot threw the thatch and the whole building seemed to explode in a huge conflagration. No one could remain in that building and live.

By now the gamekeeper was on his feet and, had it not been for the restraining hands placed upon him by the Colonel and his men, he too would have rushed to his death in the burning wreck of his home.

With a horrid fascination, they watched the flames consume the cottage. The thatch and the burning roof beams were now falling into the shell of the house. From within the building came the sound of the furniture and upstairs floor falling to the floor below. As the wall at the back lost the support of the roof timbers and cracked by the heat from the blaze, it also fell in. The gamekeeper watched too. He realised that nothing could be done to save those within that terrible conflagration. His body was still racked with fits of coughing and, in between these spasms, he stood in helpless misery, tears streaming down his blackened face as he cried in anguish for those he loved.

'Betty, oh my God, Betty....... and my little Lucy too, oh God.......' His suffering was heart rending to see.

Colonel Cressley listened, not knowing what to say and yet aware that there was nothing he could say to mitigate the horror of what had just passed. Two women; a wife and a daughter, dying horribly in that inferno, as their husband and father watched helplessly, was an experience from which no normal person could emerge unscathed. The Colonel was distraught at what he had seen and agonised over that third person, Ralph Somers, the man to whom his daughter was betrothed, hopefully dead before the searing agony of the flames engulfed him. How would Mary bear this news? He grieved for her and the misery which she must now endure and he grieved for the loss of a fine man like Ralph. His heart went out in pity to the man who stood beside him. His anguished face lit by the flames from what he once called home. The gamekeeper stood transfixed. Like a statue, he watched all that he owned and loved consumed in that all embracing fire.

As more of the roof and its timbers collapsed into the shell of the cottage, a fresh plume of flames shot upwards with renewed vigour. So intense was the heat that the onlookers were forced to retreat. Within minutes another wall collapsed on to the burning mass, to be followed shortly after by the final wall at the far end.

The masonry crashing on to the burning wood and thatch served to dampen the fire which had now passed its peak. As they watched the flames slowly die down, a shot rang out and a ball whistled over their heads. A few yards away a man turned and fell as he was struck by another ball. Looking around the Colonel's small band of men saw, to their dismay, a swiftly approaching group of Roundhead soldiers on horseback. Just as they had surprised the rebels who had fired the cottage so they, themselves, were now surprised.

Cursing his folly at not having posted a look-out, the Colonel shouted to his men to scatter and seek cover. It was too late to run far before the horsemen were upon them, striking out with their swords at the inadequately armed men. Sword in hand the Colonel sought to defend himself as a rider bore down upon him. Dodging the vicious swing of the man's blade, he thrust at the horseman as he thundered past. The sword bit deeply into the man's side. With grim satisfaction, the Colonel saw the man sway in his saddle before crashing to the ground some dozen yards away. He had little time to savour his victory for now a rebel soldier on foot rushed at him and, immediately, he was hotly engaged.

Around him, the few men left of those who had set out from Hartington Hall fought in savage, hand to hand, mortal combat,

321

but theirs was a losing battle as, one by one, they were slaughtered by the Roundhead soldiers. Even the one who sought to escape was hounded down by soldiers on horseback and cut down as he ran. The gamekeeper, possessed of a savage fury and caring not whether he lived or died, had seized a huge stake and ran like a demon to meet the charging horsemen. With all the black hate in his heart for those who had robbed him of everything that he possessed, he swung the stake aiming a tremendous blow at the first of the enemy to reach him. So furious was the impact that the soldier was lifted from his saddle as if by an unseen hand. He landed in a twisted heap on the ground where the gamekeeper continued to pound the already dead body in an uncontrollable frenzy of hate. This proved to be his undoing, for he failed to notice another rebel horseman bearing down upon him. The sword sliced into his neck, almost severing his head from his shoulders. For a moment he staggered, stake upraised to deliver another blow. Then the stake dropped from his hands and he fell lifeless to the ground.

The Colonel had, meanwhile, overcome his adversary who fell to the ground clutching the wound where the Colonel's sword had sliced open his bowels. He sank to his knees. Colonel Cressley turned to face another foe and so did not see the dying man withdraw a pistol from his belt. He pointed it waveringly at the Colonel and, before oblivion overtook him, he fired. The ball hit Colonel Cressley in the back smashing his spine and entering his heart.

Joseph Grimshaw, who had been wielding his pitchfork to some effect not far from the Colonel, saw his master fall and rushed to his side. Laying him gently on the soft turf he rose bravely to face the same inevitable fate. Pitch fork at the ready, he prepared to sell his life dearly. However, before he could strike another blow, a sword thrust from behind passed cleanly through his body. Joseph Grimshaw fell dead beside the man whom he had served so faithfully all his life.

CHAPTER 23

Spring 1959
Hartington Hall

For a moment there was complete silence broken only by the song of the birds outside the open window. Each of the five people in that richly panelled room sat quietly contemplating the words that Mary had just spoken. The logic of her argument was irrefutable. The author of those letters, sealed with the ring found on the skeleton, was undoubtedly Ralph Somers. It was, therefore, reasonable to assume that it was his remains which had been unearthed a few days ago in the rubble of that old building, some three centuries after his death.

It was Robert Somers who broke the silence.

'It's incredible, but you must be right. So those bones are the remains of an ancestor of mine some twelve or thirteen generations removed.'

He spoke thoughtfully, in awed tones, as he contemplated the discovery that they had just made.

'Well, it's almost beyond belief Mr Somers.' said General Cressley in a state of ill-concealed excitement. 'I don't suppose you expected, for a moment, to find that it was a relation of yours who has been the subject of our investigations.'

Each person in that room was filled with a sense of wonder at the evidence offered by that mute witness of a bygone age. Each person's imagination had been fired by what they had seen and heard. In silence they contemplated the many exciting questions that came to mind. What sort of people were they? What had happened to Mary, if indeed she had lost the man she loved? How had Ralph come to be entombed in the remains of that old building only a short distance from the Hall? What had been the fate of Sir Francis and his son Jack? What joys and tears had they known? What had happened under this ancient roof, indeed in this very room?

Finally, Frank Smithers rose to his feet.

'Well, sir,' he said, addressing the General. 'This has been absolutely fascinating and it has given me a splendid story. If you'll excuse me, I'll be getting back to the office to put something down on paper. If I may, I would like to get our photographer along to take a picture of Mr Somer's letter. Will that be alright with you, Mr Somers? He will call at your home, of course. Will tomorrow be convenient?' Robert Somers readily agreed.

'Won't you stay for tea?' The general was reluctant to bring this eventful occasion to an end. 'Mary, see if we can get something for our guests.'

Mary rose to leave the room.

'May I help?' enquired Robert Somers.

'Oh, yes, thank you.' replied Mary, giving Robert a smile which expressed her pleasure as well as her thanks.

Frank Smithers looked at his watch and decided that he could allow himself time for some refreshments, although he had a great deal to write about when he got back to the office. He guessed that it would be quite a while before he found time for a meal. Left on their own the General, Frank and David Gibson inevitably directed their conversation, once again, to the topic of the letters. They fell to speculating about the people concerned in those letters; what they were doing and whether they survived the war.

Soon tea was brought in by Mary and the helpful Mr Somers. The conversation continued unabated while they sat sipping tea and consuming the sandwiches and small cakes which Mary had provided. Above the buzz of conversation, a car was heard arriving along the gravel path and was seen to pass the window and come to a halt just past the front door. A moment or two later the living room door opened and the General's man servant entered. He spoke quietly into the General's ear.

'There is a Mr Martinshaw at the door. He wishes to see you in connection, he says, with the article recently published in the local newspaper. He says that he has motored over from St Ives in Huntingdonshire. Shall I show him in, sir?'

'In connection with the newspaper article, you say? Well, yes, show him in. By all means, let us all hear what he has to tell us. If it is to discuss the matter of these letters, he couldn't have come at a better time.'

The man servant left the room to reappear within seconds with the new arrival.

'Mr Martinshaw, sir.'

Mr Martinshaw was a middle aged man, whose appearance exactly fitted the popular image of Mr Pickwick. He was rather portly, small of stature, had a balding pate above a round face and a genial countenance behind a pair of spectacles through which he beamed at the assembled company. The General rose to greet him.

'Ah, how do you do, Mr Martinshaw. I'm Cressley. May I introduce Mr Smithers of the Northampton evening newspaper, Mr Somers of Preston Capes, Mr Gibson, our local historian and my daughter, Mary. These gentlemen are all here in connection with the recent discovery of a skeleton in the path of the new motorway which, I should tell you, has led to another interesting revelation. If it is on this matter that you wish to speak to me, your arrival is most timely.

Mr Martinshaw nodded a smiling affirmative. 'Yes, indeed, that is the matter which has brought me over from St Ives.'

'In that case perhaps you would be good enough to let us all hear what you have to say.'

'Of course, I hope that I do not waste your time.'

The General offered Mr Martinshaw a chair and some refreshments. Having settled himself, he began to explain the reason for his visit.

'It was a friend from these parts who brought over a copy of your newspaper when he visited me recently. He knows that I like to see the paper which, as you know, does not normally reach as far as St Ives. I read what I believe was the second article telling of the discovery of a skeleton, dating from the Civil War, and how it had been connected by a signet ring found on it with some letters, held by you General Cressley, here at Hartington Hall. The seals, which were pictured in enlarged photographs, reminded me of the seal on a document in my possession and which has been passed down in our family from generation to generation. It is a document dated May 1645, but has no address and nothing to indicate for whom it was intended, nor does it say by whom it was written. The letter, for that is what it appears to be, is from a father to his son. It tells of an illness from which he has recently recovered and reminds him of the possibility that he, the father, might be killed in the war; in which event the son would be heir to the family property. After this preamble, the letter goes on to deal with the matter for which it was apparently written. This is the part which has intrigued the Martinshaw family for years. The writer describes what would seem to be some kind of secret chamber in the family home, "wherein are documents and other things which will be of importance to you." It also sets out in detail the manner by which access may be gained to this chamber.'

'All these years', continued Mr Martinshaw, 'my family has been in possession of this information and yet having no idea where the house is to which the writer refers. It has been suggested that the document is a hoax but I cannot see why it should be. Others have suggested that it would be nothing more than a house safe containing a few dusty old papers of little interest to anyone except the owner of the house and, in any case, it was probably broken into centuries ago. All of this might well be true. However, it has intrigued the Martinshaws over the years and some have tried in vain to find out more. I imagine that those, who first obtained the letter, were the most interested to find out the location of this hiding place. As the years went by, it seemed likely that any such chamber or hiding place would have been found or the house demolished. As a youngster I was intrigued by the thought of hidden treasure, but for years the document has lain forgotten for the most part; or brought out to be shown now and then as a curio or, perhaps, in the forlorn hope that someone may throw further light on the mystery. The picture in the newspaper of the seal on your documents reminded me of my own mysterious letter, and its seal, when I thought I saw a similarity. I compared the two. The seal on my letter is not very clear. It appears not to have been imprinted in the wax with any great care and it has been broken, presumably to read the letter. Nevertheless, the similarity with the newspaper photograph is clear. At any event, it seemed like a worthwhile avenue for further exploration. So I decided to motor over to call on General Cressley, show him my letter and see if there is anywhere, in Hartington Hall, where the directions in it, to open the secret chamber, make sense. Certainly, the age of this lovely old house make it a possibility.'

'Well, bless my soul.' exclaimed the General who was, for a moment, at a loss to know what to say. David Gibson, although equally excited by this new possibility, was not quite so dumbfounded.

'That article of yours, Mr Smithers, seems to be producing some most interesting and unexpected results. I wouldn't be surprised if our next visitor was Oliver Cromwell in person.' Then he turned to Mr Martinshaw, 'You say that you have brought your letter with you. May we see it?'

'Well, not the letter itself.' replied Mr Martinshaw. 'You may imagine that, after all these years, it is in rather a poor state. I have, however, brought photographs and I have also a type written copy of the text.' He handed David Gibson a sheet of typing and two photographs.

David Gibson looked first at the two photographs, one of which was an enlarged picture of the seal. As Mr Martinshaw had said, the seal was not plainly printed in the wax and had been broken when the letter was originally opened. Nevertheless, it bore a definite resemblance to the one on the General's letter from Sir Francis Cressley. The other photograph was of the letter itself. David Gibson compared the handwriting in the photograph with the handwriting in the three letters that had been placed on the sideboard. The similarity of the handwriting in two of the letters had already been noted. The handwriting in Mr Martinshaw's letter seemed to be the same as that in the third of the three letters, that is, the one from Sir Francis Cressley. He looked next at the photograph of the imprint on the sealing wax and compared it with that on Sir Francis' letter. There was little doubt that it had been made by the same seal.

'I would say at first glance that, almost certainly, it was the same hand that wrote the other letter from Sir Francis Cressley and that the patterns on the two seals are identical.'

Frank Smithers was looking over his shoulder, whilst the others waited impatiently for David Gibson to examine the two letters to see what he could make of the new evidence. Looking again at the photograph, he could see that the document it pictured was badly scarred by time. It was torn at the edges and there was a split where it had been creased. Clearly it would fall to pieces if it were handled much more. Setting the two photographs to one side, David Gibson turned his attention to the type written sheet which he began to read aloud for the benefit of the others.

"*My dear son,*

Know that I am safe and well, but have been laid low with an ague. I would tell you more but my present circumstances prevent it. Whilst regaining my strength, I have had time to reflect upon the peril in which war places us all. Should I die, you are my rightful heir. I have no fear of death and, should it overtake me, desire only to know that I leave my affairs in good order. I would then have you know of the chamber wherein are the documents and other papers which will be of importance to you. This chamber is built into the wall on the right hand side of the fireplace which, as you know, is covered by wooden panels. Betwixt these panels, at each corner, is an ornament in the form of a carved wooden rose. Find the ornamental rose on the third row from the floor and nearest to the chimney breast. Then seek the rose that lies beneath it and to the right. Pull on the higher one as you press on the lower, when the chamber door will open.

I pray God that you will find no need of this letter and that we shall be safely together again when this wretched war is at an end.

Your loving father."

While David Gibson read the letter there was complete silence from his audience. He could see from the expressions on their faces that, like himself, they could scarcely credit what he had just read. Mr Martinshaw, on the other hand, sat beaming with some amusement at the astonishment evinced by the General and his guests.

'Most explicit, as you have just heard.' he remarked. 'The question is, General Cressley, is this the house to which the letter refers and where the chamber is to be found? I see that you have a rather large fireplace and that the room is panelled.'

Frank Smithers rose again to his feet and strode across the room to inspect, more closely, the wall on the right hand side of the fireplace. Unfortunately, much of it was obscured by a rather large, old fashioned, book case. Even so, there was enough of the panelling visible to allow him to see what he was looking for.

'Well, I'm blowed. Each of these panels does have a small ornament at each corner, a carved wooden rose. It certainly does look as though your search may have ended, Mr Martinshaw. I would guess from the seal on your letter that the author was Sir Francis Cressley and that it was intended for his son Jack who, in all probability, was the Jack he mentions in his letter to his wife.'

It was David Gibson who spoke and, as he did so, he directed his attention to one of the two letters owned by General Cressley.

'If it is the seal used by Sir Francis then that, in itself, makes it most likely that this is the house to which your letter refers and, with this panelling, this is the most likely room. However, it seems most improbable that no one has opened the chamber one way or another after all these years. What do you say General? Do you know of a secret chamber in this house?'

'Upon my word, no,' replied the General, 'but if it is here, we'll jolly soon find out. Here, give me a hand to move this book case.'

'If we take out a few of the books, we'll move it more easily.' observed Frank Smithers.

Two minutes later, relieved of its load of books, the book

case was quickly moved aside to reveal a panelled wall which, upon a closer inspection, proved, as Frank Smithers had said, to have a carved wooden rose at the corner of each of the square panels.

'Well, General,' said David Gibson, 'are you going to see if you can find this secret chamber? Perhaps Mr Martinshaw will give you the directions once again.'

'Yes, indeed.' replied Mr Martinshaw, adjusting his spectacles and taking up the type written sheet. A hush fell over the room as Mr Martinshaw began to read out the instructions. It was an expectant hush as those who could only wait and watch did so with an excitement and mounting tension that was almost unbearable.

'Find the ornament on the third row from the floor and nearest to the fireplace.'

There were no ornaments in the inside corner between the wall of the fireplace and the wall of the room, so the General selected a wooden rose that was at about eye level on the third row from the floor and one panel width, about two feet, from the corner of the recess. Mr Martinshaw continued. 'Then seek the ornament that lies below it to the right.'

The General looked uncertain for the moment.

'I suppose,' said David Gibson, 'it will be this one, diagonally across the panel.' He indicated a rose that was indeed below the other and to the right.

'Now pull on the higher rose as you press on the lower.'

General Cressley pulled the top rose with his left hand. He felt it give, as he pressed the lower rose with his right hand. Presumably, in doing so, he had released a catch which held the rose at the top in place. The top rose in his left hand came away from the wall on the end of a metal rod. It was quite stiff and the General found it difficult to extract the rod from the wall to its full extent. As he tugged at the rod, Mary exclaimed with a gasp of surprise.

'Look. That panel, to the left, by the corner; it's moving.'

Sure enough; to the great astonishment of all four people watching the efforts of the General, now assisted by David

Gibson, a panel at the corner of the wall, adjacent to the chimney breast, swung slowly open as the rod attached to the wooden rose was pulled from the wall.

'By Jove,' exclaimed General Cressley, 'fancy this being here and I hadn't the faintest idea.'

'Is there anything inside?' asked David Gibson.

'We need a torch.' suggested Frank.

'I have one handy.' The General went over to the sideboard, where he rummaged around in a drawer for two or three seconds before producing an electric torch. Shining the beam inside the dark cavity of the secret chamber, he declared, 'By George, there's something here alright.'

'Just a second,' interrupted David Gibson. 'What is it? If it is paper, it will be very brittle. Handle it with the greatest of care.'

'There seems to be an assortment of things.' replied the General. 'There are some bags. There is a loose piece of paper lying on top of a bundle of papers tied up with some ribbon. There are some rolls of paper and a number of ornaments.'

'Well, take them all out very gently and we'll put them on the table.' advised David Gibson.

Gingerly, they brought out the contents of the chamber and placed them carefully on the nearby table. The excitement was intense. All eyes were on the General, as he repeatedly reached into the mysterious depths of that dark recess and, as if it were Aladdin's cave, he brought forth yet another treasure for his audience to admire.

Finally the chamber was empty. General Cressley flashed his torch into its furthermost corners and found nothing more. David Gibson had more or less taken charge of the situation and, to be honest, the General was glad to let him do so. After all, this was David's line of business.

'Apart from the ornaments, jewellery and silver which, if handled with care, should be alright for you to look at, I think it were best if nobody touched what is left. With your permission General, I'll phone a colleague of mine who knows exactly how to handle these things. If you will allow him to take them away he can study them, decide how best to preserve them and give you a full account later of what they are. He will know how best to set out the documents so that they can be inspected without causing them any harm. As for the money bags, these gold coins should be worth a great deal. Perhaps we should make a note of what is there before they, too, are taken away for valuation. I am sure that you will wish to see all this examined and evaluated by experts.'

'Yes, indeed, Mr Gibson.' replied the General. 'I'm in your hands in this matter. Please, do what you think best. I'm afraid that this has all been just a bit too exciting for me. We're used to the quiet life here, aren't we, my dear?' He glanced at Mary whom, he was surprised to see, was deeply engrossed in conversation with Mr Somers who appeared to have wholly captured her interest in whatever it was they were discussing.

'Oh, yes indeed.' she replied, suddenly becoming aware that her father was speaking to her. 'Why, this must have been quite a shock to you, you poor dear.' she exclaimed, coming protectively to her father's side. 'I think that Mr Gibson is right, don't you Mr Somers? These things shouldn't be spoiled by our untrained hands. By all means, Mr Gibson, phone your friend.'

David Gibson made a phone call in which he explained as much as necessary to a rather startled friend, who promised a speedy departure for Hartington Hall.

'Daddy,' said Mary, 'When we have had all of this examined by the experts and we know what all of the documents are about, we ought to ask our friends to call again. Then they can hear all about them and see these documents for themselves which, perhaps by then, will have been set out so that it will be safe for us all to inspect them.'

'That's a good idea. Certainly we will my dear and, since it seems likely that this little treasure trove is worth a considerable amount, we must discuss some financial arrangements. Everyone here has played some essential part in the discovery of the chamber and its contents. Without the evidence supplied by each person, it is doubtful if the whole picture would have emerged and the secret chamber be discovered. Yes, certainly we shall have a lot to discuss when all this has been sorted out.'

When Mr Gibson's colleague arrived he was fascinated with the find. He congratulated David Gibson on the way that he had handled the various objects taken from the chamber. Rough handling, by a number of eager hands, would almost certainly have rendered the documents illegible and worthless. He estimated that a proper examination of the documents and the other finds would take at least a month. He agreed that he would have a report ready in five weeks' time, when they would all meet again at Hartington Hall.

* * *

The next day, a two column spread appeared on the front page of the evening newspaper, with photographs on an inner page where the article was continued. It began with the headlines "Treasure Trove at Hartington Hall" and then continued.

"Hartington Hall, the ancestral home of the Cressley family, was the scene of a spectacular discovery of documents, gold coins, silver ornaments and jewels hidden in a secret chamber behind panelling in the centuries old living room. Evening News reporter, Frank Smithers, was instrumental in bringing together the clues in this treasure hunt through time and was present during the amazing climax when, following directions found in an ancient document, the secret chamber was opened."

"The discovery of the secret chamber came as a direct result of the unearthing, recently, of a skeleton in the remains of the foundations of a long forgotten building which lay in the path of the new motorway. A ring, on the skeletal remains of a finger, revealed a seal engraved with a pattern identical to the one imprinted in the wax seal on a letter belonging to Mr Robert Somers of Preston Capes. It was similar to the carved decorations on the panels of the living room at Hartington Hall, which has long been in the possession of the Cressley family. It was a report in the Evening News, together with photographs of the seal, which prompted the owners of two further documents to bring these to the attention of General Cressley. One was held by Mr Somers and the other by a Mr Frederick Martinshaw of St Ives in Huntingdonshire. Both Mr Somers and Mr Martinshaw had recognised the similarity between the seals pictured in the photograph and the ones on old letters which had been handed down through the centuries within their families. Meeting at Hartington Hall yesterday, General Sir John Cressley, his daughter Mary, Mr Somers and Mr Martinshaw, together with local historian, David Gibson and News reporter, Frank Smithers, used Mr Martinshaw's letter which, without revealing where it was and in what building the chamber existed, gave explicit directions on how to open it."

The report went on to describe, briefly, the contents of the chamber which were now being assessed by experts.

'It is surmised that the results of this examination will throw a great deal more light on the history of Hartington Hall, the people who lived there and the events that took place there in the years leading up to and during the Civil War some three hundred years ago.'

The article gave a short account of the Civil War, especially with regard to Northampton and its county. It noted that one of the most important battles of the War had been fought in Northamptonshire at Naseby, but went on to say that virtually nothing was known of a skirmish that was said to have taken place at Hartington Hall. The article promised its readers that it would give a full review of the contents of the chamber, in a few weeks' time, when they had been properly assessed by experts.

* * *

Five weeks passed and, in response to the invitation from General Cressley and his daughter; Frank Smithers, David Gibson, Robert Somers and Frederick Martinshaw met again, at Hartington Hall, one evening for dinner.

Although the desire to examine the contents of the secret chamber was intense, this could not be done during dinner. Therefore the conversation was mainly of past events until the

General had led his guests back into the living room for coffee when David Gibson began his self-appointed task of telling the others what the experts had learned from the finds in the secret chamber. The value of the coins, ornaments and jewellery had still not been precisely assessed but he was assured that the value would run into five, if not six figures. Since the treasure had been found in the home of General Cressley and it undoubtedly belonged to his ancestor, Sir Francis Cressley, there was no doubt that he was the rightful owner.

David Gibson continued. 'Whilst I am sure that you will all be most interested in the monetary value placed upon the find, especially as General Cressley intends to share some of it with you, the main interest this evening lies for us in the contents of the documents and what they tell us.' He glanced across at a glass case inside which many of the documents were on display.

'All of these documents have considerable historical value, in that they throw further light on the customs of the day and add to our store of knowledge of the middle seventeenth century and of Hartington Hall at that time. However, for those of us who have been so closely connected with the developments which have led to the discovery of this treasure, the most fascinating of the documents is the letter which was found lying on top of the other contents of the chamber. It is as though it had just arrived and had been hurriedly thrown in for the time being. It is hardly the sort of letter that one would need to keep. Indeed, it is one that would probably have been best destroyed. We can therefore only wonder why it was there. Whatever the reason, it is very fortunate for us that it was kept since it answers many of the questions that have been raised and answers some points of conjecture.'

'I have a transcript of it here.' David Gibson held up a sheet of type written paper with a triumphant flourish. 'Incidentally, you will not be surprised to hear that it was sealed with that now familiar ring, the very one that was found on the skeleton, the imprint of which is also on two of the other letters which we have recently seen. This time, however, the writer has departed from his customary practice and has both addressed and signed this letter. You will understand why when I read its contents. This is what it says.

"To Colonel Sir Francis Cressley.

Sir,

You will have heard of the great battle fought between His Majesty's army and the army of Parliament at Naseby and will, doubtless, know that the day was given to our enemies. The King is fled with the little that is left of his army. During the battle your son, Jack, was sorely injured but, thank God, his wound is now healing. With rest and care he should, in time, be restored to full health and strength.

I have to tell you that my purpose in the rebel army has been discovered and it was only by God's grace that I escaped with my life.

I was impatient to convey to you some information of importance about the strength of the forces of Parliament. Your messenger had not contacted me for several weeks. I, therefore, rode from our camp at Kislingbury to the Royalist army at Daventry where I met Jack who informed me of your absence on patrol and who carried my information, in your absence, to those who could use it best. After leaving the Royalist camp, I was accosted by a Roundhead officer who had followed me, suspecting my true identity. A fight ensued when, thanks largely to Jack and his cousin Thomas, I was rescued from those who would have taken me prisoner. Since one of those who attacked us escaped, to flee back to the rebel camp, I had no other choice but to stay with the Royalist army and await your return.

We heard the following day of your injury from the lips of your Captain Richards. A day later we were with His Majesty at the battle of Naseby. When we saw that all hope of victory was gone, with Jack wounded and I in little better state, we fled with Thomas to his aunt's house

*at West Haddon. We arrived only to discover that she had
died and the house sold. In sore need of rest and shelter,
we rode a further ten miles to my house at Preston Capes
where we are at present. Jack was so weak from loss of
blood, and the pain of his wound, that we thought him
likely to die ere we found shelter. My wound, though less
severe, caused me much pain and I was hard pressed to
reach my home. Of the three of us, only Thomas
remained unscathed. For this reason, I have asked him to
carry this letter to you and return the ring which you gave
me to maintain secrecy in our communications. Since I
can no longer serve you as before, Thomas has it in mind
that you might find some use for him in my place; if His
Majesty still has such need.*

*When our wounds have healed, we will seek to re-
join His Majesty. By then we trust that you, too, will be
recovered and once more in his service. Meanwhile, I beg
that you will tell Mary that I am well, that I love her
dearly and, with your permission, which I would have
sought earlier, hope soon to claim her as my wife. Since I
am no longer under those constraints that demanded my
anonymity, I take leave to sign myself,*

Your dutiful servant,

Ralph Somers."

David Gibson ended the letter and, for a while, there was
complete silence whilst his listeners digested the wealth of
information and explanation that it contained.

The light of knowledge slowly dawned upon the faces of
those present, as the information contained in this letter
completely changed their previous understanding of these long
ago events.

'So, our skeleton is more an ancestor of mine than of yours,
Robert. He wasn't Ralph Somers after all but this cousin,
Thomas, mentioned in the letter.' said Mary thoughtfully.

'Yes, so it would seem.' It was the General who spoke and he added. 'I should tell you that I have received another letter but, before you jump to the wrong conclusions, this is not another from the past but from a gentleman who lives in Hardingstone. It seems that, having read the newspaper article, this gentleman recalled something that he had read in an old book, which he has in his possession and which was printed in 1780. The book is entitled 'Antiquities of Northampton and its Environs'. He quotes, at length, where the writer mentions a tale that he had from an old man, whose great, great grandfather was in service here at the Hall during the Civil War and whom, it seems, met his death when the Hall was sacked by Roundheads. His grand-daughter (that is the grand-mother of the old man by whom this tale was told), was only a child of twelve at the time. She was visiting the Hall and ran home, probably sent by her grand-father, when the trouble started. It seems that Sir Francis rode out to attack the Roundhead soldiers who happened by after the battle of Naseby and who were burning a nearby cottage. In the ensuing skirmish Sir Francis and his band were all killed. Only one woman survived the attentions of the Roundhead soldiers who, after dealing with Sir Francis and his men, plundered the Hall, ill-used the women and killed the few servants whom they found there. The one girl who survived, whose name was Amy, remained an imbecile for the rest of her days.'

'I had always been aware of the stories of some sort of skirmish here during the Civil War, but had never given them much credence. It now seems that they were true. Possibly, since the remains of the cottage, in which our skeleton was found, had been destroyed by fire, it was to the aid of this man Thomas, as it appears, that Sir Francis Cressley rode.'

'Well,' observed David Gibson, 'these letters have told a remarkable tale. It is clear that Ralph Somers was your ancestor, Robert, whose home was at Preston Capes. One cannot help but wonder why that letter of yours was put in its hiding place in the bureau and if, indeed, it had anything to do with the death of Ralph's father, Henry Somers. It is also now apparent, from the letter in the secret chamber, that Ralph was working as a spy for Sir Francis and had a narrow escape from the Roundhead soldiers. Had he not been so lucky, you may not have been here today. There's a thought! Sir Francis' son, Jack, certainly survived his wounds for we know that eventually, some years after the war had ended, he inherited the Hall. I suppose that knowledge of the secret of the chamber died with old Sir Francis. One might have expected that he would have told somebody the secret, but perhaps he didn't get the chance or believed that Jack had received the letter he had sent, so anonymously, with instructions on how to open it. I wonder how it came into the possession of Mr Martinshaw's family. I wonder also what happened to Ralph Somers. We have learned a lot, but there is still much that we don't know. Robert, do your local records have nothing to tell us about Ralph?

'They are far from complete in that period unfortunately. There is quite a gap after the death of Henry Somers. The church was in some turmoil during the period of the Commonwealth under Oliver Cromwell. I believe that our church was without a priest for some time. However, I will certainly look again to see if there is anything more to be found.'

'It would be interesting to know if he married his Mary after all.' remarked David Gibson.

'Oh, I expect he did.' Robert Somers spoke with a smile and cast a shy glance at Mary sitting by him on the settee. There was just a faintest blush on her cheeks when he added. 'We Somers are pretty determined when it comes to our women folk.'

CHAPTER 24

EPILOGUE

Spring 1661
The Manor House, Preston Capes, Northamptonshire

Maytime and the promise of the summer to come was fresh in the soft morning air. It was the start of a fine, sunny day. At the manor house in Preston Capes all was astir. From the hall a voice could be heard calling. 'If we are to get there shortly after midday, we should be setting off quite soon.'

Two children erupted from the darkness of the open front door into the brightness of the early morning sunshine. They were playing and quarrelling in turn as brothers and sisters do the world over.

The girl, Elizabeth, was fast growing into a young lady. Her brother, Edward, was ten, some three years or so younger.

'I shall go riding in the forest with Uncle Jack.' boasted the boy.

'He may not want to take you.' said the girl intent on aggravating her brother, whose superior attitude annoyed her.

'He certainly won't have time for you.' retorted the boy, trying not to be drawn by his sister's obvious desire to anger him.

'Come along you two and stop quarrelling. Go and see if Simon has made ready the horses yet.'

Mary was still beautiful; not with the blush of youth, but with that mature beauty which comes to some women in advancing years from the joy of fulfilment and a happy home. There were lines on her forehead it is true and, at times, a look of harassment when her two unruly offspring tried her patience. She was not so slim as she used to be but, after bearing children, that was not surprising. Where, before, from her face had shone the eagerness of youth, there now radiated the joy and contentment of being a wife and mother.

One of the servants, Simon, a middle aged to elderly man harassed by the two children besieging him with questions, led a horse and a pony, ready saddled, around to the front of the manor. Leaving them tethered, he retraced his footsteps shortly to return once more, still with the children in attendance, leading another horse and pony together with a larger animal, a pack horse, ready laden and tied by a length of rope to the larger horse.

Mary waited in the doorway enjoying the warmth of the early sun. She stepped forward to take the bridle of the small pony and assist her daughter as she climbed on to its back. Behind her Ralph appeared in the open doorway, ready at last to set off on the journey for which they had obviously prepared.

The years had treated him well. His step was not quite so sprightly and he did not leap into the saddle as in his youth, but rather heaved himself on to the horse's back. True, there was a hint of middle age spread beneath his belt, but at thirty seven he was in his prime and he felt it.

He smiled at Mary. To him she was just as lovely as the day he had first met her. He looked with pride at their two children.

'Come then, my dear. If we are all ready, we had best be on our way.' He turned to Simon to deliver last minute instructions before they left. Simon served them now in the place of Jethro who had died some three years ago and was sadly missed.

'Now, you may expect us to be gone for a week. Look after the house and keep that idle fellow at his work in the garden. You may leave all matters concerning the estate to Chisolm. He knows what's to be done.'

With waves and goodbyes, the Somers family set out to find their way along those familiar roads, country lanes and villages of south Northamptonshire which would lead them to Hartington Hall. There was good cause for the happiness which Ralph and Mary felt, as their horses carried them along the broad ridge overlooking the rich farm lands. Mary's brother Jack who, for supporting the King, had been exiled in France for fourteen years, had now returned to live once again in his native land. For nearly a year now, a new King had been back on the throne of England. Those who had supported the monarchy, and had been loyal to the royalist cause, were being rewarded and to the shame of the new king, Charles II, old scores were being settled with those who had been active in support of Parliament. For Jack, however, his reward was all that he wanted when Hartington Hall and its lands, his rightful inheritance, had been restored to him. With him he had brought back to England his French wife, Estelle, and their two boys. The family had arrived from France only a fortnight ago and were now settling into the old home.

It was a joyous occasion for both Ralph and Mary, especially for Mary. During the long sad years of the war, she had lost first her mother. Then her father had been killed and her brother, Jack, had been exiled to a foreign land. Had it not been for Ralph she often thought that she, too, might have perished. As it was, Ralph had first rescued her and taken her to the home of his aunt and uncle, where she had found a full measure of happiness, and then he had taken her to the house which she now called home, at Preston Capes. His love had sustained her in her sadness and, with the arrival of a family, the sparkle had returned to her eyes and, with it, that lovely smile which came so readily to her cheeks. Today, to complete her happiness after all these years, she was to see her brother again and to meet for the first time her sister in law and two nephews.

It was a grand day for the journey and, as might have been expected, the two children were enjoying the experience immensely. Young Elizabeth rode on the pony which had not long been hers, but which she already loved dearly. Edward rode his horse with impatience to make faster progress and, as boys must from time to time, gallop ahead to make a reconnaissance and then report back.

Mary rode side saddle and was well content to take her time. Gone were the boisterous days of youth when, dressed more like a boy than a young lady, she would gallop her horse madly through the forest and across the meadow lands around Hartington Hall. More aware now of the need for a sense of decorum and, with possibly, the responsibilities of motherhood demanding that she set a good example, she was happy to ride in the manner of fashionable ladies of her day.

For Ralph this journey to Hartington Hall, after all those years, was like the end of one chapter and the beginning of another. The past sixteen years had been hard times for many who had fought for the King. Ralph had been lucky. There seemed to be some doubt in the minds of his neighbours as to which side he had supported. Some said that they knew he had fought for Parliament, while others were sure that he had fought for the King. Others said that he was a turncoat; but let them think what they liked. He kept his own counsel and said nothing. Truth to tell, he had never felt strongly about the issues enough to want to fight as had Sir Francis and Jack. He saw merits in the arguments of both sides, but marginally favoured the King's cause. Like his father, Jack, was a committed royalist and had fought on to the bitter end. He would probably have died for the cause had he not been forced into exile for his pains.

After Naseby, Jack had remained for many weeks at Ralph's home in Preston Capes, recovering from the awful gash in his thigh. It had been a long time before he had been able to ride again and wield a sword. Ralph's wounds, though painful, had been more superficial. Within two or three weeks he had been as good as new.

After sending Thomas with news of their situation to Colonel Cressley, the two men had waited in vain for him to return. After the third day they had begun to fear that some harm must have befallen him, but then they decided that, perhaps, the Colonel had left to re-join the King and Thomas had decided to follow in search of him. Two weeks went by. Ralph was by then almost completely fit again. Jack's wound seemed to be healing cleanly with no sign of infection, but he was still very weak and in need of careful nursing lest the wound open up again. After some discussion, it was decided that some misfortune must have befallen Thomas or, by now, they would surely have heard from him. They could think of no other course of action but for Ralph to ride over to Hartington Hall to see, for himself, if the Colonel was still there and if Thomas had ever arrived. He left Jack in the good care of Mistress Gurney and Jethro. In spite of her liking for gossip, Mistress Gurney knew when to hold her tongue. Ralph had a quiet word with Jethro, who had a shrewd head on his shoulders and knew pretty well how things had been with Ralph and the Cressleys. He would keep prying eyes at bay.

It was thus arranged and so, in about the middle of July, Ralph had set out for Hartington Hall. He approached the building cautiously, wondering who he would find there. Surely it would not be deserted. There were bound to be some of the Hall servants there. However, it had occurred to Ralph that one explanation for Thomas' disappearance was that the Hall had been commandeered by Parliament and Thomas had been taken prisoner. It turned out that he need not have taken such precautions, for when he arrived at about midday and found no sign of rebel occupation nor, for that matter, sign of any occupation, he entered by a side door. Inside, the house was in an awful mess. Fortunately, the damage seemed superficial, although little of the contents were fit for use. Windows had been broken and furniture had been smashed. Only scraps of now mouldy food were left in the kitchen and, everywhere, there were signs of looting and wanton destruction. In one room, at the back, an attempt had been made to fire the building but, by good fortune, the fire had failed to take a hold. After searching every room, Ralph was able to confirm that there was not a living soul at Hartington Hall.

With no one around to talk to and ask what had happened to Sir Francis and his servants, Ralph rode into the nearby village of Quinton. Here the locals had a number of different and sometimes lurid accounts of the events at the Hall some three weeks ago, although Ralph could find no one who had actually been there at the time. It seemed that only one poor servant girl, Amy, had escaped and she could not talk after the rebel soldiers had finished with her. He spoke to Alfred's granddaughter

Susan. She could add little to what the villagers had already told Ralph. She told him of the distressed Lucy, the gamekeeper's daughter, who had told Sir Francis that soldiers were attacking the gamekeeper's cottage.

It was, therefore, difficult for Ralph to make sense of the various tales which he heard from the village folk, but it seemed that Sir Francis had ridden out to attack a marauding band of Roundhead troopers who had set fire to the gamekeeper's cottage. No one knew why the game keeper's home had been burnt. No one knew anything about Thomas, although Ralph questioned several people and did his best to describe him. Some said that it had been a cavalier soldier the troopers were chasing. Another man, who had been passing the gamekeeper's cottage at the time, and who had quickly made off when he saw that there was going to be trouble, assured Ralph that the troopers might well have gone peaceably on their way had not the gamekeeper threatened them with his gun. Though, why he should have been threatening the troopers, he could not say.

Ralph was at a loss to know what to make of it all, but it was quite clear that Sir Francis had been killed in the fight and, as far as Ralph could tell, all of those servants who had fought with him had died too. Even the servants at the Hall had not been spared by the murderous rebels who, enraged by the fight and the losses they had sustained and later inflamed by drink, plundered from the Hall and embarked upon an orgy of rape, murder and looting. Ralph was shown the newly dug graves of those who had died, including one that was clearly marked with a wooden cross upon which the name of Sir Francis Cressley had been inscribed. Other graves that were identified to him were of soldiers and servants who had fallen in the conflict, including Joseph Grimshaw and Alfred French, the only two of Sir Francis' servants whom he had known. There were also three other graves that, he was told, contained the remains of the gamekeeper, his wife and Lucy, his daughter; retrieved with some difficulty from the debris which was all that was left of the burnt cottage.

Unsuccessful in his attempt to trace Thomas, and depressed by the tragedy which had clearly happened, Ralph didn't care to

345

ask any more questions. No one, it seemed, had witnessed all of the events and a lot of what he had been told was conjecture. Furthermore, he was now anxious to ride over to Bullshead farm to see if Mary was still safe. There would be time for more enquiries later. Indeed, it was possible that she might know as much about what had happened as anybody.

Ralph turned his horse's head and set off for Bullshead farm. As he rode he tried to assimilate and make sense of the various accounts that he had just heard from the villagers of the recent events at Hartington Hall. It was hard to believe that all those who had lived at Hartington Hall had been killed. Thank God that Mary had not been there. He thought of Sir Francis, a man for whom he had worked for nearly three years but whom he had not known well. Nevertheless, the little he had known of him was enough to earn Ralph's admiration and respect. What a great pity that he had not lived longer to see Ralph and Mary married, perhaps to enjoy the arrival of grandchildren. A great sadness filled his mind as he thought of Alfred, Sir Francis' man servant, of Joseph Grimshaw and all those who had died in that last futile, but apparently heroic attempt to drive off the rebel soldiers. What misery this war had brought; not least to the Cressley family. He prayed that Jack would be spared and that there would be an end to the fighting and suffering. He began to realise that he didn't care who won or lost as long as he and others like him could live in peace.

His arrival at Bullshead was timely since it was only the day before that Mary and his Aunt Maria had arrived back from Oundle, having left her sister much restored in health. Mary was well, but devastated having already heard the news of her father's death and others at Hartington Hall. Her face was pale and drawn, her eyes were red and her face stained with tears. Pity and anguish for her sorrow welled up in Ralph's heart as he swept her into his arms. As full of grief as she was, she managed a wan smile at his coming and already the burden of sorrow was lightened. It was Uncle Charles who had had the unenviable task of telling her what had taken place at Hartington Hall and how, not only her father, but all of those whom she had loved and grown up with had perished at the hands of the rebels. Then she heard from Ralph, with horror and dismay, of her brother Jack's wounds. It was some comfort to hear that his wounds were on the mend and he was likely to be fit ere long.

Ralph stayed the night at Bullshead Farm where he discussed with his aunt and uncle the best course of action. Hartington Hall was even less a place for Mary to live safely now. She could have stayed with Uncle Charles and Aunt Maria, who treated her as their own daughter. However, the news of her wounded brother lying at Preston Capes left her in no doubt where she must go. Ralph, of course, was only too happy to take Mary back home with him. It was readily taken for granted that she and Ralph would marry just as soon as it could be arranged. Ralph's uncle and aunt were sorry indeed to see Mary leave, but they were not so selfish as to try to persuade her to stay.

So it was that Ralph brought Mary to Preston Capes. It was not how either Ralph or Mary had expected her first visit to her future home would be. All the same it was, in spite of the underlying sadness, a joyful occasion for them both as Ralph showed her around the house and gardens where she had imagined herself at home so many times during those past, lonely years. There was no disappointment in what she found, while the new life she began there did much to heal the wounds and bitter memories of first her mother and then her father's death. She had little to do for Jack who, although still weak, was clearly out of danger and would soon be fit and well again. Already he was able to walk a little, if painfully, with the aid of a stick.

Within a few weeks, in September, Ralph and Mary were married. It was not the grand occasion that it might have been and, of course, the ceremony took place in the local church. The bride left from the manor house at Preston Capes rather than from Hartington Hall. Uncle Charles and Aunt Maria, with Hugh, were able to visit for a day or two. Jack was sufficiently recovered to give his sister away. So, at last, Mary became Ralph's wife and truly became mistress in the manor of Preston Capes.

For Ralph the war was over. He felt that he had done his share for the Royalist cause and privately felt that it was now a lost cause. Had he remained single he might have seen the struggle through to the bitter end. However, married now to Mary, he was more than content to devote his efforts to building a prosperous future in the land that he had inherited with his father's death. The place needed care and attention which Ralph was determined to give it.

Jack, however, was firm in his resolve to serve the Royalist cause for as long as there was an army to take to the field. Whether Jack's zeal was through conviction, a determination to see the matter through or to avenge his father's death, Ralph was never quite sure, but Jack was in no doubt that he would fight on. He stayed with Ralph and Mary long enough to make a complete recovery and see them married. So it was in October when he finally left Preston Capes to seek the King's army. He fought in a number of small engagements, until that part of the army in which he served was forced to surrender in Cornwall during March of the following year when, like so many others who had supported the losing side, he was obliged to leave the country and seek refuge in France. Hartington Hall and its lands were seized for Parliament.

When Jack left to re-join the King he did not blame Ralph for not riding with him. Rather, he was glad to know that his sister was safely married and her husband would be staying by her side. For Mary his going was, of course, an occasion for sadness, but this time her tears were less bitter for she now had a husband and a home where she would be safe and needed.

* * *

So, gradually, memories of the horror and sadness of those war years receded and happiness blossomed in the Somers' household as time passed by. A family arrived; first Elizabeth, then, some years later, Edward. Both Mary and Ralph were contented with the quiet joy of fulfilment. Only the separation from Jack, Mary's brother, cast a shadow on what was otherwise a very happy life. Now that shadow was lifted and Mary was happy indeed.

'You have managed to replace most of the furniture I see. Ralph told me that there was little left of what used to be here.'

She seated herself in a chair by the large bay window and looked around that, once so familiar, room. Her pleasure was quite apparent. Her eyes sparkled as she smiled at her brother and his wife, who were anxious to see if she approved of their new ownership of the Hall and the changes that they had been obliged to make after its tenancy; for so many years in uncaring hands.

'It's wonderful, Jack, and I'm so happy to see you, Estelle and the boys here where you belong.' It was simply said, but it was a sincere expression of the way that Mary felt.

'As you say, we have had to find nearly all new furniture. Much of what was left did not belong originally in the Hall. It was either well used or broken beyond repair. I placed an order in Northampton for several new pieces. Some of it is still to come. It will take a while before the place is properly refurnished.'

Ralph had also been comparing the Hall now to the state he had found it in during his last visit.

'There was quite a bit of damage to the place when I came here a few days after the Roundhead troopers looted it. I don't think it stayed empty for very long, did it? We heard that it had been given to one of Cromwell's men.'

Ralph looked enquiringly at Jack.

'Yes, that's right. You remember, I also managed to make one visit here after leaving you to re-join the King. There was a lot of superficial damage. Much of the furniture was wrecked, but, otherwise, little real harm was done. It looked to be an awful mess at first sight, but a closer look showed that there was little which a good scrubbing wouldn't cure. With the help of some of the villagers, I managed to straighten the place up a bit and found someone to take care of it while I was away.'

'It did me little good, of course. When our army was beaten and I was forced into exile, I guessed that I would lose the Hall and its lands. So it proved and there was little I could do about it. For some years the place was owned by a Captain Browne, who had been on Cromwell's staff. He was a bachelor and drank a lot. His habits weren't of the cleanest.

It was some six months ago, after the restoration of the monarchy, that I petitioned the King. We heard in France how things had changed in England and how restitution was being made to many who had suffered loss at the hands of the Commonwealth. It seemed worth a visit to see if I could reclaim Hartington Hall. I was courteously received and, when His Majesty heard of the services which I and our father had rendered to his father, he readily restored all our former possessions. In fact, the Hall had been standing empty for almost a year after the death of the Captain whom, I gather, died in a drunken stupor. The place has been sorely neglected and there is much that needs to be done, but any damage that has occurred since the Hall was looted was through lack of attention, rather than wrought in malice.'

Mary looked at Estelle who had come to Jack's side as he spoke and taken his arm.

'I know that you are glad to be back home, Jack, but what of Estelle? Were you not sorry to leave your home in France?'

'Sorry, yes, I sorry, but when I see zis lovely house,' Estelle pointed at Hartington Hall. 'I forgot sorry.' She smiled happily as she hugged Jack. Plainly the main ingredient for a happy home was already there.

They had their evening meal in the dining room and then, when the children were in bed, they sat in the oak panelled living room. The fireplace stood empty and the windows were opened to let in some cool air on a warm night for May. The shadows grew deeper as the daylight faded. They talked of old times and of the people they had known. The war had been a separate experience for each of them, although none for Estelle at her home in France. In many ways this added to the interest of the discussion, especially where paths had crossed.

'I wonder what happened to Thomas.' said Ralph. 'We have never been able to trace him. He must surely be dead but how, when and where, I have no idea. Did you ever hear anything more of him Jack?'

'No, nothing. It seems likely that Thomas was in some way involved with the Roundhead attack on the Hall and it may be that he was involved in the skirmish with the Roundhead troopers, when my father and his men were killed. I say this, because it was on the day when Thomas left Preston Capes to deliver your message to my father, that the encounter with the Roundhead troops took place and when father was killed. If Thomas did arrive here and was involved in the skirmish, why then was he not found with the dead after the battle? He may have escaped, but if so why has he not been seen since? Perhaps he escaped and was killed elsewhere. The whole thing is a mystery and I imagine that it will always stay that way.'

'There was only one left alive on the estate after the Roundhead patrol left.' said Mary. 'That was poor Amy. Amy was so badly abused by the soldiers that she lost her reason and could tell us nothing. She died some few years ago. Alfred had sent his ten year old granddaughter, who had been visiting him at the Hall, back to her home in the village when he saw that there was going to be trouble. She could tell us little. All she knew was what she had heard from Lucy, the gamekeeper's daughter, when she came to seek Colonel Cressley's help and was clearly distraught because the Roundhead soldiers had fired her cottage. She knew nothing of Thomas, or any other visitor to the Hall, although she did say that the Roundhead troopers had been chasing someone. It was some of the villagers who told us that they had seen some Roundheads chasing one of the King's men on horseback and heard shots being fired. From the description of the horseman, which we got from them, it seems likely that it was Thomas who was unwittingly the cause of all the trouble.'

'It must be so.' agreed Jack. 'There are no others to tell us exactly what happened. It seems that the few men left from the estate, the wounded soldiers from father's patrol and even poor old Joseph Grimshaw, rode out with father to meet the Roundheads. Only old Alfred, and the women stayed behind. He and all the women, apart from Amy, were killed by the Roundheads when they came looting after the fight. All we know is that Lucy Jenkins came to the Hall to raise the alarm, presumably when her father's cottage was set on fire. This much we learned from Alfred's grand daughter, Susan, who was at the Hall when she arrived. As Mary said, she saw that Lucy was very distressed and that her grandfather took her to see father, but she heard little of what was said. Later, after father and his men had left, she saw Lucy Jenkins run from the Hall back towards the cottage. Susan lived with her mother in the village. So when Alfred saw that there might be trouble, he packed her off home. After the fire, two bodies were found in the rubble. These were apparently Tom Jenkins' wife and his daughter Lucy who must have gone back into the building to try to save her mother. Tom Jenkins was found outside with the other dead from the fight.'

'And that's all we know and are ever likely to know of what happened.' Ralph sighed. 'I suppose Thomas must have been killed in the fight even though his body was not found. I cannot believe that, if he had escaped, he would have knowingly left others to go to their death. If by chance he had survived, he would surely have found one of us by now to tell us how it happened.'

'Who knows how we would act when pressed?'

'He didn't act that way on Naseby field nor, I'll warrant, at any of the other battles he fought.' Ralph remarked.

Jack could only agree.

'The matter is a mystery and no doubt will always remain so.'

'Well, now the house and land are yours Jack.' observed Ralph, with some satisfaction. 'It's good to know that things have turned out well in the end. Have you deeds to prove your ownership?'

'No, they were never found; but it is of no matter. I have King Charles' own signature giving me all the land and property owned by my father. There are none who are going to gainsay that.'

'What of father's papers and money? Did you find none of those?' asked Mary.

'None at all; I do not know where he kept his valuables. I

thought that he had some safe hiding place, but I have searched and found nothing. Whatever he had must have been found, and stolen by the soldiers when they sacked the house, or perhaps his papers and valuables were found by Captain Browne.'

By the time that any of the four were ready for bed, the candles had burnt low and the hour was past midnight. There had been so much to discuss and no one had wanted to end, what had been for all four, a very happy day.

The days that followed were happy ones too. Mary was content to wander around the Hall, and its once beautiful gardens, remembering her childhood and the life she had known there more than sixteen years ago. With Ralph, Jack, Estelle and the children she rode over to Bullshead Farm. It was by no means the first visit that they had paid since Mary had left there to live at Preston Capes. She and Ralph had visited many times during those intervening years. She had bitter sweet memories of the months spent there. The family had made her so welcome that she had found happiness in spite of the loss of her mother and her constant fear for the safety of Ralph, Jack and her father. Uncle Charles was old and frail now. He had lost his wife, Maria, some two years ago. Nevertheless, he was still able to greet them with the same welcoming smile and warm hand shake of olden days and insisted that the cook should prepare a meal for them all. Hugh was now a married man living in his father's house with his young wife and baby daughter. It was another pleasant day, full of memories, so that Ralph and Mary were especially sorry when it was time to leave.

During much of their stay at Hartington Hall, Ralph and Mary were happy to leave their children in the company of Francis and Charles, being then free to wander abroad on their own. It was a mutually advantageous arrangement, for the children took great pleasure in being freed from parental restrictions. Ralph and Mary, for their part, fond parents as they were, enjoyed the peace and quiet occasioned by the absence of their off-springs. They took this opportunity of re-exploring the forest ridings on horseback and seeing, again, the places which they had known so well, where they had first met and where their love for one another had started to grow.

So the days passed all too quickly. It was on the last day of their stay, as they strolled across the meadows near the Hall, that they came upon the ruins of the cottage burnt by the Roundhead soldiers on that fateful day some sixteen years ago. There was little left now to show what it had been. It was nothing more than a low heap of charred wood and blackened stone. Some stones, it appeared, had been removed to use in building a new cottage to house the new gamekeeper and his family; some short distance away. The weeds, brambles, nettles and grass almost completely covered what remained, so that it was nothing more than a slight mound. They paused to look again, at what Mary remembered as a neat and tidy home, where she had played as a little girl with Lucy Jenkins and had been given sweetmeats and drinks of milk by the gamekeeper's wife. She shuddered as she thought of the horror which had struck both their families on that awful day.

'There's not much to show of what it used to be.' remarked Ralph. 'Not that there was much more standing when I came in search of Thomas. It must have been near here that your father died with Joseph Grimshaw and the others. I would love to know how it all happened. He must have known that he had little chance against the Roundheads, with a band of old men and cripples. Well, he died bravely and I'm sure that he would have sooner gone that way than any other. It is a pity, though, that he didn't live to see his grandchildren.'

Ralph stood lost in thought as his mind wandered over the events of that day, such as he knew them; trying, in his imagination, to visualise what might have happened.

'Poor father; he came over to see me soon after I went to live with your uncle and aunt. It is a pity that I was away during his final stay at the Hall. When I saw him last, he seemed to be missing mother badly and anxious to be away again from Hartington Hall and all of its memories. He could have lived happily with us. There would have been room, too, for old Joseph Grimshaw.' Mary sighed at the thought of what might have been.

'Joseph was quite a character.' observed Ralph. 'He was surly and had scarcely the time of day for most folk, but he was loyal to your father and would have done anything for him.' Ralph remembered the man he had known; a man of few words and one of his own will, who could be led but not driven. Ralph had known him and yet felt that he knew him very little.

'Well, they're gone now.' said Mary. 'And we are left with four more to take their place, our Edward and Elizabeth and Jack and Estelle's two lads. I wonder how many more generations of Cressleys will walk these meadows and live in that lovely old Hall.'

'Many more, I'm sure.' replied Ralph. 'Just as many generations of Somers will live at Preston Capes and farm the land there; but they won't be as lucky as I am.'

'Oh, why is that then?' Mary looked quizzically at Ralph.

'Well, those Somers won't have a Cressley as lovely as you, will they?' answered Ralph, squeezing her hand.

'Oh, stranger things have happened.' laughed Mary and, taking his arm, she led him away from the mouldering pile of stones.